FLY THE FRIENDLY SKIES . . .

Suddenly, the shuttle's crew door opened, and the crew chief pushed down the ladder. Thomas put six rounds in his chest with a double tap on the trigger of his silenced submachine gun.

Partly obscured by the dust from the engines, three teams from Thomas's recon platoon and helicopter pilot Ivan Kokovstov came out of the hole at a dead run. Once inside the shuttle, two of Thomas's teams went aft to clear out any passengers, while the third went forward with Thomas and Sanmartin to take out the crew.

A moment later, Thomas came back to the door and waved. Six specialists emerged from the ground and clambered on board. The last man carried a bucket of white sand that he carefully sprinkled over the crew chief's blood.

By Robert Frezza
Published by Ballantine Books:

A SMALL COLONIAL WAR
McLENDON'S SYNDROME
FIRE IN A FARAWAY PLACE

FIRE IN A FARAWAY PLACE

Robert Frezza

A Del Rey Book

BALLANTINE BOOKS • NEW YORK

A Del Rey Book
Published by Ballantine Books

Library of Congress Catalog Card Number: 93-90859

ISBN 0-345-38724-4

Manufactured in the United States of America

First Edition: March 1994

PRINCIPAL CHARACTERS _____

1st Battalion, 35th Imperial Infantry (Rifle)
Lieutenant-Colonel Anton Vereshchagin ("the Variag"), acting
 first task group commander
Major Matti Harjalo, battalion commander
Acting Major Raul Sanmartin, battalion executive officer
Captain Chiharu Yoshida, battalion political officer
Surgeon Natasha Solchava-Snyman, battalion medical officer
Senior Communications Sergeant Timo Haerkoennen
Senior Quartermaster Sergeant Vulko Redzup
Senior Intelligence Sergeant Resit Aksu
Lieutenant Detlef Jankowskie, special ops detachment commander
Lance Corporal Nicolas Sery, first gunner, special ops detach-
 ment
Lieutenant Victor Thomas, reconnaissance platoon leader
Corporal Vsevolod Zerebtsov, 1st section, reconnaissance platoon
Flight Sergeant Filip "Coconut" Kokovtsov, aviation platoon

A Company, 1/35th Infantry
Major Piotr Kolomeitsev ("The Iceman"), commanding
Section Sergeant Kirill Orlov, 2nd section No. 1 platoon

B Company, 1/35th Infantry
Captain Ivan Sversky, commanding
Lieutenant Per Kiritinitis, executive officer

C Company, 1/35th Infantry
Captain Hans Coldewe, commanding
Company Sergeant Aleksei Beregov
Senior Cook Katrina "Kasha" Vladimirovna
Lieutenant Gennadi Karaev, executive officer and No. 9 pla-
 toon leader
Platoon Sergeant Roy "Filthy DeKe" de Kantow, No. 9 platoon
Lieutenant Daniel "Danny" Meagher, No. 10 platoon leader
Platoon Sergeant Isaac Wanjau, No. 10 platoon
Corporal Dmitri Uborevich, 2nd section, No. 10 platoon
Sublieutenant Jan Snyman, No. 11 platoon leader
Section Sergeant Fedya "Mother Elena" Yelenov, 2nd section
 No. 9 platoon

Corporal Juko Miinalainen, 2nd section No. 9 platoon
Superior Private Dirkie Rousseaux, 2nd section No. 9 platoon

D Company, 1/35th Infantry
Major Paul Henke ("The Hangman"), commanding
Superior Private Woldemar Prigal, 1st section No. 15 platoon
Sergeant Platoon Commander Konstantin Savichev, No. 16
    platoon leader

1st Battalion, 3rd Light Attack Regiment
Lieutenant-Colonel Uwe Ebyl, commanding
Captain Ulrich Ohlrogge, A Company commander

Suid-Afrikaners
Jules Afanou, sect leader
Albert Beyers, Republic of Suid-Afrika president and Assem-
    bly member
Hanna Bruwer-Sanmartin, Assembly speaker
Christos Claassen, Assembly member and Reformed National-
    ist party leader
Nadine Joh, cowboy leader and Assembly member
Eva Moore (lieutenant-colonel, retired), hospital administrator
Pieter Olivier, businessman and Afrikaner Bond member
Gerrit Terblanche, Afrikaner Resistance Movement general secretary
Hannes Van der Merwe, Afrikaner Resistance Movement member
Jopie Van Nuys, Afrikaner Resistance Movement member

Imperials
Vice-Admiral Saburu Horii, second task group commander
Captain Tokio Watanabe, Admiral Horii's aide
Colonel Soemu Sumi, task group chief of staff and political of-
    ficer
Captain Yotaro Yanagita, task group intelligence officer
Colonel Tsuyoshi Uno, 1st Manchurian Regiment commander
Colonel Ryohei Enomoto, 6th Lifeguards Battalion commander
Lieutenant-Colonel Otojiro Okuda, 9th Light Attack Battalion
    commander
Daisuke Matsudaira, United Steel-Standard planetary director

Others
Hiroshi Mizoguchi (lieutenant, retired), public-works employee
Karl von Clausewitz, German philosopher, deceased
Quintus Sertorius, Roman general and successful rebel, deceased

Order of Battle
1st Battalion, 35th Infantry (Rifle)

| (A) MAJ Sanmartin | MAJ Harjalo | B/SGT Malinov |
| Executive Officer | commanding | Battalion Sergeant |

A Company

| LT Malyshev | MAJ Kolomeitsev | C/SGT Leonov |
| Executive Officer | commanding | Company Sergeant |

No. 1 Rifle	No. 2 Rifle	No. 3 Rifle	No. 4 Mortar
(Malyshev)	LT Degtyarov	S/LT Van Deventer	LT Sjurssen
P/SGT Korhonev	P/SGT Gledich	P/SGT Tributs	P/SGT Sausnitis

B Company

| LT Kiritinitis | CPT Sversky | C/SGT Rodale |
| Executive Officer | commanding | Company Sergeant |

No. 5 Rifle	No. 6 Rifle	No. 7 Rifle	No. 8 Mortar
SGT/PC Gurevich	LT Pajari	(Kiritinitis)	S/LT Miller
P/SGT Kyykkynen	P/SGT Aittola	P/SGT Ngo	P/SGT Soe

C Company

| LT Karaev | CPT Coldewe | C/SGT Beregov |
| Executive Officer | commanding | Company Sergeant |

No. 9 Rifle	No. 10 Rifle	No. 11 Rifle	No. 12 Mortar
LT Meagher	LT Gavrilov	S/LT Snyman	SGT/PC Traone
P/SGT De Kantzow	P/SGT Sucre	P/SGT Wanjau	P/SGT Mekhlis

D Company

| LT Okladnikov | MAJ Henke | C/SGT Poikolainnen |
| Executive Officer | commanding | Company Sergeant |

Mech Mortar	No. 14 L Attack	No. 15 L Attack	No. 16 L Attack
S/LT Fischer	(Okladnikov)	LT Muravyov	SGT/PC Savichev
P/SGT Bushchin	P/SGT Zakusov	P/SGT Liu	P/SGT Kuusinen

Reconnaissance	Engineers	Quartermaster	Aviation
LT Thomas	LT Reinikka	CPT Bukhanov	CPT Wojcek
P/SGT Drake	P/SGT Brits	SQM/SGT Redzup	F/SGT Laumer

(A) = acting rank

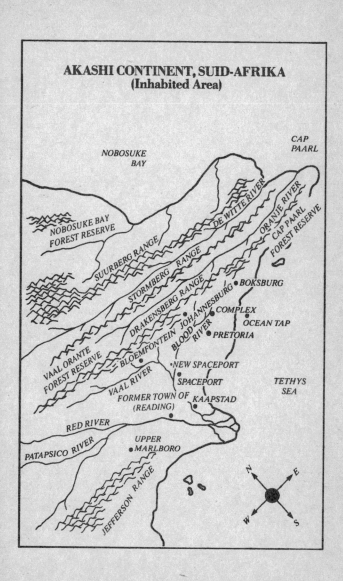

PROLOGUE ————————————————

Tokyo, Earth

IN A TALL BUILDING IN THE HEART OF TOKYO'S CHUO WARD, THE *Sankin-kai*, the president's council, of the DKU *keiretsu*, or group of affiliated companies, met, as it did each month, in the corporate dining room of the Daikichi Sanwa Bank. While the ties that bound the member companies to the Daikichi Sanwa and one another were informal, they were as close as the links between disparate divisions of a conglomerate, and each company proudly displayed the DKU emblem in its advertising.

Among the individuals present were the presidents of the Earth's largest textile company, its second-largest electronics firm, its second-largest steel maker, its fourth-largest cosmetics manufacturer, and its third-largest automaker. All of them were Japanese and male, and the youngest among them was in his late sixties. The companies they represented accounted for 8 percent of Imperial Japan's swollen gross national product.

After the plague winds of the crack-up had decimated the populations and devastated the economies of Earth's continental nations, Japan's Imperial *Keidanren*, or Federation of Economic Organizations, had effectively controlled Earth's economies and, eventually, those of Earth's colonies. Through their economic power, their manipulation of the *Keidanren*, and their close financial ties to the various factions of Japan's ruling Unified Democratic party, the men present and their counterparts in rival *keiretsu* exercised more power than any oligarchy had enjoyed in Earth's long history.

First among equals was the president of the Daikichi Sanwa—as main bank and major stockholder for each of the corporations present, the Daikichi held management rights if it chose to exercise them. After several other matters had been discussed, the Daikichi president signaled imperceptibly to the president of United Steel-Standard.

Awkwardly, hesitantly, the USS president addressed his compatriots. "I must mention that there has been an unexpected occurrence on the planet of Suid-Afrika."

Everyone in the room correctly assumed that "unexpected" meant distressingly costly, and the textile president, a decade older than the USS president and conscious of his superiority, commented, "I recall something about Suid-Afrika. You get fusion metals for our spaceships from there, heh? Five or six years ago, we requested the Imperial Government to send a military expedition there to end disturbances. Is this still a problem? Someone really should take responsibility."

Visibly embarrassed, the USS president explained, "It is a very difficult matter. The local population, which consists of Afrikaners and a nationally unhomogeneous group of peoples who call themselves 'cowboys,' is conspicuously lacking in virtue. A number of years ago, these persons set aside our authority and proceeded to act on their own, which resulted in severe losses. Although the Guardianship Council was ill advised and terminated our corporation's authority over the planet, it did send a military task force to restore order."

In a milder age, the Imperial Government had mostly used Japan's economic might to maintain its power and to further the interests of its constituent groups. Increasingly, outside Japan, that power and those interests were being challenged. Prodded by the *keiretsu*, the Imperial Government had begun using military force.

The USS man wiped his face and continued. "We have since learned that the rebellious inhabitants destroyed the bulk of the task force sent to control the situation and even destroyed warships in orbit through some trick."

"Orbiting warships were destroyed? This sounds quite serious," the aged president of a chemical firm commented.

"Because of the distance and the time dilation between events there and events here on Earth, we did not find this out until a few days ago." The USS president lowered his voice. "This left a foreign officer with an unpronounceable name—a Lieutenant-Colonel Ver-esh-cha-gin—in command of the task group. Although he claims to have suppressed the rebellion, his first action upon assuming command was to execute our corporation's planetary director. It appears that the situation there has become completely unendurable."

The textile man said, "Did I hear someone say that this Lieutenant-Colonel Ver-esh-cha-gin shot your planetary director for being stupid enough to provide ammunition to the rebels? This disruption has been going on for quite some time. I recall that your predecessor sent mercenaries there some years ago. Your company really has not had much luck with that world." He added in a politely damning tone of voice, "Perhaps we should have sent some of our guards instead."

Outside the room, *sokaiya* in ill-fitting suits with automatic weapons guarded the doors. Once hoodlums paid to prevent disruption of stockholders meetings, as the nature of Japan's economic system changed, the *sokaiya* had gradually been assimilated by the corporations they had simultaneously protected and preyed upon.

"Well, what is required to resolve this matter?" the president of the chemical firm finally asked the USS man.

"It is a passing phase, but a firm response is desirable. In the short term, the news about the rebellion will have an extremely adverse impact on our stock prices. It would be extremely disruptive to allow the price to fall," the USS president said doggedly. "The Daikichi Sanwa has approved a substantial loan to prevent this."

The eyes of a few of the presidents danced. *"Zaitech,"* the chemical man scrawled on his notepad, Japanese parlance for financial engineering, with emphasis on its less savory aspects.

The USS president pressed his case. "In the long term, it will be necessary to bring the benefits of stability and order to this planet. Due to the unfortunate political situation, metal deliveries have been erratic, and costs have been excessive. The niobium, tantalum, and other fusion metals essential to spaceship technology that Suid-Afrika provides are irreplaceable. This has made it difficult for us to fulfill contracts on schedule. Unfortunately, we have not been able to develop other dependable sources. A stable, dependable local administration would be best."

To bring the discussion to an end, deliberately eschewing euphemism, the textile man said, "So, we should persuade the Guardianship Council to send another military task force to chastise this planet's population."

"Hai," the USS president replied.

The Daikichi president nodded and began discussing another topic.

Although a respectable number of wars find their genesis in corporate boardrooms, miscalculations cause most of them.

GROUND ━━━━━━━━━━━━━━━

**Akashi continent, Suid-Afrika—L-Day plus three
hundred nine weeks
Sunday(309)**

LIEUTENANT-COLONEL ANTON VERESHCHAGIN, AT PRESENT THE
commander of the Imperial Task Group Suid-Afrika, sat on the
fallen trunk of a fern tree, meticulously carving a block of fiber
from the tree's core with short, careful strokes. In the forest
shadows of abandoned Elandslaagte Farm, the drab rank loz-
enges on his collar briefly reflected the light as he worked.

From time to time, he looked up into the sky.

For Anton Vereshchagin, it was the first day of the 309th
week since the arrival of the First Battalion of the Thirty-fifth
Imperial Rifle Regiment, the battalion he had brought to the
planet. For the Afrikaner majority of the planet's population, it
was the Day of the Covenant, December 16 on the nonstandard
local calendar, a holiday commemorating a three-hundred-year-
old victory by Afrikaner *voortrekkers* over a Zulu impi; and
since most of the Afrikaners were staunch Calvinists, they
didn't celebrate many others.

Today was also the fifth anniversary of a singularly ill-
organized revolt against Imperial rule which Vereshchagin, as
the senior surviving Imperial officer, had politely knocked to
pieces, filling more than a few graves in the process. Out of
courtesy, Vereshchagin had absented himself from the festivities.

Now that it was slowly reverting to forest, Elandslaagte
Farm was tranquil, with little to suggest that it had once been
a battlefield. The Afrikaners who had there died had been
reburied in their hometowns and cities; Vereshchagin's dead
had been cremated and either sent home, wherever home was,
or interred in the battalion's own cemetery according to each
man's final instructions in such matters. Growing swiftly in the
humid climate, fern trees had risen to replace the ones
Vereshchagin's armored cars had shot apart.

Beads of perspiration dripped down Vereshchagin's cheeks
as he worked. It was a day for remembering. In Vereshchagin's
eyes, two men had knocked the props out from under the rebellion before it consumed Suid-Afrika. One was a politician,
Albert Beyers, who had led his people away from fanaticism.
Another was a rebel general, Hendrik Pienaar, who had gotten

4

himself murdered in the process of killing the rebellion deader than rifles and 30mm shells could make it.

Vereshchagin frowned slightly. He disliked owing debts to the living, and he disliked even more owing debts to the dead.

As he gently formed the soft, native "wood," his wrist mount emitted a very mild hum precisely on the hour. Sighing, he triggered his personal radio. "One slash thirty-five point one. Break. Vereshchagin here. Matti, is this you?"

When Vereshchagin had elevated himself to Imperial task group commander, his executive officer, the irrepressible Major Matti Harjalo, had inherited command of the 1/35th Rifle Battalion. "Hello, Anton." Harjalo chuckled. "Having fun communing with nature?"

Vereshchagin smiled involuntarily. "I am. How successful have you been at kissing babies?"

The little radio conveyed a rude noise. "We had a very nice parade."

"And the bagpipes?" Vereshchagin took a childish interest in the battalion's pipe band, originally formed from survivors of a destroyed battalion of Gurkhas whose traditions embraced Highland Scottish music.

Harjalo made a noise in his throat. "The natives loved them. At least they clapped, and nobody started shooting, which I would have done if somebody had started playing bagpipes at me."

"Indeed," Vereshchagin murmured.

"After the parade, President of the Republic Albert Beyers made a nice, uplifting speech. Then Speaker of the Assembly Hanna Bruwer-Sanmartin made a nice, uplifting speech. Then four or five other politicians made nice, uplifting speeches. Then Christos Claassen and some of the loyal opposition got up on a street corner and started rousing the rabble, so Albert and Hanna got back up on the podium, figuratively rolled back their sleeves, and pitched in. A fun time was had by all."

"Was there any overtly hostile activity?"

"The Scheepers girl and some of her people went around with banners saying violently anti-Imperial things. My executive officer, one Acting Major Raul Sanmartin, handed her a bouquet of flowers and said something polite to the effect that he had bought them for his wife, but that Scheepers needed them more. The Scheepers girl has absolutely no sense of humor."

"We transported her uncle and half of her relatives for their role in the uprising," Vereshchagin interjected quietly.

"Well, she lost her composure completely and tried to hit Raul with the flowers. The cameramen caught it for the evening news and made her look at least twice as silly as God and nature intended. As I say, a fun time was had by all."

As he listened, Vereshchagin could hear singing in the background. Vereshchagin's battalion, originally recruited in Finland from Russians and Finns, had been leavened by personnel acquired on a half-dozen worlds and was now nearly 50 percent Afrikaner—in some cases the sons and brothers of Afrikaners killed during the rebellion. Despite this, the battalion had kept its traditions intact. Making a virtue out of necessity, for several years now they'd held their *Pikkujoulu* or "Little Christmas" parties on the sixteenth. The wines and vodka that Suid-Afrika produced in quantity were undoubtedly flowing.

"What about the Afrikaner Resistance Movement?" Vereshchagin asked Harjalo softly.

"Our information was correct. A couple of them tried to set off a car bomb. We have them and the bomb. Aksu interrogated them, and we were able to fold one of their safe houses. We kept it quiet—so far; Albert and Raul are the only ones who know."

"How badly did you damage them?"

"The woman we picked up is intact. The police only shot her boyfriend once, and it wasn't serious, if that's what you're asking."

"That is precisely what I am asking. Please ensure that they are fit to stand trial. What about the cowboys?"

"No one in the southern half of the continent has quite forgiven the Afrikaners for nuking them during the rebellion, and they dislike being reminded by these little holidays, but Uwe Ebyl's battalion kept them quiet and reasonably contented. Albert sent his treasury minister out in a radiation suit to the former town of Reading to lay a wreath. I'll let you know if anything happens."

Uwe Ebyl's light attack battalion was the only other major Imperial combat unit to survive the Afrikaner rebellion. For five years, Uwe had been the uncrowned king of the rancher country. Even before the Afrikaners had rebelled, he and Vereshchagin had stamped out a half-hearted rebellion by some of the cowboys, and the rancher magnates knew better than to try his patience.

"Thank you, Matti," Vereshchagin said thoughtfully. "Is there anything else noteworthy?"

"Not just yet. Enjoy your vacation, Anton. Harjalo out."

Vereshchagin resumed his careful carving, closing his mind to Suid-Afrika's political ferment. Above him, the oldest surviving fern trees formed a cool, green canopy fifty meters over his head. A small amphtile similar to the one he was carving slowly poked its head out of a pile of mold to appraise his work.

He again felt the quiet hum of his personal radio and reached up to touch the induction plate on his temple.

"Harjalo here."

"I assume this is not a social call."

Harjalo's bantering tone had disappeared. "It's not. Get yourself in, Anton. I have a helicopter on its way. There's an Imperial warship in our sky. People on Earth haven't forgotten us."

Because of the distance from Earth and the time dilation, no new orders had come since Anton Vereshchagin had assumed command of the Imperial Task Group Suid-Afrika. This was about to change.

"Will they land?"

"Not today. There's only one ship so far, and from the orbit it's taking I doubt that the new task group commander is on it. I expect we'll see more ships over the next few hours. I've contacted Albert. After he gets out of his fancy president-of-the-republic clothes, he'll want to see you. Harjalo out."

Vereshchagin nodded, a small gesture. Time dilation between colonial campaigns on eight different worlds gave Vereshchagin a unique perspective. On Earth, men born long after he had left for the colonial wars had risen to positions of authority, grown old, and died. The Imperial system had changed. Vereshchagin had not.

Vereshchagin had done well with Suid-Afrika by his own lights. Although the cowboys and Afrikaners who made up the planet's population were far from being model Imperial subjects, they were reasonably happy and prosperous. For good or ill, Vereshchagin had done as much in six years to mold the world and its people as any man could, and he sincerely doubted that the Imperial government that had inherited the results would be even moderately happy with them.

He looked up carefully far overhead into the evening sky, searching for what might have been a new star. In a curiously gentle motion he jabbed his knife into the log beside his knee. Picking up his rifle, he strode off toward the lights of Pretoria to greet the newly arrived Imperial forces and give account of his stewardship.

The rains would rust his knife, but its imprint would remain.

* * *

THE LITTLE GIRL RAN INTO THE ROOM AS FAST AS HER STUBBY LEGS
would carry her, chasing the kitten. She hit the edge of the rug
and sprawled, shrieking with laughter, as the kitten climbed the
curtains and peered down.

"Hendricka, are you chasing the kitten?"

"Yes, Tant Betje," the child answered obediently.

"You stop it, or he will scratch you," Albert Beyers's wife
said placidly from the next room in the stilted English she had
learned late in her life. "Please pick up your books before your
mother comes home from work."

"No," Hendricka said.

"You say no, and I say yes. My yes is bigger than your no,
so you pick up your books. Hurry, or your mother will be
here!" Vroew Beyers stopped what she was doing and went
into the entry room.

The three-year-old nodded solemnly, lifted herself to her
feet, and toddled off to collect her books.

Betje Beyers looked up at the kitten. "You come down from
there." The kitten suddenly let go and came sliding down as
fast as it had gone up. It plopped at her feet, and she bent to
pick it up. "If the president of the Republic must listen to me,
you do, too, little one," she murmured to the kitten.

Someone knocked on the door. "Da!" Hendricka shouted,
recognizing who was at the door by the sound.

Raul Sanmartin opened the door and stepped inside, wearing
battle dress. His daughter wrapped herself around his knees,
and he picked her up and swung her. Then he looked at Vroew
Beyers, and the pleasure left his face. "Mother, the Imperials
are here. Don't wait dinner for any of us."

Raul Sanmartin called Betje Beyers "Mother." So did her
husband and half the planet. Sanmartin's own mother was long
dead far away. He kissed the child and told her, "I have to
work late and so does your momma. Again. Afraid so. Be
good for Tant Betje." When he left, Vroew Beyers hugged her
newest adopted granddaughter very tightly.

IN THE MOTOR POOL IN A BUNKER ON THE CASERN AT BLOEMFON-
tein, Major Paul Henke, the commander of Harjalo's D Company, peered into the engine compartment of his Type 97
armored car and held his head six centimeters away from the
little turbocompressor. "We should pull the third and fourth rotors," he said, straightening and wiping oil from his hands.

Without exception, Imperial soldiers who were not Japanese called the Type 97's "Cadillacs." Although built to be almost maintenance-free, Henke's Cadillac was old.

His gunner, an ancient superior private named Chornovil, had already finished topping off the liquid propellant reservoir with fresh "fertilizer." Chornovil whistled sprightly as he methodically continued checking each round of ready 30mm ammunition.

Henke's driver, a young Afrikaner from Boksburg named Rudi Gerwig, kicked the Cadillac's sixth wheel. "But the diagnostics only said rotor three was bad."

Henke's emaciated face contorted momentarily.

"If four goes up, we can always pull it," Gerwig continued, blissfully unaware.

The wind through the open door pulled at the thin wisps of whitening hair on top of Henke's head. *Der Henker*—the Hangman—lowered his chin.

Chornovil, knowing him well, rubbed his finger on the little white gallows insignia painted on the Cadillac's side for luck and began pulling a pair of replacement rotors.

The Hangman glanced up at the sky and then at Gerwig. "Young man, you have been a recruit private in this battalion for nearly a year, but you are not a soldier. We will remedy this defect."

"Yes, sir!" Gerwig said, startled.

Monday(309)

NINE KILOMETERS ABOVE SUID-AFRIKA'S SURFACE, THE COMmander of the Second Imperial Task Group Suid-Afrika, Vice-Admiral Saburu Horii, impassively studied the new planet beneath him from the flying bridge of the Imperial frigate *Maya*. "Captain Yanagita, attend me," he said quietly into the ship's intercom system.

A few moments later, Horii's intelligence officer entered nervously.

"Yanagita, describe for me the principal officers in Lieutenant-Colonel Vereshchagin's battalion."

"Sir?" Yanagita hesitated. Normally Yanagita's superior, the task group's political officer and chief of staff, Colonel Sumi, briefed the admiral.

"Please do so," Horii said, folding his hands behind his back.

"Yes, sir. The officer now commanding Lieutenant-Colonel Vereshchagin's battalion is Major Matti Harjalo. Major Harjalo was born in Kuusamo in Finland and attended the military academy in Sapporo, graduating eighteenth in his class. He requested colonial duty with the 1/35th Imperial Rifles as his initial assignment."

"Yes, yes," Horii said dreamily. "You must learn to concentrate on essentials, Yanagita."

"Of course, sir. How stupid of me. His academy record reflects that he ranked second in his class in tactics and was disciplined three times for insubordination. Very little in his career stands out. He assumed command of the 1/35th Imperial Rifle Battalion for two days during a campaign to suppress disorder on NovySibir, following a strange incident in which Lieutenant-Colonel Vereshchagin was temporarily relieved of command and his replacement, Lieutenant-Colonel Hiroyuki, accidentally shot himself with a pistol."

"Yes. Admiral Ishizu died several years ago so that no one knows the full story anymore, but it is possible that Harjalo pulled the trigger of the pistol that killed Hiroyuki," Horii responded.

Yanagita looked at him, wide-eyed.

"Nothing was done about it. Strange things happen on the colonial fringes of empire, Yanagita. The Ministry of Defense is very far away. Go on."

"The commander of Vereshchagin's A Company is Major Piotr Kolomeitsev. Like Vereshchagin, Kolomeitsev is descended from Russians who took refuge in Finland after the crack-up. He has been wounded in action nine times. It appears that staff officers have nominated him for medals on three separate occasions, but that he has refused to accept them. His political-reliability index is extremely low, and he was ranked last in his class in tactics."

"I did not realize that," Horii reflected. "Kolomeitsev is a brilliant, but very unorthodox tactician, and his low ranking in that subject indicates a degree of stubbornness that I had not anticipated. His nickname is 'the Iceman.' "

"Why 'the Iceman,' sir?"

Horii grimaced. "When you meet him you will understand."

On a planet called Ashcroft, the natives had sworn that Kolomeitsev had the evil eye and, given his success in making corpses out of people he wanted dead, the notion had much to commend it.

"He is a very cold and very able man. Observe him carefully, Yanagita."

"Yes, sir. It appears from Vereshchagin's last report that he has made Captain Chiharu Yoshida his political officer. Yoshida was formerly the B Company commander. He is from a corporate family."

"Yes, I am familiar with the Yoshida family."

"He served for two years in the First Lifeguards, after which his request for a colonial assignment was endorsed by Colonel Kanoh."

Horii smiled. "Yoshida must have made old Kanoh very annoyed indeed."

"He was posted to Admiral Nakamura's staff and then transferred to Vereshchagin's battalion during the Ashcroft campaign, where he was wounded in the face. I am surprised that he did not return home."

"To what purpose? His career was already over. Continue."

"It appears from Vereshchagin's last report that he has made Captain Raul Sanmartin battalion executive officer. He seems very young for this. Sanmartin was formerly C Company commander. He served with the Eleventh Imperial Shock Battalion and joined the 1/35th Imperial Rifle Battalion on Ashcroft, where he was decorated by Admiral Nakamura."

"He is very young. What is special about him?"

"Very little is apparent. His political-reliability index is also low. One of his prior commanders remarked that he has a passion for zoology and oceanography but lacks propriety." Yanagita looked up at Horii. "His parents were active ecologists arrested by the Argentinian government for political offenses."

Horii nodded. "Find out more."

"Yes, sir. Finally, the D Company commander is Major Paul Henke."

"The Hangman," Horii said without inflection. "I know about the Hangman. Enough. You will find nothing in his record to suggest why he is such a dangerous man."

"What is it that you wish me to deduce from this, sir?"

Horii stroked his chin. "Until the ties between the 1/35th Imperial Rifle Battalion and the 2/35th Imperial Rifle Battalion in Helsinki were severed when the latter battalion was disbanded, Lieutenant-Colonel Vereshchagin's men maintained an unbroken linkage with the national army of Finland—*Suomi*, I believe they call it in the local language, a land of woods and snow and Russian refugees."

Yanagita dutifully laughed at the admiral's small joke.

"Conditioned by their woods and snows and racial heritage," Admiral Horii continued, "the Finns have always placed an undue emphasis on individual initiative and unconventional, quasi-guerrilla tactics, and Vereshchagin, despite his Russian name, is no exception. So, Yanagita, tell me. From all that you have read, what is the key fact?"

Yanagita sucked in his breath and stood at attention. "I do not know, honored Admiral. I am shamed by my lack of comprehension."

"You should be. The key fact is that Vereshchagin, Harjalo, Kolomeitsev, and Henke have fought six colonial campaigns— Esdraelon, Odawara, Cyclade, NovySibir, Ashcroft, and Suid-Afrika—and they have survived. They have seen more combat than any similar group of officers in the Imperial Forces. They have never failed to achieve their objectives—which are not necessarily the objectives chosen for them—and they have survived. Do not forget this, Yanagita."

"Yes, sir." Yanagita hesitated. "Sir, did you wish me to discuss Lieutenant-Colonel Vereshchagin?"

"No, Yanagita. That will not be necessary. I have reviewed Anton Vereshchagin's career myself. He is nicknamed 'the Variag,' which is an archaic word meaning *viking*. He was also nicknamed Sertorius by Admiral Nakamura after Quintus Sertorius, a rebellious Roman general of non-Roman origin known for his probity." Horii smiled abruptly. "Please look these up. You are dismissed, Yanagita."

A few moments after Yanagita left, the door opened behind Horii and *Maya*'s commander cleared his throat. Horii turned expectantly.

"Honored sir, both the United Steel-Standard planetary director and Imperial Security Colonel Sumi await your convenience."

Horii turned away to shield his slight distaste. The USS man, Matsudaira, lacked both patience and propriety. The security man Sumi was immeasurably worse. Regrettably, neither man was under Horii's command.

He looked out once again at the world that called itself Suid-Afrika and stroked his wrinkled chin. Suid-Afrika was, he thought to himself, a delicate situation, a most delicate situation.

Colonel Sumi joined Horii beside the viewscreen. Although the top of Soemu Sumi's head barely reached his admiral's shoulder, either of the thick wrists gripping the stanchion was as thick as the calf of Horii's leg. Sumi wore the gray tabs of a political officer as well as the black stripes down his pants legs that marked him as Imperial Security Police.

Unfortunately, in addition to being the expedition's political officer, Sumi was also its chief of staff, in what Horii considered to be yet another ill-advised concession by the Ministry of Defense to the Ministry of Security. Presumably, this was due to the current shortage of "suitable" line officers in the appropriate grades; Horii was skeptical.

"We should just open fire," Sumi growled.

Horii saw *Maya*'s commander stiffen. "We should open fire on friendly cities occupied by Imperials troops? How strange," the admiral said, politely baiting the security police colonel.

"The rebels here should have felt the sword. I have read Vereshchagin's report. He and his men are either cowards or traitors," Sumi said with a calculated effrontery, not bothering to look at his superior in rank.

Had Sumi been under Admiral Horii's command, rather than a watchdog placed to oversee his actions, Horii would have had him disciplined on the spot. Instead he stroked his chin. "It is indeed fortunate that I give orders here."

"For now," Sumi agreed blandly.

Maya's commander jerked his head away and left them as they watched the first shuttles land troops at the raw, new spaceport that Anton Vereshchagin had built west of the city of Pretoria. Horii reflected that he would have to make it subtly apparent to *Maya*'s commander that it was imprudent to make his dislike for Imperial Security so obvious. "The planet did present a difficult tactical problem," he commented. "Recall that Admiral Lee lost four warships and two battalions, as well as his own life."

"The Korean admiral drank too much *soju*," Sumi grunted. "That is why we do not make Koreans admirals anymore."

The USS man, Daisuke Matsudaira, joined them, wearing a gray suit and a narrow, pinstriped tie. "Admiral Horii, Colonel Sumi," he said, executing a slight bow which the two of them returned. He moved his face up close to the viewscreen. "A most excellent landing, I am sure. I myself am most anxious to arrive on the planet and begin redeeming matters for my company. Perhaps tomorrow?"

"It is difficult to say, although I am sure that Lieutenant-Colonel Vereshchagin's precipitous decision to execute your predecessor for treason has left corporate matters in some disarray," Horii said blandly, disgusted by the man's lack of manners. "I will, of course, allow you to shuttle down as soon as affairs are propitious for your arrival."

When Anton Vereshchagin symbolically broke the back of the Afrikaner rebellion by executing Matsudaira's predecessor for assisting the rebels, it won him few friends on Earth. Nevertheless, Horii quite understood the impulse.

Matsudaira glanced at him with ill-concealed hatred.

How lacking in propriety, Horii thought to himself placidly.

Sumi grunted.

STANDING BESIDE THE RUNWAY, ACTING MAJOR RAUL SANMARTIN watched as Horii's newly arrived soldiers poured out of their shuttles and formed up into rigidly disciplined parade ranks. Horii's leading elements were tough Manchurians, tall and stocky in crisp, new fatigues, part of a three-battalion regiment. Mentally, Sanmartin compared them to the worn and faded uniforms of the honor platoon he had brought from C Company.

Captain Hans Coldewe, C Company's commander, had been Sanmartin's executive officer when Sanmartin was C Company commander. Coldewe whispered, "Those big Chinese boys look sharp."

Sanmartin nodded. "I understand there's also a crack Japanese light attack battalion and a battalion of the Imperial Guard in orbit waiting to come down."

"Trouble," Coldewe said. Troops from the Imperial homeland almost always meant trouble.

They didn't waste troops like that on the colonial fringes unless someone was especially annoyed. Vereshchagin's soldiers had served continuously in colonial campaigns for twenty-six subjective years, which amounted to nearly a half century in time elapsed on Earth. His officers had few illusions, and Raul Sanmartin had fewer illusions left than most.

Before Vereshchagin had taken the reins of power, USS had owned the planet and tried to rule it ruthlessly. Shooting the USS planetary director, more than any other single act, had convinced the Afrikaners that Vereshchagin meant a fresh start. USS had just returned in the persons of these troops, and Sanmartin was convinced that the bill for peace had just fallen due.

"Shall we do it?" Coldewe whispered.

Sanmartin nodded.

Coldewe made a quick gesture behind his back, and the battalion bagpipe band launched into the stirring strains of "The

Whistling Pig," which was the battalion's favorite drinking song.

The melody—if massed bagpipes can be said to play melody—caught the Manchurians by surprise. "I love that little look of fear in their eyes when the pipes go off," Coldewe said contentedly.

The remaining Manchurians were slow in arriving, and Sanmartin stole a glance at his wrist mount. Coldewe whispered out of the corner of his mouth, "Isn't this your night to go home for dinner?"

Sanmartin grinned foolishly. His wife, Hanna, the lady speaker of Suid-Afrika's assembly, had a hellish temper when he was late. He had missed one of their infrequent meals together five years ago when an Afrikaner farmboy had planted two rounds in his thigh, and since then she tended to worry.

VERESHCHAGIN WATCHED AS THE ROOM FILLED. MATTI HARJALO and Lieutenant-Colonel Uwe Ebyl came with their key officers, and President Albert Beyers brought eight of his "*stoep* friends" who could speak for everyone on the planet whose opinion mattered. Last to appear was Eva Moore, a bridge of sorts between the two worlds. Three years ago, Moore had resigned her lieutenant-colonel's commission when Vereshchagin sent her Fifteenth Support Battalion back to Earth, accepting a job as administrator of Pretoria's hospital, which she ran for her patients' benefit with wit and an absolutely iron hand.

Beyers opened the meeting formally. "We understand that a new Imperial task group has arrived, Anton," he said in his accented English. "What does this mean to us?"

"Yes. Who will they shoot?" Christos Claassen, head of the opposition Reformed Nationalist party, asked with mock humor. Coming from him, the question was particularly apt. A banker and former member of the semisecret Afrikaner Bond, Claassen had played a leading role in the abortive Afrikaner rebellion. Although Claassen had had nothing to do with the nuclear blasts that had destroyed the spaceport, two cowboy towns, and three Imperial warships in orbit, his name figured prominently on the *Geloftsdag* proclamation of independence, and his position as a vocal leader of the opposition party made him even more vulnerable.

Beyers smiled and patted Claassen's wrist. In two elections, he and Claassen had slung enough mud at each other to build adobe houses; privately they were the closest of friends. Only

Claassen's inherent good sense kept the demagogues in his Reformed National party from staking out uncompromisingly radical postures.

"Who will they shoot? That remains to be seen," Vereshchagin told the group, quite seriously. He nodded, and Matti Harjalo spoke.

"We've chatted with the task group, and it's a big one, no mistake—the biggest I've ever seen. They have a three-battalion regiment of Manchurians, a battalion of the Imperial Guard, a Japanese light attack battalion, heaven knows how much artillery and aircraft, *and* a frigate and three corvettes. The new commander is Vice-Admiral Saburu Horii, and he came here loaded to hunt bear," Harjalo commented, using a quaint expression he had picked up on one colonial world or another. His lip curled. "They also brought along two companies of blacklegs. Maybe we could bribe one company to shoot the other."

Blacklegs—Imperial Security Police—were openly despised by soldiers and civilians alike for their brutality and venality.

Prinsloo Adriaan Smith, the Lord Mayor of Pretoria, asked an obvious question. "Matti, what do they want with so many soldiers?" Blond and extraordinarily thin, Smith invariably wore the same rumpled suit. A former journalist, he had never quite lost the habit of asking awkward questions.

"I don't know," Harjalo confessed. "Maybe paint all of the rocks white. I can think of other answers, but I don't like any of them."

Major Piotr Kolomeitsev, commander of Harjalo's A Company, looked at Vereshchagin, who nodded. The Iceman's pale eyes glittered. "I will say what everyone here already suspects. Either the Imperial Government did not believe our original report that we had the rebellion controlled, or they wish to impose a much greater degree of control over this planet and its inhabitants. USS may be greedy enough to desire this."

Kolomeitsev rarely bothered to conceal his contempt for the Imperial Government and its policies. He had achieved his present rank before the Imperial Government had begun measuring the political-reliability index of its officers, and he was prone to joke that his index was so low that he would not be eligible for promotion in any of his next six incarnations.

Vereshchagin turned to his political officer. "Chiharu, can you add to this?"

Useless as a combat commander, Captain Chiharu Yoshida was unnaturally gifted as a political officer and had helped design the government that Vereshchagin had imposed on Suid-Afrika. Although Yoshida had served under Vereshchagin for six years, Vereshchagin did not know where his ultimate loyalties lay and doubted whether Yoshida knew.

Yoshida steepled his fingers thoughtfully. "The Imperial Government has been loath to send Japanese national troops away from Earth. Previously, it has never included two Japanese battalions in the same task group, and has only sent Imperial Guard battalions to suppress colonial disorder on two prior occasions. For this reason, the composition of the present task group is a significant departure from policy. I am not, however, able to say what it signifies, so it is difficult to understand Admiral Horii's intentions."

It had taken Yoshida years to live down the highly uncomplimentary nickname "Tingrin."

The chain-smoking matriarch of a cowboy clan, Nadine Joh, commented, "Things I don't understand make me nervous. My family owns a lot of land that USS used to think it owned. USS'll have to shoot us to get it back. I'm wondering whether Horii intends to try."

"I think that we must assume that the task group was sent here to end resistance to Imperial rule, which by most definitions we have already done," Major Paul Henke, the Hangman, volunteered judiciously. "The question is how Admiral Horii defines this."

Where the Iceman was earth—stolid, preternaturally calm, and possessed of a dour wit—the Hangman was fire. Henke was possessed by nervous energy, and where Kolomeitsev wore one scar, a long one down the side of his face, Vereshchagin knew that Henke bore scars that did not show.

"So, what you are all saying is that they sent too many troops and too many Japanese soldiers to a planet far from Earth," Beyers said, summing up. "This is not hopeful."

Immensely popular, Beyers was one of the few truly honest men that Vereshchagin had ever met. He had been unstinting in his criticism of the minor irritants of Imperial rule, to which Vereshchagin had responded with waspish replies and measured retreats to the evident delight of the populace.

In fact, the two of them planned and occasionally rehearsed their more outrageous exchanges. Vereshchagin explained this by saying that if water is too pure, fish can't live in it. Beyers was even blunter, saying that his Afrikaners were entitled to circuses along with their bread.

"So, what can the Imperials do to us?" a second cowboy clan leader asked. The youngest person present, "Little Jim" McClausland had grown up quickly and headed an important family, but still asked some engagingly naive questions.

"Transport the lot of us and impose a military government," Eva Moore said flatly.

"And what of our people, then?" Hanna Bruwer asked softly.

Vereshchagin quoted an old proverb. " 'When wood is cut, the splinters fly.' "

"We know what United Steel-Standard will want. The question is how far Admiral Horii will be willing to go to accommodate them," Bruwer responded. "Let us assume for the moment that he will not. What is the worst possible case?"

Vereshchagin nodded, and Raul Sanmartin answered for him. "I can think of several scenarios. If the new USS director can't persuade Admiral Horii to put Albert's government out of business, he might try to funnel money to the Afrikaner Resistance Movement. With luck and enough money and a little heavy-handed repression from the blacklegs, the ARM boys could make it impossible for a civilian government to function and force Horii to impose a military government. Worse yet, by then, a lot of our people might want to see one."

Claassen said, rather too loudly, "The planet is mostly at peace, and its wounds have healed far better than I would have imagined possible. Even the Afrikaner Resistance Movement is tired of fighting. Should we tell Admiral Horii that if he doesn't like Albert as president, he can always have me?"

"You should have kept me from being elected when you had the opportunity, but you always were soft-hearted," Beyers said.

Claassen grinned, making no effort to deny the charge. "It was poor strategy on my part."

Vereshchagin thought not and knew that Claassen didn't believe it either. Claassen had allowed his closest rival in the Reformed Nationalist party to go head-to-head with Beyers—and Beyers had dropped the man in a very deep hole.

Everyone was nervous, and Vereshchagin could see that the meeting had lost its focus. He caught Beyers's eye and brought it to a close.

"Obviously, we will have to see what Admiral Horii intends. I shall try to make him view the Afrikaner Resistance Movement as a serious threat, which may induce him to proceed cautiously. We will consult again when we have more information."

Nadine Joh got in one parting shot. "And where will you stand, Anton, if things begin to go badly?" she asked.

"Anton will be our *amicus usque ad aras*," Bruwer said, extricating Vereshchagin from the need to reply and deliberately teasing her husband, who had picked up the habit of quoting Latin phrases on odd occasions and lived to regret it.

"This translates as, 'He will be our friend as far as the altars,' which is to say he will be our friend as far as his conscience will permit," Raul Sanmartin explained, unconsciously identifying with the planet's inhabitants.

Tuesday(309)

ADMIRAL HORII PACED THE FLOOR OF THE NEWLY BUILT SPACEPORT administration building that he had commandeered to use as his headquarters. Hearing his intelligence officer enter, without turning or changing his expression, he said, "Captain Yanagita, explain what you have learned about the political system here."

Yanagita had spent most of the previous night assembling information, and his eyes were rimmed by dark circles.

"Yes, sir. The natives are very open about their politics. We had very little difficulty in assembling data. They have a multiparty democratic system."

"Real multiple parties?" Horii asked sharply, inclining his head slightly.

"Yes, sir. In addition to Albert Beyers's Union party, which has both Afrikaner and cowboy members and controls the government, there is a strong and very vocal Afrikaner traditionalist party led by a former rebel, Christos Claassen, and two small, somewhat chaotic cowboy traditionalist parties. There is also a pro-Imperial party organized by a former USS employee. It holds no seats in the Assembly." Yanagita turned his head to cloak his embarrassment. "Other parties consider it a joke."

"Continue," Horii said, looking out the window once more.

"The president, Albert Beyers, is the chief executive. He was recently reelected to a second four-year term of office. The Assembly is unicameral and consists of sixty members, forty from Afrikaner districts, eighteen from cowboy districts, and two which represent the descendants of religious sects."

Horii nodded. "I recall that the religious sects were the planet's first settlers. Go on."

"About the judiciary, sir?"

"No." Horii looked at him directly for the first time. "I assume that Beyers has a cabinet or ministries. Who holds power? In the Assembly, who holds power?"

"In the executive office, the four ministers seem to be the president's subordinates. They are dismissed at the president's pleasure."

"And in the Assembly?"

Yanagita cleared his throat. "Currently, the Union party holds thirty-nine of the sixty seats. Claassen's party holds thirteen seats, and the two Cowboy parties hold five. The remaining seats are held by independents. The Assembly has four permanent committees and four temporary committees. The Commerce and Agriculture Committee and the Procedures Committee appear to have the most authority, as other committees have very few bills to consider. The speaker is elected by the membership. The current speaker is a woman named Hanna Bruwer who is married to one of Vereshchagin's officers. She appoints the committee heads and chairs the Procedures Committee."

"Interesting. Extremely interesting."

"Sir?"

"Observe—it is unusual, Captain Yanagita, to see a democratic system where political power is so overtly concentrated. Anton Vereshchagin is a very shrewd man."

"Sir?"

Horii ignored him. "I have directed Lieutenant-Colonel Vereshchagin, Lieutenant-Colonel Ebyl, and Major Harjalo to report to me. Let me know when they arrive." He looked at Yanagita. "It is strange, is it not? All of the senior surviving officers of the first Imperial task group were *gaijin*. Strange that only foreigner officers should survive."

"The ways of heaven are inscrutable, sir," Yanagita agreed politely.

As he spoke, the car carrying Vereshchagin, Harjalo, and Ebyl appeared in view.

Inside the vehicle, Harjalo removed one hand from the wheel and stabbed the air for emphasis. "Uwe, are you saying I should have brought along some private as a chauffeur so he can sleep in the car when he could be working? The next thing you know, you'll be telling me to make snappy salutes to impress the admiral. You're getting soft on me, Uwe, soft!"

Ebyl grinned. Ebyl was thin, bald as an egg, and possessed of an explosive temper. Like many other officers who chose a career on the colonial fringes, Ebyl had been rated politically unreliable by Imperial Security. He didn't much care. Ebyl's battalion had fought in four of the Imperial Government's colonial campaigns, and few of his men were Earth-born. They didn't much care either.

He affected a yawn. "So, Anton, so what will you do if Horii doesn't shoot us?"

"If I am encouraged to resign, I doubt that I will be encouraged to stay here on Suid-Afrika. As you know, for years now, men from my battalion have been emigrating to a planet called Esdraelon."

"Lots and lots of years," Harjalo interjected.

"I could go there to plant potatoes and philosophize."

Harjalo snorted. "People would pay money to see you placidly planting potatoes. So—when Admiral Horii fires you, do we resign, too?"

Vereshchagin winced. Matti knew just where to prick. "Please try *not* to entangle yourself in my downfall."

Ebyl made a very rude noise. "Anton, you old fraud, after what you did to USS, we will all go down, but I wouldn't have missed this if they had offered to make me a vice-admiral."

They parked the car in silence and presented themselves to the sentries at the door.

As they entered the spaceport's conference room, Admiral Horii and Colonel Sumi were grouped around a table along with the colonel of the Manchurians and seven or eight staff officers. Vereshchagin stopped a few paces away from Admiral Horii and saluted. "Lieutenant-Colonel Vereshchagin, acting task group commander, presenting myself for further orders."

Horii returned his salute. "Welcome, Lieutenant-Colonel Vereshchagin. Please be seated," he said with apparent sincerity. He nodded to his aide who pulled a small diskette from his pocket and handed it to Vereshchagin. "One of your former officers, a Lieutenant Mizoguchi, gave me this to give to you."

"Thank you, sir." Vereshchagin bowed slightly before taking a seat. He gestured to his companions. "Lieutenant-Colonel Ebyl, Major Harjalo."

"Yes, I recognize them from their files," Horii said. "This is Colonel Sumi, my chief of staff and political officer."

Sumi glared.

Horii ignored him and asked, "Lieutenant-Colonel Vereshchagin, in your estimation, what is the current military situation here?"

"As I attempted to make clear in my second report, conventional resistance has ceased. The bulk of the population has accepted the local government, but there are still several active terrorist organizations. The most dangerous one is a millenarian organization which calls itself the Afrikaner Resistance Movement—I believe that it is the third organization to use that particular name. It is well organized and well supplied with arms." He smiled, keeping his eyes on Sumi's impassive face. "Its adherents tried to set off a rather large car bomb in the city yesterday."

"Have you infiltrated them?" Sumi demanded.

"To some degree," Vereshchagin told him.

"I want their names."

"That would be awkward," Vereshchagin said serenely. "None of our contacts realize that they are working for the Imperial Government."

"I am sure that we can discuss details of security arrangements at a later time," Horii interjected. "What of the other terrorist movements?"

"The Afrikaner Order was the secret society which actually launched the uprising. We have seriously injured them, and they are currently biding their time, rebuilding their organization and awaiting a better opportunity. They may still have access to nuclear weapons."

Sitting beside Colonel Sumi, Captain Yanagita blanched.

"There are also two small anti-Imperial organizations active in the cowboy country," Vereshchagin concluded. "The secret war here is winnable, but not yet won."

"And what of the political situation?" Horii asked politely.

"Last year, as acting task group commander, I approved complete self-rule for this planet in accordance with the Guardianship Council's resolution on the matter." Vereshchagin kept his face perfectly composed, politely ignoring the fact that self-rule had never been granted to planets settled by non-Japanese.

This was too much for USS Planetary Director Matsudaira, who hissed, "You have greatly exceeded your authority by doing so!"

"Matsudaira-san, perhaps as our guest, you would like us to take a short break," Horii said, obviously enjoying the situation.

"No, honored Admiral," Matsudaira responded sulkily.

"I have asked the Colonial Ministry to rule on the matter," Vereshchagin said. "I expect to receive a definitive opinion in three or four years. Currently, Dr. Albert Beyers's Union party has a secure hold on the central government. Dr. Beyers has been very willing to cooperate in most matters and has been able to persuade his party to follow his lead. The other political parties are at least latently anti-Imperial."

"What about the New Auspices party?" Sumi asked harshly.

"The New Auspices party only exists because I continue to fund it. The local inhabitants usually refer to it as the 'Kafferboetie' party, which translates best as 'Black Brothers' party, and the expression is not intended as an endearment."

"And if I were to reconsider your action granting self-rule to be a nullity and dissolve the local government?" Horii asked, looking at Sumi.

"At best, you would have to substitute direct military government. If Dr. Beyers retired from politics, Christos Claassen would almost certainly be elected president, and his Reformed Nationalist party would probably win control of the Assembly. Heer Claassen, although reformed, is a former rebel, and he is far more moderate than many of his supporters. I would recommend against reviving United Steel-Standard's charter to govern. Both the Afrikaners and the cowboys would substitute labor unrest for political activity."

"Major Harjalo, do you concur in these assessments?" Horii asked formally.

"Yes," Harjalo replied, his nostrils flaring very slightly.

Horii looked at Ebyl. "Lieutenant-Colonel Ebyl, do you also concur?"

"Although a brilliant man, the late Admiral Lee, our previous commander, wasn't a particularly good judge of character, which is a polite way of saying he almost got us all killed," Ebyl observed. "Neither the cowboys nor the Afrikaners will stand for too much nonsense, and they hate USS." He pointed to Vereshchagin. "Anton is the pin that keeps the grenade from going off, so you'd better keep him."

"I will, of course, resign my commission if you desire this and if my actions here do not meet with the approval of the Imperial Government," Vereshchagin said politely.

Horii stroked his chin and studied Ebyl and Harjalo. "We must study the situation and take your advice under consideration before taking any precipitate action. I value your services, Lieutenant-Colonel Vereshchagin, and would ask you not to resign. You will have a place on my staff."

"Thank you, sir." Watching through the corner of his eye, Vereshchagin noted Sumi's self-control almost give way.

After discussing billeting arrangements for the newly arrived troops, they talked inconsequentially for several more hours. As they were about to leave, Vereshchagin asked Horii, "How is Lieutenant Mizoguchi?"

Horii gestured to Yanagita, who replied, "He has been discharged and leads a very productive life in his home city."

"And his eyes?" Vereshchagin asked.

"Unfortunately, his optic nerves have not responded to regenerative therapy."

Vereshchagin nodded. Moments later, he left the building with Ebyl and Harjalo. As they walked toward the car, Harjalo said, "For a moment there, it sounded like you knew this admiral."

"Yes, I recognized him almost immediately. He served on Cyclade as a lieutenant with the Third Lifeguards Battalion. He's picked up about a dozen years on us because of the time differential."

Harjalo gave him a surprised look. "The Third Lifeguards—they were the ones who got themselves shot up by the Provis."

"Yes. Horii was one of the ones who survived."

Harjalo glanced back over his shoulder. "Horii may turn out all right, but Sumi obviously has a six-*jo* mind next to a twelve-*jo* ego," referring to the straw floor mats that Japanese use to measure their homes.

"Like most blacklegs," Ebyl quipped.

As they drove away, Vereshchagin asked, "Matti, did anything strike you as odd?"

Harjalo thought for a second. "One thing did. Every officer we met was native Japanese."

"Lord of heaven, you are right," Ebyl said.

"Ten years ago, 40 percent of the officers admitted into the academies were non-Japanese," Vereshchagin said slowly, "and officers selected for colonial postings have always been overwhelmingly non-Japanese. No one with connections ever wanted to fall out of step with his year-group."

"Nobody with connections has ever wanted a posting this far out," Harjalo said bitterly. "Something's changed. Do you think that they put together a special all-Japanese lineup just for us?"

"Matti, it would worry me more if they had not selected Japanese officers just for us. It would suggest fundamental changes in the Imperial system."

"If this is the case, Anton, I am even more surprised that they did not accept your offer to resign," Ebyl articulated.

"Accepting Anton's resignation would have been a face-saving compromise," Harjalo said.

"I do not understand," Ebyl responded.

"It might mean that they don't like the political solution that we crafted and want us to help them with something unusually damned mean," Harjalo explained. "Or maybe it's something worse."

Vereshchagin stuck the disk from Mizoguchi out of his pocket and inserted it into the vehicle's stereo system. As he listened to Mizoguchi's voice, his face hardened. Although the voice was Mizoguchi's, the flavor of the words as he described the unsuccessful operation on his eyes and talked about his family's distress at his injury was not. The recording quality was poor, with a noticeable hiss. The bland phrases were jarring.

Isolated from Earth by time dilation and distance, Vereshchagin wanted from Mizo a candid appraisal of the political events that were happening on Earth. Things changed over the years, and the Variag had learned not to trust everything he heard from official sources. Political news was the one thing that wasn't on the disk.

He ejected it with a jab of his finger and stuck it in Matti Harjalo's pocket. "Mizo must have put something more on this than platitudes. Have Timo Haerkoennen work on it until we find out what it is that he could not tell us openly."

Harjalo set his mouth tightly. They finished the trip in silence.

BACK AT ADMIRAL HORII'S TEMPORARY HEADQUARTERS, SUMI erupted as soon as the staff members cleared the room. "Vice-Admiral, I protest! You had that fox-faced foreigner in the palm of your hand and let him go!"

"Governance, Sumi, consists of plucking the goose without killing it. Effective governance involves securing the most feathers from the bird with the least amount of hissing. We have the terrorist movements to contend with." He held up his hand. "It would take you months to duplicate Lieutenant-Colonel Vereshchagin's efforts. In my estimation, the situation here requires a 'Winter Campaign of Osaka.' Unless you resolutely disagree, this is the strategy that we will employ."

Sumi's jaw tightened. Bowing perfunctorily, he left the room

In 1614, the moats and palisades of Osaka castle were eight and three-quarters miles around and bristling with heavy ordnance; they stood between Ieyasu Tokugawa and domination of Japan. Besieging the fortress, Ieyasu negotiated with the defenders, simultaneously gripping their throats and stroking their backs. Negotiating a settlement that involved tearing down the castle's outer defenses, he easily seized the castle the following summer, making "A Winter Campaign of Osaka" into a proverb.

"It is good that we have an enemy here," Horii said to the walls of the room. "Otherwise, it might be necessary to invent one."

Wednesday(309)

SENIOR COMMUNICATIONS SERGEANT TIMO HAERKOENNEN CURSED softly, and mostly he cursed former lieutenant Hiroshi Mizoguchi.

Hiroshi Mizoguchi, the second son in a one-position corporate family, had been a lieutenant in B Company until he was blinded by a mortar shell. Vereshchagin had sent him home on the assault transport *Shokaku*, with a dozen other severely wounded and one hundred and fifty Afrikaners being transported for their role in the rebellion.

Unless Mizoguchi had had an operation on his head to stuff it with rocks, there should have been something more on his disk.

Haerkoennen looked at his assistant.

"Maybe Mizo taped it under duress. Or maybe he lost his nerve," the assistant speculated. "Or maybe somebody switched tapes."

"We'll talk about maybes after we check through every sound," Haerkoennen replied.

AS THE BEYERS FAMILY SAT FOR SUPPER, HANNA BRUWER NOTICED that the look on her husband's face would curdle milk. "I had to talk with farmers about their taxes, so what went wrong with your day, Raul?"

Sanmartin smiled and absently stroked her arm. "I had Ssu run a batch of the newspapers that Admiral Horii brought through the computer for me."

Ssu, a retired senior censor, was Suid-Afrika's most capable political analyst.

"Once again, in our humble and collective opinion, it's an 80 percent probability that what the Japanese people are reading is being censored pretty thoroughly, and it's a 100 percent certainty that what came in with the task group was run through a filter. The only thing I believe is the economic numbers. Stock prices are up, earnings are not, and productivity is down. If you ask three different professors of economics what that means, you'll get four different answers, but I think it means Earth's economic system is being monkeyed with more than usual, and it frightens me."

"*Radix omnium malorum est cupiditas,*" his wife added promptly. "The love of money is the root of all evil."

Sanmartin sighed. While serving with a unit on Earth that stressed "samurai virtue and Roman discipline," he had picked up the habit of quoting Latin tags on every conceivable occasion. Bruwer had cured him of the practice by adopting it.

"Have you two thought about what we should do if Admiral Horii decides to turn the government back over to USS?" Albert Beyers interjected before his wife could come in and tell him to stop talking business at the table.

"As they used to say, *Viva el Rey, y muera el mal gobierno.* Long live the king, and death to a bad government," Sanmartin commented. "We might even get away with it." He touched Vroew Beyers's battered table with a finger, reflecting that with much of Suid-Afrika's history made around it, it ought to end up in a museum someday.

"What about the troops Horii brought, how good are they, sir?" Tom Winters, Bruwer's secretary cum bodyguard, asked, old habits dying hard.

"The Japanese are well trained, but inexperienced." Sanmartin grimaced. "Manchurians are tough and tend to get used for dirty jobs. We used to joke that you could tell the Manchurians had been through when your garbage had been picked over and your dogs were pregnant."

His wife shook her head and kicked him under the table.

Beyers chuckled. "Hanna, you will never make a politician out of him if he keeps telling jokes like that."

"No, I'm half-serious," Sanmartin protested. He thought for a minute. "I don't like them. What I mean is, I think if someone ordered them to go out and rape babies, they'd do it. And they'd probably enjoy it."

Hanna Bruwer closed her eyes. "Enough! No more politics," she said forcefully, as Betje Beyers entered carrying a soup tureen. Hendricka walked solemnly at her side holding the hem of her dress.

Nicknamed the "Ice Princess" by both her friends and detractors, Bruwer was a former teacher hired to support

Vereshchagin's battalion as a translator. It was a poorly kept secret that she had pushed Albert Beyers into supporting Vereshchagin during the uprising; and Beyers had appointed her interior minister in his provisional government.

Married and pregnant, she had run in Suid-Afrika's first election and had won despite or perhaps because of her reputation as Beyers's hatchet man. The man she ran against had boasted that he was old enough to be her grandfather. She had cut him to pieces with the remark during the campaign.

In Suid-Afrika's first assembly, she had been elected speaker, partly because she was the only aspirant for the post who could be trusted not to steal the smoke off a hot fire, and partly because she was Hendrik Pienaar's granddaughter. Pienaar had been the only successful rebel general, and no one quite forgot that Hendrik had been gunned down for having the courage to say that the rebellion had failed—and had arranged to take most of the people who disagreed along with him. What Bruwer believed in, she believed in passionately, and as a politician she accepted no favors and gave no quarter.

Joining hands with Vroew Beyers, she said, "We will now pray, preferably for peace."

Thursday(309)

THE COMPLEX JUST NORTHEAST OF PRETORIA WAS SUID-AFRIKA'S main manufacturing facility, producing everything from light machine tools to household appliances to cheap fuel alcohol for the planet's vehicles. Striding its narrow corridors toward the central conference room, Daisuke Matsudaira took pride in its dimensions. He paused at the door to finger his narrow tie, and then walked into the room followed by his aides. The USS executives around the conference table, all Afrikaners, rose obediently when he entered.

Matsudaira took his seat at the head of the table and accepted papers from the aide carrying his briefcase. "Sit down, gentlemen. I am Daisuke Matsudaira. I am your new director. We will now sing the company song." After they did so, he said, "You now will explain to me the present status of USS corporate operations on this planet."

"Yes, Planetary Director," a tall, cadaverous man with close-cut brown hair said.

"And you are?" Matsudaira demanded.

"Jooste Deiselmann. Mining operations director and acting planetary director until your arrival. Lieutenant-Colonel Vereshchagin returned Heer Hosagawa, the former mining operations director, to Earth four years ago." He added by way of explanation, "Heèr Hosagawa made the mistake of violating the local election campaign contribution laws a little too flagrantly."

"I see," Matsudaira said slowly.

A man to Matsudaira's left spoke up. "Actually, he tried to bribe the treasury minister. Fairly crudely. The minister was not amused. I am Niklaas Van Reenen, light metals."

Ostensibly ignoring Van Reenen's unseemly outburst, Matsudaira made a note to himself, then asked formally, "Heer Deiselmann, how do you rate our operations here?"

"This year, for the first time in seven years, USS has the potential to actually make money here. We have scaled back most of our marginal efforts and consolidated our operations into four directorates instead of the previous nine. Despite the government's stiff environmental-damage assessment, mining and energy operations will show a small profit this year, and I project small profits for the next three years as we phase in pollution-control equipment."

"And what of our other operations?" Matsudaira muttered, deliberately studying the balance sheets in front of him so that he would not have to meet Deiselmann's eyes.

"Industrial operations will show a substantial profit this year, which is largely attributable to our joint ventures and to increased productivity from Complex. However, construction and transportation operations will fail to produce a profit, and agricultural and forestry operations will post significant losses."

"And why is this?" Matsudaira demanded peremptorily.

"Because of the land taxes and the environmental-damage assessments that the government imposes, it is uneconomical for us to continue to hold title to large, low-yielding tracts of land. There is currently no off-planet market for agricultural products, and the local market is fiercely competitive. Although we have sold off 46 percent of the land holdings that remained to us after the government survey, it would be prudent for us to sell our remaining agricultural land to individuals who are prepared to farm it intensively. We have refrained from doing so until we received approval from Earth. With regard to construction and transportation operations, this division has been too large and inefficient to compete for smaller jobs."

"We will not retrench our operations. We must expand!"

Matsudaira said firmly. "It is incumbent upon us to increase our market share rather than show cowardice at this juncture. How is it that our small competitors receive financing?"

"The government has a development fund, and they have made it known that they will provide loans at market rates to credit-worthy concerns that the banks refuse to finance." Deiselmann began tapping the end of his pen against the table, without realizing that he was doing so. "The banks have concluded that it is in their best interests to provide credit to our competitors."

Matsudaira took a gulp of water from a glass handed to him by an observant aide and asked silkily, "How is it that you have allowed the government to do this?"

Deiselmann smiled for the first time. "After the mistakes made by the late Planetary Director Tuge and by Heer Hosagawa, our ability to influence the government has been limited. In fact, the government has made efforts to further competition at our expense."

"This cannot be allowed to continue. Conceding market share is weakness which imperils the company," Matsudaira shouted. "The fate of the Suzuki *zaibatsu* shows the dangers that we face. When hard times came, her enemies withdrew money from her banks and spread malicious gossip. When the banks were forced to suspend loans, the House of Suzuki fell to pieces, and Yone Suzuki's enemies feasted at her table."

Matsudaira thrust his finger out like a sword. "You think that our company is stable, but I tell you it has many, many enemies. I tell you that continued instability here will be a source of malicious gossip. Business is war, and in war there are many casualties. A steady, assured supply of the metals this planet produces is essential, and the situation here has been a source of weakness in our company's fortress walls."

The stolid Afrikaners around the conference table waited for him to finish his tirade.

Oblivious to his audience, Matsudaira laid his hand on a stack of papers. "This instability cannot continue. I will rectify it, no matter what cost. Our first concern must be to increase our control of industrial production and construction operations so that we can either exert pressure on the government to make it recognize our legitimate interests or replace it with a more harmonious government. To do so, we must wage an unremitting campaign. My staff has begun preparing a detailed plan. Our first step will be to attack firms which have interjected themselves into the building trade. We must divert assets and cripple them, regardless of cost."

A rim man in spectacles protested immediately. "Heer Matsudaira, we cannot divert teams. We have several large projects under contracts guaranteed by the Johannesburg municipal government. If the construction falls behind schedule, the burgemeester will revoke our performance bond. Heer Matsudaira, you simply cannot do this."

Matsudaira looked down at the seating chart his aides had prepared. He said coldly, "Heer Langermann, you have a defeatist attitude. Your employment is terminated. Please leave this building immediately. Your things will be sent to you."

Slowly, insolently, Langermann pushed back his chair and left the room.

"I trust I have made my point. Is there anyone else in this room with a defeatist attitude?" Matsudaira asked.

Van Reenen glared at him. "Matsudaira-san. With all due respect, you are an ass! You have just cost industrial and energy operations its best plant manager."

"Van Reenen, is it? You are also fired!"

"You cannot fire me," Van Reenen said boldly, "I don't work for you. I am chief executive officer of one of your subsidiary operations, one of many such subsidiaries, I might add. It is very difficult for United Steel-Standard to market products under its own name on this planet." He showed his teeth in what might have been a smile. "I can only be fired by my board of directors. The man you fired had a golden parachute built into his contract and is entitled to take away the profits his division made for the last year."

Deiselmann added glumly, "Heer Van Reenen is correct, and even worse, to meet our production schedules, we will probably have to ask Heer Langermann back as a consultant. If you terminate his contract, it means that we won't show a profit for at least three quarters."

"We will break his contract! Where is our general counsel?" Matsudaira said, looking around the room.

"We don't have a general counsel. It was contracted out. A lot of things were contracted out." Van Reenen laughed. "As for breaking Langermann's contract, short of throwing out the three years' worth of laws and buying up the court system, you can't. For several years now, every contract this corporation has entered into has been written with a great degree of care. After your predecessor got himself shot for treason against the

Imperial Government, this corporation has not had nearly as much bargaining power as you might imagine. There have been a lot of changes."

Deiselmann held up a twenty-rand note apologetically. "The company is not even permitted to circulate its own currency anymore. The government's central bank prints our money, now."

When the last embers of the Afrikaner rebellion were dying, Vereshchagin did a curious thing. He took Major Kolomeitsev, Major Henke, and two dozen of his best noncommissioned officers and sent them to manage USS operations. While Henke concentrated on setting up military production facilities at Complex, the Iceman systematically screened managers and employees, reassigning the misplaced and terminating the inept and unwilling, in line with his philosophy that 5 percent of the people create 95 percent of the problems.

In doing so, the Iceman eliminated whatever remaining influence USS had over its workers. Vereshchagin completed the process by shipping out virtually all of the company's Japanese executives, allowing Afrikaners to replace them.

As Deiselmann told Matsudaira politely but pointedly, "We have laws here now, Heer Matsudaira, and USS has had to bend to those laws. Indeed, we have been pleased to follow them."

Friday(309)

IT WAS LATE IN THE EVENING, AND HARALD BREYTENBACH WAS AB-sently skimming an article in a professional journal when his telephone rang.

He picked it up. *"Hallo."*

"Liberty," a voice intoned on the other end.

Breytenbach exhaled deeply. After he calmed himself, he said in Afrikaans, "All right. What can I do for you?"

"Is your car parked out in front of your house?" the other person asked in the same language.

"Yes. Why?"

"Do not ask. You have no need to know. You do not want to know. Go out and make sure that it is not locked. In about an hour, go ahead and report it as stolen to the police. We will leave it where it can be found."

"Oh, my Lord. Why me?" Breytenbach asked in a strained voice.

"Everyone must do their part in the struggle against oppression, as much as they are able," the voice said. "Your classmates who are comrades have said that you will do your part. Will you?"

"Why, yes," Breytenbach babbled, "but still, it is my car, after all."

"Some comrades will use it and leave it. The new Imperials are not as vigilant as Vereshchagin's men."

Almost overnight, Suid-Afrika's inhabitants had begun calling Admiral Horii's men "the Imperials," while referring to the resident Imperial soldiers as "Vereshchagin's men."

"No suspicion will attach to you," the voice continued. "You will do your part, will you not?"

"My car will be there," Breytenbach said dully, chilled by some of the stories he had heard about how the Movement dealt with traitors.

"Liberty. Long live the Resistance!" the voice said.

"Long live the Resistance," Breytenbach responded.

As he hung up the telephone, he quoted softly to himself, "Liberty, liberty. What crimes are committed in thy name?" He dutifully went out and unlocked his little car.

An hour later, in a seedy part of Pretoria-Wes, Breytenbach's car slowed next to two Manchurian soldiers standing on a street corner, and a gunman in the passenger seat sprayed them with bullets. One Manchurian died, and a second was critically wounded. The police recovered the abandoned car about twelve blocks away.

Saturday(309)

COLONEL SUMI PULLED UP TO THE PRETORIA STAATSAMP WITH A squad of blacklegs.

The policeman at the door stopped him before he could enter. "I am sorry, sir. You cannot go in there armed." He was unmoved by threats.

With singular ill grace, Sumi turned his pistol over to his aide and left most of his security policemen at the door. "President Beyers is not in, but Speaker Bruwer-Sanmartin is in her office, and I am certain that she will make time to see you. It is on the first floor," the policeman said cheerily in clipped English.

Sumi went up the steps and hesitated at the top.

"Colonel Sumi? I assume that this is you," Bruwer called out crisply. "Please come in."

Sumi entered her office followed by the two blacklegs. He bowed slightly. "Vroew Bruwer-Sanmartin, I wish to see President Beyers immediately."

Seated behind a plain metal desk, Bruwer was simply dressed in a dark blue—almost black—outfit with her blond hair cut very short. The only jewelry she wore was a steel wedding band.

"Heer Beyers is unavailable at this moment. We packed him off to light a fire under some civil servants. May I assist you instead? I have ten minutes to spare for any constituent who can manage to find my door, so I can spare at least that much time for you," she said politely, still seated at her desk.

"Two of our soldiers were shot last night, and one is dead," Sumi stated harshly.

"I have heard this. Gunmen of the Afrikaner Resistance Movement," Bruwer replied, not bothering to conceal the disdain in her voice. "My heartfelt condolences to the comrades and the families of the two soldiers."

"Your police have not found the killers. The situation is intolerable and requires urgent measures. I have advised Admiral Horii that we should take hostages for the townspeople's good behavior. I will need your assistance in compiling a list of names." Sumi made no effort to conceal the menace in his voice.

"Make my name the first one," Bruwer said curtly, staring at Sumi directly.

Sumi blinked at her, momentarily taken aback.

"If you have not heard, Colonel Sumi, the Afrikaner Resistance Movement is a small band of criminal fanatics who enjoy minimal support from the population. Their goal is to destabilize the government which I have the honor to represent. This is not Earth, and taking hostages from the civilian population will do more to destabilize us than anything the terrorists are capable of doing. If you take hostages, there will be a general strike and mass demonstrations in protest."

"How do you know this?" Sumi demanded harshly, and immediately regretted the question.

Bruwer looked at him and said in a level voice, "Because I will organize the strike and lead the demonstrations." She continued matter-of-factly, "If the ARM boys see that shooting at your soldiers provokes you into doing stupid things, they will try to shoot two or three of them a week, and I would prefer to keep your soldiers alive. You do realize that whoever allowed those two boys to wander around the streets at night like that was a donkey."

Her telephone rang, and she picked it up. Cradling the receiver, she said, "One moment, dear." She looked at Colonel Sumi. "It is my husband, Acting Major Sanmartin. You were, of course, observed coming here. He bet me money this morning that you would come and suggest something like this, and he wants to know whether you have detained me."

Sumi wordlessly denied it.

She spoke into the telephone, "Raul, I think that Colonel Sumi and I have reached an understanding. *Ciao!*"

She put down the telephone and told Sumi coldly, "Please be assured that we will do all that we can to find the persons who murdered your soldiers. However, since USS controlled all shipping to this planet, you may wish to ask Mr. Matsudaira how so many weapons from Earth managed to end up in the hands of the fanatics among my people. As I have said, I am greatly distressed by this death, and I extend my sympathy and my condolences on behalf of my people."

"They are accepted," Sumi said heavily.

"So, then, Colonel. If you do not propose to detain me, I have work. I have already received eleven calls from my constituents complaining about the detachment of comfort girls your task group brought. We have laws against prostitution here, and the more God-fearing of my coreligionists are quite scandalized. Indeed, I would be grateful if you could contrive to make their presence less obtrusive. Thank you for your visit. It has been a pleasure, I am sure."

"In a manner of speaking, Madam Speaker," Sumi said, bowing with grudging respect.

"Oh, and Colonel Sumi—Christmas is Tuesday on the local calendar here. Merry Christmas to you."

"Merry Christmas, Madam Speaker," Sumi replied.

As the door closed behind Sumi's blacklegs, Bruwer exhaled deeply and closed her eyes. A moment later, she began rubbing her temples, trembling slightly.

A few moments later, the telephone rang again. Bruwer opened her eyes and picked it up, squinting at the vision screen. "Hallo, Hans. What are you up to?"

"Just checking to see that everything is all right. It never pays to assume things, as with the tango."

"The tango?" Bruwer repeated.

"Didn't Raul ever tell you the story about the tango? Husbands shouldn't keep secrets from their wives," Coldewe said with guileless simplicity.

Bruwer eyed him speculatively.

"As I'm sure you know, Finns are the shiest people on Earth. You've heard the joke about the Finnish man and woman who are stranded on a desert island for five years, and when the ship comes to rescue them, they shout, 'Thank God you've come! Please introduce us. We have so much to talk about!' "

Hans Coldewe had acquired his sense of humor in a combat zone, which most people agreed made a difference.

"Anyway, Finns of opposite sexes all go to tango clubs to meet each other, so when Raul arrived on Ashcroft, C Company naturally expected him to be an expert. The men were extremely disillusioned when the truth emerged."

As patrons of Suid-Afrika's charitable organizations had discovered at numberless benefits, on a dance floor Raul Sanmartin had the natural grace of a cheap marionette. "How much of this are you making up?" Bruwer asked wearily.

"Less than half." Coldewe coughed delicately. "I have this from several reputable sources."

Bruwer smiled sourly, as the tension from Sumi's visit began to leave her. "Where's Raul? He put you up to this, didn't he?"

Coldewe made expressive gestures, and Sanmartin moved into view. "I'm not sure anyone in Argentina under the age of ninety knows how to tango."

Bruwer eyed them both.

"It was the best we could come up with on short notice," Coldewe admitted.

LATE THAT AFTERNOON, THREE WELL-DIRECTED POLICE RAIDS ON the homes of ARM sympathizers resulted in the detention of two suspects and the seizure of ten kilograms of leaflets and three computers, but no hard leads.

Sunday(310)

SUPERIOR PRIVATE BOSMAN WAS ALERTED BY THE SOUND OF THE helicopter's engine. Crouched in the low brush, he looked at his section sergeant, Niilo Leikola. "Now, who could that be?"

Leikola had heard the same sound. "We'll see." He put field

glasses to his eyes and began methodically scanning the open land around their small kopje.

Moments later, a small utility copter touched down on the veld, and three individuals dressed in Imperial uniforms got out carrying assault rifles. They waved, and the copter abruptly rose and disappeared. They shouldered their equipment and began walking toward the forest edge.

"A hunting party, I expect," Leikola said disgustedly. He pointed. "Down the back slope and through the ravine over there. Let's see how close we can get to them."

Twenty minutes later, Lieutenant Isa Miyazato heard a bush hiss, "Please stop, sir." His two companions almost bumped into him.

Leikola stepped out from behind a fern tree. "I am Section Sergeant Niilo Leikola, number three platoon, A for Akita Company, First Battalion, Thirty-fifth Imperial Rifles. Please identify yourselves and explain your presence here." Leikola held his light machine gun a little to the side, leaving the three Japanese officers in little doubt that he could trigger a burst that would cut down all three of them.

Miyazato smiled impishly. "I am Lieutenant Miyazato of the Sixth Imperial Lifeguards Battalion. My companions are Lieutenant Akamine and Sublieutenant Kudokawa, officers in the First Battalion of the Manchurian regiment. We came for a little sport."

"This is a nature preserve, sir. Please lay your rifles on the ground and have a seat," Leikola responded.

"What is the meaning of this?" Akamine said irritably. "Can't you see that we are Imperial officers?"

"Yes, sir. This area is closed to hunting. I am authorized to detain you until a senior officer can arrive to place you under arrest. Major Kolomeitsev is on his way. *Please* lay your rifles on the ground and sit down until he arrives." Bosman stood and stepped away from the bush with his assault rifle leveled to emphasize Leikola's directive.

Miyazato glanced at his companions. They set their assault rifles aside and sat down to wait.

Ten minutes later, Leikola heard a helicopter's engines and felt a small shock from his wrist mount. Triggering his headset, he responded, "Leikola here."

"Kolomeitsev. Coming through."

A long rope snaked down a gap where a fern tree had toppled, and Piotr Kolomeitsev expertly slid down it. He un-

snapped himself, and the helicopter flew off to land in a
clearing. The three young officers hastily rose to their feet, and
the senior officer, Miyazato, saluted crisply.

Kolomeitsev returned Miyazato's salute. "I am Major
Kolomeitsev. You came here to hunt amphtiles?"

Miyazato responded automatically. "Yes, sir."

"Then consider yourselves under arrest. Hunting is prohibited here. Maps prepared within the last five years show the reserve quite clearly. The local government takes preservation of
wildlife seriously, and while our primary mission is to hunt terrorists, we assist the locals. I personally fail to see any sport in
hunting amphtiles; they have not learned fear of humans and
do not shoot back. Were you aware that this was a reserve?"

Miyazato looked away. "No, sir."

"Ignorance is not an acceptable excuse. Moreover, the Afrikaner Resistance Movement has a base camp somewhere within
fifty kilometers of here. While they are not as practiced as Sergeant Leikola and Private Bosman, they might have enjoyed being on the other end of an ambush for a change. If you had
found them before we found you, it would have been embarrassing to have to explain another three bodies to Admiral Horii."

Leikola suppressed a smile. Kolomeitsev's men, who un-
questionably had more sympathy for amphtiles than for Japanese officers, called themselves "the night shift" and had more
than considerable skill in creeping around. During the faction
fighting on NovySibir, the awed inhabitants had called them
the *"dukhi"* or "ghosts." The ARM boys had learned why.

"Any terrorists we encountered would have met with an unpleasant fate, sir! *Hai!*" Abruptly, Miyazato unholstered his
pistol and assumed an exaggerated shooter's stance and a ferocious mien. The pistol barrel drifted uncomfortably close to
Bosman.

"Lieutenant, please explain what you are doing," the Iceman
demanded sharply.

"Nothing, sir," the young officer said, relaxing his shoulders
and letting the pistol droop.

"Why isn't your pistol on safety?" Kolomeitsev asked in a
deceptively mild voice.

"Oh, it isn't loaded, sir!"

"Please place it on safety and give it to me, Lieutenant."

The young officer looked at the Iceman in disbelief and then
complied.

The Iceman held the pistol in his hand and caressed the practice grips. "A pretty gun."

The lieutenant missed the irony in his voice. "Yes, sir," he said proudly. "It is a Nakamura target weapon. I had it specially made. The trigger sear is filed down for match shooting."

"Indeed. Are you sure that it isn't loaded?" the Iceman asked, very firmly.

The lieutenant collected himself hurriedly, and the muscles in his throat moved. "Yes, sir."

The Iceman leveled the weapon at the bridge of the young officer's nose and thumbed the safety off. Then he smoothly shifted his aim a few centimeters to his right and squeezed the trigger. The pistol leaped in his hand.

The Iceman turned the pistol around to study the smoke drifting from the barrel. "You are correct. It has a very light pull." Kudokawa and Akamine looked at him in shock. The Iceman removed the magazine, ejected a round from the chamber, and snapped the safety on. He handed the weapon back to its owner.

"Do not take that weapon off safety until you are returned to your compound," Kolomeitsev directed. He began walking toward the forest edge where his helicopter was parked.

Leikola picked up the three officers' assault rifles and handed them to Bosman. "Please follow us." He added unkindly, "In the future, Lieutenant, please be more careful. Major Kolomeitsev prefers any loss of life to be intentional."

Predictably, Admiral Horii was absolutely furious when he heard about the incident, which left the Iceman completely unmoved. Even the ARM boys knew better than to hunt amphtiles in the Iceman's forest.

Monday(310)

JOPIE VAN NUYS HUNCHED OVER THE TABLE AND SLAMMED THE palm of his hand against the top for emphasis. "The only way to cleanse this planet of its Imperial stain is to execute more Imperials!"

Phillipbon drawled offensively, "Go have a beer while the rest of us deliberate, Jopie."

"Stop that, Phillipbon. And you calm down, Van Nuys," Gerrit Terblanche ruled. "We must all stick together." He looked at the other faces in the cellar with him. "No one doubts the dedication of anyone here."

The surviving leaders of the Afrikaner Resistance Movement were young but hardened. Terblanche, the eldest, was a few years out of school. Unlike his colleagues who had studied philosophy or social science, Terblanche was an engineer and tried to exercise a calming influence. Also, as one of the few Movement leaders who had not been forced underground, Terblanche had no intention of wasting all of his Christmas Eve on politics.

Withering under his gaze, Phillipbon looked down at the table and said in a more reasonable tone of voice, "Vereshchagin is sniffing at our heels. Executing a few Imperial soldiers on street corners won't help us, it only convinces people that we are gangsters."

Van Nuys slammed his palm on the table again with a whip-crack sound. "The people must be educated!"

The Movement had already uncovered traitors to the people in its ranks. Some of the bloodstains on the table hadn't washed out completely.

"Enough, Jopie," Terblanche ruled.

"We must plan our operations to achieve our goals, not to attract thrill-seekers," Phillipbon said. "If we want to execute Imperials, we should start with the new admiral."

"Why not Vereshchagin?" Van Nuys asked.

"Because we have tried twice and failed, or have you forgotten? But the new admiral will be unwary." Phillipbon grinned. "Besides, the new Imperials don't like Vereshchagin."

A few heads bobbed in agreement. "It is a good idea," someone else said.

"Jopie, are you in agreement?" Terblanche asked pointedly.

Van Nuys sucked in his breath. "We should continue street executions, but I agree that we should go after the fascist admiral. I wish the honor of carrying out that operation."

Phillipbon nodded, and Terblanche said, "All right. Come up with a plan that you can present to us."

Van Nuys nodded proudly.

Van Nuys had been a militia private in Krugersdorp during the rebellion, and had chanced to be away visiting a girl when Vereshchagin's recon men gassed his barracks. The other twenty-nine men of the Harmonie commando died that night. He remembered seeing their bodies. The nightmares came when he slept in a closed room.

* * *

LATE IN THE AFTERNOON, AN ARM MARKSMAN IN A STOLEN BAKKIE truck fired at two Japanese officers on a Pretoria street corner, seriously wounding one of them as well as an elderly shopper.

Tuesday(310)

HALFWAY THROUGH A LONG, STILTED CHRISTMAS SERMON FROM A young and earnestly liberal minister, Bruwer prodded her husband in the ribs, knowing full well that he knew how to sleep with his eyes open from his Academy days.

After church, Hendricka and her kitten filled the house with shreds of gaily colored gift-wrap, then Raul and Betje Beyers fixed Christmas dinner while Hanna completed her annual ritual of returning unopened presents to persons attempting to curry her favor. Brief notes accompanying the returned gifts explained that Madam Speaker only accepted gifts from her immediate family, that Madam Speaker's husband didn't accept gifts from anyone including his immediate family, and that Madam Speaker's daughter owned too many toys already.

Watching her husband pick at his dinner, Bruwer leaned on his shoulder and whispered, "You are as nervous as the kitten. You are not planning to work are you?"

Sanmartin squirmed impotently. "We have a night exercise planned."

"Raul, how could you? It is Christmas and raining, and after last night's festivities, half of your battalion must be hung over. Is this Piotr's idea?"

Her husband nodded. Apart from his normal concerns, the Iceman wanted to soak up some extra energy so his men wouldn't be tempted to spend the week in bars looking for blacklegs to beat up.

Bruwer sighed. "All right. Wait until Hendricka is into bed." Making sure that no one else was paying attention to them, she asked quietly, "The murder yesterday—there will be more, won't there?"

"We're still working on it," her husband said.

SUPERIOR PRIVATE JAN DE BEERS PEERED ANXIOUSLY INTO THE gloom. Although his eyes saw nothing, his ears and instincts told him that something was moving in the forest.

Eighty-four seconds later, he was "dead."

He sat down in the mud and stared at the tiny red spots on his uniform that represented simulated bullet holes, making him a simulated corpse. "Shit," he said, with true feeling.

Unfortunately, the C Company troopers who had taken De Beers out were very good—friends of his, in fact—and with De Beers taken down quickly and quietly, they would roll up No. 1 platoon like limp rope. Intercompany maneuvers were fiercely contested. "Dead," De Beers had the unpleasant feeling that he was going to be very unpopular with his messmates in very short order.

A few moments later, his worst fears were realized when Section Sergeant Kirill Orlov sat down beside him and took off his mask. Orlov's back and right side were neatly dotted with spots that were almost as red as Orlov's cheeks.

"Hello, Jan. Did you perhaps hear those street-sweepers of Coldewe's before they blew you away?" Orlov asked pleasantly. "Or were you blind *and* deaf?"

"Blind and dumb," De Beers admitted. "It was de Kantzow's section. I see what they did, now. While one of them kept my attention, Yelenov snuck up behind me and shot me up with a silenced submachine gun. I thought something was out there, but the Hangman said that the woods there were out of bounds."

"Jan, you are the dumbest soldier alive—excuse me, the dumbest soldier dead. Yes, the Hangman said the forest there is out of bounds. And I remember personally telling you that the Hangman lies to make these exercises interesting." Orlov wailed, "Oh, why did I ever become a sergeant? I must have been drunk and rolling on the ground! What a thimble-wit, I was!"

No one was as lavish with praise as Kirill Orlov—when things went right. Orlov was equally communicative when things did not. "Do you know how many months it's going to be before DeKe de Kantzow and Beregov let me live this down?" he asked rhetorically.

"Months and months and months." A glimmering of the future touched De Beers. "And every time they remind you, you are going to remind me."

"True," Orlov said glumly.

As Karl von Clausewitz once observed, given the enormous friction in war, even the mediocre is an accomplishment; and De Beers was feeling decidedly mediocre.

Settling back against a fern tree to wait for the exercise to end, he let his mind wander. "Isn't it kind of spooky out here?

What would you do if Frankenstein's monster came crashing through the thickets?"

"Thinking dumb thoughts like that, no wonder Filthy DeKe can sneak up on you. Frankenstein's monster? I saw that movie. We got a guy just like that in number two platoon. He's not so tough."

De Beers decided it might be safer not to tell Orlov that his attention had been diverted by low moans and the soft rattle of chains in the underbrush.

The 1/35th Rifle Battalion's three rifle companies had different personalities. A Company, molded by the Iceman, had always been known for dour, frightening efficiency; B Company for modest competence; and C Company for its efficient and resolute insanity. No one ever tried to explain why.

Vereshchagin, Harjalo, and Sanmartin monitored the progress of the exercise from a distance. "Nasty little firefight," Harjalo commented. "Hans is getting as sneaky as Raul."

"Sneakier," Sanmartin rejoined.

"Did you see Yuri Malinov last night?" Vereshchagin asked Harjalo.

"Our esteemed battalion sergeant sends you his compliments and wishes to know whether he can shoot Superior Private Prigal."

"What, may I ask, did Prigal do this time?" Vereshchagin inquired with the faintest hint of a smile.

"Our dear superior private got his hands on an old fuel-alcohol storage tank and somehow conceived of the notion that he should go into the business of making Christmas cheer. Unfortunately, in fixing up the tank, he wielded his torch with more zeal than skill, and nothing came out the other end."

Superior Private Prigal drove an armored car in the Hangman's light attack company. In the two seven-year enlistments of his checkered military career, Prigal had been promoted ten times from the rank of recruit private to the rank of superior private, and had been reduced in rank nine times. Mostly, this was for doing things that no one with half a brain would do, but occasionally it was for doing things that no one with half a brain would conceive of doing.

While Prigal's platoon leader, Lieutenant Muravyov, considered him to be his personal cross to bear through life, the Hangman was able to focus the concentration of his other soldiers to an extraordinary degree by asking erring troopers whether they were paying Prigal for lessons. Most people suspected—with some degree of truth—that Henke kept Prigal around for the sheer joy of seeing what would happen with him next. It was also true that in combat on at least two occasions, Prigal had done exactly the right thing for absolutely wrong reasons.

Vereshchagin closed his eyes. "Let me guess. While Prigal was trying to figure out why nothing was coming out the other end, the tank blew up."

"You apparently know more physics than Prigal does. Amazingly, he is absolutely fine, except that he has no eyebrows left," Harjalo concluded.

"Please tell the battalion sergeant that he cannot shoot Recruit Private Prigal unless Prigal tries to do this again, in which case, he has my blessing. Did Yuri have anything else to say?"

"He asked me to pass along a short private message to the effect that the *chizhiks* are back."

Vereshchagin laughed very softly. A *chizhik* was a bureaucrat in uniform. Matti had been telling non-Russian speakers for years that it was the worst swearword that Battalion Sergeant Malinov knew, and it very likely was. Then his mouth tightened, and he asked quietly, "What did the oncologist say?"

Harjalo frowned. "The same as the other one. With chemotherapy, cell replacement, and radiation treatment, he gives Yuri twelve months, no more than that."

"How did Yuri take this?" Vereshchagin asked. Sanmartin looked away.

"The same as the last time. Yuri told him politely that he would die when he was good and ready, and not before. That will be about four minutes after I certify that he is no longer fit for duty." Pain suffused Harjalo's face. "Anton, Yuri taught me how to soldier and knows more about being one than God does. How do I tell him to pack it in and die quietly because he can't do the job anymore?"

"You cannot say this to him, Matti, and I cannot, either. I have done many unpleasant things, and I have reached the point where there are a few things which I will not do." Vereshchagin had one ear to the radio and commented, "Piotr is giving Meagher's platoon a drubbing now. What do you think about the ARM?"

"Aksu, Raul, Piotr, and I all agree that they're up to something—Piotr says that the little children among them want to stretch their egos. But there won't be any trouble from the ones in the forest—they're hungry and pretty thoroughly discouraged. I expect the ones in the towns to try their hand at provoking Admiral Horii."

"Yes, it will be a race to see whether we can neutralize them before they can effect enough senseless acts of violence to provoke Admiral Horii to counter with senseless acts of repression. Please reiterate to Piotr that he should try to keep the ones he can capture alive, if practicable."

Harjalo nodded, aware that the Iceman took such requests philosophically. Although Kolomeitsev truly believed that it was a waste of effort to take certain types of people prisoner—student terrorists in particular—he was used to Vereshchagin's whims in this regard.

Vereshchagin looked at his wrist mount. "In the meanwhile, I must return to adorning Admiral Horii's headquarters. Let me know how things turn out here."

Harjalo nodded again. "I'll ask Hans to pick out some good books to read, if you like."

"Thank you, Matti, but it might be a little ostentatious for me to loll about Admiral Horii's headquarters reading books at this juncture."

"You realize that, theoretically, there's a danger that the ARM boys huddled out there in their soggy little tents may try to mix it up with us while we're shooting each other up with blank ammunition. What do you plan on telling the admiral?"

"To be candid," Vereshchagin confessed, "I had not planned on burdening him with the matter."

HARJALO DECLARED A HALT TO THE EXERCISE NINE HOURS LATER after the two companies had pretty well taken each other apart. On his way back, Sanmartin stopped by the C Company casern outside Johannesburg.

In C Company's mess, the cook, "Kasha" Vladimirovna, as round as she was tall, interrupted her mealtime choreography to greet him. Refusing to accept no as an answer from him, she sat him down a few feet away from where Letsukov was playing piano, placing a full plate in one of his hands and a cup of tea—which he loathed—in the other. Then, smiling, she took the tea and flipped it into a potted plant so he wouldn't have to wait until her back was turned.

Letsukov was playing what he called "ship" music, Beethoven's *Eroica*, which assault transport captains often played during landing operations. Suid-Afrika was the third planet his piano had been shipped to, carefully crated and consigned as medical supplies.

This week's sign in the mess read "No Peddlers or Cats." Sanmartin grinned. Not much had changed since he had given up command of C Company.

As he watched the troopers eat, he could pick out the Russians by the way they held their black bread—nibbling at it, to make it last longer. The eldest among them had been children during the *uchikowashi* after the crack-up, when a slice of bread with fillers was dinner and a second slice was supper. Time dilation had cut these men adrift as the battalion moved from colonial world to colonial world. In their thirties, mostly, they remembered an Earth that only older people on Earth still recalled. They remembered what it was like to starve, and they knew what their bread cost them.

After Sanmartin mangled Kasha's excellent food to make it look as though he had eaten, Coldewe and Isaac Wanjau, the tall and very black No. 10 platoon sergeant, came over to join him.

"Hans—Matti asked me to stop by and congratulate your people. You gave Piotr a good workout."

Coldewe laughed. "I thought we had him good, although I'll bet Piotr thought the same thing. Anyway, you're just in time!" He rubbed his hands together briskly. "We got together and voted to have a poetry contest."

Despite possessing intimate knowledge both of C Company and of Hans Coldewe's proclivities, Sanmartin twitched and pushed his plate away. "A poetry contest?"

C Company had cheerfully assisted in faunal surveys, attended presentations on marine biology en masse, and—more improbably—produced an opera in conjunction with a civic group in Johannesburg. Even so, a public poetry contest was a trifle eccentric, even by C Company's standards.

Isaac Wanjau shrugged elaborately. "Captain Hans thought we ought to get it in before the staff *vertushkas* think up things for us to do," he said, resolving the question "when" rather than "why."

Sanmartin found himself grinning. A *vertushka* was a talkative, flighty woman, and Isaac Wanjau, recruited from the rebels that Vereshchagin's battalion had shot at on Ashcroft, was an improbable source for the Russian-Finnish slang that the Afrikaner recruits copied from him. He thought aloud, "Hans

is probably right about that. I expect we'll have to make a
show of stepping up activity against the ARM."

Wanjau nodded thoughtfully. "Less time in garrison for us."

"And high time," Kasha said boisterously, eavesdropping
shamelessly. "You know what they say, in garrison women can
do everything, and men can do the rest."

Wanjau winked. "Which is mostly not to offend the cook."

Sanmartin returned to the subject at hand. "A poetry contest? Hans, I'm almost afraid to ask what you've been reading
this week."

Coldewe loved literature even more than he loved practical
jokes. "*Don Quixote* by Cervantes," he said with a sniff and a
patronizing air, "which of course has nothing to do with why
we chose to hold a poetry contest."

"Right, and Sir Walter Scott had nothing to do with the joust
you tried to talk us into. Cervantes—didn't he also write
Jurgen?"

"No, that was Cabell, not Cervantes."

"Good. When you started quoting Jurgen on women, I
thought your girlfriend was going to give you a black eye."

"My former girlfriend," Coldewe corrected, "and she did
give me a black eye, although it had nothing to do with
Jurgen. You liked Elise, didn't you?"

"I thought she was nice, but not as nice as Marta. What's
Don Quixote about?" Sanmartin asked, knowing that Coldewe
was prepared to volunteer the information anyway. "Is this another Western?"

"No, no. *Don Quixote* is a timeless tale, a biting, bitter satire
showing that only fools and madmen continue to believe in
outmoded concepts like chivalry and nobility of spirit."

"Fools and madmen," Isaac Wanjau said. "That describes us
pretty well."

As the senior officer present, Sanmartin got to pick the
theme for the poetry contest and chose "fools and madmen."
That gave an edge to Lieutenant Danny Meagher, the No. 11
platoon leader. A former mercenary, Meagher was Irish to his
very soul and claimed that this gave him a special affinity for
poetry, fools, and madmen. Meagher and Lance-Corporal
Tulya Pollezheyev from No. 10 platoon battled it out and were
declared joint winners by acclamation.

As he made his way home, Sanmartin reflected that it had
been an interesting evening, even by C Company's standards.

Wednesday(310)

IN THE EARLY MORNING HOURS, THE DRIVER OF A BATTERED SEDAN cruising the streets of Johannesburg spotted two blacklegs on a routine foot patrol. He nudged his passenger, who reached underneath the seat and pulled out an assault rifle.

As the car slowed to a crawl, the gunner released the safety. Pointing the rifle out the open passenger window with the weapon's receiver resting against his cheek, he took aim at the unsuspecting security policemen and carefully squeezed the trigger, which caused the weapon's entire forty-round magazine of caseless 5mm ammunition to explode.

The explosion ripped away the gunner's hands and lower jaw. After passing through the gunner's throat, one fragment of the plastic magazine lodged itself in the driver's skull just below the temporal bone. The driver died without ever regaining consciousness. The gunner was considerably less fortunate. Some of the less lurid photos made the early editions of the news.

Terblanche convened an emergency telephone meeting of the ARM's executive. Unfortunately, the ARM's administrative arrangements left something to be desired, and no one was quite sure what ammunition cache that particular magazine had come from. The executive suspected—correctly—that it was not the only magazine they possessed that Vereshchagin's people had arranged to doctor.

With the increasingly obtrusive presence of plainclothes policemen, presumably augmented by members of Vereshchagin's recon platoon, street assassinations were suspended, indefinitely.

Thursday(310)

WHEN CAPTAIN YANAGITA ARRIVED AT THE JOHANNESBURG staatsamp—improbably nicknamed Fort Zinderneuf—in the city's Vryheidsplein to meet with Hanna Bruwer, he was surprised to find himself directed to a small pistol range in the basement.

Venturing down, Horii's intelligence officer shook hands with her hesitantly. "I am somewhat . . . surprised to find you here."

Bruwer walked him to the firing line. "I find shooting relaxing. It forces me to concentrate and relieves stress. Also, very few of my colleagues will seek me out to discuss the sordid details of our business when they know that I have a pistol in my hand. Don't bother with hearing protection—I am using a silencer."

Bruwer was firing at silhouette targets. Yanagita peered at the tight grouping of shots in the target's breast. "You are an excellent shot. I am quite impressed. Did your husband teach you how to shoot?"

"I insisted." She smiled, reminiscing. "It is actually a humorous story. When I first came to work for Lieutenant-Colonel Vereshchagin's battalion, Raul lent me a pistol, to protect myself I assumed. After I carried it for two months, he mentioned that it was not loaded. He has been wounded twice that I know of, but I am not sure that he ever came closer to death than he did at that moment." She looked at Yanagita. "If Admiral Horii sent you to find out what my price was, please tell him that I am completely unreasonable—my husband assures me of this from time to time."

Yanagita said hastily, "Ah, no, Madam Speaker. Admiral Horii sent me to convey to you his regret over Colonel Sumi's overzealous and unseemly behavior. The admiral was deeply distressed when he heard."

"Hopefully, that means that the admiral will ensure that there is no repetition," she said with feigned levity. "I assume that you are also here to learn something about me."

Yanagita looked embarrassed, and Bruwer smiled demurely. Taking aim at a silhouette target, she fired the last three rounds from her clip. Her shots ripped open a neat hole in the torn area over the target's heart. "My husband mentioned that Admiral Horii was also distressed by one of the songs that his soldiers like to sing. Was it 'The Little Tin Soldier'?"

"No, a different song—I believe that it is called 'The Whistling Pig.' The admiral is somewhat concerned that it may not convey the proper attitude to the local populace."

Horii had been particularly annoyed by one of the more outrageous verses from the NovySibir campaign:

*The bombings and the shootings kept the pig from getting
    sleep,
But mines are very nice for keeping wolves away from
    sheep.
The admiral got impatient when the natives tried to play,
But Matti cleaned a pistol, and the problem went away!*

Bruwer explained, "As far as I know, Anton's soldiers have been singing that song for longer than the admiral has been alive. Please assure Admiral Horii that the local population is inured to it. By now, there are at least seven or eight verses in Afrikaans."

"It seems so—dismal."

"The song is quite dismal, but then so is war. My husband's battalion has been pushed off like pigs to the slaughterhouse many times, and they rather resent it."

"I see," Yanagita said, although he clearly did not.

"I am sure that the admiral will understand. I also understand that he is also somewhat concerned about the Agriculture Law."

"It seems a very curious measure for your government to require families to maintain a year's supply of food."

"Dried peas, beans, lentils, potatoes, fruit, fish, meat, and maize. Fuel alcohol, flour, sugar, salt, and powdered eggs and milk," Bruwer quoted from the enactment. "With the assistance of the churches, the neighborhood associations monitor stocks on a quarterly basis."

"The admiral wonders whether this measure was necessary," Yanagita said dutifully. What the admiral had actually said was that hungry people have no time for politics, and surplus food made Suid-Afrika's population dry tinder for rebellion.

"It appeared so at the time. You would have to ask my husband about the military reasons for enacting the law, but economically, it made a tremendous degree of sense. USS oriented Suid-Afrika to produce a large agricultural surplus for off-planet export, and the company's decision to curtail off-planet shipments nine years ago created a great deal of unnecessary economic turmoil, which helped to fuel the rebellion. Requiring people to maintain food stocks provided us with a market for surplus food, and storing the excess in people's homes is much cheaper than building silos. I am told that repealing the law would be very inflationary."

"I see," Yanagita said politely.

"I am not sure that you do," Bruwer said quietly. "During the rebellion, thousands of people were killed or lost their homes, and others were transported after it ended, although some of my fellow citizens would perhaps have liked to have seen them shot after the botch they made of things. If Imperial Security had handled things, many more would have been shot or transported. All of this resulted, Captain Yanagita, from economic mismanagement by USS. We do not wish this to recur."

"I see," Yanagita stammered.

"Is there some other matter that I can help you with?"

"The admiral was concerned that our files on you and your husband appear somewhat incomplete," Yanagita admitted. "Both of you are very young, and it is unusual for younger persons such as your husband to be promoted over the head of seniors. It would be helpful to know more."

"I assume that you have nothing on me and virtually nothing on Raul, although the commander of the unit he served with on Earth undoubtedly made a few choice comments in his file."

Yanagita looked away. "The commander of the Eleventh Shock Battalion said that your husband did not take the role of the Imperial Government or the profession of arms seriously."

Bruwer nodded as she ejected her empty clip and inserted another. "Yes, he told my husband as much. My husband dislikes tea, and I believe he told the assembled mess that the superiority of green tea is due to the relative absence of mouse droppings. His request for colonial posting was approved shortly thereafter." She assumed a firing stance. "Let me think—my husband has written seven monographs on seashell taxonomy and amphtile behavior, and he teaches at the university. He is also an anarchist of a sort."

"An anarchist?" Yanagita repeated in astonishment.

"Of a sort. He does not like governments. He accepts the fact that people would behave much worse if they did not have governments to restrain them, but he does not like governments. I am sure that you are aware that both of his parents died in Argentinian prisons."

Yanagita nodded.

"Then you understand that he did not arrive at this conviction lightly." She fired three quick rounds at the target and paused. "Raul recognizes that *all* governments—no matter how well intentioned—are ultimately based upon coercion, which is to say, the use of force and violence. Some governments do not issue their policemen guns, but their foundation is still coercive power in the last analysis. In Raul's view, what is important is whether the coercion a government applies is commensurate with the resulting benefit which in theory accrues to the population as a whole, and whether it discourages—rather than encourages—the more overt forms of hardship, mayhem, and intolerance." She fired three more rounds. "This gives Raul an unusual perspective as one of my government's advisers."

"This is very unusual," Yanagita allowed.

"And I am a pacifist of a sort."

Yanagita blinked hard.

Bruwer fired the final three rounds in her second clip. "Although I know enough history to be entitled to voice an opinion, I am opposed to the use of violence."

Yanagita fumbled for a response. "Did you not just say that governments are grounded in the use of coercive force?"

"I did, and they are. My husband and I have many virtues, but consistency is not one of them."

"Do you not find it awkward to be married to a soldier?" Yanagita asked, clearly disconcerted.

Bruwer smiled enigmatically. "It gives Raul a slight moral advantage. I am willing to die for the moral principles that I believe in, but Raul is willing to die and also to kill. He is a soldier who dislikes war, and I am a politician who dislikes politics."

Yanagita folded his hands in supplication and bowed from the waist. "May I retrieve your target? I would be honored if I could have it as a keepsake."

Bruwer nodded and watched as he went down range to retrieve it. She said to herself in a soft monotone, "How charming. How utterly charming." Her hand shook as she bent to pick up the magazine she had dropped.

When Yanagita returned with the target folded up and tucked away in his pocket, he said, "There is one matter that I should mention. When I spoke to Admiral Horii, he seemed quite concerned over the unrest that the land tax had engendered."

"No."

"No?" Yanagita responded, clearly puzzled.

Prior to the rebellion, USS had owned most of Suid-Afrika's land and left title to the rest in a state of chaos. The landrosts the company had appointed had further confused matters by impartially accepting bribes from either or both sides in every lawsuit.

After preparing a land map that confirmed the titles of persons actually in possession in most cases, Beyers had taxed developed land at a moderate rate and underdeveloped land at a prohibitively high rate. The greediest would-be land barons—and USS—promptly found themselves eaten alive by the taxes. They received little sympathy.

The tax encouraged returning land in its natural state to the government and favored small, fairly intensive uses. With help from the university, virtually all of the rancher magnates had opted to fence their land, plant it in nitrogen-fixing crops, and rotate cattle between plots. The tax left USS, as the planet's largest and least-efficient landowner, in a decidedly unfavorable position.

Bruwer looked at Yanagita with icy green eyes. "Heer Matsudaira was over to see President Beyers yesterday. Let us not mince words. Heer Matsudaira demanded concessions openly, and you are hinting that we should grant them to him. The answer is no."

"But while I would not presume to speak for Admiral Horii, if people would make accommodations in small matters, I am sure that things would work out best for everyone."

Bruwer smiled, tight-lipped. "I just finished explaining to you that I am completely unreasonable. The land tax is not a small matter, but even if it was, have you heard of the nail of Goha?"

"Goha? No, I have not."

"It is an Islamic tradition. My husband has picked up things from all over and heard the story on the island of Kalimantan. A man named Goha once sold his house, but asked if he could use a nail on the wall. It seemed like such a small thing that the new owner agreed. And each day, Goha hung something new on the nail—a basket, a coat, a stick—until it seemed as if Goha lived there still."

She looked at Yanagita steadily. "Heer Matsudaira is committed to reviving United Steel-Standard's hegemony over this planet. He was silly enough to make this known, but we would have expected this of him in any case. He intends to use any concessions we grant him as a wedge for further concessions, as I am sure that Admiral Horii understands. For this reason we will grant him none."

"This could lead to unpleasant consequences," Yanagita said uneasily.

"We are well aware that Admiral Horii could choose to dissolve our government. It will not change things." She closed her eyes. "Captain, when you recount our conversation to Admiral Horii, please explain to him that I am thoroughly unreasonable, and that in many ways, this planet is thoroughly unreasonable. Unless he understands this, he is likely to make grave errors. And you might also consider telling him that I am a very good shot—for a woman."

Yanagita said, somewhat awkwardly, "It is not that Japanese consider your sex inferior, but women seldom hold higher social status."

Bruwer allowed his non sequitur to pass unchallenged. She placed her empty pistol on safety and holstered it. "I am, by the way, a much better pistol shot than my husband is. He will tell you that it is because I have better vision and better eye-hand coordination, but the truth is that when he finds it necessary to shoot something, he likes to use something more destructive. There is one thing more—Raul has reason to believe that the ARM will try to assassinate Admiral Horii. He tells me that it is what he would do if he were in their position. Thus far, he has not been able to convince Colonel Sumi to take precautions. I would ask you to convey his fears to the admiral."

Bowing, Yanagita departed and dutifully returned to report the conversation to Admiral Horii, who closed his eyes to listen.

"The land tax—is she adamant?" Horii asked, opening his eyes.

Yanagita bowed his head. "I believe that this is so, sir."

"Matsudaira-san will be frenzied when he realizes this. How childish of him," Horii said, shutting his eyes again. "Life seems more and more to me like an illusion. There is a sense of impermanence about it. Love and hate, riches and fame, all seem evanescent as morning mist."

"Do you agree with Acting Major Sanmartin that the Afrikaner Resistance Movement will attempt to assassinate you?"

"It is of no great importance. I will never go home, I know this," Horii said with some sadness. "We are too far away. The time dilation will change things too much. I expect to remain here at my post until I die. Here, there is no love or hate, only duty. It does not greatly matter when my death occurs, although it is important not to allow the Afrikaner Resistance Movement any successes."

"Does Colonel Sumi also think this?" Yanagita ventured uncertainly.

"Surely not," Horii said, misunderstanding the question. "Sumi is an ardent follower of Go-Nichiren teachings, as many others are. He believes that after a certain number of years following the Buddha's death, Japan will be divinely called upon to take the peoples of the world under one rule in which all of the five races would live in harmony, following a final, cataclys-

mic war. While some Go-Nichiren adherents believe that this final war was the crack-up, others, like Sumi, believe that this
war is destined to occur in our lifetimes, and that they are fated
to make it come to pass. Sumi believes that the current order of
things must be purified in order to achieve its full potential. You
should ask yourself why he chose to come on this expedition."

"Is Matsudaira-sama also a Go-Nichiren believer?"

"Matsudaira?" Horii curled his lip in disdain. "Matsudaira is
nothing. Matsudaira believes in himself and money, in that order. Do you know who he is? He is a rich businessman who
had himself adopted into an impoverished branch of a distinguished family, nothing more." He·stood. "It is time. Begin
tapping the telephones of Beyers and Bruwer."

"Sir, I believe that Colonel Sumi has already done so."

"I am aware of this. I wish to know what Colonel Sumi
hears. Also, initiate discussions with Lieutenant-Colonel
Vereshchagin's political officer, Captain Yoshida. It will be important to ascertain his attitude."

"What is it that you propose to do, sir?" Yanagita asked,
once again clearly perplexed.

"First, I propose to neutralize the Afrikaner Resistance
Movement. Beyond this, it is not necessary that you know. In
attacking an enemy, it is necessary to maintain a flexible grip
and concentrate solely on cutting him, not in a preconceived
way, but by whatever means are most in harmony with the situation. For the moment, at least, it will be necessary for
Matsudaira-san to compose himself with patience. I will take
pleasure in telling him this." He cocked an eye. "Just how unreasonable is this woman—as unreasonable as she says?"

"She is very unreasonable," Yanagita said firmly.

"It will be very interesting." Horii again closed his eyes.

"Sir, there is one more matter that I would beg to report."

"And this is?"

"I noticed that the Afrikaners have a war memorial in Pretoria a few blocks away from the staatsamp listing the names
of all who died in the rebellion."

"Weak of Vereshchagin to allow them to put up such a mon-
ument, but this is hardly unusual enough to report, I would
think."

"It lists all of the names, sir," Yanagita reiterated, "including
the names of the Imperial soldiers who died."

"How very interesting." Horii closed his eyes again. "How
very unusual."

* * *

AFTER DUTY HOURS, COLONEL SUMI HELD A PARTY FOR MEMBERS of Admiral Horii's staff in a Pretoria-Wes tavern. Although English was the international language of empire, with none but Japanese present, Sumi placed a bowl in the center of the table and fined everyone who accidentally used an English word fifty sen.

In the streets outside, two plainclothes police made their presence apparent. Rather than linger, Jopie Van Nuys left.

That night, Horii committed a poem to the pages of his war diary.

> Today, as commander
> Of the guardians of the void
> In this land of dawn,
> I gaze up in awe
> At the rising sun.

Friday(310)

THE KITTEN RACED UP THE STEPS, NUDGED THE DOOR OPEN WITH her head, and bounded into the room full-tilt, in preparation for a high-speed turn and a final leap onto the bed.

Unfortunately for the kitten, the flooring was slick; when her body made the turn, the friction coefficient kept it going forward until she hit the wall. There was an audible thump, followed by a plaintive meow.

"What does that make?" Sanmartin asked, peeping out over the comforter.

"The third time this week that I know of," his wife answered sleepily. "Why do we have a cat? Nobody else has a cat."

"She's sweet!"

"She's a cat," Bruwer explained crossly from under the covers.

There was another plaintive meow from the corner.

"Did Vroew Beyers mention that she has figured out how to get into your underwear drawer? She worms her body inside. Then she gets her head caught. Every time. And she hides when people come over. Sensible cats don't like people, for the same reasons that sensible people don't like cats."

"She likes me."

"That's because she hasn't figured out that you are a person yet. Ouch, don't pull on my hair! Are the assassinations over?"

"For now."

"I spoke to the parents of those two men—boys really. For all that their sons had done, they were shocked and grieved."

"As you keep reminding me, those who live by the sword, die by the sword."

"I wish there had been some other way, some better way." Bruwer shut her eyes. "You should have told me."

Sanmartin shook his head impatiently. "The first thing that Shimazu taught both of us about intelligence is not to let the left hand know what the right hand is doing."

"I do not want to argue. Have you decided what to do about your position at the university?"

"It's time to give it up. Things are coming to a head." He smiled. "Remember when we started? The mountains of mine tailings that USS let the wind and water carry away? It looked like one big desert up there—we could have fought a battle, and it would have looked better."

She laughed. "I am sure you are right. Remember when you sent your company to repair the bullet holes in the houses along the Burgerstraat in the middle of the rebellion? Everyone in Johannesburg thought you were crazy."

"I seem to recall that you embarrassed half the town into helping."

"People are proudest of what they do themselves, with help, not what other people do for them," Bruwer said quietly. She sat up and leaned forward on her elbows. "Heer Matsudaira is putting pressure on us to dispense with the land tax which is paying to clean up the disaster his company bequeathed to us."

"The land tax does other things, don't forget. Five years ago, barely a quarter of the farmers held legal title to their land—the rest were squatters and tenants—and none of them were paying taxes to anyone. Now, all of them hold titles and mortgages, and they're actually paying their taxes cheerfully, which generally only happens in bad fiction."

"That's only because they know that USS is paying more. Raul, we have all but dismembered USS. When Matsudaira figures out how to read the balance sheets we have written for him, his heart will stop."

"Scrapping the land tax and environmental clean-up will be Matsudaira's first order of business. How much support do we have?"

"Do you want to know the truth? If this were all that he would demand, we would not have much. My fellow assemblymen do not understand. A few man-made deserts do not matter so much to them. Right now, they know that if they go along with me on environmental issues, I will be semireasonable in other matters, and they pay my price cheerfully. If I left office tomorrow, there would be other matters which would occupy their attention until the problem became too great to ignore."

Hendricka peered into the room, looking for her cat.

"Yes, she's in here, Hendricka. Come get her out so your father and I can sleep!"

Hendricka scooped the kitten off the floor and pounced on the bed. "Oh, Mutti, isn't she sweet? Just listen to her purr."

"Hendricka, I never listen to what people or cats say, I watch what they do, and if she scratches me again, she is going to be a pair of mittens. Raul, why are you laughing?"

"I think the only reason you let her have a cat is for the pleasure you get out of disliking the animal, which reminds me of Martial's formula for a happy marriage."

She poked him in the ribs, ungently. Martial had said, *Sit non doctissima coniux*, which means, "May my wife not be very learned."

It struck many people as odd that they continued to live in two rooms in the Beyers home. Sanmartin often explained that living this way lessened problems with security, but it was difficult for people to take him too seriously.

Except for Hendricka's bed, their rooms were furnished with things that Bruwer had brought from her small apartment, and the walls were bare. Sanmartin owned a pair of slacks, a suit, a sweater, several shirts, and a few personal possessions that fit inside his rucksack. Bruwer had a favored green gown she wore on state occasions and a mended kylix vase. In the intervening years, friends had given them much, but somehow never seemed to mind when their gifts ended up with people who needed them more.

Sanmartin stroked his daughter's head. "So quickly tell us what you did yesterday, before we have to go to work."

"Tant Betje took me to preschool," Hendricka lisped, "and we learned to count, and I told Pieter I wanted to be a soldier when I grew up."

Raul Sanmartin turned his head so that he wouldn't see the pain in his wife's face.

Saturday(310)

HARJALO FOUND PAUL HENKE SITTING UNDER A FERN TREE OVER-looking a pool masked by a sandbar that the river eddied around. The Hangman had a long composite fishing pole in one hand and a shorter switch with a line in the other.

"How is the fishing?" he asked.

Henke was in full field gear. He slipped off his mask and turned slowly to look at Harjalo. "It is acceptable. No better. The fish lack guile. Watch."

He pulled in his line slowly, then delicately flipped his bait into a small rill close to the bank where he was sitting. He then took a switch with a short line attached to it in his free hand and whipped the water in carefully timed strokes. The local equivalent of a fish immediately struck his hook. After a brief struggle, the Hangman pulled the fish in. Harjalo was amazed at the size.

The Hangman slapped the fish under the throat to stun it, removed the hook, and slipped it back into the water. "You see?" he gestured. "They eat the spore pods from the trees. They think the sound is food falling into the water."

"Good trick. I've never seen that done before."

"The fish are not palatable, so no one tries. I did not intend to be found. How did you find me?"

Harjalo shrugged. "I spoke with a couple of cowboys who knew the river, and they told me approximately where you would be."

"I did not realize that I was becoming predictable."

Harjalo gestured. "Why are you wearing the mask?"

"The polarized lenses improve the contrast so that I can see the seams in the water where the fish hide. Life and death," Henke added for no reason apparent to Harjalo. He put the mask on again and took it off. "I would like, when I die, to return as a fish."

"Why a fish?"

"To atone, I suppose." The Hangman placidly resumed fishing.

"Why didn't you call and tell me you wanted a day off," Harjalo asked gently.

"I thought I did. It must have slipped my mind. Things have been so confused. I have not been sleeping well, I think."

"Why not, Paul?" Harjalo forced himself to keep anxiety from showing in his voice.

"Sometimes I am terrified at night. I dream I see a missile coming at me, and there is nothing I can do to stop it. Then I see the blood pouring out. It is not a good dream—blood frightens me, even in dreams—and sometimes it makes me afraid to go to sleep. And yet it is only in my dreams that I can be a child again, and a child isn't afraid of blood because he thinks that it is just red water," the Hangman responded as he continued to ply his line. There was no expression on his face.

That was when Matti Harjalo began to realize that the best armor officer he had ever known was starting to lose his mind.

Sunday(311)

GERRIT TERBLANCHE HEARD HIS TELEPHONE RING. CURSING, HE flung his pillow at it. Then he rolled over and picked it up. "Hallo."

"Hallo, Werewolf? Liberty!"

The engineer recognized Jopie Van Nuys's voice on the other end. "This is Terblanche. Liberty. Do you know what time it is?"

"You should use your code name, Gerrit. What if someone is listening in?" Van Nuys chided him.

Terblanche rubbed his head. "This is my telephone. If someone is listening in, they already know who I am. What do you want at this hour? Unlike some people, I have to work tomorrow."

Monday was December thirty-second; like many colonial planets, Suid-Afrika had extra days in its calendar to fit its rotation. Before Terblanche could hang up, Van Nuys blurted out, "Listen, Gerrit, I can do the job."

Terblanche was instantly awake. "The big one?"

"The big one. We'll want two stoves and half a dozen heating elements," Van Nuys said, meaning he needed two rocket launchers and six projectiles.

Terblanche sniffed. "Are you sure you know how to light one of those?"

"Yes, I have had military training, remember?"

"All right. I'll see what I can do. And take precautions—no one can be certain what has or hasn't been tampered with. When and where do you want them?" Terblanche grabbed a pen and pad from the night table and cradled the telephone against his shoulder.

"I will also need a helper," Van Nuys said, reluctant to concede that he couldn't do everything himself.

"Who did you have in mind?" Terblanche asked.

"Griffin."

"Good choice. Hannes is one of the few people you don't fight with."

Hannes Van der Merwe, whose code name was Griffin, was quiet and did what he was told without a lot of back talk. He also had some commando training. They'd used him to spy on the Kafferboeties, so he knew how to keep his mouth shut as well. If truth be known, he was one of the few brothers that Terblanche would have trusted with a tough job.

As for Jopie Van Nuys, choirboys couldn't make a revolution. The Volk had to use the tools available.

"Send Hannes around to see me tomorrow at my sister's apartment. I will tell you later where to send the stoves," Van Nuys said, and hung up the phone.

Terblanche turned off the phone and rolled over. The assassination of Admiral Horii was on.

Monday(311)

CAPTAIN CHIHARU YOSHIDA, VERESHCHAGIN'S POLITICAL OFFICER, walked through Johannesburg until he reached a small house on Burgerstraat at precisely nine o'clock. He knocked and waited. A second or two later, the door buzzed, and Yoshida opened it. Removing his shoes, he bowed and said, "Mr. Snyman."

Louis Snyman was looking out a window. Acting out their ritual, he maneuvered the controls on his wheelchair to face Yoshida and nodded curtly. "Captain Yoshida."

A former dominie, Louis Snyman had been one of the men who had organized the rebellion. If he had not been shot and paralyzed, he would have been transported by Vereshchagin with the other surviving conspirators. Ironically, Snyman's son Jan was serving as a medic's aide in No. 11 platoon when No. 11 put holes in his father, and young Jan had carried his father out of Krugerdorp on his back.

Yoshida had begun visiting after regenerative therapy had given Louis use of his arms and upper body, intending to recommend transporting him if he could be expected to cause trouble. The fanatically Christian minister and the indifferently

Buddhist career officer had found a curious companionship over the years.

Waving Yoshida to a seat on the sofa, Snyman snorted. "I hear that the ships brought a new director for USS. Has that lickspittle Beyers shot the man yet?"

Yoshida barely hid his smile. "No, he has not."

"Pity, Yoshida. Pity," Snyman wheezed. "He means no good. USS forgets nothing and learns nothing, and the only people they ever send here are idiots." He waved a fat finger. "I know what you are thinking—you want to be polite and say nice things about this Matsudaira even if he is an idiot. But the Bible says, 'You shall not bear false witness.' "

After Snyman had talked him into reading the Bible, Yoshida had quoted the Eighth Commandment—often—when Louis complained about his son Jan, recently promoted to sub-lieutenant, of whom he was secretly and inordinately proud, or his daughter-in-law, Natasha. Turning the tables gave Snyman a great deal of pleasure.

"I have met Matsudaira-san, and I am inclined to agree with you," Yoshida said amiably, mildly astonished that he could find himself openly criticizing a countryman to a foreigner, even one he considered a friend. "I do not think that Matsudaira-san understands conditions here."

"If he is like the others, he will not try. The best thing that Anton Vereshchagin ever did in his life was to shoot that man Tuge. More is the pity that Vereshchagin didn't go to Earth and make a complete job of it."

Snyman hated USS almost as much as he loved his God, and the one thing men could agree upon was that he hated well. It struck Yoshida very forcefully that what would have been hyperbole coming from another man was a simple statement of fact from Louis Snyman. To Louis, Suid-Afrika was the home God had given to his people, and USS had tried to dominate it and wreck it, which Snyman would never forgive or forget.

Changing the subject, Yoshida asked, "What did Dr. Solchava say on her last visit to you?"

"That daughter-in-law of mine told me I was not doing my exercises! I gave her what for, I promise you." Snyman softened slightly. "Although, to be truthful, I am not sure she ever notices. Why Jan married her I will never understand. It was the same when that son of mine took me prisoner—you had better believe that I had some words for him when I got him home!"

"The marriage struck many other people as odd," Yoshida conceded, entirely truthfully.

Sublieutenant Jan Snyman was tall, athletic, and very handsome, having grown twelve centimeters and added fifteen kilograms to his frame since joining Vereshchagin's battalion over his father's violent objections. His wife, Natasha Alevtinovna Solchava-Snyman, Vereshchagin's once and again battalion surgeon, was exceedingly plain, moderately contemptuous of soldiers, and perpetually irritated by the frustration of binding up the consequences of other people's follies. She was also twelve years older than Jan—proof, if any was needed, that love is truly blind.

Because Solchava's rigid views on most things had caused her to transfer in and out of the battalion three times, the battalion betting line had her divorcing Jan within one year—and remarrying him within two. Jan was a popular officer, however, so No. 10 was willing to overlook his eccentricities; and marrying him had softened her enough for her to put up with her father-in-law's humors as a patient.

"I don't know what he ever sees in her," Snyman said wistfully.

"Such things are common. What did you ever see in your wife?"

"No, the question you should ask is what my wife ever saw in me." Snyman turned his chair and headed for the kitchen. "You sit here for a moment. I have a bottle of beer, and since my daughter-in-law lectured me not to drink it, I can at least have the pleasure of watching you drink it for me. Oh, and did I tell you that I sent a letter to the Bruwer girl? I complained about the usual things and told her a woman's place. She wrote me back—here, I have her letter here someplace."

Snyman wheeled over to the sideboard and pulled open a drawer, pulling out Bruwer's letter triumphantly. " 'Heer Snyman. I have received your latest missive. It is a pity that during the rebellion, neither my husband nor my grandfather found time to shoot you. In the future, please write to me on unbleached paper because it is easier to recycle. I hope that you will continue to have good health so that you can continue to bother me at regular intervals.' "

He slapped the letter with his free hand for emphasis. "Now that is a letter!" He added with grudging professional admiration, "A bunch of thieves, that is what they are. And your Colonel Vereshchagin is the biggest thief of the lot!"

Snyman was the last unrepentant "hero" of the rebellion, and the leaders of the Afrikaner Resistance Movement had made it known that they intended to install him as president of the "reformed" republic in the event that they took power, although they had no more intention of allowing him to exercise power than Vereshchagin did. The kindest thing Louis Snyman had to say about the ARM was that they were silly young puppies.

When Chiharu Yoshida left the house a half hour later, he was stopped by Captain Yanagita of Admiral Horii's staff, who wanted to discuss the political situation on Suid-Afrika, and the future role in its evolution that Yoshida would play.

DRESSED IN SLACKS AND A RUMPLED SWEATER, RAUL SANMARTIN waved to the night watchman as he and Christos Claassen walked toward a small building on the campus of the University of Suid-Afrika on the outskirts of Pretoria.

"We were not very original in choosing a name for our university," Claassen said with a smile. "Perhaps I should suggest a change to the other trustees."

"And get us both tarred and feathered, most likely."

Claassen gestured toward the watchman. "He knows you?"

"He's actually a student in the department of engineering, Cornelius Botha—really a nice kid. We usually chat a little, especially since I see more of this place at night than in the daytime." Sanmartin's frown deepened. "Most of my fellow faculty members think that he turns invisible when he puts his uniform on, which is something that the trustees might want to try doing something about one of these days."

Claassen sighed. "If we only had fifty years."

The Department of Suid-Afrikan Ecology occupied a small building on the fringe of the campus in keeping with its unpretentious status as a recently recognized discipline. As they entered, Sanmartin called out, "Simon! Maria! Karel! Come on out, I want you to meet someone." He confided to Claassen, "When Simon is working, you'd have to burn the place down to get him to notice."

Darting into the laboratory, he emerged holding Simon Beetje by the elbow and ushered him forward. Beetje was tall and extraordinarily thin. As Maria Viljoens and Karel Koekemoer joined them, Sanmartin made introductions.

"Heer Claassen, let me present Simon Beetje, who is my number two in the department, and Maria Viljoens and Karel Koekemoer, our two lecturers." Viljoens was a short woman, chubby and outwardly cheerful. Koekemoer, younger than the others and noticeably bashful, was cultivating his first mustache, which looked like greasepaint on his lip.

A politician first and a banker last, Claassen shook hands with them. "Please call me Christos. Raul has told me a great deal about you three."

A small amphtile poked its head around the corner and probed the air with its tongue, then it scuttled away.

"That's Sallust, the fourth member of our permanent staff. We named the species *Xenoambystoma hendricka*," Sanmartin explained. "We brought him in to study his ectoparasites, and he decided to stay. He's shy around strangers who don't bring him food."

"Karel here has taught Sallust how to use a litter box, which is very little short of astounding, given amphtilian intelligence," Beetje said, pushing the blushing Koekemoer forward for accolades.

"I didn't believe Raul when he told me that you would be working tonight. I am astonished at such dedication," Claassen commented.

"I keep telling them that they aren't old enough to drink, and so far they've believed me." Sanmartin jerked his head. "Christos here is on the university's board of trustees."

Claassen laughed. "And I am also the head of the loyal opposition, which means that I blackguard Raul and his wife on a daily basis, but when it comes to the university, we see through the same eyes. I met Raul during the rebellion—professionally, one might say—and Hanna's grandfather was one of my dearest friends."

"The university has changed a little since then," Sanmartin commented dryly.

The university's president, nine of the twelve trustees, and an even dozen members of the faculty were either killed in the rebellion or transported for their role in launching it. Once one of the most reactionary institutions on the planet, with changes in personnel it was now one of the most progressive.

"I cannot thank you enough, Heer Claassen," Simon stammered. "Professor Sanmartin has mentioned how much help you have been in establishing a separate Department of Suid-Afrikan Ecology. I do not know what we could have done without you."

"Oh, I didn't do so much." Claassen beamed. "Last year, I think that Professor Dr. Adam Vlok would have walked on hot coals to get Raul as far away from the biology department's budget as possible."

Sanmartin laughed and gestured. "Go ahead and tell them, Christos. Simon knows the truth and the other two are cleared for it."

"Dear old Professor Dr. Vlok had to have his arm twisted very hard, although he has since learned to recognize the sensation and acquiesce gracefully. This department is something that our people need. I doubt that Adam has had an original thought in twenty years, and the way his department avoided studying or teaching anything about Suid-Afrikan biology was criminal. We bent his nose sideways when we told him that Raul was going to be a professor, despite Raul's—"

"Nonexistent credentials," Sanmartin finished for him.

Claassen grinned mirthlessly. "I still remember the look on his face when you said that you weren't going to accept a salary."

Maria Viljoens smiled. "I remember Professor Sanmartin's first class. Oh, those clothes you wore! Wherever did you get them? They hardly fit."

"Borrowed," Sanmartin reminisced. "Thirty first- and second-year students. Ten minutes into the lecture, it dawned on them that I seriously expected them to do oral presentations in English and original fieldwork. At the first break, half of them rushed off to the registrar's office to change."

Viljoens glanced at her two compatriots slyly. "We three stayed."

"And you have done very well, since then," Claassen said gallantly. "Raul showed me your habilitation, *Genetic Analysis of Speciation among Amphtiles of the Drakensberg Region.* I confess I don't understand a word of it."

"Why don't you brief Heer Claassen on it, Maria. Nonspecialized briefing. Ten minutes in length." Sanmartin, who slept through boring lectures and expected normal people to do the same, had taught his students military briefing techniques.

Viljoens caught her breath, then launched in. She finished in nine minutes, eleven seconds.

"Amazing," Claassen said in wonder. "Most of our professors can't explain a thing about what they do in language a simple banker can understand, and there's not one of them who does not use ten words where one would serve, excepting Raul who does not count. Tell me, Maria, have you done this presentation before?"

"I gave it to the first-year students a few weeks ago." She gave Sanmartin an exceedingly dirty look. "Professor Sanmartin gave me fifteen minutes then."

"And you did an excellent job, both times." Sanmartin tapped Beetje lightly on the shoulder. "Simon, it's your turn to be up on a pedestal. I deliberately haven't shown Christos your latest work on reversing the damage that the USS mining operations did to the land and waterways."

Beetje laughed. "Sir, he practically dictated the topic to me." Composing himself, he explained, "Although ecological reclamation work has been accomplished on Earth, no one ever thought through the problems of doing so in a Suid-Afrikan context. Originally, it struck me as mere engineering— mechanic's work, so to speak. I wanted to do something, well, scholarly—some majestic addition to the sum of human knowledge, like how to apply Einstein's theory of relativity to genetics or something." Beetje gestured toward Sanmartin. "He said, 'Be different. Be useful.' "

Maria Viljoens slipped her arm into Beetje's possessively. "It required a great deal of work. Of the first dozen test projects, eleven failed and the twelfth was only a partial success."

"And as soon as Simon showed me his results, I laid my hand on the cover and asked him how we could implement them," Sanmartin interjected.

"I hadn't thought that part of it through, so that took another three months," Beetje said.

"Night and day," Karel Koekemoer said ruefully, and everyone laughed.

"When I gave it to Professor Sanmartin, he asked me if it was right. I told him that I wouldn't have given it to him if I thought it was wrong, but he just smiled and said, 'No. I'm not interested in whether you *think* it's right, I want to know if it's right.' So I spent two more months, and when I gave it back to him, he said, 'Okay. We'll begin with it tomorrow.' "

"And your plan has helped us to clean up the areas that the USS mining operations destroyed," Claassen said complacently.

"In a manner of speaking, sir. It provided a scientific blueprint, but *every* detail needed fixing up. Some of them still do."

"Oh, Simon! How can you say such things," Maria Viljoens said, pulling him close.

"It worked well enough to earn him tenure," Sanmartin observed.

"Which Professor Dr. Vlok fought, tooth and nail." Claassen looked at Sanmartin. "Dear old Adam only thought that he was ruthless and hard-headed."

"I attended classes in a tougher school," Sanmartin said mildly. "It gradually dawned on Adam that I thought what we were trying to accomplish was important, and that if he gave me any problems, I was going to rip his heart out and feed it back to him one slice at a time. After that, he was very gracious about it."

"Writing was not easy," Beetje said to fill the awkward silence. "I did not have most of the necessary knowledge. I had to work with the chemists, the agronomists, the biochemists, the faculty of the Department of Mining and Metallurgy, even Professor Vlok. At first, I didn't even know how to ask them questions. Then Professor Sanmartin made me spend two weeks at the mine pithead so that I could figure out how to do what needed to be done without bankrupting everyone concerned."

"One thing that I have never been able to worm out of Raul is how long it will take to fully restore the land that USS poisoned," Claassen said, eyeing him. "Now that I have you, perhaps you can tell me."

"If funding continues at the current level, we should have most of the work done in about twenty-five years," Beetje said confidently.

Claassen's eyes bulged. "So long," he whispered. "I did not realize."

"Most people do not realize how long it takes to repair severe environmental degradation, Heer Claassen," Viljoens said shyly, but firmly.

"So what do you think, Christos?" Sanmartin asked him.

"If these two can speak this glibly in front of the board, there should be no problem, despite their youth. And I assume that Heer Koekemoer here is next in line. These are difficult times," Claassen replied.

"You won't find people on the planet who'll do the job better," Sanmartin said. "All right, the plan is this. Effective Thursday, I am resigning my position as department head. Simon, I expect you to be confirmed in my place. Christos and the chancellor already know, and if we hear a peep out of Professor Dr. Vlok, Professor Dr. Vlok will regret it."

Simon Beetje touched the fingers of one hand to his lips and looked at Maria Viljoens. "So soon?"

"It's politics. Simon, you're already doing the job. You've been drafting the budget and handling the day-to-day stuff for six months. Well, the mission is yours now. Maria and Karel will help you out." What Sanmartin wanted to say and didn't was that men Simon's age were given command of infantry companies and expected to win wars. "Christos, is there anything you can add?"

Claassen nodded. "The mission, of course, is not merely to teach students and study Suid-Afrikan plants and animals, but also to teach our people an ethic so that we haven't destroyed what makes Suid-Afrika unique by the time the three of you are my age. Despite our political differences, Raul and I are of one heart, one mind, on this."

"I hope you understand, sir, that I will not 'carry out the mission' in precisely the way that Professor Sanmartin has done. Although I have learned from him and respect him very much, I am my own person," Beetje said.

Maria Viljoens gasped, "Simon!"

"No, young Simon is quite correct in saying this to me, Juffrou Viljoens," Claassen explained. "Raul and I expect nothing less."

"I have two boxes of original records out in the vehicle, five and a half years of fieldwork, plus some stuff from Earth," Sanmartin said lightly. "Why don't you three come get them?"

Recognizing how completely Sanmartin was severing his ties, Beetje reached out his hand and found tears running down his face. Sanmartin embraced the three of them in turn.

When they left, Claassen said privately to Sanmartin, "I wish that you would let us keep you on the faculty. We could put you on some sort of sabbatical, you know."

"Christos, I'm not a professor. We both know that the only reason that I got away with the charade for this long is that the professors who were politically reliable enough to come here were a pretty mediocre lot. Even though I've been doing this for five years, I still don't know how to be a professor, and I'm not sure I want to learn."

Christos Claassen understood, a little. Hanna Bruwer had explained. Sanmartin's mother had been a university professor of economics in Buenos Aires. On Sanmartin's sixteenth birthday, she said things in public about environment degradation and civil rights that earned her a twenty-year sentence. By dying early, she cheated the government out of sixteen years.

Sanmartin stepped off the path and gently nudged a seed fern he had planted with his toe. "Simon and Karen already know more about Suid-Afrikan ecology than I'll ever know, and I learned years ago to never look back. Did you know that a year or two ago, Simon actually wanted to join our battalion's reserve company and be a soldier part-time."

"What did you tell him?" Claassen asked quietly.

"That I needed him here. That he was this planet's seed corn."

Claassen made a small jest. "Is being a soldier so bad?"

"No. Being a soldier is fine. It disciplines you for other things. But *war* is for professionals—it tends to ruin you for anything else." Sanmartin looked over his shoulder at the campus. "I will miss this place. Oh, I meant to tell you. The Manchurians will be taking over the Pretoria and Johannesburg caserns from us tomorrow—one battalion in each casern. Call it a New Year's present."

"What?" Claassen said, taken aback.

"The order came down this morning. Ostensibly, we're concentrating the battalion in Bloemfontein to intensify our effort to root the ARM boys out of the forests. We've been expecting it—Admiral Horii asked Anton when we could be ready to move out, and Anton said tomorrow, which set a few wings flapping, I'm sure. It means that Colonel Sumi will begin taking charge of antiterrorist activities in the cities."

"What does this mean for us?" Claassen asked, his good humor erased.

"I'm sure that there's a *ringi* circulating around Admiral Horii's staff, but Anton and I haven't seen it. My guess is that Sumi is building a consensus for some pretty tough measures. I expect that we'll have to make the ARM disappear our way before Colonel Sumi gets everyone to agree to let him try to make the ARM disappear his way," Sanmartin said distantly.

Tuesday(311)

NEXT TO THE SPACEPORT SHUTTLE RUNWAY, THE TEMPORARY LODGments of the First Manchurian Battalion hummed with activity as the battalion prepared to move into permanent quarters. Elbowing his way through the crowd, Section Sergeant Ma bellowed, "Hey, Duck-Face! Lieutenant Akamine wants to see you!"

The unflattering and often descriptive nicknames the Manchurian soldiers attached to one another would have horrified their Japanese officers had they known.

Recruit Private "Duck-Face" Gu looked up. "What does that little rat-eyed pirate dwarf Pig-Snout Akamine want now?" he complained. "One-Eye" Wong began snickering in the corner of the tent.

"To scream at you, what else? When the admiral came through, he inspected your area. Don't you know how to roll a hammock?" "Sawtooth" Ma asked his subordinate.

"Oh," Gu moaned, holding his head, "all pirate dwarf officers are motherless." He looked up at his section sergeant. "What is it going to take to make Pig-Snout happy?"

"Your private parts, lightly roasted," Ma said with relish. "Of course, I could put in a word for you."

"Oh, pirate dwarf officers and all sergeants are motherless," Gu moaned. "How much?"

"Enough." Ma rubbed his fingers together. "And more for saying things like that about your old sergeant, who keeps Lieutenant Pig-Snout from making your miserable, worthless life more miserable and worthless. Besides, why do you care how much? You'll make lots of money off the locals when they start acting up."

"I thought the long-nosed barbarian colonel had the locals tamed," Gu said, reluctantly reaching for his billfold.

"All locals act up. Haven't you been in the Imperial Army long enough to know that?" Ma said complacently. "You don't think they sent the pirate dwarfs and blacklegs here to sit around with their fingers up their noses, do you? Now get moving, and remember to grovel for Pig-Snout, he likes that. And remember to hurry back! We are leaving in twenty minutes."

Similar activity was occurring at Coldewe's casern on the outskirts of Johannesburg as the men of C Company prepared to vacate the knoll they had lovingly fortified to make room for the First Manchurian.

"The Iceman can keep Bloemfontein. I don't want to move there," Corporal Uborevich complained, already two hours behind schedule. "Vosloo, admirals should be drowned at birth!"

Both Recruit Private Vosloo and his platoon leader, Sublieutenant Jan Snyman, smiled as they finished packing up their personal gear.

"You should think positively, Corporal," Vosloo said cheerfully with a wink. "I have a cousin in Bloemfontein. The girls there aren't as sophisticated as these big-city girls, so you might have some luck. Although maybe not—I hear they shave their legs and wear shoes."

Uborevich snorted contemptuously, and a few other members of his section suppressed grins. Uborevich's unbelievable stories about the women he dated grew more incredible every time he repeated them.

"I always liked the one where Bory claimed a woman came up to him at a night guard post, lifted her skirt, and told him to stand at attention," Vosloo said happily as a half dozen trucks carrying the Manchurian advance party began pulling up.

When Sergeant Ma and Private Wong hopped out of the back of their vehicle, Uborevich wiped the damp tears from his eyes. "She's a good casern. Treat her nicely."

Casting a steely eye at his section sergeant, Wong asked Uborevich in labored English, "What are these amphtiles? Are they dangerous?"

Fate had placed Uborevich at the right place at the right moment. "Oh, no," he assured Wong solemnly. "A machine gun will slow them down every time, and they only really get mean after dark. We hardly ever lose more than a few men. Of course, if they bite you, it's like that!" He snapped his fingers. "Poison. There's no antidote. You walk three steps and fall over dead."

When other C Company men nodded, the Manchurians assumed the worst. In reality, the C Company men were merely acknowledging that Uborevich actually could tell a completely unbelievable story that didn't involve a woman. C Company had speculated a lot about that.

The platoon of armored cars from Lieutenant-Colonel Okuda's Ninth Light Attack Battalion, which had accompanied the Manchurians, began pulling into the revetments. Lieutenant Danny Meagher elbowed Hans Coldewe in the ribs. "Hans, there's something odd about their Cadillacs. I've been shot at by them often enough to know," he said in a musical voice.

A former mercenary—a fairly notorious one—Meagher had worked for USS and ended up on the wrong side of the uprising after USS had left its mercs minus their pay and mostly dead. After the rebellion, Meagher had entered himself on the battalion's muster roll with characteristic bravura as "Daniel van Meagher."

Coldewe responded slowly. "The Cadillacs with 30mm guns

look all right, but there's something wrong with the 90mm guns on the others."

"Having been on the other side, I'm sure it's something we'll want to look into," Meagher replied.

IN BLOEMFONTEIN THAT EVENING, THE ENTIRE BATTALION GATHered for a muted New Year's celebration. One custom involved pouring a dipper full of melted lead into a bucket of cold water to read the future.

"Black spots mean future sadness," Isaac Wanjau, the moderately incongruous keeper of C Company's traditions, explained to some young troopers as Yuri Malinov poured the lead.

After a slight hesitation, Timo Haerkoennen announced officially, "It looks like a ship. Better make travel plans."

Meagher nudged Coldewe and whispered, "It looks more like a bullet to me."

Wednesday(311)

AFTER HANGING HAMMOCKS EVERYWHERE THERE WAS ROOM, Matti Harjalo solved the problems caused by the influx of personnel from the Pretoria and Johannesburg caserns by deploying half the battalion in the forests to crowd the ARM boys. Still, it was the first time since Vereshchagin's battalion landed that all four companies were together, and space was at a premium. A new partition split Harjalo's cubicle down the middle, leaving him barely enough room for a hammock, a field desk, and a terminal.

At the moment, the hammock was in use, and Harjalo barely opened one eye when he heard a soft knock on his door.

In addition to his other duties, Senior Communications Sergeant Timo Haerkoennen acted as a very efficient buffer between Harjalo and the rest of the universe. "Sir, Major Sanmartin's here. I'll send him in," Haerkoennen said quietly.

"What's up, Raul," Harjalo said, planting his feet on the floor and rubbing his eyes as Sanmartin entered.

"Trouble. The local police have found a body—one of our more outspoken local radicals. Nobody had seen him for a day or two. Someone put a 9mm round in the back of his head and stuffed him into a trash can. It looks like he was tortured before he was shot."

"Is the ARM cleansing its ranks of deviants again?"

"Maybe," Sanmartin said noncommittally.

"Was there anything unusual about the body?"

"One thing—someone stuffed a wad of cash in the victim's right shoe. New bills."

"Hell!" Harjalo exclaimed. "It means the frosting Manchurians did it—probably under orders. It's a very, very, very old Chinese superstition to leave money in the shoe of someone you murder so that he gets a good burial and his ghost doesn't come after you. I don't know if anyone believes in the superstition anymore, but Chinese security people leave money like that when they want astute folks to know they did a job. They probably squeezed out what the man knew, which I doubt was much, and then finished him off. Sumi's serving notice on the local rads that he plays for keeps."

"The second platoon of the Manchurian regiment's reconnaissance company is designated as a 'countersubversion' platoon," Sanmartin said slowly, "but I don't think Sumi is serving notice on the ARM as much as serving notice on us. We're already starting to get complaints about the Manchurians and the Imperial guardsmen from the merchants in town. Death squads aren't coming to help matters any."

A few moments later, as Sanmartin was shrugging out of his webbing, Timo Haerkoennen waved him over to take a call relayed from his home. "Hello. Sanmartin here."

"Hello, Raul?"

It took him a few seconds to place the voice: Anneke Brink from the faculty of music; a nice enough woman, but much too pretty and too well aware of it. "Yes, hello, Anneke. How are you?" Brink had lost a brother-in-law, a football player named le Grange, during the rebellion, and it had taken her a while to warm to Sanmartin.

"I am well enough, thank you. I am flattered that you remember me from all of that dreary committee work together."

Haerkoennen nodded and discreetly disappeared.

Sanmartin smiled. "Hanna says that I should be the politician in the family. How are you?"

"Very fine, thank you. Please say hello to your Private Erixon for me. I wish you could persuade him to turn professional for us."

That was another tie she was subtly reminding him of. Chaplain Erixon had a surprisingly good baritone voice, and Brink had played opposite him when Letsukov and C Company helped stage *Boris Godunov*.

"I'll say hello, but I suspect he's content with the two professions he already has. What can I do for you, Anneke?"

The hint of coquetry abruptly left her voice. "Raul, I am so worried. What is happening?!"

"I wish I knew." A feeling passed through him. "Listen, Anneke, do you own a place out in the country—a summer house or something away from the city where you could stay?"

"My sister has a small place outside Boksburg."

"Look, take clothes and some food and go there."

"But I couldn't possibly leave now—I already have a full set of classes!"

"Go on a sabbatical or something. Just do it!" Sanmartin closed his eyes.

Sometimes he had a feeling in his fingertips—a "pricking of thumbs," Coldewe called it—that meant something would happen. The Germans had a long, jaw-twisting word for it, having fought their fair share of wars. Sanmartin had stopped ignoring it one or two ambushes back.

"But, Raul—" she began.

"Anneke," he said patiently, more sure of himself than ever, and for a few seconds the phone trembled in his hand, "find an excuse to be away from Jo'burg for a while."

"Thank you, Raul," she said in a very different tone of voice.

"You're welcome," he said automatically, and hung up.

Thursday(311)

IN THE BACK ROOM OF A JOHANNESBURG GUESTHOUSE, A DOZEN politicians met to discuss circumstances.

With his eyes flashing under thick white brows, Wynard Grobelaar thundered, "Stealing fruit from the stalls is one thing. Murdering people is another!" Franz Vilhofer glanced at his watch. Grobelaar, the heavyset manager of a cooperative, had run unsuccessfully against Hanna Bruwer twice.

Andries Steen said patiently, "You can't be sure that the new Imperials are responsible."

"It's still a stick to beat Beyers with," Assemblyman Martin Hatting said. "The question should be asked."

Grobelaar looked around the room. "We have talked around the edges of this for an hour, now. Both parties have to take a harder line in defense of our people." Emboldened, he added,

"If we form a third party here and now, we have the power to make them do so."

Vilhofer almost choked. "Hear this straight, Wynard. Beyers can break any man here, and if you push at him, make sure you knock him over, because he will push back." He uncoiled his legs and stood. "Unless someone shows me that they can do better than he has, you will count me out. I also think that anything we do to undermine the government now will only play into the hands of the new Imperials. If the rest of you want to make a noise to no good purpose, do it, but don't include me." He rose and left. Steen and three others followed him out. Grobelaar looked around the table uncertainly.

Juriaan Joubert said tersely, "If we quarrel among ourselves, the new Imperials will swallow us whole. Franz has the right of it. *If* the Imperials begin to oppress the people, and *if* Beyers does nothing to stop it, then we should challenge him. Until then, we would be well advised to be quiet."

"Well, I won't," Hatting said. "It's time someone showed our people that some politicians are willing to stand up for them." Picking up his hat, he left and began preparing a speech for that afternoon.

When the Assembly met, hours later, Hatting rose to hurl his denunciations before the news cameras—and was promptly ruled out of order by Hanna Bruwer. For the next hour, he writhed in agony. Moments after the newsmen left, Bruwer looked right through him and called a recess.

As she left her high seat on the way to the restroom, she murmured, "Martin, you should wait for the car to slow down before you grab for the steering wheel."

"*Hexe!*" Hatting hissed, loud enough for the room to hear. It meant "witch."

Bruwer turned and said in a quiet voice that carried nonetheless, "Martin? I seem to recall that Albert and I both campaigned for you, and you owe us. I think I left my broom outside. Please polish it up for me."

When the Assembly reconvened a few hours later, Hatting found a dozen dust rags from his colleagues on his desk.

Returning home from the session, Bruwer found Anneke Brink waiting on her doorstep. Brink colored. "Oh, Vroew Bruwer. I did not expect to see you. I am Anneke Brink, I am a professor at the university. I was waiting for your husband."

"Heaven knows when he will be home. You had better come

on in." She nodded to her bodyguard. "It is all right, Tom. Juffrou Brink, this is my secretary, Tom Winters."

Stepping inside, she greeted Vroew Beyers and scooped up Hendricka. "Should I ask what my husband has done to offend you?" she asked with the child wrapped around her neck.

"Oh," Brink stammered. "It is nothing like that. When I asked him whether there would be trouble, he suggested that I take leave and move to the country." She tried to conceal her anxiety. "I thought I should discuss it with him. I learned this morning that he has resigned from the faculty."

"I will have to ask Raul when I see him next. I do see him sometimes," Bruwer said lightly, coldly appraising Brink.

Her blush deepened. "Oh, I did not mean to cause trouble. I . . . I don't want you to think . . ."

Bruwer suddenly burst out laughing. "Oh, I'm so very sorry," she said, wiping her eyes. "It just dawned upon me that you must think that I am a jealous wife."

"Well, I'm not sure that it is all that funny," Brink rejoined.

"Oh, it would be if you knew Raul better."

"You can't trust any of them!" Brink said bitterly, with the experience of two marriages behind her.

"Raul, I can trust," Bruwer said calmly. "He has many faults, but he has not lived a normal life and I doubt that he would know how to look at another woman." War had not killed Raul Sanmartin's conscience, as it had with some men; other pieces of him, perhaps, but not that. She changed the subject. "If Raul told you to take a leave of absence and go to the country, I suspect that it is good advice."

"It is an easy thing to say, but it really is a difficult choice to make. I wish that I could be as sure as you!"

Hendricka smiled at her and hid her face behind her mother's head.

"What a lovely daughter you have," Brink said lamely.

"Hendricka is more Vroew Beyers's child than mine. Don't you follow politics at all? I thought my enemies made the situation notorious several years ago." Bruwer studied Brink's face.

"Raul's battalion has a number of hard and very necessary rules, because the battalion can leave a world at any time and never return. In a way, I, too, am a soldier, you see, a most reluctant one. One rule is that married couples within the battalion must adopt children out. It is a rule they do not break."

Although Bruwer said this without effort, Brink did not mistake the pain in her voice.

"When Hendricka confounded matters by arriving a month before my first election, as Raul could tell you, I took to my bed with her in my arms and cried for three days before I would give her up to Vroew Beyers. Then I whipped the devil and the living God out of the pompous hack that Christos Claassen ran against me. I have heard the things they said and still say when they think that I am not listening."

Bruwer looked up at the clock on the wall. "But even though Betje Beyers has been a good mother to both of us, it was very hard on me. And I know that it was harder on Raul. If he told you that you should go to the country, I suggest that you follow his advice."

"Thank you very much for speaking with me, Vroew Speaker," Brink said timidly as Winters showed her to the door.

Hours later, Sanmartin let himself in. "Are you awake?" he asked softly.

"Yes. I tried to read and decided that I couldn't. Have you eaten?"

Sanmartin flipped the light on. "Kasha made me something weird and Russian. Or Finnish—I think it was a fish pudding."

"You're impossible," his wife observed. "By now, you know about Hatting. And Vroew Beyers tells me that Hendricka has been reading to herself for a week and neither one of us noticed." She sighed. "I wish there was something I could do. A magic wand I could wave for all of our troubles."

"Me, too," Sanmartin said with passion as he stripped out of his battle dress.

"Anneke Brink was by here earlier. I twisted her arm to get her to go to the country. What is going on that worries you so?"

"The ARM is about to make a move, and I don't trust Matsudaira and Sumi not to do something stupid."

"No. That is not what I meant. Something is very wrong on Earth so that people like Sumi and Matsudaira are sent here, and Captain Yanagita is allowed to make subtle threats that if I do not grant concessions to USS, unpleasant things will happen. Explain this to me so that my heart understands."

He sat down heavily on the edge of the bed. "How much do you know about politics back on Earth?"

"Obviously not as much as you think I should. We have the Imperial Government, the Japanese government, and the governments of the affiliated nations."

"Yes, and also no. About a decade ago, the Imperial ministries began working out of the same buildings as their Japanese government counterparts, and the two sets of ministries are becoming interchangeable. The affiliated governments are stuck because they can't tax or regulate international commerce, and the Guardianship Council decides what constitutes international commerce based on the advice they get from the Japanese Ministry of International Trade and Industry. Most of the time, the Guardianship Council goes along with what they're advised to do."

Bruwer waited for him to continue.

"In Japan, the United Democratic party always forms the government, but it's really just a collection of factions—*haibatsu*—which divide up the available political offices between them. The big corporations funnel money to the *haibatsu* leaders, who dole the money out to their followers, which pretty much takes institutionalized corruption to its theoretical limits. The titular leaders—the prime minister of Japan, the emperor, the Imperial Senate—don't decide anything. The Japanese call them *mikoshi*, 'portable shrines.' When a scandal breaks, as they do with regularity, a bunch of ministers resign and the *haibatsu* leaders hand their offices to another bunch." He smiled thinly. "The Japanese have always distinguished between *tatamae*, how things should be in principle, and *honne*, how things actually are."

"And the Diet?" Bruwer asked, thinking about her own quarrelsome assemblymen.

"It is hideously expensive to run for the Diet, and every election district in Japan elects the three or four people who collect the most votes. A Diet candidate who doesn't belong to a *haibatsu* wouldn't get any money to run, and if he won, his district wouldn't get anything, instead of the tunnels and roads no one needs that everyone else gets in return for their votes. So most of them are owned, body and soul, and they rubber-stamp the legislation that the career bureaucrats in the ministries put together. Everything has gotten hereditary—everybody comes from the same families and goes to the same schools."

"How does one break into this network?" Bruwer asked, frowning.

"Marry someone's daughter or get adopted."

Bruwer held her hands up to her temples, starlight from the window playing over her hair. "The Imperial Government shepherded humanity through the crazy years after the crack-up."

"Things weren't always this bad," he agreed, reaching up to

take her wrists. "If the corporations got more than their share, enough trickled down to benefit the rest of us. The Imperial system was never what it should have been, but for a long time, it meant a lot of good for a lot of people."

"Dear God. What has happened to make it change?"

"I think . . ." he said, and he thought. "I think that affiliated nations and the colonies have grown up. Their industries compete. The corporate *keiretsu* need to constantly increase their share of economic power to make the payoffs that keep the things in place. Like the Red Queen in the book that Hans showed me, they have to keep running faster and faster to stay in the same place. It isn't enough for them to dominate Japan's market and compete in external markets, they have to dominate external markets as well."

He thought of a story. "A Swiss I met on Ashcroft told me how his company once tried to set up a production line for microchips. Suddenly, nobody in MITI could sign licenses for them, and a few days later, another MITI bureaucrat told the Swiss government that there was a problem with the certification for Swiss dairy products. The Swiss aren't economically self-sufficient. They took the hint. In Argentina, when I was about five, a new government took power and pledged to end dependence on Japanese products. About a year later, they were thrown out by a coup."

"Are you saying that the corporations use the Imperial Government to attack the affiliated nations? Yes, you are. That is what is happening here."

"It frightens me that the corporations may have discovered that it's easier to use military force to keep the affiliated nations and the colonies in order than it is to use economic leverage. The corporations used to use the Imperial Government to try to beggar the nations they disagreed with. Now, I think that they have begun selectively destroying what they can't control."

"Lord God." She held his hands and stared at him gravely. "So you are telling me that unless we give in to Matsudaira, Admiral Horii may try to destroy us as a people. Are you telling me that we should give in?"

He nodded.

"But we can't!" she said, shaking him. "We can't. How can they think that it is right to do this?"

He looked at her, aware she had touched a nerve. "Love, Japanese have been telling themselves they're different from other people for so long that some of them don't think that we're human."

Friday(311)

AROUND MIDNIGHT, HAERKOENNEN FINALLY WORRIED MIZOGUCHI'S message from the tape. Recording the message backward, Mizo had raised it four octaves in pitch, speeded it up to a hundred times normal speed, and buried it in the hiss.

It confirmed what Vereshchagin suspected. Increasingly, restive Earth and its colonies were held to the Imperial way by force. The Ministry of Security had expanded its emergency powers. National battalions had been disbanded and non-Japanese officers dismissed. Worst of all, the colony on Esdraelon had been pushed into revolt. It paid the price of failure, its population reduced by two-thirds.

When Mizoguchi finished, Harjalo turned to look at Vereshchagin. The Variag was standing very still with his hands folded. His face was absent of expression.

"So this is what we've been preparing for," Harjalo said.

"This is what I feared," Vereshchagin replied. "I had hoped . . ." he started to say, and stopped.

"So what do we do?" Harjalo asked him.

"I do not know, Matti," Vereshchagin said softly. "Tell Piotr and Raul, for now. They both know or suspect most of it." Vereshchagin reached into his pocket and pulled out his pipe, gently turning it over in his hands. "Please take charge of things for a day or so. I must think on this. In any case, we must wait for the ARM to make their move. I must go back. Admiral Horii will expect to see me at staff call as usual." He stood and started to leave.

"Anton," Harjalo said. Vereshchagin turned.

"Remember what the Roman centurion said?"

"Yes, Marcus Flavinius. 'If we must leave our bones to bleach uselessly on the desert road, then beware the legions' anger!' "

Saturday(311)

FOLLOWING STAFF CALL, VERESHCHAGIN, WHO HAD NO ASSIGNED duties, was reading in his assigned quarters when Horii and his aide, Captain Watanabe, came to call.

"Good morning, Admiral." Vereshchagin rose and bowed slightly, then he snapped off the reader.

"Good morning, Lieutenant-Colonel." Apart from a hammock, a field desk, and a chair, the room had no furniture, so Horii remained standing. "What book were you reading?"

"It is a biography of Abraham Lincoln, by a man named Sandburg. It is very old, but very well written." Seeing Watanabe's lack of comprehension, Vereshchagin added, "Lincoln was president of the United States of America during the American Civil War."

"Oh, yes, of course." Watanabe nodded. "He freed slaves."

"It became necessary for him to do so," Vereshchagin replied.

"And how do you see President Lincoln?" Horii asked.

Vereshchagin waited a moment before replying. "Lincoln was a very great man and a very human one, who understood other men's weaknesses as well as his own. I am amazed by his insight into the hearts of men, and by his courage and humor."

"Yes, a most interesting man. And a most interesting rug," Horii said, pointing to the brightly colored wool rug, partially woven and partially knotted, on Vereshchagin's floor. "Very artistic."

"My *ryijy*. Some men in A Company made it for me."

"I regret that I have not been able to make time to speak with you at greater length."

"I understand completely."

They chatted inconsequentially while Vereshchagin waited for Horii to make the purpose of his visit clear. At length, Horii said, "And how do Major Harjalo's operations to eliminate the Afrikaner Resistance Movement fare?"

"I was planning to visit with him, unless, of course, you have other duties for me. One of his companies is holding an orienteering competition which they would like me to umpire," Vereshchagin said cautiously. "As to his progress, guerrilla movements are exceedingly difficult to destroy as long as conditions favor their continued existence."

"War is a dialectic of wills, Lieutenant-Colonel Vereshchagin," Horii said didactically. "One achieves a decision by producing a psychological effect on the enemy such that he becomes convinced that it is futile to continue the struggle. We must produce such a psychological effect on the members of the ARM and their passive supporters." He smiled. "Your record would indicate that you understand such movements very well. I have been told that Admiral Nakamura christened you Sertorius."

"Admiral Nakamura was very kind," Vereshchagin said, bowing.

"You are a native Russian, are you not?"

Vereshchagin nodded. "My mother was Finnish, but my father was from St. Petersburg."

"People do not realize how much the crack-up aided Russia," Horii said. "The people had no food, no hope. Although many Russian cities were obliterated and the remaining population was decimated by the plagues, the survivors emerged with a sense of pride. AIDS and other debilitating diseases almost disappeared. Russia is a far healthier nation today because of the crack-up, don't you agree?"

"In the long run, perhaps. But the cost was terrible," Vereshchagin said inflexibly.

"Sometimes harsh measures are called for in extraordinary situations," Horii said apologetically. He fell silent for a few minutes, then said, "I read from your file that you are able to recite the *Kalevela*."

"Parts of it." Vereshchagin chanted, " 'I know the origin of iron/ I know the beginnings of steel/ Air is its first of mothers/ Water the eldest of brothers/ Iron the youngest of brothers/ Fire in turn the middle one.' It mostly consists of charms and stories."

"Yes," Horii said, "in this regard it resembles our earliest chronicles, the *Kojiki* and the *Nihon-shoki*, to some extent."

"To some extent," Vereshchagin responded.

"Yes, cultural heritage is very, very important. Major Harjalo's battalion was originally raised in Finland and has been away from Earth for many years. It would perhaps be appropriate to return it there if all goes well here, don't you think?"

"I am sure that a number of Major Harjalo's men would welcome the opportunity," Vereshchagin said carefully.

"It is a difficult matter, but we must discuss the possibility again at another time. Please keep me informed of Major Harjalo's progress."

"I will do so. Hopefully, his efforts will be successful."

"We shall see. I am a pessimist, Vereshchagin. I have always been a pessimist, but I quite enjoy it. Pessimism is an art form. Military affairs are always unpredictable, but we shall see."

As Horii walked down the corridor, he said to Watanabe, "Of course, the reference to Sertorius puzzled you."

"Yes, honored Admiral."

"Plutarch compared Sertorius to Philip of Macedon, Antigonus, and Hannibal, and thought that although none of them surpassed him in intelligence, all surpassed him in good fortune. He was born in Nussa and served Rome against the Cimbri, against the Celtiberian tribes, and in the Social War where he lost an eye. In Rome's first civil war, he secured Italy for Cinna, and after finding himself a lone voice against excesses, he exiled himself to Hither Spain. He was not a fortunate man, just as Anton Vereshchagin is not a fortunate man."

"I do not understand, honored Admiral."

"Had Sertorius been born a Roman, he would have been fitted for the highest offices. As it was, despite his immense talents, he was fated to serve. He was a man of great integrity, and lived in a time when integrity was despised."

"I see the parallel. Thank you for making it clear to me."

"Vereshchagin undoubtedly is aware that foreign officers are no longer welcome in Imperial service. His first concern will be for the welfare of his officers and men. Understand that I held out hope to him in the form of repatriation back to Earth. This will make him zealous in pursuit of our interests."

Watanabe pondered this. "May I ask what happened to Sertorius?"

"You may. The Lusitanians made him their war leader, and for a number of years he defied the dictator Sulla and Rome's might. He defeated many Roman armies, including armies led by Metellus and Pompey the Great. But it ended, as all such endeavors must end, when the favor of the gods left him. He was betrayed, and grew bitter and careless. Eventually, he was assassinated by exiles he had fostered, and his state disintegrated."

"Each man must accept his destiny."

"Of course, Watanabe. I have read what Plutarch wrote very carefully. It is clear that Sertorius knew what his murderers planned for him and accepted his fate."

"It was a very subtle message you intended to convey. I hesitate to ask this, but will it be comprehensible to a foreigner?"

Horii smiled, showing all of the points of his teeth. "When I discovered that Lieutenant-Colonel Vereshchagin would be commanding the battalion here, I read all of his professional writings. His thesis at the War Collegium was entitled 'Combat as an Application of Turbulence Theory.' Turbulence theory comes from fluid dynamics. It is a way of describing interactions as controlled chaos."

"Is that so? I am not sure that I understand, honored Admiral. Isn't combat an orderly application of force to achieve an objective?"

"Yes, however, also no. The article was profoundly disturbing, Watanabe. You should read it carefully. Despite being a foreigner, Lieutenant-Colonel Vereshchagin is a complex and very subtle man."

As they reached Horii's quarters, Horii said, "Please come inside for a moment, Watanabe."

Watanabe bowed, somewhat startled. "Of course, Admiral."

As soon as the door closed, Horii pointed to a cabinet. "There is a bottle of good whiskey in there and some glasses. Pour yourself a glass and another for me. Bring the bottle here." He sat down behind a low table.

Watanabe did so, still somewhat bewildered.

As soon as Watanabe sat down, the admiral said, *"Kampai!"* and drained his glass, constraining Watanabe to do the same.

"Now, you are trying to understand the point that Lieutenant-Colonel Vereshchagin made about Lincoln, aren't you, Watanabe?"

"Yes, honored Admiral. I regret my lack of comprehension."

"Lincoln was a truly great man, Watanabe. He was born into poverty, don't you know? There was a photograph of the place he was born in Kentucky—our country was poor at the time, but you would not see many houses like that even in Japan. And yet by the time his life ended, he had become the champion of human freedom."

"But he made many mistakes, didn't he? Weren't the generals he chose very poor ones?"

"A man of true purpose, Watanabe, puts his faith in himself always. Sometimes he refuses even to put his faith in the gods. So—from time to time, he falls into error. Lincoln often fell into error, but this does not detract from his greatness. A man isn't a god. Lincoln was a very human man—he often recognized flaws in himself, which made him willing to view flaws in other persons in the best light. This inspired a feeling of warmth toward him and so aroused devotion and admiration. Only if people have this quality can they forgive each other's mistakes and help each other. But do not ever forget, Watanabe," he said bleakly. "Each man must accept his destiny. One person cannot change things."

"Of course, Admiral."

"Drink up, then, Watanabe." Watanabe did so. After the third toast, Horii finally broached the subject on his mind. "Watanabe, you listen to the other young officers, don't you?"

"Of course, one always listens to what other people have to say."

"What is it that you hear them saying, Watanabe?"

"Oh, the usual things, I am sure," Watanabe said uneasily.

"I will tell you what they are saying, Watanabe. As if I did not know what they were thinking already, a delegation of them came to see me last night." Horii held out his glass, and Watanabe filled both of them. "They are complaining about the absence of fighting, aren't they, Watanabe?"

Watanabe did not reply.

"Yes, they came here to fight a war, and there is no war," Horii drained his glass, seemingly oblivious of Watanabe. "They were sent all of this way, and if there is no war to fight, they will be behind all of their peers. They are afraid that they will never receive promotions, is this not true, Watanabe?"

"It is possible that some persons might feel this way," Watanabe conceded.

"It is important to see distant things as if they were close, and close things as if they were distant. The ones who came to see me were disturbed because Afrikaners who fought in the rebellion were not dealt with 'appropriately.' They want to cleanse this world of all 'anti-Imperial' influences. You know what they mean when they say 'cleanse,' don't you, Watanabe?"

"I have heard some persons say this, but young officers who have had too much to drink often say things that they do not mean," Watanabe said, frightened.

"And who complains the most, Watanabe? The officers of the Lifeguards battalion?"

"It is possible that they are among the ones who say the most," Watanabe admitted.

"And members of my staff as well," Horii said, reading Watanabe's face.

Watanabe tried to evade. "They are mostly disappointed that they are not allowed to take action against the Afrikaner Resistance Movement, I am sure."

"The Afrikaner Resistance Movement is nothing. A handful

of fools." Horii took the whiskey bottle out of Watanabe's hands and poured himself another drink. "So who pays for these young officers to drink and complain—Sumi or Matsudaira?"

Watanabe looked down and made no answer.

"It is both of them, isn't it?" Horii said, having found the answer he was looking for. "Careless of them. So apparent. Or perhaps they don't care whether I know. Do you agree with these young officers, Watanabe?"

Watanabe made no effort to look up. "It would appear that they have some sincere opinions which require consideration, honored Admiral."

"So how long will my young officers give me before they start taking action against the Afrikaners without orders, Watanabe?"

"Oh, I am sure that they would never be disloyal to you," Watanabe said miserably, staring at the glass in his hand.

"Yes, the delegation of young officers repeatedly assured me of their absolute loyalty. They merely disagreed with the 'bad advice' I was being given. So when will they start killing people without any orders from me, Watanabe? Two months from now? One month?" Horii radiated contempt.

"They seem very impetuous," Watanabe admitted.

"And who do they think is giving me 'bad advice'?" Horii asked.

"The foreign officers, of course," Watanabe said, astonished. "Who else would do so?"

Horii stared impassively at the wall for several minutes. "No man ever escapes his destiny," he finally said.

"Did Colonel Sumi mention to you that our technicians have tapped into Lieutenant-Colonel Vereshchagin's data bases? He was boasting of it," Watanabe volunteered, anxious to restore himself to his admiral's good graces.

"No, but it would appear to be a prudent move for us to know as much as Lieutenant-Colonel Vereshchagin does about these people," Horii said sadly.

WELCOMING VERESHCHAGIN IN, ABRAM VAN ZYL HANDED HIM A glass of wine.

"Thank you, no," Vereshchagin said automatically.

Van Zyl waved aside his protest. "I'm drinking it, and it's not good for an old man to drink alone. Besides," he smiled shrewdly, "you look like you could use a drop of something. Now pull up a chair and tell me what is going on."

A close associate of Albert Beyers, Abram van Zyl was a crafty old advocate, or so his friends said. People he had beaten in court called him a shifty old shyster, which delighted him to no end. Vereshchagin had appointed him brigade advocate, which gave him an excuse to consult him about matters which had very little to do with law.

Vereshchagin made himself comfortable on a stuffed settee. "I would have thought that you had prised that information from Albert."

"He's been quiet, but I have known both of you far too long for either one of you to fool me," the old advocate said complacently.

"Perhaps," Vereshchagin said.

"Well, I know it was not good news. I won't ask you for secrets. Tell me about these new armored cars I see."

"I am surprised that you noticed."

"How could I not notice with those fancy new guns they have. They look like something out of a science fiction film."

"Electromagnetic cannon. They impart a very high muzzle velocity to the round, much higher than our guns do," Vereshchagin said absently.

"Oh, something new then?"

"In a manner of speaking. The technology has been around for at least a century, but they have never tried to use it on Type 97s."

"Why not? You would not have to fool with gunpowder anymore I would imagine, although I understand what you use to fire your cannon is a liquid, not a powder." The brigade lawyer was proud of his military learning.

"Like anything, it involves trade-offs. For one thing, the change must have been hideously expensive. For another, an electromagnetic gun takes up considerably more internal space than a simple kinetic weapon. They had to redesign the turret and most of the internal compartmenting. It might actually have been cheaper to design and build a new vehicle." Vereshchagin considered.

"The change affected the vehicle's operational radius. While the space used for storing propellant can be used for fuel, I understand they had to convert the two forward fuel tanks. With the added weight of the increased armor on the forward glacis, the vehicle has approximately 15 percent less range than one of ours. Switching to electromagnetic guns also increased the maintenance costs. I know they have had to add an extra mechanic with specialized training for every two vehicles, although these modified Type 97s are still far less costly to ship and maintain than tanks would be."

Van Zyl grinned. "Now seriously, Anton. As tight-mouthed as this new admiral is, how can you possibly know about these extra mechanics?"

Vereshchagin leaned back in his chair. "Well, it so happens that Senior Intelligence Sergeant Aksu is an avid amateur photographer, and he persuaded a company maintenance section to allow him to take a group photo."

"Anton, I sometimes forget just how devious you are."

"Actually, I believe that that was Raul Sanmartin's idea."

"It is the same principle. I know Raul learned it from you, and Hanna learned it from being married to Raul." Van Zyl puffed on his cigar. "So tell me why this is not a good idea. It seems to me that you would want a gun that would shoot faster. Isn't faster better?"

"Not necessarily," Vereshchagin said distantly. "The muzzle velocity for our guns is quite satisfactory for targets we are likely to engage. It probably makes some types of ammunition more expensive because they have to design the rounds to withstand greater stresses without disintegrating in midflight. And remember that the increased maintenance and decreased operational radius are detriments. There is really only one application where the increased velocity would be a significant advantage."

"And that is?" Van Zyl leaned forward and ground out his cigar, conscious that he had evoked something significant from his witness.

"Antiarmor applications. The electromagnetic guns make their vehicles much more effective at destroying other armored vehicles, which no one on this planet has, apart from Uwe Ebyl and I."

"Do you mean to say that they designed these just for us?"

"Oh, no. It took years to change the design." He paused. "I am disturbed by the thought that changed political circumstances on Earth prompted the change. Many of the affiliated nations on Earth still have tanks in their inventories."

"Dear God," van Zyl said. "Are things as bad as that?"

Vereshchagin said simply, "Yes."

"Anton, I can see you sitting here wrestling with your conscience. Lawyer–client privilege, now. Tell me what is running through your mind. Let me help."

"You are my brigade advocate. I cannot very well involve you in personal matters," Vereshchagin said half-humorously.

"Anton, I am a crusty, old, and very stubborn Afrikaner. I don't work for the Imperial Government, I work for you, and I can claim to be deaf and senile when it suits me. You and I both know that I am more your court philosopher than I am your lawyer." Van Zyl picked up the cigar stub and began shredding the unburnt tobacco into a pouch. "I would like to think that I am your friend."

"Well, philosopher, let me ask a philosophical question. When is it legally and morally permissible to rebel?" Vereshchagin asked, staring at the ceiling.

"It is never legal to rebel. Unless, of course, you win."

"No, I am serious, Abram. When is it morally permissible to rebel?" He added quietly, "More importantly, when is it morally imperative to rebel?"

"Let me see. The twin principles of necessity and proportionality govern the use of force. I could twist these principles upon their tails to say that it is morally permissable to rebel when the suffering you would avert outweighs the suffering you would cause. How much of an idealist are you, Anton?"

"Very much of one, I am afraid." Vereshchagin took out his pipe and cradled the bowl in his hands. "The municipal police found the body this morning—Matti called it a stiff stiff—of a man named Breytenbach who had been tortured to death. His vehicle was used in the murders of two Manchurian soldiers, and Colonel Sumi apparently believed that he knew more about the incident than he mentioned to the police."

"Dear God! Admiral Horii strikes me as a cultured and intelligent man. How can he allow such things to occur?"

Vereshchagin smiled. "Japanese policy making can accurately be described as systematized irresponsibility. Senior decision-makers are expected to concur in the consensus of their subordinates. Admiral Horii has been ignoring most of the unpalatable advice that he has been receiving, and his subordinates are beginning to take action on their own to force him to do the 'right' thing. At this junction, if he were to issue prudent and unpopular orders, the security police and the Lifeguards would simply ignore them. He cannot subject his authority to being flouted in this manner, so he acquiesces."

"Dear God, what a system."

"It is the one that I have served all of my life, Abram, but it is becoming worse, much worse."

"I can't see as far into the future as you, Anton, but what kind of men carry out these orders, and the ones that you foresee?"

"Fanatics, of course. For fanatics, ends are everything and any means will suffice. Sumi is one. Careerists would do so as well. Some of the men I have known would pursue any policy however immoral if it would benefit them. Cynics who have lost hope would do so reluctantly, but efficiently nonetheless." He stuck the pipe back into his pocket before he continued speaking.

"But I will tell you, Abram, pity the would-be reformers who serve a corrupt regime with open eyes; for when souls are weighed in the balance, theirs will be the most damned souls in hell."

"You have been thinking about this for a long time, haven't you?" van Zyl asked him.

"Too long, perhaps. But I am very much afraid of throwing away my life to no purpose, Abram."

Van Zyl poked his finger at him. "Never try to fool your advocate, Anton. What you are very much afraid of is dragging others down with you."

"Yes," Vereshchagin said. "Yes."

Sunday(312)

AFTER WORSHIP, SANMARTIN WALKED HIS FAMILY BACK FROM church. He carried Hendricka, who carried her doll. "Call Hans?" he asked his wife.

"Call Hans," his wife responded.

Coldewe's face appeared on the telephone's tiny screen. "How was your day off, Raul? Do you realize that this is the first time one of your 'Saturdays in Chubut' actually fell on a Saturday?"

"Hans, what kept you last night?" Bruwer asked.

"We had a little moonlight yachting here."

"Night river crossing. Assault boats," Sanmartin translated.

"Easy as downhill skiing," Coldewe said.

"Hans, what would you know about downhill skiing?" Bruwer asked.

"You are jesting, of course. I was brought up in Tübingen, which is, after all, in the shadow of the Alps." Coldewe coughed. "In a manner of speaking."

Bruwer and Sanmartin looked at each other and waited for something more outrageous to come out.

"I know, for example, that the bottom of the beginner slope is a good place to look for loose change when the snow melts."

"It reminds you of Hendricka talking to her kitten," Bruwer commented. "Hans, where were you last night? We missed you."

"Oh, things got busy around here, and I decided I couldn't break away. I should have called you—"

"You should have," Hanna said firmly.

"My apologies," Coldewe said. He hung his head in false dejection. "How was the show?"

Sanmartin looked at his wife. "Well, the university band—"

"The university *orchestra*," Hanna exclaimed.

"Same thing. The university band's 'Night in Blue' was truly blue, and since she's Madam Speaker, we had to go wearing funny clothes."

"You look good in a suit. What did they play?"

"It was mostly American classical stuff. What was that one song I liked? Not the Gershwin, the other one?" Sanmartin asked his wife.

"It was called 'Blue Rondo à la Turk,' and it was by Dave Brubeck. Honestly, Hans, I cannot take him anywhere. And what were you doing with your pocket computer in there?"

"Ammunition stocks," Sanmartin explained.

"Ammunition stocks. Oh, I couldn't believe it. I thought that the couple next to us would die!" Bruwer told Coldewe.

"I thought I would, too, until you stopped trying to poke a hole in my ribs and started laughing," her husband commented. "Seriously, Hans, first an orchestra, and after that, who knows what? Sooner or later, somebody on this planet is going to try and start a ballet."

"Not that!" Coldewe said with genuine horror.

"Oh, be serious, both of you!" The frown lines reappeared on Bruwer's face. "He does these things on purpose, Hans. He doesn't think I smile enough anymore. I wish—"

"I wish we had more time," Sanmartin said firmly.

"Well, if you couldn't have come, at least you could have sent your friend Marta so that both tickets weren't wasted." Hanna lectured Coldewe to change the subject.

"Oh. I'm not seeing Marta anymore," Coldewe said.

"What!" Bruwer said sharply. "Hans, what happened?"

Coldewe refused to meet her eyes. "Oh, things weren't right

between us, so I told her that we should stop seeing each other. She wasn't very happy about it."

"I should imagine. I would have hit you," Bruwer said, staring right through him.

"Oh, she did that, too."

Sanmartin laid his hand on his wife's arm. "We'll talk with you tomorrow, Hans."

"Sorry I missed the show." Coldewe broke the connection.

"Well, of all of the silly things that I have heard! How could he? The girl loves him—very much unless I am mistaken." The "girl" in question was her own age, but Bruwer tended to overlook such things. "She should have called me. I would have said something to Hans, you can be sure!"

"I don't know that Marta would have felt comfortable calling you. It isn't as if this is an affair of state."

Bruwer laughed gently. "I keep forgetting that we do not have private lives. Poor Marta!" She eyed her husband. "Why do you think that Hans has stopped seeing her—the real reasons, this time?"

Sanmartin sighed. "I was hoping that we could put off business until morning." He walked over to his computer, which had both a voice-lock and a password access system, and printed out two copies of one file. "Here. For you and Albert. Hans has already seen them."

"What are these?" Bruwer asked, skimming the top page.

"The document on top is a transcript of the tape that Hiroshi Mizoguchi sent. Hiroshi was the blind lieutenant we sent to Earth. We asked him to report on conditions there. Underneath Hiroshi's transcript is a copy of Admiral Horii's instructions from the Guardianship Council. We pried it out of his computer—please don't ask how. It's four layers deep in euphemisms, but the general drift is viciously apparent. Finally, you have an extract of Matsudaira's working notes. Apparently, he keeps some sort of computer diary. One of his executives is at least as worried as we are, and he got Timo Haerkoennen into Matsudaira's system. It took Timo about two hours to break into Matsudaira's files. Matsudaira isn't particularly security conscious. He is unusually blunt."

"What does this all mean?" she asked, clutching the packet.

"You and Albert read it, and then we'll talk. I know what I think it means, but I want you to form your own conclusions." He smiled a wintery smile. "Most rulers would shoot a messenger who brings news this bad."

"Oh, my dear Lord," she said, clutching the packet to her-self and rocking back and forth. "Poor, poor Marta."

Monday(312)

THE AFRIKANER RESISTANCE MOVEMENT BEGAN WITH A GROUP OF students from the University of Suid-Afrika's philosophy de-partment. Only a few of the philosophy students lasted long— the philosophy department didn't offer a course in political methods, and they liked to argue with one another and every-one else past the point of prudence—but the younger, more vigorous students from other departments who took their places still formed the movement's core.

Jopie Van Nuys had been a student when Hannes Van der Merwe met him, although Van Nuys flunked out long before his political activities began interfering with his studies. As Van der Merwe was preparing to leave for work, Van Nuys pulled up in a delivery truck he had borrowed from his brother-in-law and flung a set of coveralls at him. "Get dressed, Hannes," he said curtly. "This is the day."

"What? Why didn't you tell me?" Van der Merwe said, star-tled. He added inanely, "I will be late for work."

"The less you know, the less the Imps can squeeze out of you if you are caught. Tell your employer you are sick. Now, get dressed." Van Nuys gave him a push and listened on the extension when Van der Merwe called in.

Van der Merwe changed quickly. Slightly mollified, Van Nuys said, "I didn't mean to push you that hard, Hannes."

Van de Merwe soothed him. "You were just tense, Jopie. I took no notice. The Movement always comes before personal feelings."

As they got into the truck and headed down the road, Van Nuys asked, "Did you bring the contract?"

Van der Merwe patted his pocket. "I have it here. Now what is the plan? I only know parts of it."

"You know how to use missiles, don't you? There are some hidden in carpets in the back where they won't be found. You leave me off about a kilometer from the spaceport and then drive the truck past the guards. Park it in the lot near the sign that says A-32, not too close to the other cars. That is way off to the side, so you should not have any trouble. I will meet you there."

"What about the guards?"

"You have nothing to worry about. I told you that I hid the missiles so that they couldn't be found. Just don't get nervous. We have a contract to install carpeting, and you have a clean record, so they shouldn't bother you. I would do this myself, but they have my fingerprints, and they would spot me the minute they stuck my hand in a scanner." Van Nuys's tone deterred Van der Merwe from discussing the matter further.

For renovation work that USS could not do, Admiral Horii's intendance officer had tried to throw work to companies owned by members of the pro-Imperial New Auspices party. As the ARM's spy inside the New Auspices party, Van der Merwe was ideally positioned to pick up a piece of the work, after blithely promising a cut of the profits to the New Auspices party's coffers.

Van der Merwe took the wheel when Van Nuys stopped and got out. At the main checkpoint, a small group of guardsmen made him pull over.

"Renovation contract." Van der Merwe pulled out the document and showed them. Admiral Horii clearly intended to make the spaceport into a major base, and Van der Merwe could see dozens of civilians working on various projects.

"You are doing this by yourself?" the lance-corporal asked him sharply. "Where are the others?"

"Oh, no. We have another crew coming to help me after lunch," Van der Merwe explained. "I am not supposed to start until they get here. I plan on taking a nap until then."

He obligingly showed them his identity card and his New Auspices party card. The lance-corporal shoved Van der Merwe's fingers and identity card through a scanner to make sure that the fingerprints matched the card, and that the data base had nothing adverse on him. The other guardsmen opened the back door, brushed aside the sheet hung there, and began rooting through the thick rolls of carpeting, peering through the holes in the middle. They failed to notice the tape placed over small holes on the right side of the van, or the narrow spaces that Van Nuys had cut into the inner layers of the carpet rolls to conceal two antiarmor missiles and collapsible launcher rails.

After the lance-corporal called the intendance officer to check the contract number, he grudgingly waved Van der Merwe through. Although Jopie Van Nuys was listed as a known terrorist in the data base that Colonel Sumi had copied from Anton Vereshchagin, Hannes Van der Merwe was not.

Van der Merwe parked the van on the far side of the parking lot opposite Admiral Horii's office and waited.

The crews of workmen renovating the buildings were taking dinner breaks and walking along the footpaths or chatting in small groups. Dressed as another workman, Van Nuys casually mingled with them and joined Van der Merwe in the van.

"Move the van forward about ten meters," Van Nuys whispered.

Van der Merwe did so. They stopped and went into the back.

"Good job, Hannes," Van Nuys said grudgingly.

They untied the carpets, pulled out the missiles, and began assembling the launcher rails. Breaking the silence, Van der Merwe asked, "Aren't you afraid that they will trace this truck back to your brother-in-law?"

"He's a fascist anyway," Van Nuys grunted. "He thinks that I am using it to steal things and expects me to cut him in on the profits. I will cut him in, all right. Aren't you lucky that I convinced the executive to have you join the Kaffirboeties?"

"That may be one of the things that has kept me from moving up in the Movement," Van der Merwe rejoined mildly.

"No, the reason that you have not advanced is because Troll—that man Phillipbon—does not trust you. But after today, there is nothing that the Movement will deny to either one of us. Werewolf, our general secretary, already thinks highly of you."

"I am glad of that, but I do not know Werewolf."

"Certainly you do. He is Gerrit Terblanche. You should remember him from the university."

"Oh, yes, the engineer."

"After today, you will have an opportunity to know him much better." Van Nuys's voice hardened. "As for Phillipbon, he is a right deviationist, and I think that he is a spy. We do things to deviationists and spies."

Van der Merwe looked away. Members of the executive personally "dealt with" important spies and deviationists "to show that they were totally committed to the Movement."

Working steadily, he and Van Nuys put the missiles into place inside the truck. Then Van Nuys ripped away the tape and began sighting the missiles in on Admiral Horii's office. Van Nuys had left two holes to sight through and two more for the missiles to actually emerge through. Although the holes were only a fraction of the diameter of the missiles, as

Terblanche had pointed out, the missiles would go through the side of the truck as if it were made of cardboard. It would take the resistance of the armored glass shielding Admiral Horii to cause them to detonate.

"What will happen if we kill the admiral, Jopie?" Van der Merwe asked. "I missed all of the executive meetings," he said, making a joke out of it.

"With Horii dead, Colonel Sumi becomes commander to the Imperials. He will almost certainly take action against Vereshchagin." Van Nuys spit the name out. "And against the traitors in the government. All traitors against the Volk must suffer for their treason. Never fear, when the moment is ripe, we will hunt each of them down."

Van der Merwe thought of several former friends he had broken with after they joined Vereshchagin's men. "I wonder what Sumi will do."

"Sumi will take action against our Movement that will make our eventual success possible," Van Nuys said, warming to the task of molding his colleague's opinions correctly. "The reason that our Movement does not enjoy success against the people is that they have been seduced away from their proper national-political interests. Once the Imperials oppress them properly in an attempt to destroy us, the people will begin to see their true national-political duty." He swelled with pride. "Our actions here today will make the people realize that the Movement has been acting in their best interests all along."

"Of course."

"There will be important changes after today, Hannes, never fear. Traitors within the Movement will suffer, as will Vereshchagin and Beyers and all of their creatures. You were captured once by Vereshchagin's men, weren't you?"

"Yes. Some of Captain Sanmartin's men beat me and threatened to execute me," Van der Merwe said, blushing. "Then Captain Sanmartin had them inject me with drugs and question me."

"The Bruwer woman and her fascist husband will be two of the first to go," Van Nuys exulted.

Moments later, Van Nuys finished sighting his missile in and said excitedly, "We are set, and I see people moving inside Admiral Horii's office."

Engaging the radio control that would fire the missiles, Van Nuys and Van der Merwe left the truck, locked it, and began walking up the footpath at a moderate pace.

"Are you sure that Admiral Horii is in his office?" Van der Merwe whispered.

"Werewolf has had someone watching the admiral. He is still inside his headquarters, and he is almost certainly inside his office. I will trigger the missiles when we reach the top of that rise. I saw him look out the window." Excitement bubbling up inside him, Van Nuys was almost certain of this. "Hannes, today we strike our strongest blow for Suid-Afrikan liberty, and I will make certain that the Imperials know who acted against them!"

"Colonel Sumi will probably execute hostages. I hope that he does not take any members of your family hostage."

"I expect him to execute my family members. But a true revolutionary should never be moved one centimeter from the correct revolutionary path by such concerns, Hannes. Besides, they are all bourgeois. My true family members are my revolutionary brothers and sisters. You will need to understand such things before you can be on the executive, Hannes. Even expressing such concerns can leave you open to charges of deviationalism."

"Of course." Van der Merwe stumbled. "Keep going. I think that I have a stone in my shoe. I will catch up with you in a second."

He reached under a rock and found a wave pistol that he had placed there the previous night. Running up behind Van Nuys, he silently shot him in the back.

During the rebellion, Raul Sanmartin had squeezed information out of Hannes Van der Merwe like a wet cloth. In return, he had promised to keep some of Van der Merwe's friends alive, and after the rebellion, he apologized to Van der Merwe and explained why.

"In your whole life, Jopie, you never apologized or saved a friend, did you?" Van der Merwe said quietly.

Pulling the radio control out of Van Nuys's pocket, Van der Merwe ran up the hill. Eventually, he reached a pay phone and dialed up Senior Intelligence Sergeant Resit Aksu, Sanmartin's most experienced operative. "Resit," he said apologetically, "I think that I have blown my cover."

On a ridge overlooking the parking lot eight hundred meters away, Lieutenant Thomas, Vereshchagin's reconnaissance platoon leader, set aside his sniper's rifle and breathed a long, long sigh of relief. Since the first word came through from Van der Merwe, Thomas had been waiting on the ridge six hours a day for four days. Incontestably the best shot in Vereshchagin's battalion, Thomas could have shot the buttons off Van Nuys's shirt, although the exploding rounds he was using would have had a different impact.

It was, nevertheless, a great relief to Thomas. Under the circumstances, it would have been very much a "pressure" shot, and more so if Van der Merwe had changed his mind and walked past the hidden pistol.

Moments later, Raul Sanmartin was on the telephone to Admiral Horii's aide, Watanabe. "Captain Watanabe, this is Captain Sanmartin, Major Harjalo's executive officer. Please move everyone out of Admiral Horii's office for a few hours. You might want to clear the adjoining offices as well, just in case ... It would take me a while to explain. Just tell the admiral that my armorer, Rytov, and I are on our way to defuse the situation. See you in a bit."

ADMIRAL HORII LISTENED TO SANMARTIN'S EXPLANATION WITH A great deal of interest. "And these missiles are aimed at us? Colonel Sumi will be furious, neh, Watanabe?"

"You could have been killed!" his aide responded, horror-stricken.

"You would have been with me, Watanabe, so that it would not have been any extra bother for you." Horii returned his attention to Sanmartin. "This incident will not reflect well on Colonel Sumi. He will wish to take immediate action against the ARM."

Sanmartin smiled. "We already have. We caught a man named Terblanche who is a member of their executive. We didn't want a public arrest, so we just sent a team in through his office window. I understand that he was quite surprised."

"Colonel Sumi will wish to question him."

"I would recommend against it. If I promise Terblanche to turn his people over to the civil authorities rather than Colonel Sumi, it is possible that I can use him to pull in the rest of the ARM's executive. Of course, if I made such a promise, I would have to make sure that it was kept," Sanmartin said in a carefully neutral tone of voice, watching Horii's eyes.

"This would seem to be a very difficult matter," Horii said.

"Surely it is impossible. These men have murdered Imperial soldiers," Watanabe said, outraged.

Sanmartin gave him an amused look.

"How do you propose to persuade Terblanche to cooperate, Captain Sanmartin?" Horii asked.

"We have three or four more hours before people realize that we have him. Terblanche thinks that I caught Jopie Van Nuys and persuaded him to turn his coat, so that it's only a matter of time before we mop up the ARM. He knows what will happen if I turn him over to Colonel Sumi. I think he's willing to cut a deal."

There are three elements to "turning" someone: a carrot, a stick, and a strong reason to believe that there is nothing fundamentally dishonorable about cooperating. Sanmartin had plenty of carrots and sticks in his bag, including one "revolutionary sister" who was a girlfriend from Terblanche's pre-revolutionary days and for whom Terblanche clearly felt more than fraternal feelings. But without a persuasive argument that cooperation would salvage something—the lives of Terblanche's revolutionary "brothers" from what would otherwise be a complete debacle—Sanmartin had no way of persuading Terblanche to cooperate short of breaking him into small pieces, and no interest in trying. For one thing, he had made promises to several ARM members that he and Aksu had recruited, including Hannes Van der Merwe. For another, Terblanche's girlfriend was a first cousin of Maria Viljoens.

Horii considered. "I imagine that Colonel Sumi could persuade Heer Terblanche to cooperate without the need for the condition that Captain Watanabe finds so distasteful, don't you think?"

"In this case, Colonel Sumi's methods may be counterproductive," Sanmartin said coolly. "Also, my wife has scruples, and I may have acquired some."

"Indeed." Horii studied Sanmartin for a few moments. "You may try your methods. Colonel Sumi will be very irate, I imagine. If you fail, we can allow him to try his."

Sanmartin smiled faintly. "I intend to have Terblanche call an emergency meeting of the ARM executive. It would be nice if they thought they'd succeeded in assassinating you." Sanmartin pulled the radio control out of his pocket and offered it to Admiral Horii.

"Indeed." With a glance at Watanabe, Horii pressed the button. A second or two later, a loud explosion rocked the building. Shouting and the sound of rapid footsteps filled the corridor outside.

Sanmartin stood up and bowed slightly. "With your permission, honored Admiral, I'd better get out of here before your people get too excited. I might mention a call I got from the police yesterday. Someone left a bundle of bank notes on the doorstep of a well-known ARM sympathizer, along with a typewritten note that read, 'for the cause.' He suspected a trap—probably incorrectly—and turned it in. I wonder who left it there. And why."

"I agree. It is a quite unsophisticated method of delivery," Horii murmured.

As the door closed behind Sanmartin, Watanabe asked, "Honored Admiral, you will permit Captain Sanmartin to turn these assassins over to the civil authorities?"

"Captain Sanmartin is correct to strike quickly. When you have closed with the enemy, you must hit him as quickly and directly as possible, in one timing. I will keep my bargain, Watanabe. Until conditions change," Horii said dreamily. "Colonel Sumi will be very irate."

LATE THAT NIGHT, BEYERS WAS AWAKENED FROM A FITFUL SLEEP BY a knock on his door. He pulled the coverlet over his wife and padded into the hall in his night robe. Tom Winters was already there and motioned, indicating that all was in order.

Major Piotr Kolomeitsev was waiting on the pavement outside. "My regret for disturbing you, Heer President, but it is a matter of some urgency. I have two transport loads of student terrorists, forty-seven of them, from the ARM's 'Liberation Combat Detachment,' which has been in the forests—I hesitate to use the term 'operating'—these last few months. Raul has made a deal with Admiral Horii to turn them over to your judicial authorities, and it would be prudent to hand them over before Colonel Sumi learns we have them. My landrost in Bloemfontein is not in his bed, and for once I do not know whose bed he is in."

"I will make the call," Winters said, and went to the phone.

"Yes. Raul turned over nine members of the ARM's executive a few hours ago," Beyers said slowly. "Would you care to come in, Major? I am sure I can find you a cup of tea."

Kolomeitsev shook his head regretfully. "No, I must decline, Heer President. I know my people will not sleep until I do, so the sooner I get back the better."

"Is this all of the ones in the forest?"

"No, we have another nine in bags," Kolomeitsev replied, "for a total of fifty-six."

"The poor boys." Beyers sighed, as Hanna Bruwer joined him by the door. "Which of them are the leaders?"

The Iceman smiled, slightly. "These are followers. The sheep, if you will. When the occupants of the Liberation Combat Detachment's command tent began exhorting their followers to resist us, we obliterated it, which had a salutary effect on these others."

"I hope that we can integrate them into our society after they get out of prison," Beyers said, running his hands through his thinning hair.

"These? They run to a type," Kolomeitsev said indifferently. "In six months I can make whatever you want of them. Sober citizens, pacifists, fascists, communists, ministers of God if you like. Ask Anton."

"Soldiers?" Bruwer asked.

The Iceman shrugged. "Soldiers, too. Not especially good ones, I am afraid, but yes, even soldiers." He added with glacial unconcern, "This finishes the ARM. They have sympathizers left in the cities, but in every civil war there comes a time to overlook some things."

"I will tell the landrost to give you a receipt to show Colonel Sumi," Beyers said.

"One question." Bruwer laid her hand on Beyers's arm. "Piotr, the information that led you to this 'Liberation Combat Detachment' did not come from Terblanche or the other captured ARM leaders, did it."

Kolomeitsev smiled and bowed very slightly. "No. We knew where they were. It is, after all, my forest. But as Anton said, they were feeding themselves and doing no real harm, and they were at least as miserable as they would have been in jail. With the ones in town rounded up, Anton thought it would be best to make a clean sweep. We have played the ARM card about as far as it can be played."

"Thank you, Major," Beyers said, glancing at Bruwer. "Please thank your men for me."

"I will do so. Heer President, Madam Speaker, I bid you good night." Kolomeitsev saluted and left.

Wednesday(312)

"HONORED COLONEL, I REVIEWED THE JOHANNESBURG CONFINEment facility as you directed," Yanagita said, standing stiffly at attention. "It would appear that the facility is adequate to hold the captured ARM terrorists securely."

Sumi looked up. "Sit."

Yanagita did so, nervously. Beholden to two masters, the peripatetic intelligence officer had thus far managed to serve both without offending either.

In the comfort of his quarters, Sumi was wearing traditional garb. His uniform hung where his orderly had left it out for him. He drank deeply from a flask of sake beside his elbow and resumed buffing an immaculate sword. "Do you own a sword, Yanagita?" he asked, gently stroking the bare metal.

"Only my Academy blade, honored Colonel."

"You should get yourself a really good one. See? Feel this." Sumi held his sword out for Yanagita to see.

"It is very impressive," Yanagita said, touching the weapon gingerly. "You hardly ever see such exquisite craftsmanship."

"It was made by Sukesada," Sumi said with obvious pride. "The metal has been folded over and beaten ten thousand times."

Yanagita lowered his head deferentially. "It is a beautiful weapon, honored Colonel."

Sumi drained the sake flask and flung it across the room. "The cheap trash that people make these days would bend the first time you tried to cut though someone's neck, but the man who crafted this understood swords."

He stood and took a small practice cut. "After you use a sword like this one, whenever you look at someone, you make a judgment as to whether he has an easy neck to cut or a difficult one. The best necks aren't too skinny, or too fat either. With a good neck, you cut—like so—and the head falls easily, like a flower."

Yanagita realized with a touch of panic that the security police colonel spoke from the heart and from personal experience.

"Our military forces have become degenerate in this age, Yanagita. Officers lack true Yamato spirit. Admiral Horii," Sumi said, with absolute contempt, "does not even own a sword."

He resumed polishing the weapon. "Has Matsudaira-san spoken to you about the land tax?"

"Yes, honored Colonel. At some length."

"It is shameful that this situation is allowed to continue," Sumi declared vehemently.

Admiral Horii having shown little interest in resolving the situation, Daisuke Matsudaira was beside himself.

"It is shameful," Sumi said, half to himself and half to Yanagita. "Please ensure that other young officers know this, Yanagita."

THE NEXT EIGHT DAYS PASSED RELATIVELY QUIETLY. AS HANS Coldewe pointed out with what could have passed for wit, the Assembly wasn't in session, so everyone's purses were safe.

WATER _____

Friday(313)

WALKING INTO HIS MORNING STAFF MEETING, ADMIRAL HORII NO-ticed that Lieutenant-Colonel Vereshchagin was not present. Quickly scanning the faces of his officers, he murmured to Watanabe, "Today?"

Captain Watanabe hung his head and whispered, "Yes, honored Admiral."

"Akiramemasa," Horii responded, indicating that he was resigned to the situation and accepted it.

After concluding with routine business, Colonel Sumi stood. "Honored Admiral, your staff has a recommendation on appropriate resolution of the political situation here." He walked over and placed a *ringi* in front of Horii.

Glancing at the seals on the document, Horii saw that each of his staff and senior officers had concurred in its contents.

"In that this is a political matter, I would urge you to give it careful consideration," Sumi said with politely veiled scorn.

Although Sumi's *ringi* was vaguely phrased, Horii could see that he proposed to dismiss the civil government and to take "precautionary" measures to resolve the problem posed by "foreign" officers.

"I hope that all aspects of this matter have been carefully considered," he said deliberately.

"Shall we cover our ears while stealing the bell?" Sumi demanded, referencing an incident in China's "Spring-Autumn" period. "Failure to dismiss the civil government fools no one and merely makes it appear that we lack resolve to take forceful actions."

Against the united opinion of his officers, Horii took refuge in *mokusatsu*—lofty silence. He did not agree with the advice he had been tendered, but he could avoid unpleasantness, at least for the moment.

Colonel Enomoto, the commander of the Lifeguards Battalion, noted his displeasure. "I think that it is our earnest wish to give you the best possible advice, honored Admiral. After you have had an opportunity to review the matter, we should then discuss the actual implementation."

"I agree," Horii said.

Afterward, in the privacy of the temporary quarters he had assigned himself while his former office was under repair, Horii spoke sadly to his aide, Watanabe.

"Ah, Watanabe. These things that Matsudaira wants, what do they truly matter so far away from the homeland?"

To ease his admiral's qualms, Watanabe said, "Honored Admiral, the people here are *tanin*, so perhaps it should not be viewed as a matter of great consequence," indicating that Suid-Afrika's inhabitants were not tied into the intricate web of social, business, and family contacts that bind Japanese together.

Horii reproved him. "All men are one under the eyes of heaven, Watanabe." He sighed deeply.

"I do not understand, honored Admiral. What possible danger could there be? Resistance here has been crushed twice over!" Watanabe said, genuinely perplexed.

Horii held back a smile. Instead he asked, "Have you ever heard of a general named von Moltke, Watanabe?"

"No, honored Admiral."

"You should read about him. He was a very insightful man."

"Please tell me what in particular I should read, honored Admiral."

"I suppose that I should, Watanabe," Horii said, the old proverb that a man away from home need feel no shame flitting through his mind.

"He said that officers who are brilliant and lazy make good commanders, that officers who are brilliant and energetic make good staff officers, and that officers who are stupid and lazy may be retained because they will not rise to positions of great responsibility and can be trusted to perform dull duties. However, he urged generals to immediately rid themselves of officers who are stupid and energetic, saying that there can be no greater danger.

"Colonel Sumi," he said, betraying his thoughts, "is a very energetic officer. He believes that if a bird will not sing, we should kill it."

"Perhaps we can make the bird want to sing, honored Admiral."

"Or perhaps it would no longer be necessary for the bird to sing if we waited long enough. But no man can escape the workings of fate, Watanabe. No man."

Saturday(313)

WHEN BRUWER AWOKE, SHE TURNED OVER AND FOUND SHE HAD A husband again. Tapping him on the shoulder, she said, "Raul, when did you come in? I didn't hear you."

"Around midnight." He sneezed twice and wiped his nose. "I told Matti I deserved at least one night a week at home in a real bed."

"Hendricka is probably awake by now, and if she hears your voice, she will be in here like a little rocket. What happened yesterday?"

"Our battalion's in trouble again. One of the Manchurians who tortured an ARM sympathizer named Breytenbach to death made the mistake of bragging about it in front of a couple of Sversky's boys. They smiled, bought him a couple of drinks, and then took him outside."

"Oh, no," Bruwer exclaimed.

"Colonel Sumi has threatened to execute them as an example if he can find them. I think that the admiral is amused. I'm just glad they only broke two arms and a few ribs."

"Things are getting worse in the towns. Yesterday, a woman in Pretoria was assaulted by a gang of Japanese soldiers. When two policemen tried to stop them, they were attacked and beaten by a squad of blacklegs led by an officer. Both are still in the hospital, and one of them may lose an eye. The woman—a girl, really—is shattered, as one might expect. Admiral Horii has promised to 'do the best he could to look into the matter.' " She looked down at her hands. "I read those papers you gave me. Many times."

Hanna Bruwer had almost as much military intelligence training as her husband.

"So where does this leave us?" he asked her gently.

"Albert and I fought over it for hours last night. Finally, I told him to speak to Anton, and that I would agree with any decision they could reach. I cannot believe that he is thinking about another rebellion."

"Hush! I'm beginning to worry about ears in the walls."

"It is too late for that." She rolled on top of him to look in his eyes. "Raul, if we do this—how many people die?"

"Lots. Starting with us."

"Oh, God."

"And if we don't—lots. Maybe lots more. Also starting with us. Anton has been dreading this for years."

She turned her head and began to weep.

"It's all right. It will be all right," he said awkwardly, holding her.

"No, it isn't! And who else can I cry in front of? Politicians never cry, remember?" She shook him. "You have spoken with Hans about this—I know you have."

Sanmartin scowled and kicked the sheet off his legs. "Hans was drunk as an owl, so it came out as poetry. I made him repeat it so I wouldn't forget. 'Ax-age, sword-age, storm-age, wolf-age. The pursuing wolves will swallow sun and moon, earth's bonds will crack and the mountains fall. The dwarfs will whimper and Yggdrasil tremble. The rainbow bridge will crack beneath the weight of giants, and none will flee that last battle. How fare the Aesir? How fare the elves? The sun will grow dark, the stars fall from the sky, the sea will invade the land, and fire will consume it.' I think I got most of it."

"Today would have been my grandfather's sixty-eighth birthday. I try not to think about his death, to put it out of my mind. There is never time. But today, I cannot help it."

"It isn't healthy, to wall away your grief like that."

"You transported the only decent psychiatrist we had five years ago. The ones we have left are idiots or worse. And how would it seem if Madam Speaker were seeing a mind doctor?" She laughed bitterly. "But you must know you have done no better. Sometimes we will be sitting, and you read something or hear a song and I watch the tears drip down your cheeks. It reminds you, of what?"

"My father. Or my mother. Or Steel Rudi Scheel, or Rhett Rettaglia or Edmund Muslar or a dozen others. All of them dead and gone, violently."

She got up and went to the bookshelf where she took down a Bible. Opening it, she read, " 'If a man strikes you on the left cheek, turn and offer him your right.' " She closed the book. "Every time our proud and stubborn people have gone to war, we have suffered for it."

Hearing Hendricka stirring, she left the room, leaving him deep in thought.

Sunday(314)

"WELL, MY FRIEND, I HAVE LOOKED THROUGH THE PAPERS THAT you sent to me and prayed over their meaning. We must come to the meat of it," Beyers said awkwardly.

"And?" Vereshchagin asked gently.

"Anton, I have my sources just as you do. At night, in their cups, the USS people Matsudaira brought here pay no attention to the people serving them. They speak of lists."

"Lists of proscriptions?"

"Yes. Long lists of fines, executions, deportations."

"They intend to tear the heart out of my people."

Vereshchagin said simply, "Yes."

"It is an immoral policy."

"Worse than this, it is a stupid policy."

"Heer Matsudaira wishes to own us. We would become little better than slaves, those of us Sumi does not intend to 're-move' as harmful influences." Beyers rested his hands against his sides.

Vereshchagin stared up at the soot-stained ceiling. "Yes. I expect them to dissolve your government in a few days. My battalion will undoubtedly be broken up. I will likely face criminal charges."

Beyers made no reply, and after a few moments, Vereshchagin lowered his head and resumed speaking. "Finland stopped being our homeland years ago. You have heard me speak of a planet called Esdraelon. A cold and barren world, but a home for us, nonetheless. Esdraelon rebelled four years ago. They paid the price for failure. Now, my battalion has no home."

"It seems that the peace I purchased from you is worth nothing now." Beyers laid his hand on Vereshchagin's arm. "And the rebels were right in saying that I only laid the seeds for a worse oppression. Why, Anton? Why do they do this?"

"With time dilation, nearly a half century has passed on Earth since I began serving. I suppose that trends are easier for me to see. For two hundred years, the same party has ruled Japan, and certain policies have remained long after they have outlived their usefulness. Those Japanese favored by the Imperial system have become convinced that they are entitled to more each year, and no Japanese politician will deny them this. As a result, the fabric of the Imperial system is fraying, and the economic ties which held it together are being replaced by bonds of force and coercion."

"Don't the men ruling Japan see this?"

"Some do. Many do not. Despite Japan's everpresent xenophobia, the change has been slow. The best I can say is that governments, like men, become convinced of their own self-righteousness. It corrupts them over time. The Athenians turned their allies into tributaries, and the Romans did likewise. The Japanese, many of them, have begun to see their preeminent position as belonging to them by right. Did Raul tell you that when he served with the Eleventh Shock Battalion on Earth, their watchword was 'Roman discipline and Samurai virtue'?"

"Yes," Beyers said, "that was why he learned all that silly Latin."

"It disturbs me when a nation begins to measure itself in terms of its virtue. A revolutionary named Maximilien Robespierre once said that in governing a people, terror and virtue were intertwined; and that without virtue, terror is harmful, and without terror, virtue is impotent."

"I am sure that he killed a lot of people, from the loftiest of motives," Beyers said bitterly.

"He did, indeed."

Beyers laid his hands across the table and looked at his friend. "Anton, I will tell you openly, my people will fight. They will not see all we have labored for here stripped from them or sit quietly while their friends and relations are arrested and murdered. They will fear that it will never end, and rightly so. Advise me."

"I am an Imperial officer, Albert. It is not for me to decide or advise."

"You are also an honest man."

Vereshchagin forced himself to smile. "You are very melodramatic, Albert. There are four battalions and warships in our sky. Are you suggesting that we should commit treason together in a particularly futile and useless manner?"

Beyers spread his hands, unhappily. "Tell me, Imperial officer, what choice do my people have? We will fight, Anton. Although I will sound like something out of a book when I tell you this, if you say to me there is a single chance, we will rise up so that at the least the generations to come will have hope of being free. But you are wrong when you say that it is not for you to decide or advise. You, as much as anyone, have made us who we are. You cannot easily wipe your hands of us. I know, too, that you have made preparations."

"Yes, we have made preparations, hoping this day would never come. I hope they will be sufficient, Albert. I hope they will be sufficient." Vereshchagin added lightly, as if to mask his feelings, "On Earth, there is a cycle of violence spinning toward destruction. Who are we to stand aside?"

He pulled a piece of paper from his breast pocket and slid it across the table. "Here is a list of persons. Speak with each of them. I need to know whether they will support a rebellion if we lead it, and whether they are willing to pay the price of failure. If each of them says yes, I will ask my people to follow me. I am not a pious man, but I think that we would lose our souls if we turned our backs on this world."

"Astonishing." Beyers picked up the list and squinted at it. He tapped it with his finger. "And if one of these betrays us?"

"Then Colonel Sumi will execute both of us, and the problem will belong to someone else. You realize, of course, that if we attempt this and fail, the price the Afrikaner nation will pay will be terrible beyond anything you can imagine."

"Yes, I am sure you are right in that." Beyers folded the paper and tucked it away. "Assuming that we can get these persons to agree, how do we make everyone else understand?"

"Colonel Sumi is already doing that for us." Vereshchagin smiled. "And I hope to get Director Matsudaira to help."

Monday(314)

SEATED IN HIS OFFICE, HORII STUDIED HANNA BRUWER'S FACE. HE dispensed with the usual polite banalities. "Why have you come to see me, Madam Speaker?"

"There have been any number of incidents deliberately fomented by your security policemen," Bruwer said boldly. "Matsudaira's creatures openly boast that they will dissolve our government and place chains on our people. My grandfather died to stop the last rebellion. I came to you to see if there is any hope of averting the next one."

The look on Captain Watanabe's face was one of absolute horror.

Composed, Horii merely said, "I can only promise that I will do my best to look into the issues you raise."

"I hoped that I would hear a different answer if I asked you directly." Bruwer rose and began to leave, but stopped at the threshold to ask one final question. "Why do your people hate us so?"

"It is not a matter of hating," Horii explained patiently, still seated. "A Zen master of sword fighting does not hate or harbor the wish to kill or destroy his opponent. He makes the proper movements, and if the opponent is killed, it is because he stood in the wrong place. A western psychoanalyst might say that unconsciously, the sword fighter is motivated by hate and the wish to destroy his opponent, but such a person would show little grasp of the spirit of Zen." He paused. "Regrettably, if your people suffer, it is because they stood in the wrong place."

After she departed, Horii turned to Watanabe. "An interesting exchange of views. Well, what must be done, must be done as correctly as possible, neh? So please ask Captain Yanagita whether he has spoken with Lieutenant-Colonel Vereshchagin's political officer, Captain Yoshida, to remind him of his sacred heritage and his duty."

Watanabe bowed. "I will do so, honored Admiral."

Tuesday(314)

WORKING FROM THE TERMINAL ON HIS DESK, HARJALO FELT THE hum from the induction plate on his radio and heard a familiar voice. "Vereshchagin here."

"What's up, Anton? I thought you would be in a staff meeting. Where are you calling from?"

"I am out walking and using Thomas for a relay. I have been excused from attending Admiral Horii's staff meetings, possibly for good."

"Trouble," Harjalo commented.

"Trouble," Vereshchagin agreed. "It is time, Matti. Please quietly begin dispersing noncombatants."

In five years, Vereshchagin's men had put down surprisingly strong roots into Suid-Afrikan soil. Even the non-Afrikaners among them had formed attachments, and soldiers' family members were an obvious weakness for Colonel Sumi to strike at. The wives, already partially integrated into the battalion's structure, would go to caverns carved out of the Drakensberg and Stormberg mountains. Other family members—parents, sisters, brothers, and persons with less formal attachments—

would be quietly told to move out of the cities where they were most vulnerable.

Harjalo nodded. "What do we tell them?"

"Tell them that it is merely a precautionary measure."

"They won't believe that for a moment. They're going to know."

"Then they will also understand why the less we say about this the better," Vereshchagin replied.

"All right." Harjalo slapped his hand on his desk softly. "So what happens next?"

"We wait for Admiral Horii to show his hand. And we wait for Albert's people to decide what they will do," Vereshchagin said simply. "I am meeting with them tonight. I would like you to be present as well."

"Let me know when and where. What happened last night? I heard indirectly that there were some political shenanigans going on."

"Some fun. I gather that Admiral Horii suggested to Sumi and Matsudaira that they should make a modest effort to discredit Suid-Afrika's political system before he dismissed the government, so Sumi suggested to Christos Claassen that he introduce a bill to make Afrikaans the planet's sole official language. Sumi did not go so far as to overtly offer financial support, but Christos says that the smell of money permeated the room."

"Divide and conquer. That would certainly infuriate the cowboys. How did Christos react?"

"Christos thanked Sumi very expressively, then took his people into a back room and told them that this was intended to help Matsudaira and that he would personally crucify any Reformed National party politician who so much as raised the issue."

"How nice. Is there more?"

"Sumi was a little piggish. He also had Captain Yanagita tell two cowboy clan leaders that the admiral might be willing to recognize the cowboy country as an independent state. They tipped off Uwe Ebyl."

"A cozy little puppet state. So what comes next?"

"My guess is that Sumi and Matsudaira will attempt a little discreet bribery. Hopefully our more venal politicians will at least demand cash in advance."

"Never a dull moment," Harjalo commented. "Is there anything else?"

"No. Vereshchagin out."

* * *

CAPTAIN CHIHARU YOSHIDA ENTERED A SMALL CAFÉ IN BLOEMFON-
tein. Spotting Captain Yanagita in a small booth in the corner,
he walked over and saluted. "Captain Yoshida, reporting as
directed."

"Yoshida, how good of you to come promptly. Please sit."

As Yoshida sat down, Yanagita pushed aside the tea he was
drinking. "My visit to you is informal." He waved his hand.
"Waiter, several bottles of your best beer."

The waiter, busy with other customers, ignored him.

Yoshida said politely, "My sincere apologies for misunderstanding your invitation. I deeply regret that I was forced to set
aside several very pressing matters to come and have strict orders to return as soon as practicable."

"But some orders are more important than other orders,
neh?" Yanagita said, slouching in his seat and smiling.

"Major Kolomeitsev is a very strict person in some matters,
and it would avert a great deal of unpleasantness if I returned
promptly," Yoshida said, advancing the excuse to cut short
Yanagita's pleasantries.

"I understand your concern." Yanagita sat upright and came
to the point. "Admiral Horii and Colonel Sumi believe that as
Vereshchagin's political officer you have an unparalleled
knowledge of the local political situation. The admiral regrets
the previous necessity of leaving you in your present position,
but he now believes the time to be propitious to give you a
place on his staff."

Yoshida inclined his head. "I am not worthy of such trust."

"The admiral disagrees. Indeed, he believes that all possibilities are open to you as long as you remember your heritage
and display the correct attitude."

"I do not feel that I am worthy of such honors," Yoshida responded deferentially.

"I am sure that it would please your family. They live
where, in Osaka?"

"Kyoto. I regret that my family probably considers me already dead."

"Nevertheless, with the correct degree of *nihonrashisa*, both
Admiral Horii and Colonel Sumi feel that you will be able to
make a significant contribution and believe this transfer to be
in the national interest," Yanagita said, clearly unwilling to accept no for an answer.

Nihonrashisa meant "Japanliness."

Yoshida again inclined his head. "I greatly appreciate their confidence in me. I would, however, request several days leave to put my affairs in order."

"I will relay your request to the admiral. There are, however, a few matters which will not wait, and I have been asked to obtain answers from you."

"I will, of course, attempt to reply to the best of my ability, but please understand my deepest regret that I am not always aware of all situations."

"With your experience here, I am certain that you will be able to provide us with assistance. For example, which legislators would be open to receiving financial assistance?" Yanagita pulled out a small electronic notepad.

"I would not know this."

"But surely you know whether any of them have an ostentatious life-style," Yanagita asked, probing.

"Heer Hanneman, then, perhaps," Yoshida said, unwilling to say more.

Yanagita recorded his answer. "And if an act of negative daring became necessary, who would be the best person?" he asked. "Negative daring" was an old euphemism for political assassination.

"I do not know, really. I quite regret my inability to make any reply. Perhaps one of the cowboy leaders, to reopen old wounds," Yoshida said, flustered and deeply disturbed.

Oblivious to this, Yanagita wrote down Yoshida's answer. "The rest of these questions can wait," he said, relaxing now that the difficult part of his mission was behind him. "It must have been very strange for you to work under foreign officers."

"One becomes used to most things," Yoshida said politely.

THAT NIGHT, MORE THAN A HUNDRED OF SUID-AFRIKA'S LEADERS filled a little church while a few of Lieutenant Thomas's recon boys kept a discreet watch outside. To cover bringing everyone into Johannesburg, Hanna Bruwer had called a special session of the legislature, ostensibly to discuss an emergency supplemental appropriations bill.

"Evening services," Harjalo grunted as he and Vereshchagin sat on the front step waiting for Albert Beyers and the rest of the civilians inside to finish.

"Heaven knows we will need prayers, Matti. Possibly divine intervention as well." Vereshchagin scooped up a handful of soil and rolled it between the palms of his hands.

"How long have they been at it? Three or four hours now. Most of them saw the stuff we filched days ago."

"Patience, Matti. Their lives and the lives of their families are at stake. If we are to have any chance of success, we need to have each of these people behind us wholeheartedly."

A few moments later, Albert Beyers came out to fetch them. Apparently it was warm work inside—Beyers had stripped off his coat and rolled his sleeves. His white shirt shined incongruously in the starlight. "They are ready to see you, Anton."

Vereshchagin and Harjalo followed him inside, and Vereshchagin mounted the pulpit to take questions.

Christos Claassen stood up first. "We have been speaking of revolt and revolution for the last hour, Anton. Albert and I and a few of the would-be generals here have discussed the matter, but many here have very bitter memories of the last rebellion. For the benefit of us all, if we rebel, can we win?"

"Christos, you and I and many others here know that in war, the simplest things defy prediction," Vereshchagin began carefully.

Wynard Grobelaar interrupted. "Why should this be so?" he demanded.

"Thank you. I will try to answer this before I finish my response to Heer Claassen. In war, the stresses that each man and each military unit is subject to—a philosopher named Clausewitz defined it as 'friction'—are almost incomprehensibly great. Think of a military campaign as if it were a bridge. To use my metaphor, if we rebel, our bridge will be made from straw woven together with thread. Admiral Horii will also have difficulties, so I believe that we can succeed, but I assure you that it will not be easy."

"How much of a chance do we have?" Andries Steen asked soberly.

Vereshchagin smiled cheerfully. "I would not attempt to quantify our chances. I would find it depressing."

Burgemeester Prinsloo Adriaan Smith uncrossed his legs. "Anton, some of us have never been military men. How many soldiers and tanks and things do they have, and how many do we have to place against them?"

"Matti?" Vereshchagin asked.

"So, let's count noses when the shooting starts." Harjalo looked down at the rows of faces. "We have three infantry companies, a light attack company, an aviation company of sorts, an engineer platoon, and a reconnaissance platoon. If we call out the commandos that we have integrated into our force structure, we have an additional platoon to add to each company plus an additional reserve infantry company that Christiaan De Wette runs. Christiaan, you want to show yourself?"

De Wette, a tall, bearded man, stood up and nodded to introduce himself.

"We can also count on about three hundred partially trained reservists to take over local surveillance and security duties. That gives us about a thousand trained infantrymen, sixteen Cadillac armored cars, four 160mm mechanized mortars, eight attack helicopters, and four Shiden ground-attack aircraft." He shrugged. "We have a few more armored cars and Shiden aircraft tucked away to replace losses."

"What about Colonel Ebyl's battalion?" Nadine Joh asked.

"We are talking of committing mutiny and high treason here, Nadine, and as much as Uwe's people sympathize, I don't think they want any part of it. I expect them to try to sit this one out."

At a nod from Vereshchagin, Harjalo continued, "On the other side, Admiral Horii has five battalions plus." He raised three fingers. "First, there's the Manchurian regiment, which has twelve infantry companies, a light attack company, an artillery company, an aviation company, an engineer company, and a reconnaissance company. Their companies are organized under the new system, so they're smaller than ours, but the Manchurians were shipped out here at 102 percent of authorized strength, so they can field the equivalent of 1,500 infantrymen, twelve armored cars, twelve 210mm howitzers—those are very large artillery pieces for the uninitiated—and twelve attack helicopters."

He raised a fourth finger. "Next, there's the Japanese Ninth Imperial Light Attack Battalion. Because it's Japanese, it's overstrength, with four companies of four platoons each, plus a mechanized mortar company, an aviation company, and a reconnaissance platoon. In all, the battalion has fifty Cadillacs of an unusually nasty design, sixteen 160mm mechanized mortars—those are very large and very mobile artillery pieces—and twelve attack helicopters."

Harjalo lifted his thumb and held his entire hand outstretched. "Next, Horii has the Sixth Imperial Lifeguards Battalion, which is also overstrength with four 150-man infantry companies, a light attack company, an aviation platoon, an engineer platoon, and a reconnaissance platoon. They can field about 750 infantrymen, twelve Cadillacs, and four helicopters.

Horii also has two companies of area defense troops, an aviation company with twelve Shiden aircraft, an artillery company with twelve more howitzers, two companies of blackleg security police, and four warships over our heads."

"Let no one misunderstand," Vereshchagin interjected, "these warships can see most of our movements, and once they locate our forces, they can pour down a devastating volume of fire."

"This tends to have somewhat of a chilling effect on operations," Harjalo added.

"How will we shoot down four spaceships?" Beyers exclaimed.

"We're still working on that part," Harjalo admitted. "We didn't say that this would be *easy*."

"So, Anton, what happens if our bridge should break?" Christos Claassen asked, already aware of the answer. Claassen had served as chief of logistics for the rebel forces during the uprising, and Vereshchagin's men had come very near to killing him.

Vereshchagin smiled, this time sadly. "Then like all men, we shall die untimely."

Claassen asked a final question for the benefit of everyone. "And assuming that God favors us and we win, what will the cost be?"

Vereshchagin measured his words carefully. "Trust me when I tell you that the price of victory is blood and hard fighting. The soldiers, professionals and reservists, will pay a part of this price, but please understand that the civilian population will be in the front lines of this war, and that they will pay the remainder in death and hardship. I will tell you bluntly that you must accept this formula or not wage war. And, as I have hinted, if we are defeated, the cost will be far, far higher."

Nadine Joh said very loudly, "Anton is right when he says civilians are going to pay part of the bill, but remember that we're going to pay anyway." The cowboy matriarch smiled sweetly. "Don't think USS has forgotten."

"But if we should agree to fight, what will our strategy be?" one man asked.

Vereshchagin stared at him coldly. "Please do not expect me to allow you to vote on that. If you ask me to fight for you, you will have to abide by my decisions. In the one hundred sixty-eighth year before Christ, Lucius Aemillius Paulus, a Roman general and consul, said it best: 'Commanders should be counseled chiefly by persons of known talent, by those who have made the art of war their particular study and whose knowledge is derived from experience, by those who are present at the scene of action who see the enemy. If therefore anyone thinks himself qualified to give advice respecting the war which I conduct, let him come with me into Macedonia.' "

"To clarify the issue for some of our brethren, you expect this body to give you unquestioned control over the conduct of military operations," Beyers said.

"Either give me that, or find someone else to take my place. There is no middle course," Vereshchagin said indifferently. "We do not have any margin for error or divided counsels. I will accept responsibility for failure, which is a polite way of saying that if I miscalculate, you may spit on whatever grave they allow me."

Hours later, Vereshchagin allowed his shoulders to slump as he and Harjalo waited outside for Beyers and the conclave to finish their deliberations. "Matti, I feel like the Pied Piper."

"Anton, I have no head for politics," Harjalo began. It was such an obvious lie that Vereshchagin smiled. "But I think they're going to give you everything you asked for."

"Albert and I may have persuaded the ones in there," Vereshchagin agreed, "but what of the rest of the people? The ones I have not spoken to? The ones who will do the suffering?"

Harjalo shifted his weight. "Anton, I have been talking to the little people on the streets for months, and I will tell you this. They trust Albert and Hanna, and if they say fight, the people will do it. But you? You're the magic man. You're Erwin Rommel and Robert E. Lee. The Afrikaners know that we shouldn't have whipped them with one lousy battalion. They aren't about to admit that their boys were terrible soldiers, and they know that Hendrik Pienaar was good, so you have to be that much better. Every last one of them says the same thing, 'The rebellion was wrong, and it is best for everyone that it ended when it did—but if we would have had a Vereshchagin, we would have shown you something!' "

Vereshchagin stared at him. "I am not sure whether I should laugh or cry."

"You don't really think that the nonsense that you and Albert have cooked up together fools anyone, do you? Except for the bankers and the politicians, everybody out there knows that whatever you and Albert agree on is what's going to happen.

Frosty hell, half of them probably suspect that honorably retired Senior Censor Ssu and his dandy little interactive political propaganda program write the speeches that you and Albert and Christos have so much fun delivering, which is the second most closely guarded secret on this planet. And the little people think that's fine, most of them, seeing as how we've gotten rid of most of the people who are disposed to be obnoxious. They have jobs, they're making money, and they see a little of the vision that Raul and Hanna have of the future."

"But Matti, you know the risk we run of losing. There are four warships in our sky, more than five battalions on the ground, and all of Earth behind them. I am leading these people to their deaths."

"Oh, dying isn't so bad, once you get used to it. It's not having something worth dying for that makes it hurt," Harjalo said pointedly. "Is what we've done here worth dying for?"

"Yes, Matti. It is." Vereshchagin sighed and watched the stars overhead.

After a few minutes passed, Harjalo commented, "It seems strange to be preparing for a war in a church."

"Not for Afrikaners. And perhaps this is something that human beings should pray over."

"I will grant you that. How many legislators did Albert fail to invite to this little caucus?"

"Eight," Vereshchagin said, lost in thought.

"Only eight who can't be trusted with anything important?" Harjalo snorted. "I suppose it will be a few years before the politics here gets sophisticated." He showed his teeth. "You know, I always thought I would die in a little war in some far-off place."

Vereshchagin looked at him oddly. "Matti, this will not be a little war."

Harjalo appeared surprised. Then he clenched his teeth and nodded.

Although Beyers might have won a vote, he ended the session without requesting one, wanting his people to think the matter over for a night. He advised them to pray.

Wednesday(314)

SLIPPING IN IN THE EARLY HOURS OF THE MORNING, RAUL Sanmartin found out long before he intended to be awake that one vote that Albert had not influenced was his wife's. Although Bruwer had said little to betray her feelings in conclave, she gave free rein to her anger in private.

Crawling out from under his pillow, Sanmartin tried to calm her, with predictable results.

She brushed his hand away. "I listened and I cannot believe or understand why Anton told us that we could win. So tell me—how can we?"

"It's a risk—"

"I gave a grandfather and a stepbrother to the last war, do I have to give the rest of my family to this one? Don't we have enough worldly goods to give Matsudaira what he demands?"

"Hush, hush! Don't shout," Sanmartin said soothingly. Troubled, he grasped both her wrists and held her until she calmed.

"All right." Bruwer frowned. "All right. But how can Anton say this when even now we cannot unite? The twenty or so black soldiers that you recruited on Ashcroft like Isaac— Wynard Grobelaar is going among the delegates saying how shameful it is that you force Afrikaners to obey orders from blacks, and that we should not give them citizenship. Two people have already told me. Why you and Albert insisted on including that loud-mouthed bully—"

"Easy. Easy. Grobelaar is predictable. He'll be gone. We only want to see if he'll flush anything out of the bushes before then."

"What?" Bruwer's eyes narrowed. "What do you mean 'he'll be gone'?"

"The school nurse and the district psychologist pulled his stepdaughter out of class and spoke to her, they're arranging to get her into a foster home. It seems Wynard likes young girls," Sanmartin said as calmly and dispassionately as he dared. He heard the kitten scratching at the door and hoped Hendricka was not with her.

"Dear God, what a filthy thing!"

"I gather Vroew Grobelaar knew." Sanmartin let some of his feelings emerge. "I suppose I could understand prostituting a daughter to keep from starving, but she doesn't look like she's been missing many meals."

Bruwer's mouth tightened. "How long have you known?" she demanded with fierce certainty.

"Two or three days, now. Apparently it got covered up once six or seven years ago."

"That poor girl! How could you? And why?" She shook his arm vigorously.

"Because we knew someone would raise the issue about our black troopers, and we decided Grobelaar would be perfect for the job," he shouted back.

"And I suppose that you decided for the girl that another few days wouldn't hurt!"

"As a matter of fact, we did. Colonel Sumi is going to need replacements for that comfort detachment of his, and they aren't coming from Earth. They tend to have a high wastage rate. Grobelaar's stepdaughter is about the right age. I want to spare her that."

"Dear God."

"Look, Afrikaners murdered a fair number of cowboys during the rebellion, and before that they did an even better job of massacring the sects. There are only a handful of your people the cowboys and strandloopers trust. Grobelaar is a stalking horse, our designated bigot to lure the rest of the bigots out of hiding."

"Dear God, what a filthy business this is!"

"Joh and some others wanted some assurance. I think that the quiet consensus is that if a racist like Wynard can drum up some support, this planet and the Afrikaner Volk aren't worth saving. I suspect they're right."

She pounded her fist against him. "But we can't win, can we? We couldn't even defeat one battalion and one warship before."

Sanmartin took her fist and kissed it. "That was because we were that battalion. Hans keeps quoting Voltaire to me to the effect that God isn't on the side of the big battalions, but favors the ones who shoot the best. If anyone can pull this off, Anton can. '*Suaviter in modo, fortiter in re,*' " he said absently.

" 'Gentle in manner, resolute in deed,' " she translated. She struggled with her thoughts, gesturing violently. "Sitting there, deciding who will die? Why do you trust him so very much?" Her voice trailed away. "He's so, so very smart, but our whole world depends on him, and I don't understand him and I don't understand why."

"Most of the time, Anton's place is behind the lines where he can control things and let other people do their jobs," Sanmartin said calmly, so quietly that his wife had to steady herself to listen. "But once in a very great while you'll see him doing a platoon leader's job. On Ashcroft, when I was executive officer for C Company and we were chasing cakes, cacos, 'freedom fighters'—whatever you want to call them."

He stopped speaking for a moment. "The Jebel d'Aucune was a huge cratered plateau with nearly vertical sides, and we knew a few of them were up there. Captain Samizda, who was commanding the company, thought he could slip up on them in the dark." Sanmartin tapped his nose thoughtfully. "It was the only mistake I ever saw him make."

"What happened?" Bruwer asked.

"We got ambushed halfway to the top. Samizda didn't know it, but every second cake on Ashcroft was up there. We got hit from three sides and lost eleven men in as many seconds. After Samizda took a bullet through the throat, I was in charge."

Bruwer shut her eyes tightly.

"Whenever a commander goes down like that, people wonder how the next man in line will do," Sanmartin said conversationally. "As the next man, I was wondering myself. We were scattered up and down the mountain, and they were dropping boulders on our heads and skipping bullets off the rocks. To be truthful, I didn't think any of us were coming back down, least of all me."

Bruwer nodded without speaking.

"For the life of me, I don't know how the Variag knew or timed it, but all of a sudden Lev Yevtushenko flew up the mountainside in a Sparrow, stalled the plane with its nose pointing straight up in the moonlight, and dropped Anton off, cool as ice. The cakes were so startled they stopped firing for a minute. Sparrows can do some amazing things, but I've never seen anyone fly that well, before or since." He paused.

"With the Variag telling me what to do on one side and Rudy Scheel on the other, somehow we pulled in our wounded and avoided being overrun. Then I remember Anton tapping that pipe of his and saying, 'Piotr is on his way. Let us see if we can move number eleven to the top through that chimney in the rock to our left.' "

With his arms around her, the pulse in his veins told her as much of the story as the words did.

"The cliff was so steep that while we were scaling that silly fissure the cakes couldn't shoot at us without exposing themselves, and I'm not sure they realized that we were crazy enough to try. I followed Anton up, and we turned the corner just as Piotr Kolomeitsev jumped two platoons on top of them. We chased the cakes down the mountainside and into the valley for ten kilometers until I was gray in the face." He paused again.

"The official record reads different, but that was what broke the cakes on Ashcroft. Up until then, when they ran out of ammo, they came at us with their teeth. On the Jebel d'Aucune, they had us and they knew it, and we took them. After that, they thought we could fly."

Sanmartin punched his free hand with his fist, and then let his voice fade. "After that, C Company would have followed me into hell. And I'd lead them there if Anton Vereshchagin told me which chimney to climb."

"I did not know," Bruwer said simply.

"You see him playing his kindly grandfather role, but the rest of us have seen his other side. I've often thought that every moment since then has been borrowed," he said, finishing his story. He said after a few moments, "The only person on this planet who likes fighting the war that Sumi and Matsudaira are angling for less than you do is Anton. But he can't really see a way around it, and neither can I and neither can you. What do your pupils say?"

Bruwer maintained, with a degree of truth, that the best advice she received was from her former students, the eldest of whom had just turned thirteen—they took advising her seriously and weren't old enough to rationalize.

"They don't approve of fighting, but think we should make an exception," she said, smiling through the tears on her face.

"So, do you understand, and are you still angry at me?"

"Amantium irae amoris integratio est," she said, leaning against him. "Lovers' quarrels are the renewal of love."

"Come on. Let's go find Hendricka. One three-year-old is as hard to keep track of as fifty-nine legislators."

WHEN BEYERS RECONVENED HIS "ASSEMBLY OF GOD," AS THE WITS dubbed it, Dominie Naas Van der Merwe gave the invocation and intentionally spoke to all of Suid-Afrika's inhabitants, taking his text from the verses in St. Paul's letter to the Ephesians which begin, "For he is our peace, he who made both one and broke down the dividing wall of enmity."

After the first vote, Hanna Bruwer proposed a second vote for the sake of unanimity, and this time the measure passed unanimously. As Prinsloo Adriaan Smith argued, "We must all hang together in this; or assuredly we will all hang separately."

Wynard Grobelaar did not attend, having urgent business

with the public prosecutor. After Christos Claassen, who was occasionally vindictive, foreclosed on Grobelaar's home in his capacity as banker, Grobelaar had enough of a sense of shame left to take his own life. It was convenient.

Thursday(314)

ADDRESSING HIS SECURITY COMPANIES, COLONEL SUMI SAID, "IT has become increasingly important for the population to recognize the futility of resisting Imperial authority in any manner. Labor unrest and political dissent are extremely disruptive forms of resistance. There are over one hundred thousand Afrikaners on this planet, and each of you should become aware that mining operations would proceed efficiently even if there were fewer than fifty thousand."

Major Nishiyama, commanding Sumi's No. 303 Independent Security Company, asked timidly, "Honored Colonel, when may we expect a firm decision from Admiral Horii on—such measures?"

Sumi bared his teeth. "In a few days, Admiral Horii will see the wisdom of the correct course of action."

He resolved to watch Nishiyama closely in the future for other signs that the major lacked true spirit.

Friday(314)

AT THE FIRST RECESS OF THE ASSEMBLY'S SPECIAL SESSION, HANNA Bruwer left her high seat and walked to the back benches. "Heer Hanneman, I wish to speak with you a moment."

Engrossed in drafting a speech he planned to read, "Jaapie" Hanneman, the Reformed National party assemblyman from Nelspruit, nodded and then looked up uneasily. Hanneman had not been asked to attend the "Assembly of God."

A moment later, Christos Claassen walked up beside her and folded his arms.

"Heer Hanneman, I understand that your health has made it impossible for you to continue to represent your district, and I am prepared to accept your resignation."

Hanneman made a sickly smile. "You have heard wrong, Madam Speaker. My health has never been better."

In a low, penetrating voice that carried to every corner of the chamber, Bruwer said curtly, "Heer Matsudaira has purchased your voice for his company." As the babble elsewhere quieted, she reached into her bag and threw a sheet of paper in front of him. "Heer Matsudaira maintains good records."

"But, Madam Speaker, this is all a mistake!" Hanneman protested in the booming voice that was his greatest asset as a politician. "Heer Matsudaira only paid me for some consulting work. Indeed, I was your grandfather's friend!"

"You told me once that you were my grandfather's friend," she said, cutting through his peroration. "I did not believe you then, and I do not believe you now. You have accepted a bribe." She laid another sheet of paper in front of him. "My secretary has typed up a letter of resignation for you. I wish to see your signature on it before we reconvene."

"It was a . . . contribution," Hanneman said, cringing.

"Heer Hanneman, as speaker of this Assembly, I am disturbed by what you have done. As Hendrik Pienaar's granddaughter, I am—sickened."

She walked over to her high seat, pulled out a long *sjambok* her grandfather had owned, and walked back. "If you do not sign the resignation in front of you, I will do what my grandfather would have done and whip you out into the streets."

"We drew lots as to who would actually get to horsewhip you," Claassen murmured too quietly to be understood by others in the room. "Tell Colonel Sumi that after careful consideration, you have retired from politics. And if I hear one peep from you after you have returned to Nelspruit, I swear before God that I will have you arraigned before the public prosecutor within the hour."

Sobbing, Hanneman signed as he was bidden. Two of his former colleagues led him away.

Bruwer quietly walked to the women's restroom and threw up into the sink.

Moments later, when she came back and called the session to order, there were two letters of resignation on her desk, one handwritten.

USS PLANETARY DIRECTOR MATSUDAIRA WAS ENCOURAGED TO MENtion the incident when he made his television debut on Suid-Afrika's evening news.

Prompted by his young aides and confident of his ability to explain his company's attitude to a hostile audience, Matsudaira had spent most of the morning composing answers to questions prepared by a reporter who, Deiselmann had assured him, was "sympathetic." Matsudaira had been flattered by the station's insistence that no other spokesman could adequately explain the company's viewpoint.

At one point, the newswoman conducting the lengthy interview asked him in a syrupy voice why his company's management was so competitive. Pursing his lips, Matsudaira made a pretense of considering the question deeply. "Forgive me, but you must understand that our company's management is Japanese. Excessive competition by Japanese is first and foremost due to the fact that the mental structure itself of Japanese produces a peculiar kind of excessive competition. Such racial characteristics are a product of ethnological, climatic, and historical conditions which do not easily allow rectification."

In his role as Beyers's political consultant, former senior censor Ssu had carefully prepared the questions Matsudaira was asked, then coached the interrogator. Thanks to the hole in Matsudaira's data base security, he had also reviewed Matsudaira's responses prior to airtime. As Ssu repeatedly stressed, the timing of the interview request was critical—enough advance notice to lull Matsudaira into a sense of false confidence, but not enough to allow him the luxury of obtaining other opinions.

"Some people might believe that this excess competitiveness is evil," the reporter purred "sympathetically."

"Ah! Such people misunderstand. This matter is not so much a question of 'good' and 'evil' as a problem of character," Matsudaira informed her, reassured by her demure manner and unaware that the cameras were capturing the drops of sweat running down his face and the veins popping in his neck every time he lied.

The reporter played her part skillfully. So did Matsudaira, in a manner of speaking. Judging from the shocked calls that poured into the television station, Matsudaira probably couldn't have done a better job of damning his cause if he had tried.

Admiral Horii laughed himself speechless when he accidentally caught the second half of the broadcast. "United Steel-Standard must have looked very hard to find the appropriate representative to send here," he said, wiping tears from his eyes.

ANTON VERESHCHAGIN HAD LAST ADDRESSED HIS BATTALION AS A group on a transport the day before they landed on Suid-Afrika. He spoke to them once again, as always in a quiet voice sitting on top of an ammunition box.

"As many of you know already, Admiral Horii, however reluctantly, plans to hand Suid-Afrika over to USS, and to disband this battalion and dismiss its officers, for we no longer have a place in what the Imperial system has come to be."

Seemingly embarrassed, he chose words carefully. "There is an old Kazakh folk legend about *mankurts*, slaves whose memories were destroyed by torture so that they would not remember who they were and who they had been. A man without history, without a past, cannot understand. We have lived through the past and seen history distorted."

Even the Suid-Afrikans, the Afrikaners and cowboys interspersed in the ranks, nodded silently. Suid-Afrika's old history texts had been a thin tissue of lies. As a former teacher, Hanna Bruwer had conscripted some of her former colleagues to write new texts and commissioned Senior Communications Sergeant Timo Haerkoennen to build tricks into the programming to identify the students logging on, so that she could terminate teachers and school administrators who preferred teaching lies.

"Before the crack-up, Russia was an empire of nationalities, and the Russian people forged chains for themselves to hold these peoples. Russia never quite let all of them go, and when the missiles and the plagues came, it discovered too late that it had helped lay the seeds for a holocaust. The cost of the crack-up was terrible. From its ashes, Japan helped to build an Imperial system for all of mankind, but the Japanese have begun forging chains for other nations, and for themselves."

He spoke to them carefully for about an hour, and in conclusion, he said, "For many of you, some who were born here and others who came later, this planet is home. The rest of you have nowhere better to go. Esdraelon once had a bright future. Now, Esdraelon has been wrecked and that future thrown away. I, for one, am not willing to allow the future we have built here to be thrown away."

Vereshchagin paused, and afterward, the only sound Sanmartin could recall hearing was the tapping of the Variag's pipe against his thigh.

"Unless we are very fortunate, most of us may not live through this, but whether we succeed or not, I believe that it is important for us to try. I would say that you can crush cinnabar without taking away its color, and burn a fragrant herb without taking away its scent. For once, I will ask for volunteers. Any man who does not wish to take part in this may leave, with my blessings."

He folded his arms and waited stoically.

Raul Sanmartin studied the faces around him. "What's wrong, Deacon?" he asked Roy de Kantzow.

Although Vereshchagin's battalion was somewhat unique in that it discouraged the use of vile language with an appreciable degree of success, the exception to this rule was "Filthy DeKe" de Kantzow, who hadn't managed to string two completely clean sentences together since the age of twelve.

De Kantzow struggled to refine his thoughts. "This frosting planet—first we shoot frosting cowboys so they can't shoot Imps and Boers, then we shoot frosting Boers so they can't shoot Imps and cowboys, now we got to shoot the frosting Imps. It's hard to keep track."

"Want out of this one, DeKe?" Sanmartin asked, mildly surprised.

De Kantzow looked indignant. "And miss getting paid for snuffing blacklegs? But if we'd frosting started with the frosting Imps in the first place, we'd have saved half the bother."

Sanmartin patted him on the shoulder, a little frightened, but with his faith in human nature restored. "Politics makes for strange bedfellows, Deacon."

De Kantzow nodded, having his own ideas what the quotation meant. "Yeah, they're mostly frosting boy-lovers anyway."

To no one's surprise, except perhaps Vereshchagin's, every man stayed, including Captain Chiharu Yoshida, born in Kyoto of a corporation family.

Saturday(314)

"THERE DOESN'T SEEM LIKE VERY MUCH HERE, NOT FOR FIVE BATtalions anyway," Superior Private Dinkers commented, looking around the inside of the main Imperial supply depot. The young reconnaissance trooper craned his neck to see what was stored on the third level of flats.

"There isn't," Lieutenant Thomas whispered impatiently. "Admiral Horii is a shrewd old bird. He only keeps about three or four fire units of stuff on hand where people might get to it. The rest is still up in orbit."

"You'd think that they'd have guards and sensors outside to keep people out of this place," Dinkers commented.

"Lots," Thomas said laconically. "Why do you think we had to crawl on our bellies to get here?"

"Practice," Dinkers said ruefully, based on ample prior experience.

Thomas gestured toward two banded plastic crates. "Let me show you something fun. These are urine tubes so the people in the armored cars can leak without stopping and getting out." He lit his torch, making a small glow in the darkness of the warehouse, and began heating the metal band around one of the crates. "There's about twenty thousand tubes in each of these crates. If we took the boxes, the people at the Complex could turn some more out in a few days, which wouldn't help us at all. Heating them up like this won't hurt the outer shell, but it'll melt the inner osmotic liner, which means half of them will have a blockage in the middle and overflow when the Cadillac gunners try and use them. And if the admiral's supply dinks are like supply dinks everywhere else, they'll just keep issuing out bad tubes and ignore the complaints."

After a few seconds, the metal band started glowing and Thomas switched his attention to the other crate. "When those Japanese Cadillac boys dribble in their laps two or three times, they'll start scheduling themselves comfort breaks." He looked at the young soldier. "If we have time, I want to do some things to their ammo."

"Can't we just set a bomb to blow the place up?" Dinkers asked.

"Maybe later on, but Horii's units are all putting in requisitions, and for now I want to get to the stuff they plan on issuing out in the next couple of days."

Dinkers scratched his head. "How do we know what stuff that is?"

Thomas ignored his question. "I brought you here to work, not talk, you know. We need some stuff. Pull out your shopping list. Fuses are down aisle fourteen, and I want one box of everything listed there. Try not to drop anything."

Grabbing a hand truck, Dinkers scampered off to comply. As he did so, he observed Senior Communications Sergeant Timo Haerkoennen, the third member of their party, patiently disassembling a field diagnostic kit for an armored car. "What's Timo up to?" he asked.

"Ah, that's mother's little secret," Thomas said.

Another war party paid an unofficial visit to Daisuke Matsudaira's sedan. The next morning, when the ignition was switched on, it took the air conditioning system sixty-seven seconds to fill the vehicle's interior with soapsuds.

Sunday(315)

"THE ASSEMBLY EXPELLED TWO LEGISLATORS FOR PRO-IMPERIAL sympathies. All the officers are discussing it. I think it is an intolerable affront," Captain Watanabe declared in Admiral Horii's hearing.

Horii smiled, knowing the true facts better than Watanabe, as he checked his reflection in the mirror. "Where is Lieutenant-Colonel Vereshchagin today?" he asked.

"I have not seen him for two or three days now. Not since Colonel Sumi asked him to cease to attend staff meetings. His bed appears to have been slept in. Should I inquire?" his aide responded.

"No, that will not be necessary, Watanabe."

"It will be pleasant when repairs to your quarters are completed," Watanabe said wistfully.

Horii made a noise to indicate agreement. A few moments later, he asked, "What else are the young officers saying, Watanabe?"

"Admiral," Watanabe said nervously, "they are concerned that we have not dissolved the civil government. While I disclose my respect from my inmost feelings, I earnestly feel that continuing to evade the issue might lead to unpredictable consequences. I—also share their opinions."

Horii stared at his aide for a long moment. Finally, he said, "We have always undercompensated our officers. Perhaps more so now, with inflation. This is a weakness of ours. How shortsighted of us." He closed his eyes.

Without the expense accounts and annual bonuses that most Japanese workers took for granted, young officers were perennially short of money, perhaps intentionally so. "How much did Matsudaira-san give you, Watanabe?"

Shamefaced, Watanabe pulled out a packet of elaborately folded sheets of colored paper and opened it to display the money inside.

"How shortsighted of us." Horii sighed and again closed his eyes. "One person cannot change things. What must be, must be. Please inform Major Harjalo that I wish to inspect his command this afternoon."

"At once, honored Admiral!" Although mystified, Watanabe hastened to obey.

* * *

WHEN ADMIRAL HORII ARRIVED IN BLOEMFONTEIN, MAJOR HARJALO met him at the airstrip with an honor guard.

"I expected to see Lieutenant-Colonel Vereshchagin with you," Horii commented as they drove to the spacious hill where the Bloemfontein casern was located.

"I thought that you had Anton," Harjalo commented. "Maybe he's checked himself into the hospital for a short rest. He told me several days ago that he wasn't feeling well."

"Indeed. He should take good care of his health," Horii said politely.

Harjalo led him through the bunker he was using as his headquarters and then led him through A Company's barracks.

"Your men appear sullen, Major Harjalo," Horii commented.

"This is the Iceman's company. Dour. Dour Finns and Russians, that's what we are," Harjalo said jovially. "The bear is our national symbol, *metsän omena*, the apple of the forest."

Horii wondered idly how much of Harjalo's open, blustering manner was feigned. "Where are the rest of your men?" he asked.

"I have most of two companies out in the forests. We don't have room for them here, and I want to make certain there aren't any more members of the ARM 'Combat Liberation Detachment' wandering around," Harjalo explained as he led Horii toward C Company's cantonments.

A high proportion of the battalion's Afrikaners were out in the forest, on the odd chance that Horii or one of his staffers could distinguish one group of round-eyes from another. Harjalo wasn't particularly interested in having Horii realize just how high a proportion of the battalion's present strength had been recruited locally.

"I am sure that all of your men are concerned about their future," Horii commented.

Harjalo grinned. "Most men are, honored Admiral. Most men are."

Coldewe and Company Sergeant Beregov were waiting when they reached the C Company area. "This is Captain Hans Coldewe, my C Company commander."

Coldewe bowed politely. "Welcome to our humble abode. We're still in the process of fixing it up," he said, leading the admiral inside.

As Horii entered, he spied a large fishbowl, part-full of slips of paper. A little sign said, IN CASE OF EMERGENCY, BREAK GLASS.

"What is this, Captain?"

Coldewe shrugged. "Sir, it belongs to Corporal Uborevich. He has special permission to keep it."

The admiral said nothing, but raised his eyebrows.

Coldewe flashed a sudden grin. "Uborevich makes more of an effort to cultivate the locals than most of our men do, but Bory looks moderately simian and doesn't have much luck with the ladies. Whenever some woman tells him to take a walk, he throws her phone number into the pot."

Horii smiled at the jest. Moving on to the next building, Coldewe said with obvious pride, "This is our sauna. It took us most of a week to move it here and get it set up again."

Again, Admiral Horii lifted an eyebrow. "A sauna?"

"It's hard to keep Finnish troops happy without a sauna," Coldewe explained. "I rather like it myself. Of course, in a hot climate like this, we had to alter the design."

He led the admiral inside and rapped on the doors. "This is the washing room, and this is the steam room."

"Most ingenious. It surely must have been difficult for you to obtain the wood," Horii responded, peering through the glass. He straightened and delicately touched a slender branch lying on a small stand. "And these?"

"Birchwood *vihtas*." Coldewe picked one up and swished it to demonstrate. "The Finnish boys say that a sauna without a *vihta* is like eating food without salt. A few of the farmers keep greenhouses, and we persuaded one of them to grow some birch trees for us."

Private Kriegler's father could and would grow anything, Coldewe had discovered, if you were willing to listen to him tell you how impossible it was.

"Most ingenious," Horii said politely.

Coldewe gestured. "Next to it is the cold room." The cold room was ten centimeters deep in snow with a dark pool of water at the far end.

"Remarkable," Horii said, looking through the frost-rimed glass.

"Lieutenant Reinikka, our engineer platoon leader, figured out how to make it snow. To save on energy, we use the heat we pull out of the cold room to warm the steam."

"Indeed," Horii murmured. "One might think the snow excessive. Would not a simple cold shower do as well?"

"It would, but there's not much snow on this planet, and it makes it feel a little more like home. Reinikka worked out the sauna design on a planet called Ashcroft which was mostly desert, and nasty desert at that. It helped keep our people from going crazy."

"Indeed. And is that building your armory, Captain Coldewe?"

"Let me show it to you." Coldewe escorted him into the old farmhouse, down two flights of steps, and through a steel door. "This is Company Armorer Rytov."

The armory's interior was half-full of ammunition boxes of varying dimensions. A number of weapons were neatly racked against the far wall. Rytov was seated behind a long table filing down a trigger housing. Although his whiskers were grizzled badger-gray, Rytov's white hair gave him almost an angelic expression. His life extended by time dilation and the icebox, Rytov was one of the children evacuated from St. Petersburg and had actually lived through the crack-up. He nodded meekly when the admiral entered, but made no effort to rise or otherwise acknowledge his presence.

"Senior Ordnance Sergeant Rytov and I have met," Horii said. "Acting Major Sanmartin brought him to defuse the missiles which were aimed at me."

"Want some caviar?" Rytov pushed the *zakuski* plate in Admiral Horii's direction.

"The orange?" Horii asked, amused.

"Is trout. Farmers raise them in ponds."

"And the red?"

"Is fake. Color it with carrots."

"We're a little short on ammo, sir, and we would appreciate whatever you could deliver. So far, we've had trouble getting our supply requests filled," Coldewe said.

Horii nodded, well aware of the reasons why Coldewe's ammunition requests had not been filled. He walked through, looking at the shelves. "Yes, yes. I quite agree. You appear to be very short of ammunition. I will direct my intendance officer to see to this matter. I notice, however, that you have an unusually large amount of liquid artillery propellant on hand."

"That we make for ourselves," Harjalo explained. "The nitrate factory outside Johannesburg runs an evening shift for us."

"Indeed." The admiral pointed languidly to a piece of equipment in a corner. "What is this?"

"It's a pump. In case we get leakage," Rytov volunteered, lying smoothly. He held his fingers four centimeters apart. "In the wet season, we get this much rain in an hour."

"Indeed. I will mention this fact to my intendance officers. It might assist other units in avoiding such damage." Horii cocked his head. "You served on Cyclade, did you not? I was there."

"Cyclade. Yes, Cyclade was bad," Rytov reminisced with the air of a connoisseur. His eyes glazed over. "Ashcroft was worse. There was a hell-world. When one boy died, we joked that he asked the Devil if he had to go back. Maksakov, his name was. Yes, Unto Maximovich Maksakov."

Horii looked at Rytov thoughtfully, having seen what he came to see. "Major Harjalo, please prepare detailed plans for turning over your heavy weaponry and embarking your battalion on the assault transport *Chiyoda* to return to Earth."

"Yes, sir."

"That will be all, Major. Please have your plan ready to show to me on Wednesday. Captain Coldewe can see me off."

After Harjalo bowed and left, Horii said, "Captain Coldewe, I imagine that your company will be anxious to see Earth again."

"It has been a long time. We've jumped around a lot. I imagine a lot of us will want to think about emigrating to other colonial worlds."

"Possibly, possibly," Horii said genially. "I would consider this if I were much younger. Tell me, Captain Coldewe, what do you think will happen with the political situation here?"

"I imagine that USS Director Matsudaira wants to do some things that will get the people here stirred up," Coldewe said with perfect candor. "Very stirred up, if you understand me."

"Ah! But the people here should understand not to challenge the Imperial Government." Horii gestured. "The Finnish have fought many wars against Russians and know that ants should not challenge elephants, is this not correct, Senior Ordnance Sergeant Rytov?"

Rytov nodded, lost in thought behind his workbench.

"You would like to return home, would you not, Senior Ordnance Sergeant Rytov?"

"Home?" Rytov looked up. He said fiercely, "With all my heart."

Horii allowed Coldewe to escort him to his plane. Horii failed to realize that "home" to Rytov meant long-dead St. Petersburg. Absent magic to bring the dead to life, Rytov didn't intend to leave a C Company armory until someone drove a stake through his heart.

More interested in weapons than people, Rytov didn't remember what he wanted to say about ants and elephants until several minutes after the admiral left.

"Sosialististen Neuvostotasavaltojen Liito voitti hyvänä kakkosena tuli maaliin pieni sisukas Suomi," he muttered to himself as he worked. It was a famous line from a novel about Finland's Continuation War—"The Soviet Union won, but spunky little Finland came in a good second."

Monday(315)

ADMIRAL HORII'S MORNING STAFF MEETING WOULD HAVE BEWILdered any foreigner. Because Japanese affect to believe that they are a "unitary race" with a "homogeneous existence," many of them think that they have "anticipatory perception" which enables them to intuit what other Japanese are thinking. Thus, a peculiarly Japanese way of negotiating compromise between opposing viewpoints is to negotiate "through the strength of one's personality" rather than by arguing the matter. At best, *haragei*, as it is called, involves considerable ambiguity; at its worst, it can be described as communication devoid of communication.

Because both Admiral Horii and the advocates for immediate action were determined to avoid an open breach, much of the "discussion" was unspoken, and the remainder was shockingly imprecise. As Horii observed to Watanabe, "Thoughtlessly using the imperfect medium of words would have ended up pouring cold water on a unified understanding that was only achieved with great difficulty."

Unfortunately, Admiral Horii left the meeting with the impression that Colonel Sumi agreed that further delay was necessary, while Sumi left with the assumption that Horii had tacitly approved of seizing Vereshchagin and Beyers so long as it could be accomplished without stirring up things too much.

The few officers present who believed that seizing Vereshchagin and Beyers—either now or later—was stupid and unnecessary did not feel it appropriate to make their views known.

Tuesday(315)

AFTER CHECKING THE ROOM FOR WIRETAPS, COLONEL SUMI TOLD the officers of his two security companies, "You see copies of an operations order on the table in front of you. Please review your part. Its purpose is to arrest Lieutenant-Colonel Anton Vereshchagin, Albert Beyers, and their principal subordinates.

I have been informed that Vereshchagin will meet with Beyers this evening at the president's residence, and we will arrest them there. The Manchurian regiment will place a battalion of men around the casern in Bloemfontein to ensure that Vereshchagin's men do not interfere."

Major Nishiyama said hesitantly, "We are indeed eager to carry out your orders. I am certain that you and Admiral Horii have thought through all of the uncertainties in such an operation."

Sumi marked Nishiyama for replacement at the first opportunity. "I will take full responsibility," he barked. "These men nurture treasonous intentions. We are at an extremely crucial juncture in history. The mission of the people of Yamato is to prevent the human race from becoming diabolic. You must endeavor to arrest these men with the least amount of disturbance so that opposition may be speedily crushed!"

He glowered at his men. "You will repeat after me, 'For existence and self-defense, our nation has no other recourse but to appeal to force of arms and to crush every obstacle in its path.' "

The officers present did so dutifully.

"We will sacrifice everything to our nation's cause," Sumi chanted rhythmically. "We resolve to dedicate ourselves, body and soul, to the nation. The key to victory lies in faith in victory."

His officers repeated this litany.

Holding his sword high, Sumi concluded, "We pledge ourselves never to stain our glorious heritage, but to go forward until the eight corners of the world are under one roof."

Two hours later, the blacklegs and Manchurians began moving out.

IN A CAVERN IN THE UPPER STORMBERG RANGE, TIMO HAERKOENNEN left his equipment and unceremoniously pushed open Matti Harjalo's door. "Sir, Lieutenant Thomas says that five companies of Manchurians are on the move, apparently on their way to Bloemfontein. Also, several truckloads of blacklegs are leaving the Pretoria casern, heading downtown."

Stretched out on his hammock fully dressed, Harjalo opened his eyes.

"They took down the phones and began jamming all frequencies very, very heavily about five minutes ago," Haerkoennen added.

Harjalo thought quickly. "This is it, then. Tell everybody to execute plan A for Akita. Anton is with Raul and Albert. What is their status?"

"They have not reported in. Lieutenant Thomas is trying to reach them directly."

Harjalo sprang up. "All right, Timo. Let's get everybody moving."

VERESHCHAGIN, BRUWER, SANMARTIN, AND ALBERT BEYERS WERE sitting in Beyers's study when Tom Winters came in. The nominal secretary had a silenced submachine gun in his hands and two more slung over his shoulder. "The street outside is filling up with blacklegs."

Hanna Bruwer glanced anxiously at her husband. Vroew Beyers appeared cradling Hendricka.

"Out the back?" Vereshchagin asked, accepting one of the weapons.

Winters shook his head. "The men on the roof spotted them there, too."

"Out the tunnel, then," Sanmartin said, arming himself and pushing Albert and Betje Beyers ahead of him. Vereshchagin patted Bruwer on the shoulder to move her along.

Hendricka squirmed in Betje Beyers's arms. "My kitten," she protested, aware that something was not right.

"You must be quiet, and you must be brave," Betje Beyers whispered in her ear as they hurried down the cellar steps.

Inside the tunnel, dim, blue, bioluminescent light made it possible to see a few meters. Vereshchagin shut the door and bolted it. "Please put on the shoes and jackets there."

Sanmartin gave his daughter a pill to take, wrapped a blanket around her, and slung her into a harness he could wear on his back.

"There's no water," she complained.

The muted sounds of rifle fire penetrated from the street above, then the roar of a command-detonated mine.

"This is important. Just chew it, honey. It'll make you sleepy," he coaxed, holding her head gently but forcefully.

"Please do this right now, Hendricka," Bruwer said, struggling into ankle-high boots.

A moment later, the child was asleep. Sanmartin led the party, leaving Vereshchagin to bring up the rear.

The tunnel had been put in at the same time that the sewer had been laid, and Betje Beyers used the sewer pipe to steady herself. "Is Tom coming?" she asked.

"Please whisper. The pipe may make it possible to hear our voices," Vereshchagin said. "The mine means that Tom did not like what the security policemen had to say. I am afraid that he is dead."

"He was a good trooper. A lousy typist. I hope that the boys on the roof get away," Sanmartin said, knowing full well that they would stay, to buy time.

"I wonder if the admiral knows about this," Albert Beyers said.

"I'm not sure that it matters," Sanmartin said. "I think we're committed, either way."

A moment later, Betje Beyers turned around to look behind her. "Where is Anton? Should we wait?"

Sanmartin smiled. "He'll catch up. He's arming the booby traps. Just in case."

They emerged into a safe house nineteen blocks away.

"Is there a car here?" Beyers asked.

"Yes, but we won't be taking it," Sanmartin replied. "They probably have enough sense to cordon the roads and check passengers. We'll rest here for a moment and then walk to where we can be picked up." He put his arm around Betje Beyers and brushed away the tears forming at the corners of her eyes. "It is all right, Mother. Everything will be all right."

FEELING SELF-CONSCIOUS, LIEUTENANT LANGERMANN WALKED UP to the factory gate. Three of Langermann's sixteen reservists hadn't shown up at the rendezvous, and he hoped that they would eventually catch up. The plant's lights were on, and Langermann could hear the sound of machinery indicating they were running a third shift.

The night watchman was reading a mildly pornographic book and didn't notice Langermann until he rapped on the glass.

"It is all right. We are the good guys. We have a warrant from President Beyers," Langermann assured the watchman, pointing to the *Vierkleur* flash and Vereshchagin's salamander crest hastily sewn on to his battle dress. Langermann and his men had exchanged their old, worn uniforms for new ones, which would better shield them from sensors; Langermann's itched. Unable to resist the temptation, he said, "Take me to your leader."

With one eye to the assault rifle under Langermann's arm, the watchman lost no time unlocking the gate and escorting him to his shift manager. As they entered the facility, Langermann's men fanned out on their separate tasks.

"Heer Kemp, this man needs to see you," the watchman told his boss timidly.

Langermann cut in, "Heer Kemp, I am an officer in the Army of the Republic of Suid-Afrika. I forget—is this our third or fourth republic? In any event, I have a warrant here from President Beyers to remove certain components from your heavy equipment, and a proclamation for you to read to your employees." Langermann passed the papers over.

"It is all right, Jan. Go back to work and don't tell anyone about this just yet," Kemp told the watchman absently as he studied the documents and ran his finger across Beyers's unmistakably flamboyant signature. "This is a rebellion," he exclaimed.

"It is all we are left with, I am afraid. The Imps tried to arrest the government a few hours ago. But Colonel Vereshchagin is on our side, this time." Langermann smiled behind his face shield. "We need to immobilize your production facilities by pulling the microchips from the equipment. If we win, we will put them back. If we lose, the Volk will have other problems to worry about."

Kemp looked up at him uncertainly. "Heer Langermann? Is this you?"

"Oh, damn it, Kemp!" Langermann pulled off his face shield. "You weren't supposed to recognize me. If the Imps know, they may take reprisals."

"Sorry, sir. I will not mention it." Kemp rose and shook Langermann's hand. "It is good to have you back anyway. Ah, you had better let me read the proclamation to the men. Your voice is distinctive. How is your family, sir?"

"I sent them off to the country last week. And yours?"

"Very fine, sir." Kemp reached into a drawer. "If Oom Albert says that we are starting a rebellion, I guess that we had better drink to its success."

"No, thank you. We are in a hurry. Is that young puppy Matsudaira put in to replace me here tonight? I sent two of my men to check my old office."

"Yes, sir. He likes to work late." Kemp glanced out in the hallway and saw a soldier driving an electric cart. A Japanese man, blindfolded, bound, and gagged, was strapped to the back. "That looks like one of your men with him, now."

Hearing Kemp's voice, Matsudaira's man began writhing on

the cart. Only small noises escaped his gag. The trooper driving the cart ignored his antics. Kemp waved.

Langermann hastily refastened his mask. "Ah, Kemp, when you read that proclamation, ask your people to help give my boys a hand. A few of them are farm lads, and they understand the theory of pulling microchips better than they understand the practice, although we did slip in here for a few hours of hands-on training when you were closed last Sunday." He sighed. "It feels strange to be doing this. It will take me a few days to get used to it."

"Good luck, sir."

"No, good luck to you, Kemp. Good luck to all of us."

An hour later, after Langermann and his men had disappeared into the night, Kemp wandered through the plant and found a casting machine purring away that Langermann's men had somehow overlooked. He shut off the machine and reached inside to pull out the microchip that told it what to cast. Shrugging, he dropped it on the floor and ground it under his foot.

ANOTHER GROUP OF FOUR RESERVISTS ENTERED THE PRETORIA GAOL armed and handed the flustered turnkeys a stack of pardons.

"Former terrorists, out of your sacks!" the corporal in charge, a bearded young Afrikaner, called out as the prison guards hastened to separate the ARM men and women from the petty thieves.

As the door to his cell opened, Gerrit Terblanche grabbed the corporal's arm. "What was that you said? What is happening?"

"Suid-Afrika and Colonel Vereshchagin are rebelling against the Imps, and President Beyers thinks that if we leave you in here, they'll shoot you straightaway. I am all for it myself, but Oom Albert isn't, so we are accepting volunteers for the infantry. All of you who can get yourselves moving in the next five minutes are welcome to help us fight."

"Hey! What happens if we don't like being in your army?" one ARM member called out.

"Hey, yourself! If we don't like having you in our army, we boot you out." The corporal reached in his pocket and pulled out freshly minted currency. "The Hangman will supervise your training, so I have twenty rand that says none of you last a week."

"Well." Terblanche looked around at his former comrades. "Does anyone else want a piece of that bet?"

* * *

AROUND ELEVEN O'CLOCK, AFTER TWO SQUADS OF BLACKLEGS manning roadblocks around Pretoria failed to report in, Colonel Sumi finally woke up Admiral Horii. Comprehending the situation almost instantly, Horii flew into an absolutely murderous rage and coldly ordered Colonel Uno's Manchurians to probe the defenses of the Bloemfontein casern.

Within an hour, a chastened Colonel Uno reported that Vereshchagin's men had evacuated the casern literally under his nose. Dressing down a hapless Colonel Sumi did not improve Horii's temper one whit.

Horii formally declared a state of siege and announced the suspension of the elected government for its close ties to Vereshchagin and his mutineers. Sumi roused his weary blacklegs and sent them out to seize control of newspapers and television and radio stations. Despite what he considered to be the obvious futility of such a request, Horii asked Suid-Afrika's district officials to reassure their people and await instructions from Imperial authorities.

Wednesday(315)

"AH, LIEUTENANT AKAMINE," HORII SAID, "I UNDERSTAND THAT Vereshchagin's casern was evacuated during the night without anyone noticing. Please report how many casualties we suffered in the process of occupying it."

Lieutenant Akamine had been the first of Colonel Uno's officers to set foot inside the deserted Bloemfontein casern, and Uno had sent him to Horii's headquarters as a sacrifice.

Akamine glanced uneasily at Colonel Sumi and Captain Yanagita, who had obviously already experienced the admiral's wrath. "We suffered very few casualties, honored Admiral. It would appear that Vereshchagin's men departed hurriedly, and the engineers were able to remove most of the booby traps that they left without great difficulty."

"That is a small consolation. Please explain how this evacuation was effected."

Akamine floundered for the correct words. "It is Colonel Uno's belief that this was a well-laid plot. We found a tunnel had been constructed which led to a secluded area nearly half a kilometer from the casern perimeter."

"On a planet so addicted to mining operations, this is perhaps not entirely surprising." Horii gave Sumi a malicious glance. "Colonel Sumi has already assured me that Vereshchagin laid careful plans, and I certainly hope that this is true. It would be extremely disquieting to discover that he was able to improvise such a disappearance. What about his vehicles and aircraft?"

"A number of trucks were left behind, as well as two helicopters and four Type 97 armored cars." Akamine hesitated. "The vehicles were rendered unserviceable, while the helicopters and armored cars were stripped of components."

"How thoroughly stripped? Shells?"

Akamine nodded unhappily. "They were completely stripped, honored Admiral."

"A Potemkin village," Horii said, with evident amusement.

Akamine handed Watanabe a two-sided leaflet to give to the admiral. "Children have been distributing these throughout the town of Bloemfontein. Colonel Uno requests instructions as to how he should deal with this."

In Horii's opinion, Uno was a weak character who spent too much time listening to his chief of staff, a blackleg lieutenant-colonel. "They are being distributed elsewhere," he said without touching the document. "The only inhabitants who are not familiar with what President Beyers has to say by now are undoubtedly blind and deaf, neh, Colonel Sumi? Please instruct Colonel Uno to ignore this matter. What about the armory, Akamine?"

"It was empty except for a small quantity of liquid propellant. The ammunition and weapons stored there were missing."

Horii turned and asked blandly, "What do you think of this, Captain Yanagita?"

Yanagita replied stiffly, "Sir, it is my belief that Lieutenant-Colonel Vereshchagin removed the bulk of his soldiers and equipment undetected prior to last night."

"I agree." Horii turned back to Akamine. "Tell Colonel Uno that I will not hold him to blame."

"Thank you, honored Admiral," Akamine said, bowing low.

"Akamine, one final question. What about the saunas?"

"The saunas?" Akamine appeared puzzled.

"It is not important. You are dismissed. Please advise Colonel Uno that I wish to see him immediately."

"Yes, honored Admiral." Akamine saluted and left.

Horii folded his hands in front of him. "The birds have taken wing. Somehow, I doubt that Colonel Uno will find them. Captain Yanagita, what else has occurred overnight?"

"Sir. It appears that a preplanned program of sabotage

went into effect. Vital machinery at all facilities appears to have been immobilized by the removal of small parts. USS plant managers uniformly assert that they cannot operate. Matsudaira-san also reports that three of his executives have been kidnapped."

At the great Mariental mine northeast of Bloemfontein, USS employees had shown Yanagita hundred-ton excavators and thirty-ton haulers, capable of leveling mountains, that had been stripped of the computer chips that regulated each stroke of their engines. The chief engineer had quipped that with wheelbarrows and overtime, it would only take him fourteen years to fulfill his daily quota, assuming, of course, that someone could get the smelter running in that amount of time.

"Lieutenant-Colonel Vereshchagin is a very shrewd man. He has succeeded in delineating the nature of our conflict."

"Sir?"

"Observe. My objective is to eliminate resistance and ensure continued deliveries of fusion metals. Even though we have control over the populace, he has arranged matters so that we cannot deliver fusion metals without defeating him—and perhaps not then. An ingenious touch on his part. Is there more to relate, Yanagita?"

"Yes, honored Admiral. We have control of all strategic points except the ocean tap and two mines which are occupied by small parties of rebellious soldiers. Colonel Sumi respectfully recommends that we assault these positions."

Sumi remained uncharacteristically silent.

Horii snorted. "Vereshchagin is denying us access to the ocean tap and the deep mines. He knows that it will be years before we can restore production if we provoke his men into wrecking them. I will take Colonel Sumi's recommendation under advisement. Until I decide otherwise, you will take no action against these men."

Yanagita swallowed hard. "Sir, may I respectfully emphasize these soldiers are not Japanese and they have no means of escape. In my opinion, a quick assault would cause them to surrender and place these facilities in our hands with minimal damage."

"And if you are wrong, Captain Yanagita, and they blow up themselves along with these facilities?" Horii asked sardonically. "Will you rebuild them for me?"

Horii paced the room. "Vereshchagin did not need to leave these soldiers behind. He expects me to test the resolve of these men, and expects that they will die. He does this to remind me not to underestimate his spirit. Do you know anything of Russian history, Yanagita?"

"Very little, sir. They were defeated in the First Pacific War."

"Russia endured the Tartar yoke, the communists, and the worst of the crack-up. Tens of millions of them died. Vereshchagin reminds me of this. Issue strict orders to leave the men at these locations alone."

Again, Horii began pacing. "In effect, Vereshchagin challenges us to a duel. The forces left behind are to ensure that I understand this. It is quite simple. If we crush his command, his rebellion will end. Have you relayed my orders to Lieutenant-Colonel Ebyl?"

"Yes, sir. I regret that he states that it is impossible for him to comply," Yanagita replied, looking even more discomfited.

"I thought as much. It is a bee sting on a face in tears," Horii said, quoting an old proverb. "Ebyl wishes me to know that his men will neither help nor hinder. He will suffer for it after we have collected Vereshchagin's head, as he is undoubtedly aware."

Horii sat down and tilted his chair back, looking up at the ceiling. "We must not permit Vereshchagin to dictate the terms of our conflict. When an enemy has few men, you must crush him straightaway without allowing him space for breath. It is essential for us to locate his main force before he can mature his plans."

"Sir, I will guarantee discovery of his location," Yanagita declared.

"Please see that you do. Preferably within one week. Please leave now."

After Yanagita closed the door behind him, Sumi said belligerently, "Admiral, I stand by my conduct. A hasty stroke often goes awry. I believe that my actions helped to bring this treasonous plot into the open."

"Inasmuch as Vereshchagin appears to have forestalled every action that you attempted to take against him, I shudder to think how much more danger he would have been had you allowed him more time to prepare. We will discuss your insubordination and lack of attention to detail at another time. Until then, I still have use for you. What is it that you want?" he asked, knowing the answer but wanting to hear Sumi ask anyway.

Sumi swallowed his anger with a measurable effort. "I wish to lead an attack against these traitorous mutineers."

"You may do so. I will, of course, expect you to ensure that all of my officers display a more obedient attitude in the future."

Sumi forced himself to say, "Yes, honored Admiral."

A few moments later, the building was rocked by a loud explosion that more or less obliterated the supply depot that Thomas's men had visited a few nights previously.

Horii smiled. "A worthy opponent," he murmured.

IN EVERY ARMY, THERE IS ALWAYS SOMEONE WHO DOESN'T GET THE word. In the 1/35th Rifle Battalion, that person was frequently, although not invariably, Private Prigal.

On this morning of all mornings, Prigal was driving a bakkie to the Bloemfontein casern with a load of cooking oil purchased in Upper Marlboro. Using the initiative and ingenuity which had earned him his less-than-exalted rank, he had managed to connect his personal radio to the local "Top 50 Hits" station rather than to the battalion net.

When Prigal reached the gatepost and honked his horn, he noticed that the guards were Manchurian about the same time that they realized he wasn't and began chambering rounds. As Prigal threw the pickup into reverse and wheeled it around, the same providence that protects drunks and little children caused one bullet to pass ten centimeters to the right of his body and another to pass twenty centimeters to the left.

Leaking cooking oil, the truck bumped down the street on three tires. Two of the three Manchurians pursuing Prigal promptly slipped in the spilled oil. An awed Afrikaner in the druggist's shop down the street later expressed regret that she didn't have her video camera running.

Ditching the truck, Prigal found a safe house and called in. After his section sergeant figuratively removed 2 centimeters from his backside and everyone else literally laughed themselves silly, Matti Harjalo complimented him, with a discernible twinkle in his eye, on carrying out his orders despite circumstances that might have caused a lesser man to quail.

Prigal, who had secured himself yet another modest footnote in battalion history, understandably concluded that he would have been better off getting himself shot.

SUID-AFRIKA'S RESPONSE TO ADMIRAL HORII'S SIEGE PROCLAMATION and suspension of the civil government was immediate and well coordinated. Street signs and house numbers disappeared overnight. The district governments stopped functioning, refusing to send in reports or answer phones. The border police quit to a man.

The populace collectively forgot their English and declined to communicate in any language except Afrikaans. They declined to communicate effectively in that language, as Japanese officers with translators discovered to their mounting exasperation. Afrikaners have always had a collective talent for dumb insolence. In one old man's words, "What the blacks did to our ancestors, we can do to these Imps."

Vereshchagin's men provided them with technical advice. Mohandas Gandhi drew lessons from the civil disobedience campaign that the Finns waged against the czarist government in the early twentieth century, so as Hans Coldewe expressed it, "It runs in the family."

FIRE _____

Thursday(315)

DEEP UNDERNEATH A DRAKENSBERG PEAK, IN THE CAVERN THAT had become the seat of Suid-Afrika's government, Hanna Bruwer and a quorum of evacuated assemblymen passed a package of laws to make legal most of the things that needed doing. Albert Beyers signed it into law a few moments later. One legislator whose pet notions included a new constitutional convention was unceremoniously told to shut up and sit down.

One statute that Bruwer and Beyers rammed down the Assembly's collective throat was a Militia Act, which provided for military ranks, law, pensions, and pay to resolve whatever questions remained about the status of Vereshchagin's men, scattered by platoons in the huge forest reserve that took in the western Drakensbergs and the upper Vaal and Oranje valleys.

Predictably, the less-experienced among Vereshchagin's men were bored within the first twenty-four hours.

"HOW MUCH TIME BEFORE WE MOVE OUT, DO YOU THINK?" recruit Private Vosloo asked his hammock mate, Kriegler, as they leaned against a fern tree together.

"You heard Captain Coldewe the same as I did," Kriegler retorted. "You think I read minds?"

"You're right. I should know you don't read." Vosloo thought for a minute. "How much ammo are you carrying?"

Kriegler patted his webbing. "Three hundred sixty rounds. That should be enough, don't you think?"

"I don't know. Sergeant Orlov made it sound like we would want more."

"Look, they issued us two ammunition pouches which hold four magazines each, plus one more in my rifle. Nine times forty rounds is three hundred sixty rounds. It stands to reason that if they wanted us to carry more, they'd have given us more pouches, right? It's not as if we're not carrying enough," Kriegler said, thinking of the single-shot rockets, grenades, mines, and extra machine gun ammunition he had been handed. Food and water was definitely an afterthought.

"It seems like a lot, but I don't know."

"Look, why don't you ask Bory how much ammo he's got? I bet he's only got three hundred sixty rounds."

"You're on. Five rand says he's got at least four hundred."

Kriegler snorted. "More fool you. Last week, he kidded me because I was carrying a full tube of toothpaste. Hey, Bory! How much ammo have you got?"

Corporal Uborevich looked up with interest.

"We've got a bet on," Kriegler explained.

"Well, let's see. One in the gun." Uborevich considered himself above such trivia as the ancient distinction between a rifle and a gun. He opened up the ammunition pouches on either hip. "Eight more here." He reached up and opened the breast pockets on his jacket. "And eight more here."

Vosloo noticed that Uborevich had sewn little loops in his pockets to hold the magazines in place. "That's six hundred eighty rounds."

"You win," Kriegler said disgustedly.

"Hold it." Uborevich began patting his pockets. He found three more magazines in a thigh pocket. Then he wrinkled his nose, obviously perplexed. "You know, I can't think of what I did with the rest of it. Maybe I left it in my rucksack. Well, it doesn't matter. Orlov always carries extras, and I can borrow a few from him."

"Got some thread?" Vosloo needled his friend.

Uborevich winked so that only Kriegler could see and whistled, perfectly imitating the sound of an incoming artillery shell.

Vosloo immediately dived into the nearest hole, which, like most holes in the upper Vaal Valley, contained about six centimeters of standing water. Several seconds later, he realized that he had been had. "Damn you, Bory, that's hard on a man!"

"Good practice, good practice." Uborevich chuckled. He immediately heard a voice over his radio. "Wanjau here. Bory, is that you fooling around?"

"Yes, Platoon Sergeant." Uborevich sighed.

"I thought so. Wanjau out."

"What did the platoon sergeant want?" Kriegler asked.

Uborevich sighed again. "Based on past experience, I think the platoon sergeant wants me to show you kids the best way to dig a latrine. Or maybe several."

RAUL SANMARTIN ASSEMBLED THE POLITICIANS EVACUATED TO THE Drakensberg caverns and stood on an ammunition box to address them. "If I may have your attention." He studied them as he waited for the murmuring to quiet.

"My wife tells me that some of you have been complaining about the menu here, which pretty much consists of stew today, stew tomorrow, and stew twice on Thursdays. I regret that this is not a hotel. I assure you, you are eating what I am eating, which is the same thing that the soldiers are eating when they get to eat."

He paused. "Our battalion does not have very much in the way of an administrative element. A number of years ago, Lieutenant-Colonel Vereshchagin asked everyone whether they'd like more amenities and things like beer in the field, or fifty extra people carrying rifles at the sharp end of things. The vote was unanimous. After we took it two or three times. If you would like to organize yourselves to help out with the chores around here, we would appreciate it."

He turned them over to Betje Beyers, who chose Eva Moore as her first assistant.

As Sanmartin would have admitted if anyone had asked, they could have brought in some extra civilians to do drudgery, but leaving a few hundred politicians and notables without meaningful labor did not strike anyone as particularly intelligent.

Friday(315)

WORKING THROUGH THE NIGHT, ADMIRAL HORII'S STAFF PUT TOgether a plan to launch probes north of Bloemfontein into the foothills of the Drakensbergs, feeling that Vereshchagin's men could not have traveled very far. The plan was adopted at Admiral Horii's morning staff meeting without significant discussion. The First Battalion of Colonel Uno's Manchurian Regiment was assigned the mission under Colonel Sumi's overall direction and given twenty-four hours to prepare.

"We will smash them!" Uno exclaimed exultantly as the meeting broke up.

Horii grinned at his aide, Watanabe, as soon as the room cleared. "The first drum makes courage, neh, Watanabe?"

"I do not understand, honored Admiral," Watanabe admitted sheepishly.

"Our strategy should be to make a show of being slow, then to attack Colonel Vereshchagin without warning when he is not expecting it. You must research this, Watanabe," Horii said placidly.

WHILE COMMUNICATIONS WERE STILL RELATIVELY SECURE, HANNA Bruwer and her fellow politicians organized a human chain, from Upper Marlboro in the south to Boksburg in the north, as a peaceful protest.

Rejecting Colonel Sumi's advice, Admiral Horii chose to largely ignore the demonstration and only allowed the Manchurians and blacklegs to use batons. As a result, only two civilians died.

Saturday(315)

SIPPING TEA FROM THE MUG IN HIS HAND, SENIOR COMMUNICATIONS Sergeant Timo Haerkoennen watched Matti Harjalo playing solitaire on a small field desk. "I hate sitting around waiting for something to happen," Harjalo announced loudly.

"Patience, sir. Patience," Timo Haerkoennen kidded Harjalo, knowing the source of Harjalo's discontent.

Harjalo stared at his cards and then threw them in in disgust. "All right, Timo. Anton says that they'll send company-sized probes through the highlands, either today or tomorrow. What say you?"

"Today, if they're moderately incompetent. Tomorrow, if they're grossly incompetent."

"Tomorrow, but it won't be a company-sized probe. Horii will want to end this quickly, so I expect him to try and find us and then pile on." Harjalo began dealing out another hand.

The communications board that Haerkoennen and his assistant, Communications Sergeant Esko Poikolainnen, manned in shifts was the battalion's nerve center, and never more so than at present. Admiral Horii's signals section had the best communications detection and intercept equipment that Earth could produce, forcing Vereshchagin to dot the countryside with clusters of short-range relay nodes—the rough equivalent of stringing telephone wire to each unit—to keep radio messages from being jammed, or worse still, used to pinpoint the location of the senders.

Poikolainnen shook Haerkoennen by the arm. "Something's coming through garbled."

Twirling around in his chair, Haerkoennen helped him make delicate changes in the relay path. Harjalo came over and stood behind the two of them. The radio crackled. "Bad jamming," Haerkoennen said quietly. "Okay, we have them. This is Haerkoennen. Go ahead."

It was Lieutenant Thomas, the reconnaissance platoon leader. "Thomas here. I've had trouble getting through. A flock of aircraft just took off from the spaceport on a 348-degree heading. One group just took off consisting of four Shidens, four choppers, two Sparrows, and twelve, repeat twelve, transports. There are two more gaggles of equal size waiting to go."

"Four Shiden, four choppers, two Sparrows, twelve transports, the first group of three groups on a 348-degree heading," Haerkoennen repeated.

"Correct. It looks like the Shidens in the lead group are armed with a normal load. Thomas out."

Vereshchagin had somehow divined the need for his presence and joined them from the side passage that served as his bedroom.

"We have company coming. No, actually, we have about three companies coming. The middle Drakensbergs, do you think?" Harjalo asked him.

Vereshchagin tapped his unlit pipe against his thigh. "Yes, it would appear that they are going to pick out a landing zone or two to explore after a few course changes to throw us off the track." He picked up an electronic pointer and began tracing patterns on the map. "The Shidens aren't carrying the munitions they would need to manufacture landing zones, so they have about a dozen choices."

Another call came through from a different sender. "Mintje Cillie here. There's an armored column leaving the spaceport barracks and heading north on the Pretoria road. It looks to be battalion size."

Harjalo looked at Vereshchagin.

Called to duty a few days ago, Cillie, an economist, was a member of Vereshchagin's reserve reconnaissance platoon, the "Baker Street Irregulars," whose mission was to provide information that Vereshchagin needed to fight. Like the other members of her platoon, Cillie was not trained to fight like a soldier. She was trained to die like one if it came to that.

"Harjalo here. What vehicles so far?" Matti asked her.

"Six slicks and seven Cadillacs, so far. They are keeping hundred-meter intervals, but there are a lot more coming. A lot more."

"Very fine. Let us know when you have a complete count. Harjalo out."

The road network through the Drakensbergs was largely undeveloped, and the armored column filled in one piece of the puzzle for Vereshchagin. "They will land here, or here," he said, framing two relatively open areas north of the village of Valkenswaard on the electronic map. Part of Ivan Sversky's B Company was posted there. Looking at Harjalo, he asked the all-important question, "Where are the warships?"

"About thirty-five kilometers up. They started drifting north in a tight diamond formation about ten minutes ago," Harjalo said.

Several dozen observers with a varied collection of astronomical equipment kept Admiral Horii's warships in constant view and constantly communicated changes in their positions.

The warships and the geosynchronized satellites they used for targeting were superbly equipped with visual and thermal detection gear that could penetrate all but the thickest clouds or vegetation. Vereshchagin's men and vehicles were shielded and as well hidden in the forests as they could contrive. However, as rebels had discovered on a dozen worlds, the heat of weapons firing showed up unbelievably well to warships overhead.

"Admiral Horii will use the Manchurians in the transports to flush the game for his ships," Vereshchagin commented.

"We'll need those ships heading in some other direction if we want to play hell with the Manchurian boys," Harjalo replied. "Timo, tell Thomas to initiate the feint we talked about, then get me Sversky."

Thomas had one section of his recon platoon waiting patiently near the east end of the spaceport runway where the Imperial Guard battalion maintained an outpost. Thomas's men would give the unlucky guardsmen a small dose of concentrated hell and then disappear, leaving behind enough exploding fireworks to simulate a continuing attack. Hopefully, Admiral Horii would mistake it for an assault of major proportions and divert the warships to support them.

If the warships turned around and the Manchurian assault force did not, Sversky's men would have a window of opportunity.

A SHALLOW UNDULATING BOWL OF OPEN AREA TWO-THIRDS OF A kilometer in diameter, the landing zone arbitrarily designated Gifu Chiba was framed by forest and the mountains looming to the north. Riding in a two-man ultralight Sparrow aircraft, Colonel Sumi circled the LZ; his tiny plane, built from radar-absorbant materials and fitted with panels that matched the ambient light, was virtually invisible.

As Sumi watched intently, two Shiden ground-attack aircraft followed tiny Hummingbird reconnaissance drones over the landing zone, dusting it with antipersonnel bomblets and raking the north tree line with cannon fire. When the thunder of the bomblets died away, two more Shidens dropped canisters of liquified fuel that spread into a sticky blanket and exploded a few meters off the ground, searing the scrub vegetation and creating an overpressure that would detonate any mines laid.

The fire quickly burned itself out, and helicopters took up overwatch positions at the four corners of the LZ to cover the troop landings. "We observed no secondary explosions, nor did we receive return fire," the Shiden flight leader told Sumi. "We will proceed down the valley."

Sumi called Colonel Uno, riding a Sparrow a thousand meters lower, and directed him to proceed.

Moments later, a single tilt-prop landed, the four huge propellers on the front and back of its wings pointing skyward to lower it gently. It spilled out sixteen nervous Manchurian reconnaissance troopers who immediately fell prone. As soon as the tilt-rotor took off again, two more transports landed and disgorged the remainder of a Manchurian recon platoon. The Manchurian recon troopers spread themselves out in the blackened, waist-high ferns and began cautiously probing.

Unknown to the Manchurian troopers, far to the south, Lieutenant Thomas's men had turned a quiet afternoon into hell, sending a sleepy platoon of Imperial guardsmen sprawling into their shelters. As they fired at their unseen opponents, the guardsmen frantically requested maximum artillery and warship support.

Working from hastily crafted contingency plans, artillery shells from the 210mm gun-howitzers at the spaceport pounded the area around the outpost, and Admiral Horii's four warships turned and sped south. Despite the suspicious timing of Thomas's attack, a "real" threat to the Japanese national troops at the spaceport was a higher priority than the potential threat to the Manchurians.

As the Manchurian recon troopers reached the tree line to the north and east of the glade, they began to relax, and Sumi impatiently directed Colonel Uno to proceed.

Moments later, loaded with D for Date Manchurian company and part of a mortar platoon, a tight, nine-ship wave of transport aircraft came floating in. As the tilt-rotors grounded, the Manchurians poured out and began fanning out in all directions under the watchful eyes of Colonel Sumi and Colonel Uno, who were monitoring the company radio net to countermand or revise orders.

Elated as his transport touched down, Section Sergeant "Sawtooth" Ma jovially told his men, "Now, remember to find a few souvenirs for your old sergeant." Like the Manchurian recon troopers, Ma failed to notice the sensors that Captain Sversky's B Company had inconspicuously placed in the treetops.

From prepared positions in the tree line to the southwest, an eight-man half section from Sversky's No. 7 platoon watched and reported the Manchurians' progress to Sversky, a dozen kilometers away.

"Pihkala here. One platoon and one company so far. The company is half unloaded. We're prepared to engage with remotes."

Ivan Sversky looked at his company sergeant, Rodale. "Engage. Sversky out."

Seconds later, two 7.7mm general-purpose machine guns opened up on the Manchurians from the *east* side of the landing zone, chewing holes in the grounded transport aircraft and scattering surprised Manchurian infantrymen.

With four platoon leaders, a company commander, a battalion commander, the helicopter company commander, Colonel Uno, and Colonel Sumi all in evidence, the Manchurians on the ground were immediately deluged with orders. They laid down a base of fire and prepared to assault while the helicopter gunships nearest the disturbance plastered the east tree line with fire.

Unfortunately, the enemy they were preparing to assault literally wasn't there. Vereshchagin's armorers had mounted a few-dozen spare gp machine guns on concrete pedestals, wrapped them in composite matting, and equipped them with camera eyes and electronic triggers to command the more obvious landing sites. Undeterred by the heavy fire, the Pihkala's soldiers on the *southwest* side rotated the seven-sevens with joysticks, firing sporadically to make the carefully camouflaged guns difficult to spot and to keep from burning out the barrels.

While the two machine guns in action were not inflicting many casualties, they helped the bemused Manchurians reach the natural and erroneous conclusion that the s-mortar rounds that Pihkala was dropping almost vertically onto their positions were also coming from the eastern side of the LZ.

Repeated helicopter strikes succeeded in knocking out one of Pihkala's guns. Reaching agreement, Colonel Sumi and Colonel Uno ordered two sections of No. 16 Manchurian infantry platoon to move into the north tree line and maneuver around what they perceived to be Pihkala's flank. Immediately, two more remote-controlled machine guns opened up from the southeast and northeast corners of the perimeter and caught them in a raking cross fire.

From his vantage point high over the battlefield, Colonel Sumi counted the general-purpose machine guns peppering the Manchurian company and reached an understandable and perhaps predictable conclusion. He opened up a channel to his senior officers. "Colonel Sumi here. Attention! We have succeeded in engaging at least two platoons of Vereshchagin's men. Date Company will lay down a base of fire and pin down the enemy forces. Beppu Company and Chiba Company will proceed to Landing Zone Gifu Beppu and move on foot to trap the enemy. Crush all resistance. Sumi out."

LZ GB was a good four kilometers away through terrain cut by ravines and cloaked in dense forest; it would take the two companies at least two or three hours to "trap" Pihkala's force. While Sumi's maneuver was not a battle tactic that Vereshchagin would have employed, it was what the textbook called for, which meant that it was exactly what Vereshchagin expected.

Even as Sumi was issuing his orders, Lieutenant Per Kiritinitis was moving the rest of No. 7 platoon into place around LZ Gifu Beppu. "Bee point command. Break.

Kiritinitis here," he reported through bursts of static from the jamming. "Ivan, we're in place and so are the two Cadillacs. The firing positions have a little water in them, but they're in pretty good shape. The Manchus are about to land—are the mortars up yet?"

Sversky balanced himself precariously on a tiny utility vehicle carrying a 105mm mortar and its crew as it bumped along a narrow trail cut between firing points. "Sversky here. We'll be there. I'm moving a section of number six to reinforce you." Moments later, the vehicles with the four mortars of Sversky's No. 8 mortar platoon reached their initial firing points and lowered their little spade feet so the mortars could fire.

As Kiritinitis watched beneath the fern trees, the section from No. 6 platoon filtered into place from the depths of the forest. In the clearing ahead, clouds of red, green, yellow, and violet smoke expanded like the petals of a flower as the Manchurians advanced toward the tree lines on all sides. "Kiritinitis here. Number six is in position. The second wave is about to touch down. The Manchus are firing off colored smoke grenades, but I can't think why."

"It's so the people in the choppers can keep the formations tight," Sversky responded. "They must think we're a bunch of savages. You initiate."

When the lead elements of the Manchurians were no more than sixty meters away, Kiritinitis keyed his wrist mount and whispered, "Bee point Akita. Break. Kiritinitis here. Fire on my signal. They're setting up an artillery counterbattery radar in the middle of the LZ. That needs to go—Toivo, you take it. Flak launchers, go for the overwatch choppers—first section number seven, southeast; second section number seven, southwest; second section number six, northeast. Cadillacs, take the transports. Everyone, hit the people in your sectors. Everyone set?"

As No. 7, the second of No. 6, the mortarmen, and the Cadillacs acknowledged, Kiritinitis quietly released the safety on his weapon and privately intoned the infantryman's prayer: "Call us, Lord, but not just yet." When the eight tilt-rotors of the Manchurian second wave slid into position, Kiritinitis whispered into his wrist mount, "Number seven and attachments, fire!"

Three surface-to-air rockets leaped out to pull down three of the four overwatch helicopters at almost point-blank range. The fourth hesitated a few fatal seconds before beginning a firing pass that killed a launcher crew and three riflemen; two more surface-to-air rockets struck it almost simultaneously and ripped it apart.

A few meters from Kiritinitis, the first section eighty-eight roared, obliterating the Manchurians' counterbattery radar, while machine gun and s-mortar fire shot the Manchurian platoons to pieces. In the space of forty seconds, sixteen 105mm shells from the B Company mortars landed inside the Manchurian perimeter.

With most of their troops still aboard, the second wave of transports frantically tried to gain altitude. From a knoll two kilometers off, 30mm and 90mm rounds from a pair of lurking Cadillacs tore into them. Four of them crashed and a fifth spun away trailing smoke; the rest scattered wildly.

The Manchurian officers overhead shouted out conflicting orders as the deadly ambush took its toll. Unnoticed through the wisps of colored smoke, a fifty-meter gap had opened up where every Manchurian in two sections had been killed or wounded.

Spotting the gap, Kiritinitis called Sversky. "Bee point one. Break. Kiritinitis here. I can move a section inside the Manchurian perimeter and clean them up."

"Do it! Five minutes," Sversky ordered.

Six kilometers away, his company sergeant was vainly trying to reach him through the intensified jamming to relay a message from Vereshchagin.

"I can't reach them," Rodale told Harjalo with pain and frustration in his voice. "I sent a vehicle."

"Tell him to get everybody out," Harjalo said with deadly intensity, knowing that by the time Rodale got to Sversky, it would be too late. "Admiral Horii smelled a rat in the arras, and the warships are going to be over your head any minute now. Harjalo out." He put his hand over the transmitter and looked at Vereshchagin. "Here's where we pay for bad habits."

"Indeed," Vereshchagin murmured.

The moment that B Company's mortars fell silent, Kiritinitis pushed his first section through the gap in the Manchurian perimeter. Skillfully using the dead ground, they moved into the center and shot up the Manchurian command group. Seconds later, one of the remaining flak launchers shot down the Sparrow with the Manchurian battalion commander. As first section began crawling away, the surviving Manchurians around the edges of the perimeter began shooting through the center and into each other.

Retribution came ten minutes later from the sky. Angry, buzzing helicopters flattened the top of the hill from which the Cadillacs had sprung their ambush, and the warships in the upper atmosphere began their approach. Moving in, two corvettes plastered No. 7 platoon's tree line to a depth of five hundred meters, methodically concentrating on each individual firing position. From fifty kilometers away, long-range artillery from the Johannesburg casern pounded the mortar positions that the warships had spotted, wiping out two of Sversky's mortar crews.

As the forest around them sizzled, most of No. 7 platoon died. Kiritinitis led the survivors away.

To the south, Lieutenant-Colonel Okuda's Ninth Light Attack Battalion pushed north to interdict the farm roads and seal off B Company's retreat, while Sparrow reconnaissance aircraft and Hummingbird drones combed the area. When the Manchurian soldiers at LZ Gifu Chiba finally knocked out the last of Pihkala's remote-controlled machine guns, Sumi diverted the remaining transports there, and Manchurian Company D for Date belatedly took up the chase.

One Imperial Hummingbird spotted the third section of Sversky's No. 5 platoon escaping through the forest. Moments later, a flight of Shiden ground-attack aircraft converged and loosed a flock of small seeker missiles that homed in on individual soldiers. In seconds, fourteen of sixteen men were killed or wounded.

As B Company continued its retreat, Sparrows from Thomas's recon platoon slipped in and out of the cloud cover, bringing away the seriously wounded. Alert to the danger posed by the Ninth Light Attack Battalion, Sversky set up a road block with the sixteen men of the first section of No. 6, which stopped them cold for two hours with a loss of four vehicles. Sversky and the first section of No. 6 died to a man.

As afternoon lengthened into evening, Manchurian Company D for Date slogged through the swamps trying to reestablish contact. Private One-Eye Wong panted and wished he were light-years away as he listened to Lieutenant Akamine mumble orders. Exhausted, Wong had already thrown away most of the jewelry he had taken from Johannesburgers.

"Only a little farther . . . a little faster . . . and we cut them off and destroy them," Akamine told his tired soldiers. "Remember, 'the nimble foot gets there first.' "

Wong hoped Pig-Snout was right.

The forest frightened him. Already, two men had been shot

by snipers, a dozen more, including his tentmate, Duck-Face Gu, had fallen out with heatstroke—and the amphtiles he had heard so much about were waiting.

As they reached a clearing, Wong suddenly heard the whine of s-mortar rounds exploding, and the men ahead of him began dropping. Akamine stood speechless.

"Dig in!" Wong heard Sergeant Ma shout frantically.

Wong immediately ripped off his entrenching tool and began scooping away soil. A few centimeters down, he struck water and immediately understood why the enemy had waited to ambush them. He said something in Mandarin that any soldier would have recognized. Presently he died, the last casualty of a bitter day, without even the consolation of having Lieutenant Akamine precede him.

Later that evening, one of his mates remembered what Sergeant Ma said about finding some souvenirs for their old sergeant and left a badly burned boot beside Ma's rucksack. A blackened foot was still inside.

NURSING A WOUNDED THUMB AND A SPRAINED SHOULDER, PER Kiritinitis brought out what was left of B Company. About half of them made it to the safety of the mountains, including three of sixteen flak gunners. They brought out their wounded. They left behind most of their dead.

Harjalo, Vereshchagin, and Battalion Sergeant Yuri Malinov listened in silence as B Company's survivors reached their checkpoints and reported in through the jamming.

Radiation and chemotherapy had cost Malinov his hair and thinned him terribly. Malinov knew most of the men in B Company well, and Company Sergeant Rodale best of all. "I hope Rodale makes it. I lent him money," he said.

Vereshchagin knew that Malinov had little use for the money he was paid and probably would have hit Rodale if he had tried to repay the loan.

"Another victory like this will ruin us," Harjalo said.

A few moments later, Paul Henke approached. Henke's company had lost the two Cadillacs and the two slicks attached to B Company.

"Paul, what are you doing here?" Harjalo asked.

The Hangman's voice was calm and his face was perfectly impassive, but Vereshchagin was astonished to see streams of tears running down his cheeks.

"We must train new crews," the Hangman said, oblivious to the drops of water dripping down the front of his uniform.

ADMIRAL HORII HELD A POSTMORTEM AROUND MIDNIGHT, WAVING his officers to their seats. "Colonel Uno, what have you learned from today's operations," he asked, clearly enjoying Colonel Sumi's discomfiture.

"It was like fighting a cloud," Uno grumbled.

Officially, the Manchurian regiment had recorded in their war diary that they lost "more than a slight number of men, but less than a considerable number, the number falling within the normal range of fluctuation for a difficult attacking operation so that it does not represent a setback."

Uno gestured to Captain Aoyama, the commander of the Manchurian engineer company.

"I have something to bring to the admiral's attention." Aoyama held up an object that looked like two small wheels pasted together and balanced it delicately on the end of one finger. "We have taken a number of these from the bodies of rebel soldiers. Each one weighs approximately one and a half kilograms and has a tiny alcohol-fueled motor as you see."

"What is it?" Sumi asked.

"It unfolds into a bicycle," Aoyama said, demonstrating.

"Amazing," Admiral Horii said. "So much strength and so little weight. What is it made out of?"

"A fine wire matrix of nickel-chrome-molybdenum steel latticed with a ceramic-metal composite," Aoyama replied. When his audience manifested incomprehension, he added, "It appears to be virtually identical with the armor on the Type 97 armored car."

Colonel Sumi exploded. "This is impossible! You must be mistaken. The composition of Type 97 armor is secure information!"

"I deeply regret bringing this information to your attention," Aoyama stated with the faintest hint of malice.

"No, you were entirely correct to do so," Admiral Horii said. He asked, "Could the material have been scavenged from destroyed armored cars?"

"I am unwilling to make a pronouncement on so weighty a matter without much more evidence," Aoyama said, "but the data accumulated would appear to indicate that Colonel Vereshchagin has established a production line. It would be important to learn if he has received assistance from Complex personnel, but this would appear to be a security matter."

"The uninhabited portions of Suid-Afrika are largely trackless. The movement of vehicles is significantly restricted in many areas. Possession of such bicycles would give Colonel Vereshchagin's foot soldiers a significant advantage in mobility," Horii conceded.

Sumi objected, "This is nothing new. Japanese soldiers used bicycles to advantage during the South Seas campaigns of the Great Pacific War, and possession of such toys will not make up for the absence of Japanese spirit."

"Yes, of course," Admiral Horii said. "However, this does not mean that we should ignore this accomplishment. We will have to adjust our aerial tactics to compensate for this increased mobility of his men. The remotely operated machine guns were quite ingenious. I wonder whether Vereshchagin has other surprises in store for us. Captain Yanagita?"

"The soldiers we encountered were from the enemy's Beppu Company, which was destroyed in the engagement. Unfortunately, we were only able to capture one soldier alive and were not able to obtain very much useful information from him before he succumbed to his wounds. However, from the paths of retreat taken by the survivors of that company, we now have a general idea where the rest of Vereshchagin's battalion is concentrated." Yanagita tapped his map for emphasis. "This is extremely important information."

Admiral Horii smiled very faintly.

At the end of the meeting, Colonel Sumi sought out Admiral Horii. With only a trace of his customary arrogance, Sumi said, "Honored Admiral, my security police are prepared to launch simultaneous attacks on the two mines and the ocean tap. My officers believe that they can take these objectives without substantial risk."

Sumi's initiation into infantry operations had not humbled him, and Horii studied him, wondering whether Sumi was consciously or unconsciously grasping at moonbeams in an effort to cleanse the stain placed on his reputation.

"Colonel Sumi, I decline to authorize this. The men that Vereshchagin left at these three points have clearly indicated that they will die rather than yield them."

"It is my belief that foreigners boast a great deal but lack the necessary resolve," Sumi said stiffly. "My officers have prepared excellent plans which will undoubtedly result in swift and decisive success."

"And if you have failed to correctly gauge the military spirit these men possess, Colonel Sumi, the likely outcome of such an operation will be the destruction of these facilities. Does Matsudaira-san desire to run such a risk?" Horii said irritably. He had reviewed the preliminary reports emanating from the Manchurian regiment. With a lifetime's worth of experience, he understood the grim reality conveyed by the vague, flowery phrases the Manchurians' officers had used. He suspected that Sumi did not.

"I have discussed this with Planetary Director Matsudaira. He wishes to take this risk."

Like most other major Japanese companies, USS had a long-standing arrangement with the government to send its annual intake of young university graduates through military basic training to instill the proper corporate discipline in them. This had the unfortunate effect of convincing many salarymen that their brief exposure to military life made them experts on military matters.

For twenty-five years, Matsudaira had taken inordinate pride in being the honor graduate of his basic-training company, and Admiral Horii had already divined that Matsudaira felt himself fully qualified to present him with strategic and tactical advice. Admiral Horii, of course, rarely solicited advice from recruit privates, which is what Matsudaira's experience qualified him to be.

"I earnestly hope that Matsudaira-san comprehends that a military operation is less predictable than a tea ceremony," Horii said casually, conveying a subtle double insult: As a civilian Matsudaira could not be expected to comprehend military operations, and as an adopted parvenu he could not be expected to comprehend the way of tea. "I will authorize an assault on one of the occupied mines. If this operation is successful, we can discuss further operations. If Vereshchagin's men unexpectedly display spirit, the destruction of one mine will not distress us nearly as much as the destruction of the ocean tap, so it is much more prudent to do things this way, don't you think?"

"Yes, Admiral." Sumi saluted and left.

Sunday(316)

SUMI'S BLACKLEGS OPENED THE ASSAULT ON THE CALVINIA MINE by forcing mine employees to use the only functioning tunneling machine on the planet to drill a new shaft into the base of the mountain that the mine lay under.

Deep underneath the surface, Superior Private Dirkie Rousseaux watched the needle jump on his seismic meter. Before joining up, Rousseaux had worked two seasons in the mines. "Wake up, Section Sergeant. They're digging a hole."

"Mother Elena" Yelenov, rolled over and rubbed the sleep from his eyes. "We must have missed a tunneler."

"It looks like they're trying to connect up with passage B. It's only about a hundred meters from the surface in spots," Rousseaux explained.

"Miinalainen is up there." Yelenov touched his wrist mount. "Nine point two Akita. Break. Yelenov here. Juko, they are drilling a tunnel to connect up with passage B at . . ." He looked over at the map of the mine that Rousseaux was holding up. ". . . somewhere between Beppu 3535 and Beppu 3545. Put out a camera and two or three directional mines, and then get down here. Everyone else, just get down here. Yelenov out." After listening for every one of his men to acknowledge, Yelenov turned back to Rousseaux. "Time to go, Dirkie."

THREE HOURS LATER, MAJOR NISHIYAMA TURNED TO COLONEL Sumi. "We are prepared to proceed, honored Colonel." Nishiyama tried but failed to hide the trepidation in his voice.

Sumi grunted, "Proceed, Major." He looked at Nishiyama coldly. "To ensure success, make certain that you are the first one into the mine."

Nishiyama nodded. Before issuing his final orders, he left a lock of hair with his executive officer. Moments later, his blacklegs flooded the mine with gas and a swarm of small seeker missiles and then entered at two points, the main entrance and the newly cut tunnel, pushing mine employees ahead of them.

If the situation had required it, Yelenov would have ordered his men to shoot down the mine employees to get at the blacklegs. Since Yelenov wasn't planning to stay, he didn't bother. Untroubled by the gas and the seeker missiles filtering through the upper levels, he triggered the remotely operated machine gun on the ceiling near the entrance for a few seconds' worth of unobstructed shooting, then touched off one of the directional mines as soon as the employees ducked clear. The results were mildly gratifying.

After flipping the central fuse, Yelenov led his seven men sideways out the mine's narrow "back door," a thin passage cut a few days previously that led to a brush-choked ravine on the far side of the mountain. Ten minutes later, charges strapped to every support pillar in the mine's lower levels exploded, collapsing the ceiling and filling the mine's galleries with rubble.

The blacklegs only suffered a handful of casualties. One of the dead, however, was Major Nishiyama.

As they crouched in the ravine, Rousseaux whispered to Yelenov, "I still don't understand, Section Sergeant."

"Ah, Dirkie, lad. The Imps think that we blew ourselves to frosty hell a minute ago. If the boys holding the ocean tap were attacked, they would have to blow themselves and the tap to frosty hell, which neither the Variag nor the Imps want to see. This way, the Imps know that they can't attack the ocean tap. Everybody's happy, if you understand what I am saying."

"Yes, Section Sergeant," Rousseaux said unconvincingly.

"Good lad. Now be quiet until dark. It's a long ride back."

Already beginning to doze off, Miinalainen commented, "On these putt-putt cycles, it's going to feel like the Tour de France."

Monday(316)

BILLOWING CLOUDS OF PARACHUTES DOTTED THE SKY AS ONE OF Admiral Horii's shuttles began aerial resupply operations. As it drifted over Akashi continent at a suitable altitude, a stream of one-ton pallets rained down on Admiral Horii's caserns.

Two corvettes patrolled alertly, ready to pounce on any attempt to disrupt the operation, along with a flock of Shiden aircraft carrying antiradiation missiles that would home in on radar signals as soon as Vereshchagin's men attempted to lock on to a target.

The resupply operation proceeded without interruption until the shuttle reached Bloemfontein. As the Manchurians gathered below, a single flak missile—unguided, with a modified antiarmor warhead—arched into the sky and struck a pallet of mortar ammunition. Squashing itself against the pallet, the warhead exploded and sent a stream of liquid metal into the mortar rounds.

The resulting detonation spilled the air out of some chutes and split others open. Frantic Manchurians ducked out of the way of the one-ton loads that came dropping onto their heads. One crashed into a bunker and completely flattened it.

"It appears to have been an excellent shot," was Admiral Horii's comment when he was informed.

"WELL, WE KNOCKED DOWN A LOT OF AIRCRAFT AND CHEWED UP most of two Manchurian companies, but B Company is wrecked. Admiral Horii probably considers it a good exchange," Matti Harjalo commented when Vereshchagin was able to gather his officers together. "Raul, what do we know about that new bomblet they're using?"

"I have Rytov and Reinikka looking at the pieces we picked up, but it probably homes in on human pheromones," Sanmartin responded.

"Yes. We field-tested something similar during the Cyclade campaign," the Iceman said. "Apparently, they have figured out how to make it work."

"Add to the debit side of the ledger the fact that Horii now knows about the bicycles and the gimmicks with the machine guns," Sanmartin interjected. "Eventually, it's going to dawn on someone that we've been making preparations for a long, long time, and if they start thinking about some of the other surprises we have for them, we're in trouble."

"Where are the warships?" Harjalo asked.

"I don't know. We lost sight of the warships last night when it started raining, and nobody has reported their positions yet," Sanmartin confessed. "Horii has figured out that we're tracking their movements rather closely and started getting shifty on us."

He watched Per Kiritinitis's hands tremble. It had been a long day and night for Kiritinitis.

"Thus far, their use of reconnaissance aircraft has been sloppy," the Iceman said.

"Timo tells me that they have most of their Hummingbirds out combing the Drakensbergs under central direction, which is inexcusably sloppy under the circumstances," Harjalo commented. "Think it's time we did something about them?"

"I think so," Vereshchagin agreed. "It will be a few days at most before Admiral Horii discovers that the data he stole from our computer is corrupted, and after that, it is only a matter of time before someone uncovers the rest of it." Everyone else nodded except Per Kiritinitis, who didn't know what they were talking about.

Timo Haerkoennen stuck his head in and interrupted the meeting. "Lieutenant-Colonel Ebyl reports that his casern is under attack. Warships have already destroyed several bunkers and inflicted heavy casualties. Reserve reconnaissance platoon personnel report that aircraft are leaving the spaceport and heading south. It appears to be a strike force of three companies and eight Shidens."

Admiral Horii was using the warships to pin Ebyl's battalion in place while he maneuvered the rest of his force into position.

"Well, that saves me from asking everyone what Horii's next move is," Harjalo said with forced levity.

No one stated the obvious. The cowboy country was short of population after the losses they suffered during the rebellion. Having taken in only a handful of recruits to replace the personnel who had been killed or discharged, Ebyl's light attack battalion had barely half its nominal strength. With the warships to pen Ebyl's vehicles in their revetments, the aircraft and infantry that Admiral Horii was sending would easily breach his defenses.

"Apparently, they did not take Uwe's protestations of loyalty seriously," the Iceman said.

"I told Uwe to go when we sent off what was left of the Gurkhas," Vereshchagin said, pained by the memory.

"I think that Uwe was tired of fighting colonial wars," Harjalo responded.

"But why would they attack him? It must be obvious to Admiral Horii that even though he sympathizes with us, he isn't going to do anything to help us. Strategically, it makes no sense," Kiritinitis questioned.

"From a purely logical standpoint, Admiral Horii can utilize a victorious operation like this to rebuild the morale which must have been shaken by the losses his forces suffered yesterday," Paul Henke said. "However, I do not believe that he will leave a garrison in Upper Marlboro. This would be a useless diversion of resources."

The Hangman's comment struck a jarring note. Sanmartin tried not to stare. "Call it an exercise in terror, Per. He's trying to intimidate us."

"He's making a good job of it," Harjalo commented.

Ebyl went off the net several hours later. Out of the 250 men in his battalion, about sixty escaped the trap. A very bitter captain named Ulrich Ohlrogge took command of the survivors. The Manchurians who conducted the operation took most of their casualties when Ebyl's ammunition bunker blew up. They took no prisoners.

Horii left instructions with his staff that he was to be awakened if there was any countermove from Vereshchagin. About a half hour later, thirty-seven reconnaissance drones that he had scouting the jungle simultaneously crashed themselves.

Tuesday(316)

HORII WAS DOZING FITFULLY IN HIS PERMANENT QUARTERS, HIS ENgineers having finally finished repair work, when he heard footsteps in the corridor outside. He sat upright. "Watanabe?"

Watanabe entered the room highly agitated. "Admiral, a helicopter was shot down in the Stormberg Mountains about forty kilometers north of Steenfontein. Our aircraft are attacking and are receiving return fire. This would appear to be a major contact."

Instantly alert, Horii rose and allowed Watanabe to dress him. Calling up his electronic map, he tapped the touchpad to focus in on the valley where the helicopter went down, carefully studying its contours. "Has Captain Yanagita discovered the problem with our reconnaissance drones?"

"I regret that he is still researching the matter, honored Admiral." Watanabe pointed excitedly to the map. "We have intercepted signals from individuals moving around the valley there. Colonel Uno has two companies waiting to board transports. We could easily block both exits and land troops along the ridges to trap Vereshchagin's forces, but if we delay, they will escape."

"Do we have pilots overflying this valley?"

"Yes, Admiral."

"Let me see it."

Surprised, Watanabe hastened to make the arrangements with the aviation company commander. A few minutes later, he splashed the image from one helicopter's camera eye onto the admiral's electronic map.

"Heavily forested," Horii grunted.

"But there are good landing zones along the ridge line and

on the valley floor, honored Admiral," Watanabe responded. "May I give Colonel Uno your approval?"

"A good swordsman intuitively sees the origin of every real action, Watanabe," Horii said inflexibly. He pointed. "What is that? There, on the side of the mountain."

"I do not know, honored Admiral."

"That is an old lava flow on the side of a volcano, Watanabe. Perhaps it is not such an old one. Some volcanoes build up pressure inside until a weak place bursts and then spew out gases or superheated mud. Such flows can travel at 120 kilometers an hour, faster than men can run. Tell Colonel Uno to stand down. Have the warships attack instead."

"Honored Admiral?"

"It is a trap. If there is a volcano on this continent that Vereshchagin can cause to erupt with the proper explosives, it is this one, Watanabe. This is the origin of his action."

Watanabe folded his hands and bowed. "Yes, Admiral."

"Both a low spirit and an elevated spirit are weak, Watanabe. You should not rush in at your enemy's first movement, nor should you flinch from him. You defeat an enemy in battle by knowing his timing and using a timing that he does not expect. That is the lesson you should learn from this."

"Yes, Admiral."

"Tell Colonel Uno that he may send a survey party with instruments to determine the condition of the volcano in a few days if he wishes."

When evening fell, Watanabe made one final check on Horii before retiring and found the admiral in a contemplative mood.

"Look at the starlight, Watanabe! Isn't it beautiful? What strange constellations!"

"Honored Admiral, Colonel Sumi is still waiting to see you. He wishes to discuss taking hostages from the populace."

"I will see him in a few moments."

"I will tell him this. May I turn on the lights?"

"No."

"Honored Admiral, surely you shouldn't sit here in the dark," Watanabe urged, the same way he coaxed Horii to eat when the admiral was in a foul mood.

Horii chuckled. "I was nearly killed in this room. What would happen if watchers outside could see inside?"

Watanabe rushed to the window and peered out. "The Life-guards have two platoons on that ridge there," he said, pointing. "Surely there is no danger. If there is, you should be moved!"

"There is no danger. If I were killed, Colonel Sumi would take my place. If Sumi were killed, Colonel Uno would do so; and if he were killed, Colonel Enomoto would do so. They would take actions against the civilian population that Vereshchagin wishes to avoid. Vereshchagin knows this."

"I am not certain that I understand. The civilian population provides the water in which Vereshchagin swims. Wouldn't attacking them be a good idea?"

"The proverb is, 'When the lips are destroyed, the teeth are cold.' I do not agree, Watanabe. Destroying the will of the people to resist will cripple him, but merely attacking them will only defeat them superficially. We must penetrate to the depths and extinguish their spirit."

Horii rose leisurely and walked over by the window. "Colonel Sumi is developing a ferocious hatred for this world and its people, which perhaps blinds him. One cannot hate and be a good soldier, Watanabe. It weakens one's spirit. Hatred is something that belongs to living persons. The way of war means choosing death whenever there is a choice between life and death. Once you have become accustomed to death, you can keep your spirit correct and pass through life without possibility of failure."

"I admit that I have been worried by the disharmony between you and Colonel Sumi," Watanabe said, expressing what most of Horii's officers felt, but few dared voice.

"If a carpenter knows the strengths and weaknesses of his workmen and their tools cut well, he should deploy them so that the finished work turns out well. It is the same with soldiers. A commander must know the abilities and weaknesses of his men. I know Colonel Sumi's strengths and weaknesses and intend to use him to best advantage." Horii turned away from the window. "What do my technicians say about the Hummingbirds that crashed themselves?"

"They still profess themselves mystified, Admiral. They have grounded all such aircraft and are wondering whether this could be a manufacturing flaw."

"That is nonsense, Watanabe. Tell them that I demand answers."

"I will do so, honored Admiral. Also, Colonel Enomoto reports that he has identified Lieutenant-Colonel Ebyl's body."

"Please tell Colonel Enomoto that it is my express desire to have the body buried with appropriate honors." Horii's tone of voice made it clear that the disposition of Ebyl's body was not open to further discussion. "Are there other matters?"

"One other, honored Admiral." Watanabe fumbled with his notecase and produced a document. "Matsudaira-san has been interrogating his employees and has information which he believes to be of importance, as well as a plan of operation that he wishes to suggest to you."

"Matsudaira-san believes whatever his employees tell him. I find this humorous." There was too little light in the room to read Matsudaira's missive, so Horii let it fall into a wastebasket. "Tomorrow, please remind me to compose a suitable reply thanking him for his efforts."

"May I fetch Colonel Sumi, now?"

"Yes. Do so."

As Watanabe turned to leave, he noticed a woven object rolled up in the corner, and curiosity got the better of him. "Honored Admiral, what is this?"

"Lieutenant-Colonel Vereshchagin's *ryijy* carpet. I am returning it to him. Recall that it has sentimental value."

"Honored Admiral, he is an enemy!" Watanabe protested.

"Of course, Watanabe, but an honored one." Again, Horii looked out the window into a darkness misted by the halos of the spaceport's lights. "He was an Imperial officer before you were born. He remembers a different Imperial system. He was born Japanese in another life—of this, I am sure. More than anyone else, I believe that he understands that in some ways Earth is too far away from us to matter. A few weeks ago, he asked me politely what difference it would make to Earth if Matsudaira got what he demanded. The same metals would go to Earth in the same ships, and nearly the same finished goods would be shipped here. The only difference would be in the cost to the people living here. Matsudaira-san cannot understand this way of thinking, unfortunately. You must honor the spirit of your enemies, Watanabe. The *ryijy* is a small matter."

"I am not sure that I understand," Watanabe said, disturbed by the admiral's bizarre humor.

"Remember, Watanabe, that I know Anton Vereshchagin. I was a lieutenant in the Third Lifeguards Battalion on Cyclade, and Vereshchagin was a major. Time differential has altered things between us as you see. On Cyclade, some young Lifeguards officers were frivolous."

Horii waited a moment so that Watanabe would make the comparison with his own young officers. "These officers did not take the way of war seriously. The rebels there, the Provisionals, understood this. With no real strength, they destroyed one Lifeguards company and part of another. Major Vereshchagin was brought in to explain to us the nature of war. In this way, our fates have become entwined." He turned. "That is all, Watanabe."

When Sumi entered a few moments later, Horii said, "Colonel Sumi, I understand you wish to further discuss taking Afrikaner cultural leaders as hostages."

"Yes, honored Admiral," Sumi replied politely, impatient with delay and prepared to argue the point.

"I concur. Please issue the necessary orders to have two or three hundred selected persons taken into preventive detention to ensure proper behavior from the population."

As Sumi left, Horii once again lost himself in contemplation of the night sky.

During the night, Sumi's blacklegs fanned out to detain every Afrikaner identifiable as a community leader, using the master population list taken from Vereshchagin's data base. Problems developed immediately as the security policemen were unable to find the persons in question at the addresses listed for them in the central data base. In some instances, they were unable to find the addresses themselves.

New lists and frenzied discussions failed to resolve this. Blackleg patrols brought in people, but it rapidly became apparent that few, if any, of these people were the cultural leaders that Sumi wanted.

Part of the problem was identified when one sharp-eyed corporal noticed that one address on a printout did not match the same address on a printout made several hours before. After several hours of tests, it became apparent to Horii's computer technicians that data in files copied from Vereshchagin's data base was literally migrating from file to file. The technicians' elation rapidly turned to confusion when they discovered that data was migrating from files which had not been copied from Vereshchagin's data base.

Wednesday(316)

HORII FOUND OUT ABOUT THE COMPUTER GLITCH AT BREAKFAST, which put him in an exceedingly foul mood by the time Captain Yanagita came to report progress.

Yanagita saluted. Then he bowed. "Honored Admiral, we have uncovered the problem which caused our Hummingbirds to crash. It would appear that the central data base has been infected with a computer virus."

Yanagita looked and felt awful, having been up all night with the computer techs.

"Is this perhaps the problem which induced Colonel Sumi's security policemen to detain two sixteen-year-old boys as leading citizens of the community last night?" Horii demanded.

Blacklegs were not selected for their intelligence, and a number of Sumi's patrols had chosen to believe the printouts they were given rather than what their eyes told them.

Before Yanagita could respond, Horii snapped, "How was this done, Yanagita?"

Yanagita shifted his feet uncomfortably. "It would appear that when we copied data from Lieutenant-Colonel Vereshchagin's data base, we also copied the virus, which recopied itself into data files and executed operations to corrupt data and programs. It is very sophisticated. Whoever created it knew our systems well enough to evade our controls."

"Of course they did. Vereshchagin uses an earlier version of the same program." Horii turned his back.

"Regrettably, the virus allowed Vereshchagin entry into our systems, which permitted him to issue commands, such as the one which caused our Hummingbirds to crash themselves. We are indeed fortunate that we uncovered this problem before he was able to cause more extensive damage," Yanagita said, fervently wishing that someone else had been tasked with reporting this to the admiral.

"Are our backup files corrupt?"

"There is a distinct possibility that many of them have been contaminated as well," Yanagita admitted.

"So—Vereshchagin possesses more accurate information about our forces than we do."

"Our technicians have uncovered the enemy program, honored Admiral. Even as we speak, they are eliminating it from the system!"

"You fool," Horii hissed.

"Admiral?"

"Pick up the telephone and call them. Immediately."

The intelligence officer did as he was bade. A moment later, his face turned ashen. He held his hand over the receiver. "Admiral, every data base has been erased."

"Quite predictable, I assure you," Horii said coldly. "Please deal with the situation. And Yanagita—please be exceedingly careful with the backup data, given the skill that Colonel Vereshchagin's personnel have thus far displayed."

The young officer saluted and bowed, twice. He left the room visibly shaken.

When the door closed, Horii turned to his aide, Captain Watanabe. "There was a Greek legend of a wooden horse, and we appear to have taken one in. Shall we talk of poetry?"

A few moments later, the telephone rang. Watanabe answered it. He turned to Horii. "Admiral, the Third Manchurian Battalion reports that their mine fields appear to have activated themselves and cannot be disarmed. They have incurred two casualties."

Horii's mouth gaped. "It never occurred to me. How utterly ingenuous! What an exquisite touch."

His aide stared, uncomprehending.

"When we uncovered Colonel Vereshchagin's virus, it activated our mine fields at the same time it erased our data. Colonel Vereshchagin has able programmers. Please inform Colonel Sumi that he is to discontinue his efforts to bring in Afrikaner notables and refrain from initiating other operations. Inform Captain Yanagita that within the hour I wish to know what other damage this virus may have caused. Then see that I am not disturbed."

Seeing the look in Horii's eyes, Watanabe hastened to obey.

Thursday(316)

OPERATING IN THE VICINITY OF JOHANNESBURG, SUBLIEUTENANT JAN Snyman's platoon executed a textbook daylight ambush on a Manchurian convoy that no one on Horii's staff had thought to reschedule. In slightly less than five minutes, they destroyed a dozen trucks and most of the light attack platoon escorting them.

When an elaborate search and sensor scan of the area failed to uncover Snyman's men, Colonel Sumi ordered the Manchurians to burn the ten houses closest to the ambush site.

Horii remained in seclusion while his forces marked time. Meals left outside his door remained untouched. At dusk, Horii's staff sent Watanabe to remonstrate with him.

Entering the room timidly, Watanabe found Horii seated cross-legged, lost in reflection. After a few moments, Horii noticed his presence.

"Oh, it is you, Watanabe. Come sit."

"Honored Admiral, your loyal staff wishes—"

"I said sit, Watanabe. I did not say talk."

Watanabe sat. Finally, Horii deigned to speak. "The movements of large numbers of men are easy to predict, but the thoughts of one man are not. Vereshchagin is not given to quixotic gestures. He strikes shrewd blows that appear aimless. He must have prepared a plan that would allow him to succeed. I cannot, however, think of such a plan." He cocked his head. "What has Sumi done in my absence?"

"Colonel Sumi has obeyed your order to refrain from initiating new operations. He has attempted to make contact with members of the New Auspices party."

"The Imperial-lovers. What of it?"

"He regrets that his efforts have met with less success than one might otherwise hope. It appears that Vereshchagin has circulated details of the payments he made to the party's leaders. Neighbors of party members have induced most of them to renounce the party. Only a few members have taken refuge in our caserns. While Colonel Sumi plans to use them as penetration agents, he concedes that Vereshchagin will easily counter this move."

Horii grunted. "They are useless. How ironic that the only purpose the party served was to identify and neutralize potential Imperial agents." He again lost himself in thought.

Watanabe took a deep breath. "Honored Admiral, perhaps Lieutenant-Colonel Vereshchagin planned this result."

"Hmm? That is a disquieting notion."

"Consider, honored admiral, that he continued to fund the party long after its uselessness was manifest," Watanabe said doggedly.

"Possibly. Possibly. I wonder when Vereshchagin first conceived this mutiny of his?" Horii mused, stroking his chin. "I wonder if he has somehow become aware of conditions on Earth."

"He might also have heard about the incident on Esdraelon. His battalion has numerous ties to that planet."

"It is just possible that Vereshchagin has been maturing a plan in secret for a lengthy period of time. Even so, how does he expect to win?" Horii thought for a moment and then gasped. "I wonder—it is just possible."

"What is it, sir?" Watanabe asked, agitated.

"Have Captain Yanagita report to me at once. I wish to know whether it is possible that any corvettes survived the destruction of the frigate *Graf Spee*."

Hours later, Yanagita found the answer in records of personnel returned to Earth on USS freighters and brought it to Horii.

"Honored Admiral, it appears that one corvette survived, the corvette *Ajax*," Yanagita said stiffly with one eye on Colonel Sumi.

"Where is it?" Horii asked, then waved his hand diffidently. "It does not matter. It could be hiding anywhere in the system."

"But honored Admiral, where would he find a crew?" Yanagita exclaimed.

"The corvette is not in orbit. Therefore, he has managed to train men capable of moving it out of orbit. Observe, Yanagita, how carefully Lieutenant-Colonel Vereshchagin plans. It is an exquisite plan he has composed, neh?"

"I deeply regret my inability to comprehend." Yanagita bowed low. "I am ashamed by my unworthiness."

"I would not expect you to understand," Horii said, enjoying Yanagita and Sumi's disquiet. "In his career, Lieutenant-Colonel Vereshchagin has shown a proclivity for swift, decisive action. He has a corvette, but even with the element of surprise, a corvette cannot hope to successfully engage three corvettes and a frigate. Even if the Afrikaners have provided him with nuclear weapons, Vereshchagin does not have a delivery system capable of striking a warship. How then can he hope to meet with success?"

Yanagita looked at Sumi helplessly.

"If our warships spotted an enemy corvette, what would they do? They would group together for mutual support and then attack. You will observe, Yanagita, that some of the attacks that Afrikaners made during the rebellion were suicidal in nature. I assume Vereshchagin could find other such Afrikaners."

"Divine wind!" Yanagita mouthed, awestruck.

"Precisely. Unfortunately, Lieutenant-Colonel Vereshchagin erred in leaving soldiers behind at two mines and the ocean tap, allowing me to discern the details of his plan." Horii paced the floor.

"When our warships mass to subject Vereshchagin's corvette to superior firepower, it will ram the frigate *Maya*, with its fusion bottle cycled to critical mass and presumably with one or more small atomic weapons fused to detonate. The resulting explosion would eliminate all of our warships, a suitable application of Chaos Theory, wouldn't you think, Yanagita?"

"But we would still have a superiority in ground forces," Yanagita protested.

"How unfortunate for Lieutenant-Colonel Vereshchagin that you are not his opponent, Yanagita," Horii said, baiting his unfortunate subordinate. "Vereshchagin has carefully hoarded aircraft and has attacked our aircraft at every opportunity. His strategy has been to encourage us to disperse our forces chasing phantoms so that when his corvette strikes, his aircraft can suddenly seize command of the air. With command of the air and the positions of our scattered forces known, Vereshchagin would be in a position to defeat us in detail. Recognizing his stratagem, we will of course take actions to counter it. Nevertheless, his plan is quite brilliant."

"How will we do this, honored Admiral?" Yanagita asked meekly.

"The volume of space where Vereshchagin's corvette can hide is too vast for us to seek it out without leaving our own forces open to attack from space. I will, of course, issue orders to ensure that our warships maintain distance from each other and are prepared to destroy the intruder when it appears. As for Vereshchagin, we can easily forestall him by finding his hidden headquarters swiftly and crushing him."

"I understand, honored Admiral," Yanagita said, bowing.

"See that you do, Yanagita. Work with Colonel Sumi's security forces. I wish to have Vereshchagin found," Horii said. "You are dismissed."

Bowing low, Yanagita hurried off.

"Colonel Sumi," Horii said.

Sumi spoke for the first time. "Yes, honored Admiral."

"When you are fighting, and there are obstructions so that it is difficult to cut your opponent, you must stab him at his heart with the necessary spirit," Horii observed. "Lieutenant-Colonel Vereshchagin has purposefully taken up a position in which I find it difficult to cut at him. I need information. You wished to take hostages. Begin doing so, three or four hundred, men and women at random. No more than one from any single family."

Sumi swallowed the implied rebuke. "I will have the hostages interrogated as soon as they are brought in, honored Admiral. Anything that they know, I will know."

Horii waved a cautionary finger. "I appreciate your zeal, Colonel, but I have a different thought. Please do not interrogate the hostages. Instead, please stress personally to each of your officers and men that I wish them treated with extreme politeness."

Horii went on to explain his thought, and the frown on Sumi's face turned to delight.

By midnight, Sumi's blacklegs had pulled in several hundred hostages. He began posting their names in lists of fifty.

Friday(316)

HANNA BRUWER SEARCHED HER HUSBAND'S FACE. STRAIN AND lack of sleep had etched itself into lines. "Something is very wrong," she said, reading him accurately. "What is it?"

"Admiral Horii found the worm we embedded in his computer yesterday."

"The worm?"

"We knew that Horii would want to copy our data bases, so we buried a surprise inside—it was Timo Haerkoennen's idea. Heaven knows why Timo stays with us considering the money he could make on the outside. I asked him once. He says he likes the food."

Sanmartin shoved his hands into his pockets in an unmilitary fashion. "Horii is showing himself to be a very good chess player. He's going to chip away at our pawns while he waits for us to make a mistake. And if we do, we die." He grinned mirthlessly. "I was hoping that we could coax him into running an operation before he got his systems scrubbed out—we could have really screwed with his tactical radios—but he's patient. I'm beginning to think that we ought to try and kill him, but if we do, Sumi takes over, and I'm sure he'd do a Nanking."

Bruwer shook her head to indicate that she did not understand. "What is a 'Nanking'?"

"Sumi would send a battalion or two into Pretoria and Jo'burg to rape and murder in the hope that we'll either get ourselves slaughtered trying to stop him, or surrender and get ourselves shot."

Bruwer shut her eyes. "What kind of man is he?"

"A fanatic. A nasty one. Truth is, if Horii thought for a moment that the trick would work against Anton, he'd do it, too. The difference between Horii and Sumi is that Sumi would try it even if he didn't think it would work." He shrugged. "Horii's soldiers are inexperienced right now, but the ones who live long enough are going to get very good very quickly. If we can hang on for a few weeks, we have a few things to try, and if they work, we win. If they don't, we get to see who runs out of soldiers first."

"Attrition."

"Attrition. We've got to be ready for a long war." He began speaking to himself. "If you're not the Iceman, or the crazies in number two platoon who don't understand complicated concepts like fear, you say, 'All of my friends are going to die.' And you want to stay to keep them alive until you realize that death is random and that you're going to die, too, sooner or later. Then you get careless."

She touched his arm. "What happened this morning, Raul?"

"A skirmish. *Maya* found a section of one of the reserve platoons. Horii's ships destroyed a half-kilometer's worth of forest to get them. Someone made a mistake, I suppose. Or maybe Horii's intelligence people put enough puzzle pieces together."

"Who was it?" Bruwer asked, understanding.

"Two retirees from C Company who came back for one war too many. Plus one of my former students."

"Why do we human beings do such things to each other? What kind of responsibility must the people who steal young lives bear? I cannot think about such things without thinking about God, and God commanded us to love."

Sanmartin made an effort to turn it into a joke. "As Hans would say, 'Four things greater than all things are, women and horses and power and war.' "

A furrow appeared between Bruwer's brows. "Hans has never seen a horse in his life."

"I know. And he hasn't done very well with women," Sanmartin said, which struck him for the moment as the funniest thing and he began laughing hollowly. "Anyway," he finished, "it's going to get worse from here on out."

"Why?" she asked, suddenly frightened and suspicious.

"Sumi's blacklegs began taking hostages last night. No rhyme or reason to it. He's putting up lists of fifty names of people he intends to execute in a week. To get a name off the list, someone has to give Imperial Intelligence a piece of useful information that checks out. Then, of course, Sumi takes a name off and puts someone else's name on instead. Nasty little idea. I wonder who dreamed it up."

"Fifty people each day? My God."

"The question is which fifty people. People are already beginning to bend over backward to ransom their family members off those lists. If enough of them bend, the names on those lists are going to start turning over several times a day, and eventually Horii is going to be able to put together enough seemingly unimportant scraps to massacre us." Sanmartin frowned. "I talked to Albert. He's prepared to prosecute anyone who gives out information, although I doubt whether Admiral Horii will be considerate enough to tell Albert who to prosecute."

"How do we tell frightened people that they cannot try to save their own family members?"

"Particularly when Admiral Horii's people will very likely take pains to reassure them that the information they provide is harmless. Maybe we can't, but enough tiny clues—what we bought, who did some of the work, the names of our soldiers—and Horii will fry us."

Sanmartin grasped his wife's hand tightly. "I can tell you what we tell every recruit, which is that military operations require *maskirovka*, deception, to succeed. A campaign of deception has to be *ubeditel'nyi* and *pravopodobnyi*, persuasive and plausible—something the enemy is predisposed to believe. And it has to be *rasnoobraznye*, varied, so that every conduit carries the enemy the same message. And finally, it has to have *nepreryvnost*, continuity, and *svoevremennost*, timeliness, so that it climaxes at the appropriate moment. We're not ready. We're badly outnumbered and badly outgunned, and I can already feel our mask starting to slip."

"You are afraid that these lists will kill us," she said, reading him. "How do we stop this?"

"I don't know. Neither does Albert, and neither does Anton. We'll take reprisals, but Horii knows that we'll run out of Japanese employees of USS long before he runs out of Afrikaners." He released her wrist before his fingers left marks. "I don't know."

ONE NAME ON THE FIRST LIST BELONGED TO ASSEMBLYMAN MARTIN Hatting's press secretary, Niccoline De Klerk, who was also his mistress. Hatting was one of the new assemblymen who had not been evacuated, largely because no one could locate him the night that Sumi attempted to arrest Beyers.

After struggling with his conscience for several hours, Hatting called in and spoke with a very agreeable intelligence sergeant for several minutes, providing the man with a fictitious name. Hatting was just congratulating himself on getting Niccoline off the list in return for information of no value when

Captain Yanagita and several blacklegs appeared at the door of the house where he was hiding.

"Heer Hatting, may I come in?" Yanagita said ingratiatingly.

"How did you find me?" Hatting croaked.

"Yesterday, we built up a nice little voice library from the television station's file tapes. When the computer told us that it was you, we traced your call. Admiral Horii has listened to several of your speeches."

The latter comment was a polite lie, but Yanagita was confident that Admiral Horii would convert it into truth by the time he returned. He patted Hatting on the shoulder. "Admiral Horii is looking forward to meeting with you."

Numbly, Hatting allowed himself to be led away.

By nightfall, after speaking with Horii and with Niccoline De Klerk, Hatting had allowed himself to be persuaded to become president of an Imperial "Republic of Suid-Afrika." As Horii had repeatedly assured him, it was best for his people if someone was prepared to accept the inevitable.

In his first television address, "President" Hatting laid stress on the benefits of a "homogeneous cultural and racial heritage" that both Afrikaners and Japanese enjoyed.

Saturday(316)

IN THE COURSE OF THE AFTERNOON, ONE DESPERATE MOTHER COMpromised a member of Vereshchagin's reserve reconnaissance platoon, and a schoolteacher identified a bunker complex near Johannesburg. Although guilt-stricken, the teacher contacted the wife of a member of one of the reserve platoons to keep anyone from using it.

Captain Yanagita's intelligence staff also spoke with two men who had worked on hollowing out Vereshchagin's caverns under the mountains. While they were able to say something about the construction, the crews had been flown out for one month at a time and had no idea where the sites were located.

Although the initial results from his hostage policy were modest, Admiral Horii was quite pleased.

Sunday(317)

FOLDING HIS HANDS, CAPTAIN CHIHARU YOSHIDA WATCHED MATTI Harjalo skim his report on the impact that Horii's measures were having on the Afrikaners.

"Good job, Chiharu." Harjalo set the report aside, still mildly amused that Yoshida insisted on preparing things in writing after all these years.

Yoshida asked a question that had been bothering him. "Sir, I heard a disturbing rumor that Admiral Horii has adopted a new formation for his ships."

Harjalo nodded. "Horii's spreading his ships out. He has his freighters and transports in a loose diamond formation around *Maya*, and then he has the three corvettes in a triangle on top."

"Does this mean that he suspects?"

"Yes, he knows we have a ship."

"This will make it difficult for us," Yoshida said, outwardly calm.

"A classic understatement. Sorry you threw in with us?"

"Duty is never easy."

"I understand Louis Snyman was taken hostage today. I know he was a friend of yours. I'm sorry."

"Thank you. Yes, it is a great pity, although it was perhaps inevitable that he would be selected." Beneath Yoshida's imperturbable demeanor lay an indefinable sadness. "A few weeks ago, he offered to baptize me. I regret that I did not agree. It would have given him great pleasure."

"You'd make a good Christian, Chiharu." Harjalo tapped Yoshida's report with a finger. "Does this mean what I think it means?"

"Yes. The morale of the Afrikaners is crumbling steadily."

HORII WATCHED JULES AFANOU THROUGH SLITTED EYES. THE gaunt, dark-skinned sect leader and his followers lived a simple life along the middle reaches of the De Witte River, but he was clearly no simpleton. Indeed, Horii reflected, he understood the art of "belly language" as well as any Japanese.

The cultists were Suid-Afrika's first settlers. Over the years, the original five sects had fragmented into a dozen or more. Their military power was negligible, but from generations of occupation, they knew the back country between the Drakensberg Mountains and the north coast better than any of Suid-Afrika's other inhabitants, and this knowledge was a form of power. One of the few cultists willing to deal with "gentiles," Jules Afanou led one sect and had close ties to the leaders of several others, which made him eminently worth cultivating.

"We have many, many aircraft such as the one we sent to pick you up," Horii said, making a show of impressing his visitor.

Afanou waved his hand negligently. "In the eyes of the One, the Creator of all, such things are trifles. Only men and the reverence in their hearts matter."

"Yes. It is in matters of the spirit that Japanese have always excelled."

"Do Japanese truly believe in the Spirit? I had not known this," Afanou exclaimed.

Sensing an opening in Afanou's guard, Horii responded resolutely, "Of a certainty."

"All within the Spirit are brothers. The Afrikaners are not people of the Spirit, yet there are a few men among them that are of goodwill. My heart would be troubled if a dark fate befell them," Afanou said cautiously, exposing his interest.

Horii probed delicately, certain that Sumi had swept into his net a few men that Afanou had reason to want released. "Obviously, we would wish to cherish such men."

Afanou lowered his head. "May the Spirit fill them."

"Unfortunately, we lack knowledge possessed by ones who have lived here all of their lives."

"May the Spirit grant you wisdom," Afanou intoned piously.

"I have heard that at times, Afrikaners have taken up arms against your people," Horii said to prolong the game. "And of a village called New Zion."

During the years when USS's authority was crumbling into anarchy, a secret faction among the Afrikaners had released plagues to devastate the crops the cultists depended upon and encouraged Afrikaner commandos to raid the sect villages. At New Zion, the Bothaville commando had herded the people into a shed and turned them into human torches.

For a moment, Afanou's eyes blazed. "Although all of us are brothers and sisters in the Spirit, one of my father's sons died at New Zion, and several of my father's daughters died in the Starvation Time. May the Spirit grant them justice!"

His people called the trail they had taken across the roadless Stormberg Mountains "The Path of Unnumbered Tears."

Horii drank a little of the sake that Afanou had politely refused. "I would desire to know this land better. Its people. Its paths." He paused. "It is rumored that you know these paths well."

"Once, I did. I have walked the land these many years."

"Could you find them on a map, perhaps?"

"A map? I do not understand such things," the sect leader said serenely. "Lines on a piece of paper mean nothing to me. In the mountains, the paths change as the Spirit wills; when the waters flow or the mud slides down the hillsides, then perhaps the paths lead nowhere at all. And the mountains have many names; my people call them by one name and the lowlanders by others. Once I knew these paths, these mountains. If you wish to find something, perhaps my feet could show you. But who can ever truly know land that belongs to other men?"

Horii smiled, catlike, and leaned forward with anticipation. "Who can truly possess land? The Spirit that touches all things can decree a different owner in an instant. Yet, if this were to occur, how would we know that your feet would not deceive you, that perhaps they might deliver us into the hands of evil men?"

Afanou folded his arms. "My son came with me. If my feet were to lead men of yours falsely, it would be fitting for him to die."

Afanou's son was waiting outside, as patient as the native people Horii had seen in the hills of Luzon. A slender youth with bushy hair so different from Afanou's own, he was dressed in clean but ragged clothing with a metal pencil incongruously stuck behind his ear.

Now, it was time for the bargaining to begin in earnest. In Horii's view, it would be entirely fitting for the Afrikaners to reap full measure of the crop they had sown, and whatever he promised Afanou would undoubtedly elicit a pleasurable amount of whimpering from Matsudaira.

A FEW HOURS LATER, PAUL HENKE COLLAPSED AND IN THE DARKness had to be flown out of the Drakensberg Mountains in a valley-hopping Sparrow.

Monday(317)

VERESHCHAGIN GREETED HARJALO OVER MORNING TEA, WHICH was put out by custom an hour before dawn even though dawn was moderately irrelevant beneath the roots of the Stormbergs.

Reading the set of Harjalo's shoulders, he asked quietly, "What is wrong, Matti?"

"This is an awkward time to bring this up, but I think Paul has lost it."

"Do you know why he keeled over yet?"

"Natasha thinks it's mostly from lack of food and lack of sleep. Paul hasn't said."

"I will take care of it, Matti," Vereshchagin said in a soft voice.

"What else is going on?"

"Well, I have a note here from a woman who claims that God sends her messages and wants her to relay one to us," Vereshchagin said with a deadpan expression. "I had to explain that we could only receive instructions from higher authorities through the proper chain of command, and advised her to write to Albert."

Harjalo ran his fingers through his hair as he tried to keep the grin off his face.

"How are we fixed for personnel?" Vereshchagin asked him.

"I commissioned the four extra Cadillacs we had stored away and put them under a captain of Ebyl's named Ohlrogge—you've met him. Ohlrogge's boys are manning three, and I gave Mikhail Remmar the fourth."

Remmar was a former rifleman with a prosthetic knee. "Where did you find a crew for Mikhail?" Vereshchagin asked, engaging half of his mind.

"I didn't. He found one for himself. His wife and her cousin. Or is it her cousine? I forget whether English differentiates between genders." Harjalo eyed Vereshchagin speculatively, daring him to question his action. "Marie is a better driver than Mikhail will ever be, and her cousin is a natural marksman—you wouldn't believe her reflexes. You should see her on a video game."

"I will not criticize you, Matti. If they have the necessary skills, well, it is their planet, too."

MUSIC ECHOED IN THE VAST NATURAL AMPHITHEATER FORMED BY C Company's cavern as Letsukov softly played the piano that his admirers had somehow contrived to bring along and secrete in a side passage. Hans Coldewe stopped to admire. "What are you playing?"

"Oh, whatever the boys ask for. Remember?" Letsukov ran

his fingers up and down the keyboard in a rapid glissando. "You said, 'Them that pays the fiddler, gets to call the tune.' "

"I think I was quoting something," Coldewe admitted, momentarily taken aback.

Letsukov smiled slyly. "It's all right, sir."

"What is this? Your third war, Dmitri?"

Letsukov fingered the keys for an instant and stopping playing. "Fourth." He gave Coldewe a look out of the corner of his eye. "You know, sir, war is like Wagner. It's loud and it lasts too long, and you can only smoke during intermissions."

For a moment, even the normal bustle of business ceased in the cavern's still air. "Matti is right," Coldewe said, half to himself. "We are crazy."

A few of the boys had already built a papier mâché wall to hide Letsukov's piano so that it could be recovered in the event that the Drakensberg caverns were compromised. When Coldewe thought about it, it cheered him to think that they were that confident.

AS A BONA FIDE PATIENT, PAUL HENKE WAS ENTITLED TO A REAL bed, and Vereshchagin sat down on the edge of it, balancing a cup and saucer and a plate. "No, don't get up, Paul. I brought you tea and a sandwich."

The Hangman looked up and nodded, the lines worn into the corners of his taut face showing clearly. "I was just resting. I will be out of here in a few hours."

"Eat something. Otherwise you are not going anywhere." Vereshchagin said, deliberately forcing Henke to stretch. As Henke grasped the saucer, his hand trembled violently, spilling tea over the edge of the cup.

"Excuse me, Anton," he said awkwardly.

Letting Henke grasp the cup, Vereshchagin took the saucer away and put the sandwich in Henke's other hand. "Paul, we know what the problem is."

Henke's voice struck a note of false cheer. "Oh, it is nothing, Anton. A little nerves. I have seen the doctor."

"Paul," Vereshchagin said quietly, "in this battalion, we do not lie to each other, or even to ourselves. I have spoken to the doctor. You are not eating or sleeping, and you are drinking too much—"

"Very little!" the Hangman said forcefully.

"Perhaps in an abstract sense, but you are drinking more than you ever have, which is very much too much for you,

Paul." He rested one hand on Henke's shoulder. "Paul, we have been through a great deal together, but there is a breaking point for each of us. You are perhaps the best officer I have ever known, and you are my friend, but you cannot command a company if you cannot command trust, both from me and from the people you lead." Beneath his hand, he felt Henke shake violently. "I need an operations officer desperately, and there is no one better."

"A few days' rest, perhaps. I admit I have missed a few meals."

"Paul, these are symptoms. They are not the problem," Vereshchagin said as gently as he could.

After a moment or two, Henke stopped trembling. "Am I really cracked, then?" He said wistfully. "Funny, I would have resented that from anyone else."

Vereshchagin nodded. "I know, Paul. We are all a little mad, I think, but one must have moderation in all things. Tell me, is Sergei Okladnikov ready for a company?"

"He will do." The Hangman ruminated. "Will I have to see a psychiatrist?"

"You should try. Also, Dr. Solchava has been threatening to teach me how to meditate to relieve stress. We can try this together."

"What will the men say when they find out that you have an insane operations officer?" Henke asked with one piece of his mind.

"It will merely confirm what they had believed for years."

A few moments later, after Henke fell asleep, Vereshchagin straightened his whitened hair and left him in Solchava's care.

Solchava allowed him to take on light work late that afternoon after she watched him eat a real supper. Together with Battalion Sergeant Yuri Malinov, who could work five or six hours without excessive pain, Henke began adding detail to the plan that Vereshchagin had been contemplating.

UNDER COVER OF THE OVERNIGHT RAIN, A ROVING PLATOON OF armored cars from the Imperial Ninth Light Attack Battalion engaged two D Company Cadillacs, one mounting a 90mm main gun and the other a 30mm gun, as they were moving to a new hiding place. In the darkness, quick gunnery allowed the D Company vehicles to get off the first shots. The 30mm shells from the lead vehicle did no harm; the 90mm shell from the second struck the lead Imperial vehicle at an acute angle and scored the turret without penetrating.

Electromagnetically enhanced projectiles from two of the Imperial armored cars smashed both D Company vehicles in a matter of seconds.

Tuesday(317)

HANNA BRUWER FOUND RAUL SANMARTIN IN THE SMALL KITCHEN-ette attached to their quarters, the only luxury she had insisted on. "Raul, have you been eating my cake?"

"To tell the truth, I'm not sure." He calmly licked his fingers. "It was very good."

"I wanted to frost it." She reached up to brush the crumbs off his battle dress. "And now tell me the truth."

"If you do the politics, I'll bake."

"It's been so long—I wish there was a convection oven here." Bruwer examined her lumpy concoction. "I hope it won't disappoint Hendricka."

"No, she'll be excited. With enough icing, she'll never notice."

"Don't be sure. She asked me yesterday whether good kittens go to heaven. One cannot lie to a child. I told her the truth. Dogs, perhaps—but cats, never."

Apparently unable to believe that their quarry had escaped, Sumi's blacklegs had spent hours with sensors in Beyers's house. Thomas's men, creeping back in, found Hendricka's kitten in the sock drawer with its head beaten in. Hanna's kylix, the last of the things she had brought from Earth, was smashed beyond mending.

Sanmartin looked at her oddly. "Why are you baking a cake? Did I forget a birthday or something?"

"No, you did not forget a birthday," she said, not meeting his eyes. "Tell me, did our radio messages do anything to halt this trading of information for hostages?"

"No. It didn't," Sanmartin said, suddenly frightened.

She put her arms around his neck. "I thought of something I could do that might stop it."

"No," he said, understanding her. "Nobody's asking you to. We need you here."

"You need me there more." She let him hold her. "The people don't understand. They think that soldiers fight wars, and that they are somehow insulated."

"The ones who were out on that human chain and in the cities know better."

"No. You are wrong."

"That's not true!" Sanmartin shouted, his reserve finally cracking.

"It is, Raul. It is," she said very softly. "If I offer myself as a hostage, perhaps then they will understand."

"Damn them. Every one of them."

"There are things that you, or the Iceman, or the Hangman cannot do. These are my people, and I am what Albert and Anton and my grandfather, and yes, even you, have made me. I am a soldier, even though I carry no gun. We cannot escape it." She touched his face. "Please, Raul. I am frightened. Please do not make this hard. I am so very frightened."

He closed his eyes. Trained by Senior Intelligence Sergeant Shimazu, both of them knew what it was like to undergo interrogation.

"Raul, I know that my way of fighting—without violence—would never work with people like Sumi and Matsudaira, but your way will not work either unless my people—all of them—understand. I have to show them."

"I hate them!"

"No, don't. Raul, please understand. Someone has to act."

"No—"

"And if somehow we come through this," she continued, "I only want one thing. I am tired—tired of being Hendrik Pienaar's granddaughter, and Madam Speaker, and Heer President's hatchet man, and the battalion executive officer's wife. For a while I only want to be Hanna, and maybe Raul's wife and Hendricka's mother. And if that requires a superextraordinary dispensation from Anton Vereshchagin or Albert Beyers or even God Almighty, well, we will have bought and paid for it."

His voice softened. "I'm sorry. I guess this hasn't been much of a marriage, has it?"

"It has been a better one than most," she said, pulling on his nose. "Remember the good times. That restaurant you took me to."

"Die Koffiehuis."

"They asked me afterward whether you meant it when you said you would burn the place down if the meal wasn't perfect."

"I probably did. I was so nervous."

"You were and I was. Here we both are nervous again. Just hold me."

He did. He asked, "Who have you talked about this with?"

"Albert and Anton." She put her fingers over his mouth. "They both agreed it was the only way. I knew if I came to you first, I would never be able to go through with it. Anton thinks that the sooner I go, the better chance we have. I won't see Hans and Katrina and Isaac, so you will have to tell them."

Once Bruwer got over the shock of meeting a "Bantu," she had come to like Isaac Wanjau very much, and she was the only person alive who called Kasha Vladimirovna by her given name, Katrina.

He began to say something and she said, "Hush! Timo knows we are not taking calls from anyone. I told him that for the next five hours, it is 'Saturday in Chubut.' "

AS SHE WAS WAITING FOR THE PLANE THAT WOULD CARRY HER OUT of the mountains, Bruwer entered two verses from the Gospels into her engagement book: "Jesus was stripped naked before his enemies, tortured, and killed," and "Father, if you are willing, take this cup away from me; still not my will but yours be done."

Raul Sanmartin had had one other girlfriend in his life, in Argentina when he was fifteen. After his mother had enrolled him in an Imperial military academy and gotten herself arrested for preaching sedition, he had written her several times. She never wrote back.

ADMIRAL HORII HEARD THAT EVENING AND IMMEDIATELY WENT TO confront Colonel Sumi. "Colonel Sumi, I understand we have captured Assembly Speaker Bruwer-Sanmartin."

"Yes, she came to protest our hostage policy. How foolish. I have begun interrogating her personally." Sumi had a bowl of rice with plum pickles in front of him, and pushed it aside, half-eaten. "She claims she has poison in her body that will allow her to die if we mistreat her too severely, but this is obviously false."

"Please discontinue interrogating her. You will discover nothing useful."

"I have been quite gentle. A few more hours—"

"She is quite unreasonable."

"Yes," Sumi finally agreed.

"Indeed," Horii mused, "it would be prudent to simply release her. Please do so."

Sumi locked eyes with Horii. "I regret that I cannot comply with your wish. She is an enemy of the nation. Regrettably, this is a security matter, not a military matter."

With ill humor, Horii let the matter drop.

Wednesday(317)

SITTING IN A METAL CHAIR IN A WAREHOUSE CONVERTED INTO A cell, Louis Snyman watched Hanna Bruwer as she moved from person to person, speaking with each of them in turn. Even from a distance, Snyman could see faint bruises on her heart-shaped face.

Sensing his eyes upon her, she came over. "Heer Snyman."

Snyman nodded. "Vroew Bruwer. Please excuse me if I do not get up."

Bruwer quirked one side of her mouth into a smile. "Yes, well, when we were discussing a woman's place, I suspect we both had something different in mind."

"How is my son?" Snyman asked, unable to conceal his anxiety.

"Jan and Natasha are both fine. Raul says that he is a fine young officer, and you will be pleased to know that he has been annoying the Manchurians."

"Thank God for this." Snyman noticed that the other hostages, most of them ordinary men and women, were listening without being obtrusive. He settled back, content. "Thank you, Vroew Bruwer. How are you feeling?"

Bruwer grimaced. "Colonel Sumi made an effort not to leave marks. He was also in something of a hurry. I suspect that I owe Admiral Horii for this." The electrical shocks had been the worst, and her hands twitched involuntarily. "Is there anything I can do for you, Heer Snyman?"

"Yes. Please get those savages to give me back my wheelchair."

"I will see what I can do."

Curiosity got the better of Snyman. "Why are you here?"

"Admiral Horii wants hostages."

"What kind of information will it take to buy your freedom, I wonder?"

Bruwer dusted off an area of the floor and sat down. "If the only thing they asked was my husband's middle name, the price would still be too high. We must stop this trade in information."

"It is trafficking with the devil."

"If it does not stop, we will lose our chance at freedom. So I came to stop it. It sounds very melodramatic coming from a woman sitting on a concrete floor, doesn't it?"

"I understand," Snyman said.

"Perhaps you do, Heer Snyman. Perhaps you do. I imagine that they will shoot us in a few days."

"It is all in God's hands."

"Yes, I know. Everything is always in God's hands."

Snyman studied her. "You meant that, didn't you? I did not know you were a woman of faith."

Bruwer smiled mischievously. "Did not Saint Paul say that women should keep silent in the churches?"

"I shall be sure to mention this in my next letter to you. You are a lot like your grandfather, you know. Why are you being so kind to me?"

"Well, Scripture does say—"

" 'If your enemy is hungry, feed him; if he is thirsty, give him something to drink; by doing so, you will heap burning ashes on his head.' " Snyman finished for her. "You know, for years I hated you and Beyers and Vereshchagin, and could not understand why God permitted the broken pieces of me to linger this way."

Snyman lifted the blanket that covered his withered legs and allowed Bruwer to see them.

"I forgot that the foolishness of God is wiser than human wisdom. Now I know that He saved me so that one Afrikaner would be spared this place. This much has been granted me. I wish you to know that I have forgiven you, and I pray that you have forgiven me."

Bruwer turned her head so that she wouldn't see the tears in Snyman's eyes. "In Ephesians, it says, 'All bitterness, fury, anger, shouting, and reviling must be removed from you, along with all malice. Be kind to one another, compassionate, forgiving one another as God has forgiven you in Christ.' " Bruwer looked around at her fellow prisoners. "Perhaps all of us would like to pray."

Several of the persons listening were released that evening. Two of them found the courage to refuse release and had to be carried out of the warehouse. As intended, the message spread.

Thursday(317)

HENKE AND MALINOV PASSED AROUND THE PLAN THEY HAD worked up. Henke confessed, "We worked in the crazy parts that Raul and Hans suggested, but there is a problem which Yuri and I have not been able to resolve, which is the Ninth Light Attack Battalion."

"In open country, their electromagnetic guns can chew us up," Harjalo commented, glancing through the plan. "And if we don't come out and challenge them, they have a hundred thousand civilian hostages. At best, we have a stalemate. At worst, we have a massacre."

Hans Coldewe said, "Maybe they'll leave if we ask politely."

The mood was tense, and no one laughed.

"ARE YOU CERTAIN, SENIOR COMMUNICATIONS SERGEANT?" ADMIral Horii's chief signal officer asked his principal subordinate.

"Watch the map, honored Major. The signals we are intercepting last approximately two seconds in duration and are repeated four times daily."

The map was tied into the network of geosynchronized surveillance satellites. Each radio signal that the Imperials locked onto as it cycled between frequencies appeared as a white cross.

"It would be very unfortunate if this turned out to be another balloon incident, Mogi," his superior cautioned.

Senior Communications Sergeant Mogi had been very excited about the signals intercepted in "Volcano Valley" until someone pointed out that all of Vereshchagin's men appeared to be traveling downwind at a steady speed.

"No, we are quite certain, honored Major. We have been plotting the movements of individuals for the last day and one half."

"Strange that Vereshchagin would have his men report in at such regular intervals. Have you been able to decrypt these signals?"

"No, honored Major. Vereshchagin appears to have made modifications to his personal radios. We are intercepting strings of numbers in a code we have not been able to crack. Nevertheless, we are able to locate over two hundred individual radios to within two hundred meters four times each day."

Suddenly, Mogi's map burst out in pinpoints of light. Brushing his hands across the controls, Mogi focused in on a heavily forested stretch of the upper Oranje Valley dotted with white crosses.

Friday(317)

AS AGREED PRIOR TO DEPARTURE, THE CORVETTE *AJAX* LEISURELY practiced an unobserved return to Suid-Afrika on the side of the planet opposite Akashi continent.

The ship's commander, Lieutenant Detlef Jankowskie, was manning sensors. "Things must have gotten interesting while we were away. There are a bunch of ships in orbit."

"I hope everything's all right. I don't know about you, but the first thing I plan to do is to eat a five-course meal in a hot tub," his first gunner, Lance-Corporal Nicolas Sery replied.

During the rebellion, when the frigate *Graf Spee* was induced to take aboard a large cube of platinum containing a fission device, *Graf Spee* and the corvettes *Achilles* and *Exeter* disappeared in the blink of an eye. Lucky *Ajax* survived. This, however, created its own difficulties.

A corvette is a short-range vessel, essentially a manned fusion bottle. Although a corvette's fusion drive could theoretically take it anywhere, it lacks the navigation instruments and the storage capacity to travel between solar systems. A frigate would normally carry up to three of them across the void.

The destruction of *Graf Spee* left *Ajax* and her crew of eight enlisted technicians and four officers in an awkward position. Although a corvette can dip lower into a planet's atmosphere than a frigate and possesses devastating firepower in the form of two missile launchers on the underside of the hull, and a ground attack laser and composite particle dispenser underneath the nose, a corvette is not intended to operate independently for any great length of time.

Making the best of the situation, Vereshchagin detailed Detlef Jankowskie and seven undersized infantrymen to form a second crew. With a degree in robotics, Jankowskie had been the least unqualified of Vereshchagin's officers. The ship's commander objected mildly, but as Vereshchagin explained, it was the first time that the Imperial Navy had managed to lose a frigate in a colonial operation, and a novel situation required a novel response.

Three years later, after Jankowskie and his "seven dwarfs"

had made themselves proficient, Vereshchagin allowed the ship's original crew to return to Earth.

Jankowskie had tried not to act surprised when Vereshchagin suggested sending *Ajax* on an exploratory cruise around the system's outer planets towing a pod with water and supplies to last the trip. Politely, Jankowskie thought that the Variag had lost his mind; when he announced the voyage to his dwarfs, they politely thought that he had lost his. Nonetheless, as Jankowskie observed in one of his infrequent reports, although privacy and creature comforts did not measure up to navy standards, for the infantry, it wasn't half bad.

"I'd like to find out what has been happening. Moushegian keeps asking me whether I think the Engineers whipped the Springboks this year. We should be close enough to check in," Jankowskie told Sery, who was manning the communications board while the primary communications specialist slept. Unlike the rigidly stratified navy, Jankowskie had insisted on crosstraining each of his men to do every job, especially his own.

"I'm ahead of you," Sery said as he made contact with a four-man communications center Vereshchagin had stuck on an island in the middle of nowhere on the planet's far side.

The reply came back, "Very good approach. The Variag says he has a dozen bottles of beer for each of you."

"What do they mean by that?" he asked Jankowskie.

Jankowskie whistled loudly. "It means all hell has broken loose. There's an Imperial task group down there to put down a rebellion that we're on the wrong end of."

"What?!"

"Hold on, there's something else coming through."

"Eighty-nine, eighty-nine, eighty-nine. Twenty-nine, twenty-nine, twenty-nine." Sery rubbed the top of his head. "What does that mean?"

Jankowskie pulled a tiny cipher book out of the pocket of the T-shirt he was wearing and began flipping through it. "It means four Imperial warships, two freighters, and two transports. They want to know if we can take them out. Reply 'eleven,' which is 'Who knows?' Nobody's ever fought a battle between warships in space. Our detection and fire-control isn't up to the job, and neither is theirs. Of course, there are four of them and only one of us."

"Eleven, it is."

A moment later, the station responded. "One-forty-seven,

one-forty-seven, one-forty-seven. Two, two, two. Why the repeat?" Sery asked.

"It would be embarrassing to have the numbers come
through garbled. Maybe a bit more than embarrassing,"
Jankowskie replied distractedly, flipping through his book. He
whistled again.

"What is it?"

"One-forty-seven is a plan, that's what it is." Jankowskie
looked at Sery directly. "It's an awfully furry one, too. Better
get everybody in here so we can talk over the whys and
wherefores of mutinying against the Imperial Government." He
added, "Two means 'We're awfully glad to see you.' "

A month or so before the Afrikaner rebellion, Detlef
Jankowskie had innocently put a rocket into what turned out to
be the second-largest ammunition dump on the planet. He
hoped that this might turn out a little less spectacular.

Saturday(317)

IN THE EARLY HOURS OF THE MORNING, ADMIRAL HORII RECEIVED
a radio message from Captain Chiharu Yoshida asking plaintively whether there was some way to compromise the differences that separated Horii from Vereshchagin.

A few moments after they finished speaking, Colonel Sumi
appeared at Horii's door. "Honored Admiral, I understand that
you have communicated with traitor Yoshida. From a security
standpoint, this gives rise to uncertainties."

Horii noted that Sumi was wearing his sword and smiled in-
wardly. "Yoshida is torn between loyalty to Vereshchagin and
his duty. He wishes to know whether there is any possibility of
compromise. Of course, there is not, but one makes use of tools.
Unfortunately for Vereshchagin, we were able to trace the location of the call to an area in the central Stormberg Mountains.
Please direct Captain Yanagita to contact Heer Afanou. Our
eyes are beginning to focus. It is necessary for us to act."

Reassured, Sumi bowed and left.

PULLING A HEAVY BOX MARKED WITH AN AMMUNITION TREFOIL
out of *Ajax*'s stores, Sery and Moushegian suited up and
hauled it out the air lock where Jankowskie was waiting for it
impatiently. Securing the box to a stanchion, they began passing its contents "up."

One of the two-meter cylinders broke free of Moushegian's grip and began drifting off in the general direction of Arcturus, which, with extreme good fortune, it might have reached in ten or twelve billion years. Cursing, Jankowskie kicked himself free of the corvette's skin and used a hook fashioned from a bent tie-rod to bring the flak missile back while his backup man watched anxiously.

Sery almost turned white as a few more projectiles tried to free themselves. Quickly, he and Moushegian regained control, dangling the missiles like flies from a safety line. Flipping on his suit-to-suit radio, he asked Moushegian, "Why do the warheads on these flipping things look nine months pregnant?"

"Because they're stuffed with a whacking great antiarmor charge, Nicolas," Jankowskie cut in. "Please save aimless questions until we get back inside."

"Sorry."

When the job was finally done, Jankowskie's dwarfs came outside to admire their handiwork in the quiet reaches of space. "We look like a Christmas tree," Moushegian complained.

From each of the corvette's four steering pylons, a fifteen-meter rod projected, hung with four flak missiles pointing backward. Connections run through the duplicate wiring in the pylons ran to an ungainly control panel mounted on the first gunner's seat.

"Want to try her out?" Jankowskie asked.

Reentering the ship, his crew took up positions, with Moushegian poised at the air lock holding a bundle of magnesium flares. At Jankowskie's command, he pulled the tab on the flares and pitched the bundle hissing into the void.

Opening up the main jet, Jankowskie moved the corvette forward. Sery manipulated his breadboarded control rig. After a moment, he said in disgust, "Abort. The pitching things have locked on to our jet, not the flares."

Jankowskie shut down the main jet. "Aborted. What now?"

Moushegian stuck his head through the access door to the bridge. "We have enough rods to stick them out another five or six meters. If that doesn't take us out of the target acquisition angle, we'll have to dismount four missiles." He shrugged. "You didn't actually expect this to work, did you, Lieutenant Detlef, sir?"

Jankowskie threw the ration bar he was chewing on at him.

Their second practice missile took their fourth and last package of flares out of space in a wild cascade of sparks.

"So much for the easy part," Jankowskie said. He noticed that Sery, who didn't smoke, had pulled out a cigarette—something strictly forbidden on Imperial warships—and was trying to light it. "Nicolas, when you get that thing going, give me a puff."

BEFORE THEY WERE TAKEN FROM THEIR WAREHOUSE PRISON TO THE execution ground, Snyman, Bruwer, and their fellow hostages inscribed in the dust on the windows, "If I speak in human and angelic tongues, but do not have love, I am a resounding gong or a clashing symbol. And if I have the gift of prophecy, and comprehend all mysteries and all knowledge, if I have faith so as to move mountains, but do not have love, I am nothing. If I give away everything I own, and if I hand my body over so that I may boast, but do not have love, I gain nothing. Love bears all things, believes all things, hopes all things, endures all things. Love will never fail."

Sunday(318)

"ARE WE PREPARED TO STRIKE YET, HONORED ADMIRAL?" CAPTAIN Watanabe asked as he presented Admiral Horii with the overnight summaries.

"One must be prepared to make deliberate haste, Watanabe," Horii said, carefully scrutinizing them.

At morning staff call a few moments later, Horii asked, "Captain Yanagita, were you able to contact Heer Afanou, and is he prepared to guide us into the mountains?"

"Yes, honored Admiral."

"Then we should attack immediately."

For a moment, his officers sat stunned except for Horii's logisticians who had been tipped off to begin preparations. Then Sumi rose and led them in shouting *"Banzai!"*

Horii alone remained seated. When the room quieted, he said, "That sly fox Vereshchagin will throw out a rear guard and disappear quickly if he discovers that we are on to him, so the best chance for success is to deploy overwhelming force."

Lieutenant-Colonel Okuda, the commander of the Ninth Light Attack Battalion, stood up. "Honored Admiral, I respectfully request the honor of leading for my battalion. With native guides, we could cross the backbone of the Drakensberg mountains in a matter of hours."

Horii nodded. Even if Vereshchagin had scouts in the area and attempted an ambush, with warships in support, Okuda would have more than enough firepower to fight his way through. He looked at Colonel Uno. "When Lieutenant-Colonel Okuda reaches the Oranje River, we will airlift the Manchurian engineer company to assist him in crossing if you consider Captain Aoyama's successor to be equal to this task."

Aoyama had been accidentally shot by a nervous sentry. Fighting an unseen, aggressive foe wearing essentially the same uniform, Horii's troops were averaging one "own goal" a day. Thus far, only abysmal marksmanship had kept the toll from rising more quickly.

"Yes, honored Admiral," Uno replied.

"Finally, as soon as Lieutenant-Colonel Okuda pinpoints Vereshchagin's location, we will establish airheads and land the Lifeguards Battalion to reinforce him. To initiate this operation, we will launch air strikes at the men located through the untiring efforts of our efficient communications personnel," Horii directed. "Please prepare the necessary orders."

Captain Yanagita was chosen to compose the message accompanying the attack order, which concluded, "Exalt the glorious tradition, transmit glory to posterity."

Noting that the stream of information from relatives of hostages had begun to dry up, Admiral Horii judged that the hostage policy had served its purposes. After executing a final group of fifty hostages, he directed Sumi to discontinue taking hostages and to release the remaining ones he had gathered.

Monday(318)

"WILL NOT COLONEL VERESHCHAGIN HEAR YOU WHEN YOU USE THE voice box? He has many ears," Jules Afanou asked Captain Itaya.

Itaya, the commander of Lieutenant-Colonel Okuda's Akita Company, smiled at the old man's naïveté. "It is almost impossible to detect short-range radio transmissions from one vehicle to another. These Vereshchagin will not hear. We are maintaining radio silence on all longer-ranged transmissions."

"Ah, I see! The sons of Dai Nippon are very wise in the ways of war," Afanou said.

Itaya had protested sharing his armored car with "a jungle bunny." Ironically, the sect leader had violently objected to the "mechanical" smell inside the vehicle, and it had taken all of Captain Yanagita's charm to persuade him to get inside.

A message came in from Itaya's lead vehicle. "Armored car *Taiko* here. Honored Captain, another large tree has fallen, blocking the road."

"Captain Itaya here. Can you move it aside?"

"Please excuse, honored Captain, but it is even larger than the last one. It is easily a meter and a half in diameter." There was awe in the voice of the lieutenant commanding the armored car.

Next to Itaya, Afanou nodded. "It happens as God wills. The biggest trees have shallow roots and often fall. It will be several hours' work for men with axes."

"Acknowledged. Itaya out," Itaya said crisply. He thumbed his radio. "Engineers point three. Break. Itaya here. There is another fallen tree blocking the trail. Please clear the way. Itaya out."

"We are delayed again. The forest fights for Vereshchagin," Afanou said.

"It fights weakly," Itaya said, smiling. "Command point one. Break. Itaya here. Honored Battalion Commander, we are temporarily halted by yet another obstacle in the road. My engineers will clear it in a matter of moments. I recommend that we adopt a herringbone defensive formation in the unlikely event we are attacked."

Lieutenant-Colonel Okuda issued the necessary orders, and each vehicle in the column turned slightly to face left or right. They sat there with their engines idling in the heart of the forest until the engineers were able to cut through the huge tree with their power saws.

Moving past the break, Itaya noted, "We are behind schedule, but not excessively so. These paths through the jungle are like a maze."

"We make them to follow the slope of the land, not for visitors," Afanou said.

"Our armored cars will make quick work of them."

"Heer Yanagita suggested to your admiral that you should give me a radio and have me signal when I got close to Vereshchagin's lair. I told them that it would take many days for me to walk there, and that Vereshchagin's men would surely stop me and question me along the path," Afanou declared candidly.

"What a silly idea," Itaya said, smiling.

Even as they were speaking, a well-organized strike by all four Imperial warships and more than twenty aircraft struck the forests of the upper Vaal and upper Oranje valleys, killing or wounding more than one hundred and fifty amphtiles wearing telemetry collars fashioned from condemned military radios.

THE FRIGATE *MAYA* HAD MADE ONLY ONE MISTAKE THAT SAN-martin could see. It was a minor one, and perhaps a predictable one.

Frigates are uncomfortable to live in during extended operations, and corvettes are even less pleasant. *Maya*'s commander had arranged for shuttles coming up to the freighters to dock with *Maya* and let off fresh food before continuing on.

With Admiral Horii ready to make another push, it was natural, almost foreordained, that his intendance officers would want to top off their ammunition stocks—especially since several of them had less ammunition on hand than their computers had reported a week ago—and it had been over a week since *Maya* had taken on a food consignment.

It was a very thin thread on which to hang lives, and possibly the fate of Suid-Afrika. Still, nobody in their right mind would expect someone to step out of a hole in the ground and hijack a shuttle in broad daylight without anyone noticing. Or at least that's what Sanmartin hoped.

As he waited with his knees pressed against his chest in the crawlway underneath the runway, Thomas tapped him on the shoulder and whispered, "They're loading crates of eggs!"

Thomas's men had thoughtfully strung a landline through the crawlway. Sanmartin picked up the phone on the end of it. "Sanmartin here. We're going in. Tell Matti to tell Detlef. Sanmartin out."

As the ground crew began to leave, rendered almost invisible by a slight dip in the ground, Thomas began crawling stealthily toward the shuttle. The shuttle began test-firing her engines as he reached the runway's edge. Creeping up under the wing-root, Thomas jammed a long-bladed knife in the space behind the shuttle's left quadruple landing gear.

The shuttles the Imperial Navy used were a proven design, but they had a few flaws, including a tendency to suck branches and other small debris up under the wheel wells during landings, which the ground crew was supposed to clear.

Two minutes into the takeoff sequence, Thomas's knife would show up on the preflight check-down as a minor malfunction. At that point, the pilot could either shut down the engines, abort the takeoff, and bring the maintenance crew out—or he could curse out the ground crew and send his crew chief to clear what was probably a loose branch.

Sanmartin was betting on the latter. It was the only way to get on board without causing a commotion by shooting the place up.

"If they cut the engines, we run like hell," Thomas repeated to himself as he leaned against the landing strut with a silenced submachine gun across his knees. Shielded from the tower by the shuttle's bulk, he waited to see if the door would open.

Two minutes passed. Sanmartin listened for the engines to shut down. If they did, Thomas had, at most, twelve seconds to grab his knife and get underground.

Suddenly, the shuttle's crew door opened, and the crew chief pushed down the ladder. Before he could take his first step, Thomas put six rounds in his chest with a double tap on the trigger of his silenced submachine gun.

Partly obscured by the dust from the engines, Sanmartin came out of his hole at a dead run, followed by three teams from Thomas's recon platoon and helicopter pilot Ivan Tsukernik, who swore he could fly anything and would have an opportunity to prove it. Once inside, two of Thomas's teams went aft to clear out any passengers in the seats in the upper cabin while the third went forward with Thomas and Sanmartin to take out the crew.

A moment later, Thomas came back to the door and waved, and six specialists emerged from the ground and clambered on board, including Platoon Sergeant Liu from No. 15, who knew less about shuttles than he knew about playing a fiddle but whose Mandarin and Japanese were flawless. The last man carried a bucket of white sand that he carefully sprinkled over the crew chief's blood.

The ladder came up. The shuttle took off on schedule, on a hope and a prayer, and a message went out to *Ajax*.

CAPTAIN ITAYA'S RADIO CRACKLED. "ARMORED CAR *TAIKO* HERE. Sir, we have reached a fork in the trail. Both paths run roughly northwest. Which way should we take, the left or the right?"

Itaya looked at Afanou who said, "Your directions mean little to me. We must go and see, and I will tell you."

"Captain Itaya here. I will personally reconnoiter the paths ahead. Itaya out. Command point one. Break. Itaya here. Honored Battalion Commander, please halt the column for a few moments so that we can check our course. Itaya out."

The armored car moved to where the trail forked. As the vehicle slowed, Itaya looked up as Afanou reached to open the hatch.

"Your vision screen is a wonder of God, honored Captain, but it means nothing to these old eyes. I must get out and see." Sprightly as a monkey, the old man slid out the hatch and down to the ground.

Itaya followed. "I think—" he began to say as a burst of silenced submachine gun fire from the side of the road took him in the throat and Afanou literally disappeared into the undergrowth.

Several kilometers back down the trail, Miinalainen, perched in a tree, effortlessly hoisted his big 88mm recoilless gun and carefully sighted through a gap in the forest canopy created by a fallen tree. "So many of them, and so few of us," he murmured, making a very Finnish kind of joke, "how are we ever going to bury them all?"

Coldewe's voice crackled over Miinalainen's radio. "Coldewe here. Hit them!"

Miinalainen's first round ripped open a fuel trailer towed by a stubby little amphibian utility vehicle. The trailer erupted in a pillar of fire fifty meters high. Up and down the column, from both sides of the trail, eighty-eight rounds struck fuel trailers and armored cars indiscriminately.

The Ninth Light Attack Battalion responded with trained precision. Surviving armored cars crashed into the forest on either side and opened up with a torrent of fire. Thirty- and ninety-millimeter rounds ripped into the trees, stripping away the foliage at ground level.

Ignoring his orders, Miinalainen awkwardly reloaded his eighty-eight and put a second round into the fuel trailer just ahead of the one he had destroyed, sending another five thousand liters of fuel alcohol billowing skyward. Then, unstrapping himself from his tree, he jumped, arms windmilling, shielded by its bulk. Grunting in pain from an awkward landing, he crawled into a hole at its base and pulled a carefully camouflaged steel lid over his head.

Crouching in the darkness and the water as the Cadillacs continued to tear the heart out of the forest, Miinalainen muttered to himself, "I'm getting too old for this stuff."

Passing over the column from above, four Hummingbird reconnaissance drones took advantage of the confusion to begin gently touching the armored cars on either side of the road with laser designators. On Coldewe's further order, Bushchin's No. 13 platoon rolled its four 160mm mechanized mortars into a clearing and pumped out forty antiarmor rounds—every one that Vereshchagin possessed—over the tops of the fern trees and almost directly down on the embattled Cadillacs, guided by the laser designations. Twenty-five of the Ninth Battalion's Cadillacs, two of its mechanized mortars, and its last remaining fuel trailer were struck—a few of them more than once—within the space of two minutes.

Immediate counterbattery fire from the other Ninth Battalion's mechanized mortars knocked out one of No. 13 platoon's vehicles and damaged another, which did little to alter the fact that after losing half its fighting vehicles and all its reserve fuel, the Ninth Light Attack Battalion had been wrecked as a fighting unit.

The rear of the column where the Ninth Battalion's slicks were concentrated was struck by 105mm mortar rounds from No. 12 mortar platoon, which damaged five of them. Significantly, the armored infantrymen at the rear of the column heard Mekhlis's mortars scattering mines on the trail behind them. With the road ahead clearly a death trap and the road behind blocked, Lieutenant-Colonel Okuda found himself in an unenviable position.

"Base point one. Break. Okuda here. Honored Admiral, our mission has been compromised. I say again, our mission has been compromised. We have been betrayed by our guide and have serious casualties. For these reasons, I do not consider it feasible for us to attain our objective. I request immediate air and naval fire support and further request permission to break out across country and return to Bloemfontein by way of Leiden Pass. I will inform you further after we verify our position." Looking down at the gauges in front of him, he added, "I also anticipate possible fuel shortages. I request arrangements be made for aerial fuel resupply."

Moments later, Miinalainen heard a tree broken by an electromagnetically enhanced 90mm round land on top of his hole with a pounding thud. He repeated to himself, "I really am getting too old for this sort of thing."

As Admiral Horii received Okuda's message, in the next room Afanou's purported son grabbed the pencil behind his ear—actually a painted rod of tungsten steel with a needle point—and flung it into the heart of the guard standing a few meters away. Scooping up the guard's rifle, he sprayed Admiral Horii's communications personnel with 5mm caseless rounds.

As he paused to claw a fresh magazine out of one of the dead guard's pouches, a wounded staff officer who had fallen behind a desk pulled out his pistol and placed three bullets in his chest. Despite mortal wounds, the man calmly reloaded and shot the staff officer dead. Seconds later, a security squad burst into the room and riddled him.

Horii entered a few moments later and observed the carnage. "Remarkable," he said. A thin line of blood crawled across the floor and stopped against his shoe.

BREAKING A TRAIL THROUGH THE FOREST OF THE UPPER ORANJE Valley, Lieutenant-Colonel Okuda again pleaded for air and naval support, and especially for fuel resupply. With the operation's secrecy already compromised, Horii had no difficulty granting his request, and sweating logistics personnel hastened to send off strike aircraft and two tilt-rotors fitted out as refueling platforms.

However, the naval support Okuda was expecting was abruptly diverted.

ONE PROBLEM INHERENT IN SPACE WARFARE THAT DETLEF JANKOWskie recognized as he plotted his approach was that his corvette would have to shed most of her speed and come almost suicidally close to the Imperial ships in order to make her weapons effective.

The five-hundred-kilogram precision-guided projectiles that his missile launchers could fire were virtually useless against anything moving at a ship's speed, while his ground attack laser, although excellent for incendiary work, was relatively ineffective against protected targets. Even Jankowskie's composite particle—or "chicken seed"—dispenser, which could spew out hundreds of two-gram pellets charged with fusion energy each second, could only be expected to score a respectable number of hits at close range. Jankowskie's chances of doing significant damage depended upon his being almost literally yardarm to yardarm.

The initial problem with fighting a space battle, Jankowskie brooded, seemed to be getting the other side to cooperate. Unfortunately, since the other side had four warships to Jankowskie's one, that might not be too much of a problem.

Moments later, he got a signal relayed by the four bored "coconut counters" out in the middle of nowhere. It ended with the plain text message, "Good luck!"

"Ready, everybody?" Jankowskie inquired. When no one dissented, he tapped Moushegian, whose nickname was "Sniper," on the knee and told him, "Take her in, Snipe."

Using the planet as a huge shield, *Ajax* swung on a wide elliptic and swooped in from a sunrise direction across the sea toward Akashi continent, picking up speed in the process.

Her appearance almost caught Admiral Horii's ships by surprise—almost but not quite.

By scattering his ships, Horii made it impossible for *Ajax* to penetrate into the center of his formation and ram *Maya*, causing a double fusion bottle explosion that would empty a considerable amount of space in every direction. Unfortunately, it left the freighters and transports screening *Maya* virtually motionless in comparison to *Ajax* and exceedingly vulnerable.

The first ship that Jankowskie encountered was the freighter *Los Angeles Maru* on the sunward point of the diamond around *Maya*, and Jankowskie barely had to slow. Even though the freighter's fusion bottle was effectively armored to withstand the enormous internal stresses, she was packed to her beam with fuel and munitions in compartments that were not. She couldn't move fast, and she couldn't shoot back.

Dropping perhaps half his relative speed, Jankowskie came in close and directed a fourteen-second stream of composite particles and two missiles from *Ajax*'s launchers at her. Although both of the missiles missed, nine of the nearly four thousand chicken-seed particles that Jankowskie launched struck, with devastating results when two of them impacted on cases of 210mm artillery rounds.

As the *Los Angeles Maru* quietly blew apart, Jankowskie maneuvered to engage the transport *Chiyoda* on the right side of the diamond, which unaccountably was still heading in his direction, apparently convinced that Jankowskie was going to allow it to remain a spectator to the battle.

Passing as close to the transport as he dared, Jankowskie rapidly disabused it of the notion. Struck by nearly two dozen composite pellets, and raked by Jankowskie's laser, *Chiyoda*'s skin peeled away, and it began drifting, helpless.

"That's two!" Sery exulted from his gunner's station.

Jankowskie ignored him. The corvettes *Yahagi*, *Kasumi*, and *Asashimo* had been flying top cover "above" *Maya* with respect to Suid-Afrika's surface, and the three ships were closing in on him in a broad inverted V.

"Time to get out of here, Snipe," Jankowskie ordered.

"Trouble," Moushegian commented, and Jankowskie immediately realized why. With more thrust built up than *Ajax*, the pursuing corvettes were rapidly closing the gap in between, and with *Ajax* lower in Suid-Afrika's outer atmosphere, Jankowskie had more friction to contend with, as well as one direction where he could not go. In a stern chase, Admiral Horii's ships would soon catch up. While the race does not always go to the swift nor the battle to the strong, that's the way to bet.

"The ships on the wings are changing course to intercept, skipper. Maybe two minutes to contact," Moushegian announced glumly.

"Nicolas, it's Christmas tree time," Jankowskie said.

"Yes, sir," Sery said automatically. Anticipating his order, Sery was already engrossed with his jury-rigged firing controls.

A corvette's weapons were designed to be fired forward, and the sole purpose for the eccentric array of flak missiles that Jankowskie and his crew had hung on *Ajax* was to permit her to fire a Parthian shot at ships pursuing her. Although nimble at low speeds, *Nagara*-class corvettes were pigs under full thrust, which was just as well since even a slight evasion would cause the missiles to miss at the relatively low speeds their rocket engines could generate. With luck, they might cause the pursuing corvettes to veer off.

"Targets acquired, missiles one, two, seven, eleven, and fifteen," Sery announced. A new light came on. "Twelve!"

"The middle corvette has opened fire," Moushegian mentioned.

Sery fired. A second later, he shouted "three" and fired once more. One missile spun out of control immediately. The other six "sped" off aimed at two of the three pursuing corvettes, although the corvettes were moving toward the missiles at eight times the best speed the missiles could manage.

Seconds later, with maddening lack of response, Jankowskie jerked the ship left to dodge a thrust of fusion energy from *Kasumi* immediately astern and held his breath, not knowing how well the corvettes' sensors would pick up the tiny missiles against the clutter, and whether the corvettes' crews would recognize them if they did. Half a minute passed.

Seconds before impact, *Kasumi* and *Yahagi* recognized the danger. *Yahagi*'s commander pulled his nose away and easily avoided the missiles aimed at his ship. Intent on his prey, *Kasumi*'s commander ignored the missiles for a few seconds too long. His panic reaction at the last instant dodged three of the slow missiles moving toward his ship and impaled his ship on a fourth.

The twenty-kilogram antitank charge that Armorer Rytov had stuffed into the missile's warhead squashed itself against the vessel's hull and exploded, boring a finger of white-hot metal deep into the ship's side. Most of a corvette's interior is taken up with the fusion bottle, and by luck and the grace of God, the molten metal pierced it through. The ship disappeared in a cloud of light.

Kasumi having disintegrated and *Yahagi* having taken herself out of the fight, Jankowskie prudently turned the ship to evade *Asashimo*, which managed only a few insignificant hits with composite pellets before her target eluded her.

A few seconds later, when Sery realized that he was going to live to see another birthday, he whooped and pounded Jankowskie on the back. Jankowskie, still intent on his instruments, banged his head against the display.

As Jankowskie held his nose with a hurt look on his face, tiny globules of blood began floating across the bridge.

"Sorry, sir," Sery said contritely.

Minutes later, *Ashashimo* and *Yahagi* gave up the chase, as increasingly anxious calls for ground support came to them from the planet below.

During the battle, *Maya* had not moved from her initial position, and now she drifted, tilted slightly. To an anxious *Yahagi*, she broadcast, "Have been damaged by sabotage. Render immediate assistance."

As *Yahagi* and *Asashimo* acknowledged and closed to dock, missiles and clouds of composite particles from the heavier-armed frigate knifed out and slit open both corvettes.

ON *MAYA*'S BRIDGE, SANMARTIN SAT IN THE CAPTAIN'S CHAIR, WITH the corpses of her bridge crew wedged to one side.

With silenced submachine guns, breaching charges for interior doors, and eighteen gas grenades apiece, it had taken Thomas's men, veterans of house-to-house fighting in Krugersdorp and Nelspruit during the rebellion, less than seven minutes to penetrate to *Maya*'s bridge, and less than twenty to clear the ship.

Sanmartin turned to his commo man, a brainy, ship-trained

young Afrikaner. "All right. Tell the freighter and the transport to surrender or we'll cut them open."

Predictably, the two ships tried to escape. In a matter of minutes, the freighter *Zanzibar Maru*, much too close, was run down and destroyed. The transport *Hiyo* built up speed and disappeared into space on a vector that would carry it far from any jump point.

"Let them go," Sanmartin said, staring at the lump of brain on his sleeve.

"So that was a space battle," Thomas said, wondering.

"The very first," Sanmartin replied. He absently tried to wipe his sleeve. "Someone ought to tell these navy boys that people sometimes shoot back."

A few minutes later, after studying *Maya*'s control panel, he began systematically destroying the network of reconnaissance satellites that operated as Admiral Horii's eyes.

On the planet below, the battle reached its crescendo.

MATTI HARJALO WALKED UP TO LIEUTENANT MURAVYOV'S Cadillac, which was draped in live seed ferns. Muravyov sat on the rim of the hatch where he could give Harjalo a hand up.

Crouching beside the turret, Harjalo asked, "The Ninth Light Attack is on its way. Your people ready?"

Muravyov had four Cadillacs and four slicks—two-man scout vehicles—from his own No. 15 platoon plus Savichev's two Cadillacs from what was left of No. 16. He nodded.

"Good." Harjalo patted him on the shoulder. He sniffed the air inquisitively. "What is that I smell?"

Muravyov stared off into space with a disgusted expression. "Recruit Private Prigal's lunch." He eyed his driver. "Prigal and I were just discussing that a few moments ago."

Harjalo smiled. "Chicken! Where might it have come from?"

Muravyov's gunner turned his head and began making sputtering noises like a teapot.

"I, ah, found it while I was out scouting, sir," Prigal responded, peering up from his seat like a turtle.

"Indeed." Harjalo looked down at his wrist mount. "Well, we have ten or fifteen minutes yet. Recruit Private Prigal, I call this field court-martial to order. Yet again, what do you have to say in defense or in mitigation?"

Prigal thought for a minute. "Sir, the chicken refused to identify itself when I challenged it."

"Very imaginative. The farmhouse up the road?"

Prigal nodded guiltily.

"I vote for boiling him in oil if we live through this," Muravyov said, looking daggers at Prigal.

"Since you're still a recruit private, I can't very well demote you, can I?" Harjalo announced. "I just spoke with the farmer up the road there, and he is a very nice man. I think he's one of Jan Snyman's cousins. Sometime next week, go knock on his door and tell him I told you to pay double what he asks for."

"Yes, sir," Prigal said, holding his head between his hands.

Harjalo looked at Muravyov. "Set?"

"Yes, sir."

"Remember, your job is to set them up for Stash Wojcek."

"I will." Muravyov smiled, his aged eyes glowing. He shut the hatch behind him.

Moments later, Muravyov summoned his vehicles to battle as the Hangman had always done. "Hear me, my brothers. The winds of paradise are blowing. Where are you who long for paradise?"

Like a man challenged by a wasp, Lieutenant-Colonel Okuda delayed his refueling operation and moved to meet him, throwing a platoon against each of Muravyov's flanks to drive away the covering slicks so that his battalion could crush Muravyov, Cadillac to Cadillac. Overjoyed at the prospect of pitting his electromagnetic guns against an armored foe, Okuda purposefully did not use his waiting air power.

As soon as Okuda went for the bait, Captain Stash Wojcek's four helicopters materialized from bunkers built into the back side of the Drakensberg Mountains. In a matter of seconds, they shot down the two waiting fuel transports and the two helicopters escorting them. Then two of Wojcek's helicopters peeled off to engage the attention of the Imperial Shidens with help from flak gunners hidden on the ground, while the other two made a quick, but devastating, attack on Okuda's flank platoons.

Wojcek's wingman, Kokovtsov, heeded Wojcek's instructions to make his firing run count, banging his left wheel on a Cadillac's turret a second or two after his gunner had finished pumping it full of holes.

Weaving in and out to discourage pursuit, Wojcek's three surviving copters flew off to the north. Kokovtsov's gunner grinned feebly. "Hey, Coconut. I thought for a minute there you wanted to join the infantry."

A thin smile played around the edges of Kokovtsov's mouth. "Me, a groundhog? I fly. Serves them right for living on the ground. Good run," which was the most his gunner had heard him say at one time in seven years.

Sergeant Platoon Commander Konstantin Savichev, who took command after Muravyov's Cadillac blew up, used the respite to break contact. Lieutenant-Colonel Okuda had to be physically restrained by his battalion sergeant. Halfway up the Leiden Pass, his remaining vehicles began running out of fuel. Less than a dozen of them limped back to Bloemfontein.

When the Shidens flown off to support Okuda returned to the spaceport, *Maya* caught eight of them, damaging or destroying six in a running chase.

NINE MINUTES LATER, THE FULL GRAVITY OF THE SITUATION BEcame apparent to Admiral Horii's staff when snipers picked off two of the Lifeguards Battalion's flak gunners and an extended-range round from an 88mm recoilless gun crashed into the spaceport radar. It cleared the way for four of Vereshchagin's Shidens.

Crammed with ordnance, they came in low—with fern fronds dangling from the engine nacelles—and pulled up over the spaceport to unload indiscriminately on troop positions, parked aircraft, and supply depots. Custom-made drag-plates attached to their bombs gave the fuses time to arm and the aircraft barely enough time to clear the buildings before hell came loose.

As Colonel Enomoto mobilized his men to fight fires, Admiral Horii, watching through his window, commented to Watanabe, "The situation is quite serious, isn't it?"

Moments later, the flight of Imperial Shidens that *Maya* had shot up appeared and immediately came under intense small-arms fire from Enomoto's jittery guardsmen. While most of the flight circled and attempted to identify themselves, one plane streaming fuel from a ruptured tank tried to land and was struck several times. As it touched down, it began sliding and burst into flame when it fell off the runway.

"Another own goal," Horii commented.

In a smoke-stained uniform, Colonel Sumi prepared an order of the day that read, "Due to unexpected setbacks, soldiers must hold their positions without fail. This is a contest of spiritual strength. Continue in your mission until all your ammunition is expended. When it is expended, use your hands. If they are broken, use your feet. If your feet are broken, use your teeth. If there is no breath left with your body, continue to fight with your spirit."

He went to present it to Admiral Horii for signature.

MORE OR LESS REENACTING HIS ORIGINAL ENTRANCE INTO BLOEM-fontein, Piotr Kolomeitsev returned in the back of a borrowed bakkie truck. Traveling down the Venterstadt Road, he spotted a group of about a hundred men and boys armed with a miscellany of weapons off to the side and signaled his driver to slow the vehicle.

An older man with a decrepit shotgun saluted. "Major Kolomeitsev, we were expecting you. Most of us have weapons."

The Iceman carefully studied the way they held themselves and said with what passed in him for kindness, "Please. Go home."

"We want revenge!" one man shouted, brandishing a rifle. A few others echoed him.

"Many of us have lost relatives," the older man said soberly.

The Iceman's voice could cut like a knife when he chose. "The dead are dead. Hanna Bruwer would not have wanted this. Please—go home. We professionals will ask for assistance if we need it." His smile was chill as he left them.

Matti Harjalo was waiting for him by the fountain in the Krugerplein, having "reoccupied" the town, already under sporadic mortar fire from the nervous Manchurians in the casern, with the pilot of his Sparrow.

Harjalo grabbed Kolomeitsev by the shoulder as soon as he arrived. "Piotr, how long will it take your men to deploy?"

"Give me fifteen minutes, and I will have two platoons in position. What is the situation?"

"The Manchurians are holed up here and in the Pretoria and Johannesburg caserns. We got lucky—one of De Wette's platoons managed to stampede the garrison company out of Complex, so we took it intact. Also, tell your boys to be careful—some farmer already mistook Thomas for an Imp and tried to part his hair with a shotgun. He was thouroughly indignant."

Harjalo concluded, "The people flying transports are breaking their backs, so Coldewe and De Wette may have their people in place in about an hour."

The Iceman nodded, acknowledging the sincerity of the statement, and began positioning his men. In truth, it was another three hours before Coldewe and De Wette could put any semblance of a ring around the other two Manchurian-occupied caserns.

As soon as Harjalo reported that his men were ready, Vereshchagin nodded impassively to Timo Haerkoennen and took the microphone from him. "Colonel Uno, this is Lieutenant-Colonel Vereshchagin. As you are aware, your warships have been captured or destroyed. Further military action on your part is useless. I wish to arrange for the peaceful repatriation of the force under your command. Please respond." Vereshchagin repeated his message three times. He deliberately avoided using the word "surrender."

Haerkoennen shook his head. "No response, sir."

"Signal Raul."

On cue, *Ajax* dipped low and showered the Johannesburg casern with chicken seed, while *Maya* did the same to the Pretoria casern.

"Colonel Uno. Please respond," Vereshchagin repeated.

"We're getting a response from Bloemfontein, sir," Haerkoennen said.

Vereshchagin recognized the reedy voice of Lieutenant-Colonel Bukichi, Uno's blackleg chief of staff. "As Imperial soldiers, we will never give up our positions!"

"Lieutenant-Colonel Bukichi, please allow me to speak with Colonel Uno or Lieutenant-Colonel Okuda. If the Manchurian regiment accepts repatriation, I will return its officers and men to Earth. If it refuses, I regret that it will be destroyed," Vereshchagin said inexorably.

Unknown to Bukichi, Timo Haerkoennen had tapped into the Manchurian regiment's radio net, and every soldier trapped in the three caserns was able to hear their exchange.

"We will fight to the end as befits Imperial soldiers," Bukichi said shrilly. "And at the first sign of attack, we will shell the towns of Bloemfontein, Pretoria, and Johannesburg. This discussion is at an end."

"Tell Matti," Vereshchagin told Haerkoennen quietly. "Bloemfontein first."

The Johannesburg and Bloemfontein caserns were built on hills made of deeply veined and fissured quartzite, and before leaving the two caserns, C Company Armorer Rytov had carefully pumped thousands of liters of liquid artillery propellant into the rock, forcing it deep into the hairline cracks. One result was that neighboring farmers found displaced water flooding their fields, and it had taken Raul Sanmartin some effort to soothe them over.

Of greater import, the artillery propellant had turned both knolls into huge bombs. It was a fairly spectacular variant on Rytov's usual task of preparing a dead-man's switch to blow up his armory to keep it from being captured.

At Harjalo's command, Rytov sent a radio signal to ignite the charges he had left to touch off Bloemfontein casern, and the nitrate-impregnated rock erupted, detonating the ammunition stored in the armory above it for good measure. It left an irregular crater eighteen meters deep and four hundred meters in diameter. The shock wave set off the casern's mine fields and broke virtually every window in the city. People as far away as Upper Marlboro felt the ground tremble.

One Manchurian, stripped of his clothes but otherwise uninjured, landed on top of a neighboring farmhouse. It was four hours before he was able to speak with sufficient coherence to identify himself.

A Company had little trouble mopping up the dazed survivors.

"I didn't think it would work," was Rytov's comment.

Moments later, Vereshchagin explained how his men had destroyed the Bloemfontein garrison and again called on the Johannesburg and Pretoria garrisons to accept repatriation.

"It's a shame we couldn't do anything with the Pretoria casern," Haerkoennen commented.

"We may not need to," Vereshchagin replied.

The Japanese major commanding the Johannesburg garrison curtly refused. Inside one of the bunkers that Coldewe's men had built, Section Sergeant Ma and his section listened surreptitiously.

Cement had flaked off the bunker's ceiling when Bloemfontein exploded. "That will be us," Little Jia said.

Licking his dry lips, Ma studied the pale faces of his men and cautiously approached Lieutenant Akamine. "Honored Lieutenant—"

Akamine turned away from the bunker's vision slit.

"Perhaps—"

Akamine read the expression on Ma's face and backhanded him across the face before he could finish. "Silence! We will die like men, not dogs!" He contemptuously returned to his study of the terrain outside the bunker.

His cheeks red, Ma looked at each of his section members

in turn. Duck-Face Gu took out his billfold and threw a sheaf of bills on the floor.

Picking up his rifle, Ma calmly shot Akamine three times in the back. His men quickly tied a pair of cotton underpants to a length of pipe and raised it over their bunker. Within minutes, a dozen other bunkers had up white flags.

The Japanese major directed the men with him to fire on Ma. When they hesitated, he ripped an s-mortar out of one man's hands and began firing himself. Return fire from an eighty-eight killed him. A full-scale fire fight broke out inside the Manchurian perimeter.

Twenty minutes later, after the Manchurian battalion sergeant and the last two Japanese officers killed themselves with grenades, the remaining defenders surrendered to Coldewe.

The lieutenant-colonel commanding the Pretoria garrison quickly recognized what had happened. Assessing his men's state of mind, he retreated into the armory and blew it up underneath him. De Wette's men moved swiftly to take possession.

In Bloemfontein, Matti Harjalo spread his portable map over the wing of his Sparrow and listened as reports come in. Wearing the arm band of the reserve reconnaissance platoon, Mintje Cillie walked up behind him and tapped him on the shoulder. "Ah, Major Harjalo, sir—excuse me, Colonel Harjalo." She made a clumsy attempt at a salute.

Harjalo turned his head. "Oh, hello. Cillie, isn't it? What can I do for you?"

She held out a little notebook. "Please, sir—may I have your autograph?"

On his face, Harjalo could feel airborne bits and pieces of the Bloemfontein casern and its defenders drifting down. "Your timing is pretty awful. This isn't exactly a battle we'll want to remember."

"Please, sir, it's for my little brother. He's very keen on football. Please say, 'To Jan-Pieter.' "

Harjalo usually added himself to the engineer platoon's roster when they played their annual exhibition matches against the local club sides, and he had scored on the Bloemfontein team two years running. He had the grace to look embarrassed when he took the notebook from her.

"ADMIRAL, THROUGH SOME DEVILTRY ON THE PART OF Vereshchagin, we have encountered an unexpected situation," Sumi stated coldly.

Horii smiled. "If by this you mean that our warships have been turned against us and our soldiers have been resoundingly defeated, I quite agree with you. It would appear that Lieutenant-Colonel Vereshchagin is a formidable antagonist. He understands that when an enemy starts to collapse, he should be cut down utterly."

"There is one way for us to rectify this situation. I have directed my security companies to take up positions in the towns of Pretoria and Johannesburg. I am quite certain that Vereshchagin will be dissuaded from following up the advantage he has gained after a sufficient number of logs have fallen," Sumi said, fingering the hilt of his sword.

Horii turned to Captain Yanagita, who had followed Sumi into the room. "Spirit is like water, Yanagita. It adopts the shape of its receptacle. Sometimes it is a trickle, sometimes a raging flood. We have lifted the lid on a teapot and brewed a typhoon." He raised his voice. "And if you are wrong, Colonel Sumi? What then? Regrettably, Lieutenant-Colonel Vereshchagin is a professional and will not yield to misplaced pity for those 'logs.' I forbid this. Please countermand your instructions." He turned his back on Sumi.

"I will not!" Sumi shouted.

Horii smiled at Yanagita. "Are you prepared to disobey me as well?"

Yanagita loosened his pistol in its holster. "No, Admiral."

Sumi did not seem to know how to take this. Horii stepped over by the window. Sumi followed, silently unsheathing his blade. As Sumi did so, a bullet came through the reinforced glass and took him just below the right eye.

Yanagita threw himself to the floor and pulled out his pistol. "Admiral, get down!"

"A large-caliber sniper's rifle, no doubt. It was a very good shot from that distance, don't you think, Yanagita?" Horii said conversationally. He smiled again and moved away from the window. "If Lieutenant-Colonel Vereshchagin had wanted to kill me, he would have done so before now."

Yanagita shakily returned the pistol to its holster. "Honored Admiral, how could—"

"I did not know." Horii pointed toward the small rise, nearly eight hundred meters away. "But lacking the men needed to hold an extensive perimeter, I removed the troops there a half hour ago, as Vereshchagin's watchers undoubtedly observed. It seemed likely that they would take advantage of this."

Two officers appeared at the door with drawn weapons.

"Colonel Sumi has been shot by a sniper. You two, please remove his body," Horii said, loftily overlooking their astonished expressions.

As they left, half carrying, half dragging Sumi's corpse, Horii nudged Sumi's fallen sword with his toe. "If this were a genuine Sukesada blade, Yanagita, it would be a national treasure and I would direct you to pick it up. But of course it is not, so you might as well allow it to lie there. It is time. Please begin destroying our papers and data files."

Yanagita picked himself up. He paused as he reached the threshold. "Admiral, should I also destroy the money in the safe? We are accountable for it."

Horii grinned. "Leave it. We will need some of it for the ferryman over the river Styx."

As soon as Yanagita left, he drew the curtains over the windows and whispered to himself, "In the universe what is there but dream and illusion? Those who are born in the morning die before night, and those who are born in the evening are dead before dawn. Is there anyone who is born and does not die?"

He entered one last poem, a *jisei*, into his war diary before he burned it.

> Why then should I cling?
> to a life that is fulfilled
> when nobly given
> for the love of country
> for the sake of the people

The blackleg company in Pretoria imprudently holed up in the two-story brick bank building they had sequestered to use as a headquarters. *Maya* sent four thousand-kilogram bombs through the building's thin roof, gutting it and its inhabitants. Part of the other blackleg company was ambushed by a section of the reconnaissance platoon as it attempted to reach the spaceport. The survivors were hunted down.

Reprise—Week 318

THE SIXTH LIFEGUARDS BATTALION STILL HELD THE SPACEPORT IN A perimeter bounded by the administration complex and low hills to the south and east. Horii assigned one Lifeguards company to each hill and formed his service and supply troops into provisional infantry companies to guard the low ground to the west. He retained the remaining two Lifeguard companies and his howitzer company to defend the area around the administration complex.

Fixated on offensive operations, Colonel Enomoto's guardsmen had failed to fortify the spaceport. This neglect cost them dearly.

Vereshchagin did not intend to allow them time to profit from their mistakes. He placed the reserve company, a composite platoon from B Company, and the reconnaissance platoon in a loose net around the spaceport, where they harassed the Lifeguards with intermittent but intensifying sniper and mortar fire as the Lifeguards sweated to dig in. Then he used *Ajax* and *Maya* to isolate the administration buildings and began systematically to rip the defenses apart in a bitter two-day struggle of artillery and engineers.

A half dozen former ARM members were assigned to assist the mortar crews with the rest of Henke's half-trained recruits. The conflict was by no means one-sided; Recruit Private Gerrit Terblanche was one of the casualties.

After Reinikka's engineers cleared approaches, and direct fire from Okladnikov's Cadillacs tore down the walls, A Company and C Company crawled slowly and painfully into jump-off positions. When the wind shifted, weighted with grenades and explosive charges, they launched a well-rehearsed assault under the Iceman's personal direction, covered by billowing clouds of phosphorus smoke to obscure their visual and thermal outlines.

The Iceman's No. 2 platoon spearheaded the attack. No. 2's platoon leader was Lieutenant Tikhon Degtyarov, A Company's second officer of that name. Degtyarov had been born on Esdraelon, and his men included most of Vereshchagin's Cadmus soldiers—the ones who loved combat rather than respected it. They were perhaps the only men in the battalion who carried bayonets and expected to use them. Normally, a three-to-one fire superiority is necessary to ensure a successful assault. Captain Stash Wojcek's aircraft and helicopters, flying suicidally low, provided the necessary margin.

In the ruins of the administration building, Section Sergeant Niilo Leikola of the Iceman's No. 3 platoon spotted Lieutenant Isa Miyazato's Nakamura target pistol next to a headless body. Leikola had lost several friends. "How's the hunting?" he asked. He left the pistol lying there.

Out of the three Imperial companies defending the area around the administration building, there were two survivors, both badly wounded.

After Coldewe's men raised the *Vierkleur* flag over the rubble, Vereshchagin watched it flutter through a patch in the smoke from the smoldering pyre of the helicopter that Wojcek had flown and repeated a poem by Basho that Horii would have recognized.

> Withered summer grass
> is truly all that remains
> Of the dream of the warriors

Horii had broadcast one final order just before the Iceman's men finished clearing the buildings, directing his soldiers crouching in dugouts to the east, south, and west to "please report to Lieutenant-Colonel Vereshchagin to assist in the process of returning the remains of fallen comrades to the homeland, as it has become extremely difficult to continue our efforts here." His body, like many others, was never positively identified.

Virtually ammunitionless, they did so, and Paul Henke took charge of them.

Separating out the officers and noncommissioned officers among the prisoners, Henke put the Japanese to recovering and cremating the bodies of the dead, and used the Manchurians to repair some of the damage. Mixing the two groups would have significantly increased the death toll.

He placed the officers and noncommissioned officers in individual cells so that the zealots among them couldn't try to shame the others into committing suicide, and Chiharu Yoshida spent hours talking to them. A week later, they were released into a camp called "Rebirth" and introduced to group self-criticism. A handful of obnoxious ones were left to quietly rot; most of them took the easy way out.

Eva Moore took charge of the Thai and Filipino prostitutes of Sumi's "comfort detachment." Like many areas on colonial worlds, the cowboy country had a population imbalance of roughly three men for every two women. With Beyers's approval, Moore picked out a few who had not been addicted or thoroughly brutalized and conditionally offered to let them stay. The rest would go back when transport could be arranged, together with the captured soldiers and what was left of Matsudaira's staff.

In orbit over Akashi continent, *Maya* still had over a hundred bodies aboard, most of them gassed in the crew areas. Lacking the manpower to move them, Sanmartin shut off the crew deck's life support systems and allowed them to freeze. When the tempo of operations allowed, he moved a crew of civilian volunteers on board to clear out the dead and their personal possessions. It was grim work.

Without being asked, Vroew Beyers bought up several hundred pottery vases and turned them over. They made tolerably good urns.

BOWING TO PUBLIC OPINION, ALBERT BEYERS HELD VICTORY REviews in Johannesburg, Pretoria, Bloemfontein, and Upper Marlboro. Lest anyone forget, Vereshchagin had his men march with spaces left in the ranks for the dead and severely wounded.

Saturday(318)

SIX POLICEMEN TOOK DAISUKE MATSUDAIRA FROM THE OFFICE where he'd barricaded himself, imperiously ordering up hot meals from the Complex cafeteria. They placed him in handcuffs and formed a wall to get him past his employees, who pelted him with wads of paper as he went by.

At the front door, Matsudaira clumsily took a poison pellet from his belt and tried to place it in his mouth. One of the policemen slapped him hard on the back and knocked it away. "If you wanted to do that, you should have done it before. Now, behave yourself! We are going to have enough trouble getting you to the gaol in one piece."

"Please," Matsudaira begged brokenly as he listened to the jeers.

The policeman squeezed his shoulder jocularly. "Oh, no. Everyone is far too annoyed with you for that."

IN SOME WAYS, MARTIN HATTING'S FATE WAS THE CRUELEST OF ALL. He hid out in a shack behind his house waiting for the police to come arrest him, but no policemen came. Instead, his neighbors and friends began pretending he didn't exist. A byelection was announced to fill his assembly seat. Instead of his salary, his wife began receiving a widow's pension. Eventually, she began pretending he didn't exist.

He tried to file a lawsuit, but the landrost's court sent it back stamped, "Petitioner Deceased."

For an ambitious politician like Hatting, a bullet would have been far kinder.

ALBERT BEYERS ARRANGED FOR HANNA BRUWER'S FUNERAL. RAUL Sanmartin was persuaded, with difficulty, to attend. As Anton Vereshchagin had realized long ago, a victory is the greatest tragedy, except for a defeat.

WIND _____

Sunday(319)

DESPITE THE ELATION IN THE STREETS, THE MOOD OF THE SOLDIERS that Vereshchagin gathered to discuss the future was somber.

Captain Ulrich Ohlrogge spoke first for the survivors of Ebyl's battalion. "My men have taken a vote." Ohlrogge looked at the faces of Vereshchagin's officers. "We'll keep our flag and other things, but we want to reorganize ourselves as a light attack company in your battalion. The Third Light Attack Company, so we can keep what we can of our name."

"Does anyone disagree with this?" Vereshchagin asked. "It is so moved. Shall we move on to matters of strategy?"

Matti Harjalo gave everyone else a second or two to speak, then said, "*Hai*, O-Anton-sama. Let's move on to strategy."

The Iceman said with mock levity, "Having declared war on the universe, how do we propose to win?"

"The transport that got away took off at high speed in the wrong direction. This will give us a couple of extra months of breathing space. We may have as much as six or seven years," Henke pointed out.

Harjalo shook his head. "We'll be lucky if we get more than five, and they'll know we have warships the next time around."

"Chiharu, for the benefit of us all, what is the likelihood that the Imperial Government may simply decide that Suid-Afrika is not worth the cost to pacify?" Vereshchagin asked.

"Very low, I regret to say." Eschewing corrective surgery, Yoshida had begun wearing steel-rimmed reading glasses. He took them off and began polishing them.

"United Steel-Standard will, of course, view recovery of its position here as essential and will make every effort to induce the Imperial Government to act. As it is presently constituted, the Imperial Government will conclude that its prestige will not allow it to avoid a confrontation. The Imperial Defense Forces and the Ministry of Security will undoubtedly view pacification of Suid-Afrika as a matter of honor, while expansionist elements will argue that control of Suid-Afrika's fusion metals is essential for national security and that allowing rebellion to succeed here will undermine the foundations of the Imperial way."

"You would think that people there would realize that we are serious about keeping USS out," Christiaan De Wette commented.

"What about the Japanese public?" Per Kiritinitis, newly promoted to captain, asked.

"It is doubtful that the Japanese public will pay any attention to the matter," Yoshida responded. "Information about colonial wars does not circulate freely, and apart from persons who enter the military and the security services, very few Japanese pay attention to colonial matters. The persons governing Japan, I regret to say, have become narrowly Japanese in their focus, and do not have a realistic understanding of how they are perceived by other cultures, which is very distressing. Although I hope that reforms will be implemented, it may take a significant shock, perhaps a shock similar to our defeat in the Great Pacific War, to correct the cultural and psychological narrowness that has led us to present Imperial policies."

"Conquering this planet looks cheap on paper," Matti Harjalo added. "The Imperial Government has already put out two task groups, and the more effort they put into conquering this place, the less likely it is that they'll quit. I think that we can expect to get hit at five- or six-year intervals until they finally bury us."

"We can still hope that the Imperial Government will implement reforms," Yoshida said.

"Chiharu," Kolomeitsev said, with unaccustomed gentleness, "once a self-perpetuating system of repression has established itself, it cannot be reformed, it can only be toppled. My people lived under communism for four generations and under the systems that succeeded it for four generations more, and I would tell you from the heart that you cannot reform something that is corrupt at its roots."

Ohlrogge asked, "In five or six years, can't we bastion the planet so that they can't take it?"

Henke nodded. "I have begun working up a plan for a national redoubt, modeled on the Swiss strategy. Briefly, in years one and two, we would dig cavern complexes and prepare the population psychologically. In years three and four, we would begin shifting industry and storing additional food; and in years five and six, we would begin shifting the population itself, destroying the facilities we leave behind. I envision enrolling all adult males into the militia, and a significant percentage of the juveniles and adult females into supporting services."

"The problem with a national redoubt," Harjalo argued, "is that the Imperial Government will either nuke it until it glows and send a batch of reliable settlers out, or even worse and more likely, they'll keep trying out biological agents until they find one that we can't stop. We can't replace warships, and we can't count on being able to ambush the next couple of frigates they send. We might be able to wreck a task group or maybe even two, but eventually we're going to lose."

"Hans?" Vereshchagin said mildly. "I see that you have been waiting to speak."

" 'You may triumph on the fields of the Pelennor for a day, but against the Power that has arisen there is no victory,' " Coldewe declaimed triumphantly.

Harjalo suppressed a smile. "Hans is right. We can't take on a new expedition from Earth every six years forever."

"Another thought which has occurred to me is that we might export revolution to other colonial planets and force the Imperial Government to disperse its resources in this manner," Henke said.

"No good." Harjalo shook his head. "At least no good for the people here. By the time the Imperial Government finds out that we've launched revolutions in three or four other places, there will be a task group on our doorstep."

Vereshchagin spoke. "Raul? Now that we have run through other possibilities, I believe that it is time for you to outline your idea."

Sanmartin nodded. "First, I think that Chiharu is right when he says that USS and the people running things in Tokyo are going to believe that letting us go will cause other planets and nations to get wrong ideas. Second, if the Imperial Government takes us seriously and wants us badly enough, they can bury us. I think they'll take us seriously, so the only way for us to win is to go to Earth and persuade them not to want to come here."

Ohlrogge almost fell out of his chair. "With one battalion, we're going to attack Earth?"

The Iceman's eyes gleamed. He patted Ohlrogge on the

shoulder. "You will get used to this sort of thing around here, Ulrich."

A glimmer of a smile touched Sanmartin's face. "While there is a modest disparity in odds, to quote Virgil, *'Possunt quia posse videntur,'* which means, 'They can do it because they think they can do it.' "

Seeing De Wette eyeing him skeptically, he continued, "When I first got to this battalion, Steel Rudi Scheel told me the battalion had *sisu* and lots of it. I had to ask him what *sisu* was, and he told me that it was mostly being too ignorant to ever know when you're beaten. Our people think that they can take on the known universe and win. They may be right."

"Comments?" Vereshchagin asked, looking around the table.

Kolomeitsev folded his arms. "Raul is correct. Having let the jinn out of its bottle, we must go to Earth. We cannot win here, and if we lose, it scarcely matters how. We have three assets: surprise, warships, and a small cadre of excellent soldiers. As someone said, 'With a lever long enough, I can move the world.' There comes a time to smash the cauldrons and scuttle the boats. I think that time has come."

"I agree it sounds quite risky," Yoshida said calmly. "However, there is an expression, 'To capture the baby tiger, you must enter the mother tiger's lair.' "

"If we succeed, with luck we buy time for humanity to mature," Vereshchagin said. "And time, to a man who has great objects in view, is the most precious commodity of all."

"Who said that?" Harjalo asked.

The Variag winked. "According to Plutarch, Quintus Sertorius did." He looked around the room. "First, who precisely is our enemy, and what precisely are our objectives?"

"The last time I checked, I was shooting at Imperials," De Wette said. "Aren't we fighting the Imperial Government? I think that they would take us seriously if we burned down Tokyo."

Yoshida said icily, "My sister's family lives in Tokyo. The Imperial Government is a glove that many hands wear. Cut the hands, not the glove. Our enemy is United Steel-Standard."

"USS is part of the DKU *keiretsu* and is financed by the Daikichi Sanwa Bank. I see no reason to leave them out of any reckoning," the Iceman commented.

"What is a *keiretsu*?" De Wette asked.

Captain Saki Bukhanov, the battalion's logistical genius, had dabbled in running the banking systems on two different worlds, and he recognized that Vereshchagin had brought him to answer such questions. "A *keiretsu* is a loose grouping of companies under one of the major banks. The bank provides financing to its companies and owns substantial amounts of the stock. The directorships interlock. The bank has the right to appoint management, and senior officials move between companies. In effect, USS is one tentacle of a very large octopus."

"So, in effect, we are declaring war on a number of corporations," Henke observed. "How do we fight them? They do not have bodies or souls to punish. If we blow up a factory, the insurance company will pay off."

Coldewe grinned. "Insurance companies don't cover war risks."

"The DKU group is *big*," Sanmartin said. "You aren't even thinking close to the proper order of magnitude. Knocking off a factory is a small pinprick to these companies."

"Captain Sanmartin is correct," Yoshida said. "The Daikichi Sanwa is Japan's largest bank. It must have more than a trillion yen in assets, without counting its subsidiaries and its *keiretsu* companies."

"Add some zeros," Bukhanov commented. "The DKU group has a larger GNP than some continents on Earth."

Harjalo said, "I understand the point, and I'm still a simple soldier. How do we hurt them?"

Sanmartin sucked in his breath. "Well, corporations don't bleed. People do. To use Chiharu's analogy, we need to strip away the glove and take a cleaver to the fingers. These corporate groups are larger than any army, but only a few people make the decisions. If we target them, and quantities of the politicians and ministry bureaucrats who keep them powerful, they will feel the pain."

Yoshida stated with artful simplicity, "I wish for Japan to survive. I do not believe that this will occur unless the ministry officials and corporate leaders who control the Imperial Government change their thinking."

"If we shoot enough of them, they'll get the message," Harjalo said. "I gather we're talking about a quick tip-and-run raid on Tokyo."

"Yes, the bureaucrats and corporate heads concentrate there. The city of Tokyo is extremely large, roughly a hundred kilometers in diameter. I do not believe that we could take control of more than a few points with the manpower available," Henke said doubtfully.

He thought for a moment. "There are only a few battalions

of troops billeted within the city, but there are at least a hundred thousand riot police—*kidotai*—stationed there, and perhaps an additional ten thousand security police. Both the riot police and the security police have some infantry training, and the riot police hold regular earthquake drills. I suspect that the National Police Agency could evacuate and cordon off the entire city center of Tokyo in two or three hours."

Jankowskie, the junior officer present, spoke up. "Do we even need to send people in? Why not just hit them from space?"

"The question is a fair one, but I believe that the city has defenses against attacks from space," Kolomeitsev said.

Yoshida nodded. "There are always a number of warships at Yamato Station, and even though Japan demobilized its space-based missile defenses several decades ago, there is still a ring of missile interceptor sites around the Tokyo metropolitan area. They were intended to knock down intercontinental ballistic missiles, but they can also destroy orbiting warships. They would keep us at a distance, and we would undoubtedly cause severe civilian casualties in attempting to destroy the ministries and the USS Building."

"Well, we might not even have to hit them at all," Jankowskie persisted. "If we took out Yamato Station, we could always threaten to mix a nuclear-tipped missile in with enough other stuff to saturate the defenses. Or we could threaten to hit some other city if Tokyo turned out to be too tough a target."

"Detlef, I am fairly certain that they would not believe that we could hit Tokyo with an atomic missile unless we actually demonstrated that we could do so. And I will not use a nuclear weapon on a city, no matter what," Vereshchagin said with simple finality. "I have always said that we should only kill the ones we cannot reform. Moreover, war is the controlled application of violence to achieve political objectives, and I do not believe that we have one chance in a thousand of altering the Imperial Government's policies unless we selectively prune some of the persons presently controlling the Imperial Government."

He absently tapped his pipe against his knee. "As a final thought, there is something indefinable about what we are doing. Warships are very impersonal. If we simply blast away from the relative security of space, I suspect that the Japanese will perceive us as less than fully committed. Above all, we wish to make this a very personal matter for the Japanese people."

"Yes, sir," Jankowskie said, nodding agreement.

No one spoke for a moment or two. Then De Wette said flatly, "It all sounds impossible, Anton. And even if it is not, I think that attacking Tokyo would give them even more of a reason to crush us."

"As Raul has grasped, our war in truth is not against the Japanese people or even against the Imperial Government, it is against certain people who have caused a war to come into existence," Yoshida said.

De Wette shook his head. "Maybe I am still missing the point here."

"Look, winning means convincing whoever is running the Imperial Government that they really don't want to apply the force they need to pound us into topsoil—agreed?" Harjalo said, pointing his finger at De Wette.

"Agreed," De Wette said, nodding slowly.

"No victory we win here is going to change things in Tokyo. Even if we win, it'll be years before anyone knows, and at best, somebody nonessential like the prime minister will resign. If we sit back and wait for the Imperial Government to come to us, all we can try to do is absorb whatever punishment they can mete out. Esdraelon is an example of what happens when they get tired of fighting fair. Eventually, their ability to mete out punishment is going to exceed our ability to absorb it—agreed?"

"Agreed," De Wette said reluctantly.

Harjalo stared him down. "To put it baldly, whatever we try has a high risk of failure. If we go to Earth and shake things up, they might fall out the right way. If they don't, we might as well die gloriously so that the civilians here maybe have an opportunity to surrender on reasonable terms."

Vereshchagin said, "Christiaan, in terms of your own people's history, if someone had assassinated Rhodes, Beit, Milner, and Chamberlain in 1898, it is quite possible that Britain would have never gone to war with the Transvaal and the Orange Free State. Raul, can you add to this?"

Sanmartin laid his hands on the table in front of him. "We win by convincing the Japanese people that they don't want to win. Sometimes the Japanese act like a school of fish swimming in tight formation—all of a sudden, they turn around and swim the other way. If a few of them are half-convinced already, well, maybe we can get all of them turned around."

Yoshida nodded. "The psychological effect of an attack on USS and the ministries in Tokyo would far outweigh the military effect. I believe that it is essential for us to convince the

Japanese people of our sincerity in acting and the purity of our motives, and that in doing so, as Raul suggests, we will alter the consensus impelling the Imperial Government to send yet a third task group to Suid-Afrika."

Jankowskie gave him a quizzical look. "I am not sure I understand what you mean when you talk about our sincerity."

"From a Japanese point of view, the sincerity of individuals is often equated to their willingness to uphold principles in the face of overwhelming disapproval, or even to die for them."

"The forty-seven ronin," Kolomeitsev said.

Yoshida nodded again. "The *Chushinguru*—the *Treasury of Loyal Retainers*—is the story of the forty-seven ronin of Ako, and it excellently illustrates this point. When the young lord of Ako failed to pay off a corrupt courier of Shogun Tsunayoshi's government, the courier caused him to be disgraced, and Ako tried to kill him. Ako was ordered to commit *seppuku*. His retainers secretly swore to avenge him."

Sanmartin took up the thread of the story. "They waited three years to allay suspicion, then the forty-seven of them who stayed with the program sealed a pact in blood, turned the courier and his guards into dog meat, and presented themselves to the shogun for execution. The Japanese people collectively went nuts over the incident. Their grave site is a national shrine. Whether or not they were right, the Japanese agree that they were sincere about it, and they've been writing stories, songs, and plays about the forty-seven ronin for the last five centuries."

Yoshida nodded yet again. "If we were able to present an assault as revenge against USS and their creatures, our sincerity, as evidenced by our attacking our enemies in the heart of Tokyo, will make it much harder for the Imperial Government to justify an expedition against us. Possibly, it would also strike fear in the hearts of ministers who would order such an expedition."

De Wette finally nodded. "It is a strange way for people to think, but all right, you have convinced me."

"Matti?" Vereshchagin asked.

"Unless someone has a better idea, I know where we want to go. Let's go back to talking about who we want to hit when we get there," Harjalo said, looking around the table for contradiction.

"I believe that we should target every individual in USS corporate headquarters, Daikichi Sanwa's corporate headquarters, the Ministry of International Trade and Industry, and the Ministry of Security," the Hangman said, counting off on his fingers.

"There will be no shortage of volunteers to go after the blacklegs," Kolomeitsev said. "In addition, I would suggest eliminating the bureaucrats in the Ministry of Finance who set banking policy, and the people in the Ministry of Education, who promulgate that execrable *kokugaku* history which justifies all sorts of villainy. We also should kill a few political bosses—it would gain us a certain amount of public sympathy, and I would personally find it very satisfying."

"How about the Ministry of Defense?" Kiritinitis asked.

"The MoD would be a tough target, maybe a tougher target than the Ministry of Security—guards, deep fortified shelters, filtration systems," Harjalo admitted, "but to be honest, unless things have changed a whole lot, the people there pretty much do what they're told to by the ministries with real power."

"Agreed," Vereshchagin said. "However ironic this may appear, I do not see any reason for us to view the Ministry of Defense as a military target. Moreover, in the event that we are successful, they will be fully occupied providing explanations. Are there other suggestions?"

"Perhaps we should also attack the Ministry of Construction. It is the single largest source of corrupt deals to use in bribing politicians," Yoshida said.

"I think not, Chiharu. To be comprehensible to the Japanese people, our actions should take the form of action against the centers of power which have directly influenced the Imperial Government to subjugate Suid-Afrika," Vereshchagin said. "The use of the MoC as a source of bribes would appear to be a problem for the Japanese to resolve, rather than our problem."

"There is also Dentsu-Hakuhado to consider," Sanmartin said at length. "I think that we need to address them as well."

"What is Dentsu-Hakuhado, Raul?" Henke asked.

"An ad agency, the world's largest. They essentially have a monopoly on advertising on television stations and in major magazines, which gives them ties to all of the major corporations and politicians, and enormous leverage over the media. As an extra service, Dentsu-Hakuhado pressures newspapers and magazines into modifying stories that might embarrass their clients."

Yoshida nodded agreement. "In effect, my country has two censorship systems, a public system managed by the Ministry of Security, and a private one administered by Dentsu-Hakuhado. Inasmuch as we will wish people to know our side of this matter, Raul is correct to say that we should deal with Dentsu-Hakuhado."

"Hakkaa Päälle," Matti Harjalo said. It was an old Finnish battle cry. It meant, "Cut them down." "USS and the other big corporations have been fighting a lot of dirty little wars. It's time that we showed them how to wage one properly."

"Detlef, can the transport *Chiyoda* be repaired quickly?" Vereshchagin asked.

"I am not sure," Jankowskie answered soberly. "Raul made an awful mess of her bridge, but most of the other damage is superficial."

"That gives us a frigate, a corvette, and possibly a transport. Does anyone have another proposal for us to consider?" Vereshchagin asked deliberately.

No one spoke, and he nodded approval. "I thought not. Raul, Piotr, and Chiharu, please stay behind so that we can work up a plan to discuss and to present to President Beyers and the government. I thank the rest of you for your efforts," Vereshchagin said, bringing the meeting to an end.

Monday(319)

COLDEWE'S COMPANY TOOK UP RESIDENCE IN THE VILLAGE OF Platkops. As Coldewe cheerfully explained, the last tenants of the Johannesburg casern left it a mess. Arguing that the sauna and the kitchen were the two things too important to be left to officers, he turned the task of reestablishing them over to Wanjau and Kasha.

Coldewe was both surprised and disturbed when Raul Sanmartin appeared with his bergen and a hammock under his arm.

"Raul, what are you doing here?"

"Moving in with you. You want to find me a room?" Sanmartin walked past him into the building. "Isaac said that there's a nice one on the first floor that nobody's claimed."

"It's next to mine." Coldewe caught up with him. "Why aren't you home with Albert? Don't tell me you want to bring Hendricka here. She'll have a hundred uncles in residence, and we'll never get anything done."

"I left her with Mother—Tant Betje. I couldn't stay there, Hans." Sanmartin walked into the room Coldewe indicated, dropped his bergen, and leaned his rifle against the wall.

"Where's your personal stuff?" Coldewe asked.

Sanmartin smiled, ever so slightly. "I gave away the suit and left my singlestick for Hendricka. The rest I burned."

Coldewe blinked. "It took forever to get you into clothes that fit."

"I won't be needing them. If the Variag approves, we'll be leaving in about thirty days."

"What about Hendricka?"

"Albert and Betje are really her parents. It's better this way."

"Look. Raul, I understand that you're upset. Grief is a natural thing, but you can't—"

"*Nascentes morimur*, every day I die a little," Sanmartin said woodenly. "Apart from the soldiering, nothing makes sense to me anymore. Too many ghosts around here, Hans— Rudi, Rhett, Edmund. Now Hanna, always Hanna."

Coldewe quietly shut the door.

Sanmartin leaned his back against the wall. "Hans, this time the pain won't stop. Something's broken inside. Say something poetic. Say something funny."

"Raul, if that's true, Earth is the last place you should be going," Coldewe temporized.

"The brain still functions, and that's what matters. All I need to do is get through the next thirty days until we up ship."

"What about Hendricka? How old will she be when you get back? How old will you be? If you drop out of her life now, she'll never let you back in!"

"What about Marta?"

Coldewe scowled at him. "That's not fair, Raul, and it's not the same. This is your daughter."

"I tried to tell Hendricka where her mother went. Heaven is difficult to explain to a three-year-old. We adopted her out, remember? She belongs to Albert and Betje."

"Look, if you stay, you don't have to be a soldier. Why don't you think about going back to the university?"

"Live a normal life, you mean?" Sanmartin laughed a little and closed his eyes. "You lose your sense of time in the icebox. It rubs the edges off. It leaves marks. You can't see them, but they're there. Besides, you and Anton need me on this one. There are no better military minds than Paul and Piotr, and you're not so bad yourself, but our problem is political, not military, and that's where I fit in. By definition, what we're trying to accomplish is crazy, and I'm that. Soldiering is what fits me, Hans."

"Look, Raul—nobody can take Hanna's place, but there'll be somebody for you. I know it. Don't cut yourself off. What about that woman who was hanging all over you at the funeral?"

"Anneke Brink. I felt like hitting her."

"Well, maybe not her, but somebody. What about Daniela Kotze? You like her. She lost a boyfriend in the rebellion and a husband this time around. Try consoling each other over a cup of coffee."

"No, Hans."

"There are lots of fine women out there. Heaven knows Marta deserves someone better than me."

"You don't understand, Hans," Sanmartin said with deceptive mildness. "It wouldn't be fair."

"To whom?"

"To anyone. It's too soon. It'll always be too soon. Everything inside me is gone. I can't just pretend that nothing happened. I resent the living a little, the ones who didn't suffer. Remember years ago, when I told you I felt like cleaning this world off and starting over? I feel a little like that now." His eyes chilled. "And I understand this—if I don't go, Hendricka may not have the chance to grow up."

Coldewe made one last attempt. "If you go, where does that leave Albert? Who's going to fix the environment?"

"Simon, or Maria, or no one. Anyone but me." Sanmartin looked up. "You don't understand, Hans. Albert will keep things going for a few more years, but he's lost control of the legislature. It'll take them awhile to muster the courage, but they'll run him out, sooner or later. And Claassen's lost control of the Reformed Nationals. It's only a matter of time before the people here start squabbling over the spoils." He smiled wistfully.

"For five years, we had a dream that we woke up to every morning. Now, the best thing I can hope for is that the people who come after us don't do too bad a job." He shook his head emphatically. "But I can't stay to see that."

Isaac Wanjau knocked on the door and opened it. "Captain Coldewe," he said with a straight face, but with deep compassion in his eyes. "I think we need you out here to help us decide how to fit the sauna in."

"Thanks, Isaac," Coldewe said automatically.

Tuesday(319)

CHRISTOS CLAASSEN, ELECTED EMERGENCY SPEAKER OF THE ASsembly with only a modest amount of chicanery, called a special session to discuss the plan to go to Earth, which Beyers had approved as commander-in-chief. Beyers and Claassen privately made two things clear: The expedition was going, regardless; and if anyone played politics with the debate, there would be repercussions.

Vereshchagin and Sanmartin were called upon to testify. The member from Linden wanted to know why they couldn't simply fight a defensive war; she was gently asked if she was volunteering her home and front yard for the next battlefield. The member from Annapolis wanted to know why the expedition couldn't confine its attacks to "military" targets; he was politely told that the distinction had gotten a little blurred.

Sanmartin explained the theory behind the expedition as the "mule" theory. A mule responds very well to gentle coaxing—once you get the mule's attention with a sufficiently big stick.

He didn't slip until one member made a long speech, in the form of a question, exulting over the prospects of hitting Tokyo and making lots of the "little yellow monkeys" pay for their sins. Sanmartin rejoined tersely, "If this doesn't work, I hope you're the first one to fry."

The exchange was omitted from the official record.

Wednesday(319)

WHILE THE ICEMAN BUSIED HIMSELF ARRANGING LOGISTICS AND reviewing potential landing sites, Sanmartin began working on the technical side of things. Before he was fairly started, Dr. Natasha Solchava dropped by.

"Hello, Natasha. I was meaning to see you. I need to talk to you about Yuri Malinov."

"I have burned out three malignancies along Yuri's spinal cord and two more in his brain, but even with his iron constitution, this is too much. He is dying."

"How long will he be able to function?"

"Depending on how he deals with the pain, three months, perhaps. Perhaps six."

"And if he went into the icebox?"

"The cooling would retard the growth of the tumors, perhaps even cause them to regress slightly." She looked at him sharply. "Yuri asked me the same questions yesterday, but he would not tell me why. What are the two of you up to?"

"We're going to Earth in twenty-nine days. I want to take Yuri with me. It's a nine-month trip, and I can afford to keep him on ice for seven months of it. I want someone to handle *Ajax*'s weapons systems when we get there. All Yuri has to do is shoot, and if you can keep him functioning for three hours in combat when we get there, that's all I need."

"It is not a question of me keeping Yuri functioning, it is a question of Yuri keeping himself functioning, but yes, I can do things to dull the pain. But can't you let him die in peace?" Solchava asked pedantically.

"Yuri has been a soldier for twenty-four years. He didn't think much of the Imperial Government before and he thinks less of it now."

Solchava softened. "Yes, I know. I doubt that anything would give him greater peace than to go with you. But Hans didn't ask me here to discuss Yuri Malinov. Hans is concerned about you."

Sanmartin looked at her. "Natasha, can you imagine what it would be like to lose Jan?"

"Yes. I know that they make jokes about me behind my back, but they do not make words to describe what I would feel if I lost Jan."

"Just do the same for me that you're doing for Yuri, Natasha. Get me to the battlefield and let me function for three hours."

"Jan tells me that you want him along on this expedition. He has already asked me to allow him to go. You will need a surgeon along, I imagine."

"Yes, I want both of you."

She smiled painfully. "How kind of you to ask."

After she left, he called Resit Aksu—the Turkish Senior intelligence sergeant and team were busily interrogating prisoners on the latest changes to Tokyo's topography. Then he went to find Aleksei Beregov, who was acting as battalion sergeant in Malinov's place, and Lieutenant Meri Reinikka, the engineer platoon leader.

He caught Beregov by the arm as he passed him in a corridor. "Bery—can you find me nine men who look and sound Japanese?"

Beregov rubbed his chin. "Including Aksu, Liu, and Captain Yoshida, maybe eight."

"Nine would be better."

"Maybe we could use Soe."

"He looks Japanese. Maybe Aksu can work on him enough so that he acts and sounds mildly retarded instead of obviously foreign."

Slapping Beregov on the shoulder, Sanmartin flew up to see Meri Reinikka and gingerly took a seat on Reinikka's hammock. Reinikka had found himself a computerized drawing table somewhere and worked from it standing up, which made watching him an interesting process.

"Meri—some technical questions. If we wanted to use our ships to thoroughly wreck some buildings, from top to sub-sub-basement, how would we go about it?"

Like most engineer officers, Meri Reinikka enjoyed blowing things up a great deal more than he enjoyed building them in the first place. He pursed his lips. "It would take an awfully long time to reach underground with composite particles."

"We won't have it. There are six missile-defense centers ringing Tokyo. With a little luck, we can take out one or two with assault teams and clear a lane into the city, but if we circle around and try to pound buildings into rubble, the centers we don't take out will lob missiles over the horizon at us. We're also going to have to hit the central air defense command and control center, which is almost certainly a hardened target."

"*Maya* has precision munitions, doesn't it?"

Sanmartin made a face. "The projectile mix they sent *Maya* out with was mostly light stuff, and she's already fired off the biggest things in her arsenal. Most of what she has left is only good for antipersonnel work."

"Nukes?"

"We have one nuclear artillery shell that we inherited from the former Republic of Suid-Afrika that we can attach to a missile, but using nuclear weapons on buildings in the heart of Tokyo is something that I'd rather not do—it's a little indiscriminate."

"Possibly," Reinikka conceded.

"If we sent assault teams into the city, is there anything they could carry with them that would do the job? How about a dust initiator?"

"To take out a really big building?" Reinikka shook his head. He called up a window in the corner of his electronic table and consulted a table. "Probably not. A kilo of explosive, another kilo of incendiary mix, and eighty kilos of surround—coal dust, flour, powdered coffee, tapioca, what have you—will cover about sixteen hundred cubic meters. That's maybe one floor of a building that's twenty-eight meters on a side. I could build you something to pump the dust, but that's an awful lot of weight to lug around. I don't know that conventional explosive would work either; you need too much for a team of men to carry, and it would take a lot of time to put the charges in place."

He thought for a minute. "Of course, I could probably build you an air-to-ground projectile that would do the job."

"We don't have time to set up a production line."

"I could do it in a couple of weeks from stuff we have on hand. Listen, for the body of the missile we take the barrel off one of the 210mm howitzers we captured—those gun tubes are made of extremely hard alloy, and thirty-two calibers times 210 millimeters is nearly seven meters long. You can pack an awful lot of HE into a tube that big." Reinikka warmed to his task.

"Put a fuse with a time delay in the tail, pull the motor and the laser guidance system off one of the smaller guided projectiles, fabricate some wings and a nose cap, and presto—you have something that goes off in the basement. The shell of the building will still be there, but the insides will be a wreck. I could slap one together and test it on a rock someplace to make sure it goes off. Of course, a projectile like that wouldn't travel very fast, so you would have to launch it from where the missile defenses can't knock it out of the sky."

"If you can fit a couple of them to a corvette, we could launch them from in close."

"On a corvette?" As an engineer, Reinikka had all sorts of strange things loaded into his data base, and he promptly called up a diagram and scanned it. "I don't think we could mount them externally—the heat and stress when the ship entered atmosphere would likely snap them right off. On a corvette, there isn't much internal space to work with. Maybe I could squeeze one or two in. Doesn't a corvette carry a little boat of some kind? We could pull that out and use the platform as a launch rail."

"Talk to Jankowskie and the people over at Complex and work up a plan. Now the big question: The hardest target we want to hit is the Ministry of Security. Would one of these missiles you're talking about take it out?"

Reinikka consulted his computer again. "All the way to the bottom? No, at least, I don't think so," he said after a pause.

"Why not?"

"The MoS was built before the crack-up. Half a dozen nations had cruise missiles. I can build you something that will crash through six meters of solid concrete, but I'm guessing that they have at least one and probably two basement levels with sealed armor plating to survive a hit from anything short of a fairly big nuke. The 210mm penetrator I was talking about would take out the mice on the top floors, but the rats would stay snug in the deep basements until somebody came to dig them out."

"Maybe if we built something bigger."

Reinikka shook his head emphatically. "Not unless we put a nuclear warhead on it. We'd need a larger hardened tube and a bigger motor, which we don't have, and we still wouldn't be able to invest enough kinetic energy in it to make it punch through two layers of armor—it would break up. It just wouldn't be dense enough. I could build you something that would penetrate, but I couldn't build anything that would penetrate *and* blow up."

"We'll have to go after the MoS with assault teams then."

"I wish I could be more helpful." Reinikka wrinkled his nose. "I've got another bit of bad news for you. I talked to some of the people over at Complex."

"And?" Sanmartin shifted his weight on the hammock.

"The USS Building was put up right after the crack-up. It may also have a reinforced basement level."

Sanmartin leaned back, lost in thought. After a minute, he said, "Okay. Thanks, Meri. Get Rytov to start pulling the barrels off those two-tens for you."

After Kasha forced him to eat lunch, he and Chiharu Yoshida went to see Vereshchagin to discuss acts of "negative daring."

Vereshchagin did not trouble to mince words. "Which politicians do you suggest we assassinate?" he asked them quietly.

"Chiharu and I agree that it should be these two." Sanmartin laid two photographs copied from magazines on the table.

Vereshchagin picked up the top photograph of a fat man with gray hair.

"Schunichi Gyohten is head of the most openly expansionist UDP faction. Interestingly enough, he's never been elected to public office, although he's been UDP secretary general twice. He's described as being warm friends with the leaders of two right-wing extremist groups, which means that he finances them and uses them at election time," Sanmartin said. "They call him the Money Man."

Vereshchagin slid one photograph under the other. "And the other?"

"Osachi Abe. Abe leads what is either the third or fourth largest UDP faction. He's headed up ministries in four of the last five cabinets. He's the fifth generation of his family to be elected to the Diet from Niigata." Sanmartin shrugged. "Most current Diet members are the sons or sons-in-law of former Diet members, but the Abe family seems to carry hereditary service to extremes."

"Why Abe?" Vereshchagin asked.

"While Japan has had thirteen different prime ministers over the last twenty-eight years, it has only had seven different secretaries general of the United Democratic party," Yoshida explained. "Unless a scandal occurs prior to our arrival to bring down the government which was just installed, Abe will be the only faction leader of his generation who has not served a term as UDP secretary general, and he has only picked one prime minister."

Sanmartin added, "In a word, when the most recent cabinet gets pushed out of office, it's his turn at the trough."

"If our assault is successful, the current government will be discredited and forced to resign," Yoshida continued. "The current generation of faction leaders has exercised power for nearly thirty years, and a younger generation of politicians is openly restive. Assassinating Abe will almost certainly lead to a succession crisis within the UDP as younger, less-tainted politicians attempt to push aside the aging faction leaders."

"This might help us," Vereshchagin said, laying the photographs down.

"Rattling the dice," Sanmartin said as he picked them up.

Moving to the last person on his list, he went to see Timo Haerkoennen about creating a computer simulation that would allow them to work through the rough spots in the plan.

Haerkoennen was an absolute genius when it came to communications and computer systems, and utterly disinterested in virtually everything else. After reviewing the initial design criteria, Haerkoennen voiced one terse criticism. "You're looking at this wrong, sir. We're going after people, but we're not going after information systems. Your plan doesn't call for us to screw with the companies, if you know what I mean."

Sanmartin shook his head. "Come again?"

Haerkoennen squared his shoulders impatiently. "I mean, we're killing the people who run USS and Daikichi, but we're not really touching the people who *own* these companies."

"Good point. Go on."

"I mean, companies like Daikichi have been manipulating Japan's stock market for decades. We ought to return the favor." Haerkoennen smiled crookedly. "I got some ideas. Just remember that you need me along when it comes time to choose up personnel, sir."

Sanmartin nodded. "I read once that every ship should have a Finn aboard to calm storms and call up a wind, and you're the closest thing we have to a wizard."

After Haerkoennen explained his ideas twice, Sanmartin threw up his hands and took him to see Vereshchagin, who smiled and set Haerkoennen and Saki Bukhanov—the nearest thing the battalion had to a financial expert—off to see the only professor of economics at the university who understood stock-market modeling.

Thursday(319)

SANMARTIN LOOKED UP FROM THE FIELD DESK WHERE HE WAS working when Isaac Wanjau ushered Pieter Olivier in.

"Major Sanmartin, do you have time to see me?" Olivier asked.

"Yes. Pull up a chair." Sanmartin looked around his tiny room.

Wanjau reached one huge hand outside the door with a flourish and produced a straight-backed chair for Olivier to sit in.

Olivier watched in fascination. Then recovering himself, he sat down. "Heer Sanmartin, I am very sorry about the death of your wife." Having some idea of Sanmartin's temper, he refrained from making comments about Wanjau that Sanmartin might find offensive.

"Thank you. What can I do for you?"

"I am sure that you are aware from your spies that I am the current head of the Afrikaner Bond."

The Bond was a semisecret and fervently nationalist Afrikaner organization. One faction of it, the Afrikaner Order, had launched the rebellion. Olivier had been involved up to his neck, and Raul Sanmartin had personally accepted his surrender.

Sanmartin nodded, neither confirming nor denying Olivier's statement. "What brings you here?"

"I owe a debt of gratitude to you for keeping me alive and not transporting me, and as much as I dislike Colonel Vereshchagin and his policies, it occurs to me that I owe a greater debt to him for preserving the Volk," Olivier said formally, the sour expression on his face betraying his somewhat mixed feelings.

"And?"

"Christos Claassen tells me that you are preparing an expedition to Earth. Our interests coincide. I can offer you our assistance." He opened his briefcase. "We have control of several hundred million francs invested in Zurich. It represents the last remaining portion of the gold and foreign currency reserves of the former Republic of Suid-Afrika. While the interest goes to fund various activities for the Afrikaners remaining on Earth, our organization retained control of the actual trust principle. Heer Claassen seems to feel that you could use this money."

Sanmartin leaned back. "Are you sure that the people we transported haven't cleaned out your accounts?"

Olivier smiled slightly. "To ensure that this money was not diverted to improper uses, the access number to the account has always been divided between the Bond's treasurer and assistant treasurer. After the rebellion, the assistant treasurer refused to give his portion of the number to anyone being transported."

"That's right. They murdered his brother-in-law." Sanmartin thought for a moment. "Timo Haerkoennen came up with a scheme. Do you know, we might even be able to turn a profit. Is there someone in your organization you can trust to send to Earth?"

"Yes," Olivier said. "Me."

"Hmm?"

"My children are grown. My wife left me several years ago."

Sanmartin studied his face. Olivier's cheeks were puffy, and he had put on some weight, but traces of the man he had been were still there. Sanmartin shook his hand firmly. "Welcome to the party."

Friday(319)

WITH THE ASSAULT PLANNING COMING TOGETHER, SANMARTIN BEgan working on other aspects. Late in the day, he brought a university professor in a simulated tweed jacket to see Hans Coldewe.

"Hans, this is Dr. Jacob Van der Wurte. Jac is a lecturer in astrophysics, and I've asked him to help us with the problem of bringing your shuttle down on Japanese soil without anyone noticing. Jac, Hans will be commanding the assault group."

Coldewe shook Van der Wurte's hand. Eyeing Van der Wurte's bushy hair with distaste, he said to Sanmartin, "I'm not going to like this, am I?"

Van der Wurte enthusiastically set up a portable display screen he had brought along. "I think that you will be pleasantly surprised once I explain my concept to you, Heer Coldewe. Now, Sol systems has a great deal more orbiting debris than most solar systems, and a lot of it is man-made junk orbiting around Earth. Although a ship would stand out—"

"Like a clown at a funeral," Coldewe interjected.

"A shuttle is much too small. So, if you cut loose from your frigate at a point just inside the outer Van Allen belt with a great deal of initial velocity and make your approach to Earth via the planet's south axis—there's an ice continent there—no one will notice that you are not just another stray piece of rock."

"What about astronomers?"

"Someone's equipment may register you, but it's not as though people expect to see shuttles appearing out of nowhere," Van der Wurte said with an academic's certainty.

"We're painting you with a black, silicone-based paint to confuse your radar signature, and you won't have to fire your engines for most of the trip," Sanmartin said reassuringly.

"The paint will burn away when you enter the atmosphere, which will make you look even more like a meteorite." Van der Wurte pointed to his display. "Your actual entry will be at a point northeast of an island called, ah, New Zealand. From there, it will be an easy trip. You overfly an island called, ah, Guam to let Heer Olivier off and then head for Japan."

Coldewe put on the smile he wore to charm people. "Doctor, you were born here on Suid-Afrika, weren't you?"

Van der Wurte beamed. "Why, yes. How did you know?"

"A lucky guess." Coldewe looked out the window. "Doctor, just out of curiosity, how much of a safety margin will we have in terms of things like food, oxygen, water?"

"Well, not a great deal. Of course, if something goes wrong, you might be able to ditch on one of the islands there," Van der Wurte admitted.

"And just how long is this trip going to take?" Coldewe asked suspiciously.

Van der Wurte brushed a stray piece of lint off his jacket. "Oh, roughly three hundred forty hours."

"Raul—we're going to spend three hundred and forty *hours* inside a shuttle?"

"It beats walking."

"Major Sanmartin and I have discussed installing things like a shower, a recycling plant for water, an extra tank for liquid oxygen—" Van der Wurte began to say.

Coldewe shut his eyes, evidently in great pain. "This is going to rival the Black Hole of Calcutta, isn't it?"

"After you string hammocks, it will be tight but manageable," Sanmartin said firmly. "Five will get you ten the boys start a nonstop tarok game back there."

"All this comes from letting the inmates run the asylum," Coldewe complained.

Saturday(319)

VERESHCHAGIN REVIEWED THE DRAFT PLAN HE WAS GIVEN AND made a number of changes. The most important one was to cut down the number of men involved to 140. "It is enough. Taking more will not appreciably increase our chances of overall success and will only increase our casualty list in the event that we fail."

"This isn't very many men to invade a nation of a hundred and seventy-five million," Coldewe complained.

" 'The Midianites, Amalekites, and all the Kedemites lay in the valley, as numerous as the locusts. Nor could their camels be counted, for these were as many as the sands on the seashore,' " Sanmartin quoted.

"All right. He's Moses, and you're Gideon. I stand corrected."

Sanmartin nodded. "While I am thinking about it, the ladies of Johannesburg have sewn us a battle flag—real silk. It's not bad, the salamander on it even sort of looks like a salamander."

The battalion emblem was a white salamander with three black spots and emerald green eyes on a black field.

"How nice of them," Vereshchagin said.

Malinov grinned like a skeleton.

"I hope you asked them why they waited until the war was over," Harjalo demanded. "What are we going to do with it? We're a rifle battalion. We have a crest—it's nicely broken in, too. Rifle battalions don't carry flags. This isn't another silver samovar, is it?"

The neo-Baroque samovar he referenced was a parting gift from the citizenry of Orenburg on NovySibir. It came out of storage once a year on May Day. Its aesthetic qualities were of the sort that took years to fully appreciate.

"Thank the ladies kindly, Raul," Vereshchagin said firmly. "Perhaps someone will build a museum we can offer it to."

Sunday (320)

WHEN HARJALO ANNOUNCED THAT THE BATTALION WAS GOING TO Earth, there was a second or two of silence and then a deep-throated roar. Their people kept it going for nearly a minute until Matti started tapping his foot.

"They're interested," Coldewe observed.

Then Matti announced that only 140 men would go.

The battalion immediately began whistling—the Russian equivalent of booing—and began a chorus of "Matti's got a bald spot, Matti's got a bald spot!" which was the traditional and rather silly way they dealt with any unpopular pronouncement from on high.

Then Vereshchagin asked for volunteers. Half of the battalion knew what the icebox meant, and Vereshchagin made certain that the rest knew what the time differential would do to the relationships left behind. He also made sure that would-be volunteers knew the odds against success.

It was a difficult decision for some, and Vereshchagin forced the ones who volunteered immediately to think it through overnight.

He ended up with a few more than three hundred volunteers to fill the 140 places. Only five of the reservists in De Wette's company volunteered, while the surviving hard cases in Degtyarov's No. 2 platoon volunteered to a man. Vereshchagin went among them, man by man, and quietly thanked the ones he would ask to stay behind. He accepted a fair number of Afrikaners and a few cowboys, but if he mostly selected veterans who had been with him for a half dozen years or longer, no one begrudged him this.

Meagher, Snyman, Karaev, and Thomas would command elements of the assault force under Hans Coldewe's control. Degtyarov and Savichev would command the elements of the Iceman's support force. Jankowskie would command the frigate, and Sanmartin would fly the corvette.

Choosing men who had worked together as the nucleus of the assault groups, Vereshchagin selected most of the men from first section, No. 1; first section, No. 2; second section, No. 9; and the recon platoon. He also took a mortar team from No. 4, and light attack men. A scattering of men came from the other rifle platoons and from the engineer and aviation platoons. Some men Vereshchagin chose because they could pass for Japanese; the rest he picked for their skills and experience.

Matti Harjalo would stay to form a coherent force from the ones who remained behind.

Monday(320)

JUST BEFORE THE EXPEDITION LEFT, THE QUESTION OF RENAMING the warships arose in the Assembly. A proposal to rename the frigate *Maya* the *Hanna Bruwer* was gently rejected, and an accompanying proposal to rename the corvette *Ajax* the *Louis Pretorius Snyman* was withdrawn.

After considerable discussion, *Maya* was renamed the *General Hendrik Pienaar*, and *Ajax* was sensibly rechristened the *Corporal Lightwell Gomani* after a dead A Company trooper from Ashcroft. Vereshchagin's men were already calling the 210mm penetrators that Reinikka was loading aboard her "Lightwell's pencils."

When Jankowskie's men painted the new names and tiny *Vierkleur* flags on the ships' hulls, they also painted a small, white gallows insignia on each for luck.

Thursday(323)

ESCORTED BY A LARGE CROWD INCLUDING CHILDREN RELEASED from school, the last shuttle left the spaceport to the wail of bagpipes from the battalion band. With all of the confusion, the legislature hadn't gotten around to adopting a national anthem, so instead the band played the "The Little Tin Soldier," "The Whistling Pig," and finally, the Finnish anthem "Our Land."

As Matti Harjalo watched the shuttle recede into the sky, he turned to Per Kiritinitis and said, "Okay, tell the pipers that that's enough. I can see little kids sticking fingers in their ears."

Outbound

A FRIGATE LIKE THE *HENDRIK PIENAAR* IS NOT A TROOPSHIP, NOR IS it designed for an eighteen-month voyage—nine months out and, assuming luck, nine months back—without resupply. Nevertheless, a frigate is not a small ship. As *Maya*, the *Hendrik Pienaar* had carried a crew of 130 to enable her to conduct around-the-clock operations, plus an additional thirty-six men to man her three corvettes. Because a reduced complement was more than sufficient to steer her between planets, she had a ninety-six-space hibernation unit.

In place of the two missing corvettes, Vereshchagin could carry two of Suid-Afrika's last three shuttles, both stuffed with equipment, and a pair of supply pods. Putting Kolomeitsev's support group and a scattering of other personnel into the icebox gave him enough room for Coldewe's assault group to live and train for their part of the mission. Yuri Malinov went into the icebox.

Lightwell Gomani's nickname had been "Speedy," which soon became the corvette's nickname as well. The patrician *Hendrik Pienaar* became known to her crew as "Granddad."

Sanmartin and Kolomeitsev made strenuous efforts to refine the plan further. The first four times they ran Haerkoennen's simulation, there were varying levels of success and few if any survivors. They made appropriate changes.

When Sanmartin brought the third set of changes back to Haerkoennen, he asked one question. "Timo, I noticed when we were running through the assault on the Ministry of Security Building, there was a little cutaway on the screen that said, 'Press Tab N for Option G.' What was that all about?"

"Try it and see," Haerkoennen said, turning his chair and proffering his terminal.

Sanmartin entered the last simulation he had saved and moved ahead to the Ministry of Security. Haerkoennen had stolen the graphic images for the buildings from some architectural program, and the screen portrayed an amazingly realistic aerial view of the ministry.

"The architect who built that deserves jail time," he commented as he pressed Tab N.

The building rotated until Sanmartin found himself looking south-southeast toward the reclaimed land in the Port of Tokyo. Suddenly, a huge reptilian creature lifted itself out of the waters of the harbor. Stepping out onto Kaigan-dori Avenue, it began moving toward the Ministry of Security in a series of measured, menacing steps.

Sanmartin folded his arms and looked at Haerkoennen.

"Captain Coldewe suggested it," Timo said gleefully as the simulation began counting down how long it would take to scramble aircraft from the military airfields in the vicinity of Tokyo.

Approximately one month into the voyage, Captain Chiharu Yoshida asked Lutheran lay minister Erixon, who was also serving as spiritual adviser to the Dutch Reformed adherents on board, to accept him into the Dutch Reformed faith. Superior Private Erixon, a tolerant soul handy with a machine gun, agreed without hesitation.

PERHAPS THE MOST MACABRE TOUCH DURING THE LONG TRIP WAS the "casualty pool." For a five-rand bet, troopers pulled out numbers ranging from 0 percent to 100 percent. On the return trip, half the pot would go to the soldier whose number most closely approximated the percentage of casualties suffered during the operation; the remainder would go to charity.

A hulking farmer's son in the Iceman's Support Group, Superior Private Kobus Nicodemus, drew the ticket that equated to 100 percent casualties and observed, "Now I know what they mean by mixed feelings."

WHEN THE TIME CAME TO TURN COLDEWE'S SHUTTLE LOOSE, RAUL Sanmartin's prediction about a nonstop tarok game turned out to be dead on.

VOID ————————————————

The Pacific Ocean, Earth

SUCKING OXYGEN FROM THE ATMOSPHERE RATHER THAN FROM ITS almost empty internal tanks, the shuttle skimmed along a few meters above the rough waters, barely cresting the tallest waves in the darkness. Although the lights in the cabin were turned off and instrument lights dimmed, the shuttle's nose still glowed very faintly from its burning passage through the upper air.

As the pilot, Kokovtsov, made a course correction to head the craft almost due northwest, Hans Coldewe commented from the command seat, "You know, I never realized you could fly a shuttle this close to the water."

Kokovtsov broke his habitual silence. "You're not supposed to."

His copilot, Zerebtsov, one of Thomas's recon boys, said reassuringly, "Don't worry, sir. If something goes wrong, it'll be over so quick you'll never notice."

"Thank you very much," Coldewe said, fingering the nondescript civilian clothes he was wearing underneath his uniform.

An hour and nine minutes later, Kokovtsov said, "Get the civ ready," and Zerebtsov went back into the main compartment to awaken Pieter Olivier.

From his seat next to the right emergency exit, Olivier's face looked grayish under the blue cabin lights. He looked around at Coldewe's troopers who were mostly asleep. "I keep asking what I have gotten myself into."

"We'll be passing over the island of Guam in eleven minutes. We're not slowing down, so I'm pushing you out the door in nine," Zerebtsov told him. "Try not to miss the island."

"I will try not to," Olivier assured him.

"One question—are you *sure* you never played tarok before?"

Olivier grinned. Moments later, he found himself drifting down. He opened his parachute and glided to a landing on a very wide white beach as the shuttle sped away into the night.

Slipping out of his harness, Olivier bundled his chute and stuffed it in a large green trash can. Walking a few hundred meters up the beach, he took off his coveralls and stuffed them into a different trash can. Straightening his tie, he walked up the hill to the lifeguard station and used the map there to orient himself as Thomas and the other reconnaissance troopers had taught him. Selecting the proper coin, he called an all-night taxi company to pick him up from the road.

An hour later, he checked himself into a medium-size hotel. Computing the time difference in his head, he placed a call to the small Berenger et Cie Bank in Geneva. "Hello. I have updated instructions for account 0110-7342-8119."

"Yes, monsieur." The clerk punched up the account on his terminal. "May I have the first phrase, please."

The clerk had a hair-thin mustache and an insouciant air that vaguely irritated Olivier. "The first phrase is 734-0021-7622-0912."

"That is correct, monsieur. And the second?"

"The second phrase is 482-9093-6550-3218."

"A moment, monsieur. Yes, that is correct. What may we do for you?"

"What is the current value of the account?"

"At current prices, that would be 345,632,873.37 ECU." Deftly noting Olivier's slight hesitation, the clerk added, "That is European Currency Units, monsieur."

"Very good. Please convert the trust principle. I wish to sell short the stock of the following companies . . ." Olivier rattled off the names, beginning with United Steel-Standard. "Put one hundred million francs into USS and split another one hundred million among the remaining issues, with a delivery date thirty days from now."

By selling "short," Olivier was paying to "borrow" stock shares to sell at the current price, while promising to deliver the same number of shares in thirty days.

The clerk made a slight gasp. "These stocks are doing quite well at this moment, monsieur. Are you sure that they will make such a dramatic turnaround so quickly?"

"These are my instructions. I have my reasons. Will your bank carry them out?" Olivier asked patiently.

"One moment, monsieur. I really should speak with my director. May I have your name?"

"Please tell him that I am Jopie Fourie," Olivier said. He spelled out "Fourie" for the clerk.

A few moments later, the clerk came back on the line. "We will comply with your wishes, monsieur."

"Next, please place another one hundred million into selling sixty-day DKU Group index futures contracts, and another twenty-five million into selling short the Japanese yen." Olivier smiled sourly. "You may keep the remaining trust money as a margin reserve so your director will feel more comfortable."

The clerk swallowed. "As you wish, monsieur."

"Thank you. I expect prompt execution. I will call again in a few days to find out how you have done." Olivier smiled thinly. "If you have any money of your own, you might consider selling United Steel-Standard stock short."

"Oh, no, monsieur. That would not be proper. My director would not approve."

"I assume that you are recording this conversation. I have told you nothing improper. Tell your director *he* might consider selling USS short," Olivier said and hung up the phone.

The hotel was a good business-class establishment. Olivier turned on the monitor and called up the stock markets to find some good newspapers to buy up in the days and weeks—and years—ahead.

Ago Bay, the Japanese Pacific Coast

THE SHUTTLE CONTINUED ON ITS WAY UNTIL THE LAND MASS OF Honshu, Japan's main island, rimmed by tiny islands cloaked in pine trees and the white gossamer of waves breaking against the cliffs, rose abruptly out of the night.

"Passing Ago Bay, sir," Zerebtsov said. He pointed his thumb at the glow of lights on the horizon. "The Kashikojima resorts."

Kokovtsov altered course a few degrees and lifted the shuttle's nose to begin climbing the coastal mountains. He leveled off just above the height of the tallest trees. Dipping into a valley, Kokovtsov muttered, "Thank heaven we don't have a full load."

Coldewe nodded. The minutes passed, and he dozed fitfully until the copilot tapped him on the knee. "Sir, there's Mount Asama. We're almost there."

"Oh. Yes. Tell everybody in back to get ready." Coldewe snapped completely awake and peered out the window to study the terrain through his night-vision glasses. Moments later, he spied the first potential drop zone they'd selected from the maps, a tree-lined meadow overlooking a mountain lake. Lit by a small sliver of moon, the lake glistened. An unpaved road led away from it toward the Ise-Shima Skyline Drive that ran along the highest part of the ridge in front of them.

They circled the meadow twice slowly, scoping it for irregularities. Finally, Coldewe nodded. "Try not to drop us on top of any hikers." He began moving to the rear of the shuttle.

Kokovtsov whipped the ungainly shuttle around and climbed high enough for the parachutes to deploy. Then he slowed almost to stalling speed, opened out the clamshell doors in back, and hit the jump light. As he circled the meadow, fifty-four men and a miscellaneous collection of equipment came raining out of the sky.

As the shuttle spun around for its final pass, Kokovtsov closed the clamshell doors and slipped a programmed course into the automatic pilot, then he and Zerebtsov exited through the side door.

Twenty-five seconds later, the shuttle obediently turned

around and flew itself back out to sea, where a calculated jag
would cause it to ditch itself.

Drifting down, Coldewe watched it go. There are three essential elements to a really good raid: getting in, wreaking
havoc, and getting back out. "I hope we find another one of
these when the time comes," he murmured under his breath.
As he landed and struggled from his chute near the forest edge,
the first of the equipment chutes touched down with a gentle
thump that was absorbed by its break-away pallet.

Leaving his lieutenants to organize matters unhindered,
Coldewe ambled through the trees out to the road and sat down.
He was quickly joined by a security team. Almost a half hour
passed. Then he froze at the sight of approaching headlights.

The vehicle stopped a good distance away. A uniformed man
got out and walked up the path shining a flashlight back and
forth. Coldewe held his breath and motioned to the security
team. The team leader acknowledged. As the man approached,
a recon trooper materialized in front of him and stood up.

The park custodian waved his flashlight uncertainly. "Who
are you? What are you doing here?" he snapped in Japanese.

The soldier cradled his weapon and placed his palms together as a gesture of supplication. Then he held one finger,
signaling the man to wait, and beckoned into the shadows.

As the man started to say something, Senior Intelligence
Sergeant Aksu stepped forward, hidden behind his face shield,
and the rifleman faded into the gloom.

"I am Major Yosuhiro, Imperial Security Police Special Detachment," Aksu said, his Japanese marked by a slight trace of
the thick Kagoshima *ben*. "What is the problem?" He deftly
turned his body so that custodian's flashlight caught the black
stripe down the side of his pants leg.

"You shouldn't be here! I was never told—" the man stammered with a shade less authority.

"Please excuse me, but where precisely is 'here'?" Aksu
asked him mildly. "Our pilot may have made a slight error in
navigation. I am disoriented."

"This is Ise-Shima National Park."

"*Shimata!*" Aksu grunted and slapped his hand to his head.
"Please excuse me, we are not even in the right prefecture."
He explained, with complete sincerity, "This is quite serious,
and you should not be mixed up in it."

"But—" the custodian started to say deferentially.

"Please! Let me think," Aksu said quietly but forcefully.

"As I have said, this is quite serious." He pretended to ponder for a moment. "Can I trust your judgment and discretion? This is extremely secret!" he barked out assertively.

The man nodded, like a puppet.

"For the next ten days, say nothing to anyone about this, not even your wife. It would be . . ." Aksu paused delicately. ". . . highly embarrassing. We should be elsewhere at this moment." He reached into his pocket and pulled out paper and a pencil. "Let me take your name and address, and I will have a letter sent to you commending you for your assistance. For the next day or so, ignore anything unusual you see here."

After chatting for a few minutes to discover what the man had observed, Aksu packed him off. As soon as the man disappeared from sight, Aksu motioned for two of the recon boys to follow him and watch.

Coldewe joined him. "Good job."

"He thinks he saw four chutes, honored sir. We are not compromised. My life on it."

"It is." Coldewe paused. "And if he'd smelled a rat?"

Aksu patted his silenced submachine gun.

"Just checking." Coldewe squatted and flipped open a notepad.

Aksu's curiosity got the better of him. "Honored sir, what are you doing?"

"Writing him his letter of commendation. I'll pick up an envelope somewhere and drop it in a postbox just before we go in."

"Of course," Aksu agreed blandly. He pulled out his own notepad. "Would you like his name and address?"

"Not just yet. If we get blown, it might save him a lot of explaining if they didn't find it on my body."

Aksu nodded thoughtfully in the gloom as he began taking off his uniform.

Lieutenant Danny Meagher joined them. "We're set for the night. Most of the equipment made it in one piece. One of the Sparrows is junk, and we lost two fuel bladders."

Coldewe nodded. "Well within tolerances." He jerked his head toward the lake below. "Get rid of the pallets and the chutes. What about jump casualties?"

"Two sprains. Nothing serious," Meagher told him.

"Good enough," Coldewe responded as he pulled off his mask. "Get the drivers into civvies. Aksu and I are going to find ourselves a phone booth. Time we rang up Mizoguchi."

Aksu looked at him. "I confess that this is the part that I do not like."

"I know." Coldewe pointed to the stitches stretching the skin around his eyes. "How do I look?"

"Fortunately, it is very dark."

They found a phone booth in front of a *robatayaki* full of late diners on the outskirts of the town of Uji. Accompanied by a nervous Aksu, Coldewe ambled over and began thumbing through the phonebook.

"See," he said, pointing to the entry on the tiny screen, "easy as sipping beer."

"Let us hope that it is the correct Hiroshi Mizoguchi. It has been eight years for him, after all," Aksu commented.

"One way to find out," Coldewe replied, dropping coins in the slot and dialing the number. He pressed a button so that the connection would be sound only.

A sleepy guttural voice answered.

"Hello, Mizo? This is Hans. Long time, it's been." Coldewe cradled the receiver against his shoulder. "What say we get together." He suddenly looked up at Aksu. "Damn," he exclaimed incredulously, "Mizo dropped the phone."

Mizoguchi lived in Nagoya, about an hour away by train. He arranged to meet with Coldewe five hours later in the town of Ise-shi in the back room of a *nabemone* restaurant. When Coldewe entered, Mizoguchi was seated at the table. Beside him were two bowls of *kabe-nabe* and a bottle of *amakuchi* sake. The ubiquitous television screen in the corner was showing a cartoon show about a family of sea otters. Uncomfortable in his civilian clothes, Coldewe sat down on the *tatami* and squeezed his knees under the table opposite the sightless man. "Hello, Mizo."

"Hello, Hans," Mizoguchi said, an older Mizoguchi than Coldewe remembered, with deep lines in his face. "The owner here is a cousin. He can be trusted. I had my wife drive me to the train station. I told her that you were a former colleague and that you might have a better job for me. I will take the train back, and she will pick me up when I call her." The blind former lieutenant stared through Coldewe. "How can you be here? I never expected to see you."

Coldewe picked up the *amakuchi* bottle, poured out some of the sweet liquor, and looked around the room to see if Mizoguchi's cousin had left out any *o-tsumami* worth nibbling on. "Actually, I'm not here." He gave Mizoguchi a second or two to digest that statement. "First off, the Variag sent me here to thank you. We owe you. If you hadn't told us what was going on, we would have been wearing our trousers around our ankles."

"Then . . . Admiral Horii's expedition arrived before you left."

"This is good stuff." Coldewe listened to the sounds from the kitchen to make sure that Mizoguchi's cousin wasn't eavesdropping. Then he changed his tone of voice. "Mizo," he whispered, "do you remember when we used to get tipsy and talk politics? What are yours, these days?"

"I am a pensioner. I have none," Mizoguchi said bitterly in the English that he had almost forgotten he knew. He tossed down a shot of the liquor.

"How are things for you?"

"They are well," he said automatically.

"Funny. You can usually tell when someone's lying to you by the way that their eyes dart up and away. You're blind, so I didn't think it would work with you. How bad is it?"

Mizoguchi did not speak for a few minutes. Finally, he said, "I have adjusted, Hans. I do the cooking—my wife says that I cook better than she does. I have never seen her, but I know what she looks like—my hands and my body see her. So I don't need eyes—after all, you close them when important things in your life are going on. If I were a painter, I would, but I have other senses. Look at how many sighted people cannot see. I was more blind when I had eyes." He said fiercely, "I am well, Hans. I am well."

Coldewe took a deep breath. "Mizo, I asked about politics for a reason. How interested are you in shaking things up?"

Mizoguchi gaped.

"Mizo," Coldewe said very quietly, "you can forget you ever saw me. I have an envelope here stuffed with cash which you can consider a small token of our esteem. Or you can come in. All the way in. Call your wife and tell her that you'll be away for three or four days." He grinned. "Tell her that it might be the opportunity of a lifetime."

"And afterward?" Mizoguchi asked in a low whisper.

"Truth is, Hiroshi, if you come in, there might not be an afterward. We came here to do some crazy stuff. I told Raul and the Variag that we didn't need to bring you in. That we really didn't need you, and that you were a security risk—a bad one. And the Variag looked right through me and said, 'But he is one of our own.' And Raul looked right through me and said that anyone who would send the message that you did wouldn't change in six years or sixty. Do you have children to worry about?"

"No, but my wife is ... kind. Not every woman would marry a sightless man." Mizoguchi began talking quietly to himself. "Things are not good. Because of the time dilation, my family and my friends are older. They changed, and they do not like it that I did not age as they did. There is also resentment that I am holding a position that a sighted man could hold. Jobs are difficult to find, even though they have begun conscripting young men for military service. There is also much discontent. The people are very unhappy with the state of affairs." Mizoguchi turned his head toward Coldewe.

"People say they have seen Oshio Heihachiro stalking the foothills of Mount Fuji. This is ridiculous—most people no longer remember who Oshio Heihachiro was, but they believe that more and more their needs are being ignored. Taxes are very high. People talk about lowering the taxes on smaller businesses and individuals, but the government does not do anything about it. Everywhere, officials are supposed to set an ethical example and to do things to benefit the people, yet everyone repeats the proverb, 'Officials are honored and the people despised.' "

He clenched his fists. "But I think that if it is this bad here, it must be worse elsewhere. We Japanese have become too inward-looking. I know what it was like in other countries and on colonial planets. People outside Japan must be very, very angry, Hans. It frightens me. The politicians, the companies, the ministry bureaucrats have seduced us with their leavings. We Japanese have lost our spirit."

Mizoguchi took a deep breath and struggled to fit his thoughts into an alien language. "People do not speak about these matters. With the police everywhere it is too dangerous. You could only talk about such things with close friends after you had both drunk a great deal, and at such moments words are unnecessary. But I think that most people believe that what we are doing must stop."

"And?" Coldewe asked slowly.

"I also think that Colonel Vereshchagin knows me better than I know myself. I will call my wife." He paused. "If we live through this and the opportunity presents itself, I would like you to see her. I wish to know if you think she is pretty. I have often felt her face, but I wish to know."

"I will," Coldewe promised. He cautioned, "Just tell her you think that you have something good lined up, and that you'll be out of touch for three or four days. The less you tell her, the better it will be for her."

"Yes, I understand."

"I will try to make sure you get an opportunity to explain everything to her."

"Yes. It is not necessary, but—thank you, Hans."

"Anton says that he asked you to register a company and to get to know some reporters."

"It has been so many years. Yes, the company still exists, and the money that he gave me all of those years ago has been safely placed in an account. I know two reporters. They are not friends, but they are acquaintances."

"Good. Large wads of cash make people nervous, and we'll need the reporters. Here are your business cards." He set a pack of them in Mizoguchi's hand.

Mizoguchi ran his finger across the raised surface of one of the cards. "Senior Executive Managing Director?"

"Sounds impressive as hell, doesn't it? After the sun comes out, we'll buy some vehicles and give your reporter acquaintances a call." He looked at his watch. "We'd better get back. I have Aksu waiting about a klick outside of town."

"Where did you camp?" Mizoguchi asked, suddenly suspicious.

Coldewe fluttered his hand nonchalantly so that Mizoguchi would feel the movement of the air. "Up in the hills. Not too far from here."

"Here?" Mizoguchi twisted his head and said in a hoarse whisper, "You landed in Ise Park?!"

"We were looking for something far from the maddening crowd. There aren't that many untenanted sites on the Pacific seacoast of Honshu, and we didn't want to pick a place that somebody had just built on."

"It is ... somewhat sacred," Mizoguchi said awkwardly.

"I know. According to the guidebook you have about a hundred and seventy-nine shrines up there, including the grand shrines. I stopped on the way in and left a donation on behalf of the battalion."

Mizoguchi began rubbing his temples in short, circular motions.

"I also picked up one of those little, cloth-and-paper traffic amulets. You know, with the suction cup to stick it to your windshield." Coldewe made little movements with his hands.

"The way Prigal drives—you remember Prigal?—I figured we might need one."

As they stood up, Mizoguchi's cousin timidly stuck his head in the door. "Is everything all right?"

"Very fine," Mizoguchi said. "More than fine."

L-Day plus one

MIZOGUCHI BORROWED A BATTERED TOYOTA FROM HIS COUSIN. After daybreak, he and Aksu went to a bank in Ise and added money to the account Mizoguchi had invested for Vereshchagin. After picking up three Japanese-looking drivers that Coldewe sent, they went to a local car dealership and dickered the price down on three minivans in assorted colors.

The vans were seven-passenger models, with the usual modular seating and smoked glass on the side and rear windows. Mizoguchi asked the dealer to install privacy screens between the driver's seat and the passenger compartment, and extra rear seats in two of the vehicles.

The dealer balked at the extra seats, explaining apologetically that he had none in stock, but that he could guarantee delivery in three days. Responding to a touch on the elbow from Aksu, Mizoguchi expressed his sincere thanks for the dealer's efforts despite the current recession, and his deep regret that they would not be able to conclude the sale.

The dealer immediately pulled seats out of the last minivan he had on the lot. Mizoguchi and Aksu put 25 percent down and financed the balance over four years. They politely declined an offer to put a corporate logo on the vehicles for what was alleged to be a nominal price.

Aksu then motioned his drivers to get the minivans off the lot, whereupon Recruit Private Prigal, who had been made up and deodorized well enough to pass for a Hokkaido native, promptly climbed in on the passenger side of the vehicle and began looking for the steering wheel, having forgotten that Japanese drive on the left-hand side of the road.

Aksu covered. "It is indeed fortunate that Buddha looks out for the weak-minded."

The dealer responded with a knowing wink and a penetrating observation about the wits of country bumpkins. Prigal, of course, *was* a country bumpkin, although from a different country, and the wounded look on his face as he slid across the seat transcended cultural barriers.

Renting a utility trailer for the third mini, Aksu and Mizoguchi sent the three of them to Coldewe, one at a time, together with an assortment of road maps and boxed *bento* lunches.

"What's next?" Mizoguchi asked.

Aksu smiled. "We buy ourselves a subscription to the evening edition of *Nihon Keizai Shimbun* and radio the access code to Timo Haerkoennen. Then we make a few phone calls and go to the library to validate information about some people and buildings."

After paging through some books on Tokyo architecture and reading up on who was who in the current government, Aksu made a dozen phone calls and radioed Coldewe to tell him to put refueling plan two in effect. He had Mizoguchi set up a meeting with his journalist acquaintances in the lobby of Tokyo's New Akasaki Prince Hotel at seven the next morning.

One serious problem surfaced when Aksu discovered that Osachi Abe was off campaigning in his home city of Niigata, on the Sea of Japan.

"Niigata is another one hundred kilometers north of Tokyo as the bird flies," Coldewe said. "Frost and damn. I will have to get back with you, Resit. Coldewe out."

Thinking quickly, Coldewe said to Chiharu Yoshida, "If we gave up the Ministry of Education, we could get Zerebtsov up there in a Sparrow, but he'd have to steal some fuel to get back. That's no good. Is there some other politician worth taking down instead?"

Yoshida had been tasked to interact with the reporters and explain Suid-Afrika's reasons for rebelling. "None that fits our purposes so closely," Yoshida responded. "It is clear from what Aksu told us that he is the only politician of his generation who is still entitled to an opportunity to become UDP secretary general, and his campaign appears designed to cultivate greater exposure to the electorate."

"Hmmm, I wonder what policies he's promoting up there?" Coldewe said aloud as he thought through the tactical problem.

Yoshida gave him a puzzled look. "Why would Abe have policies?"

"Well, yes. Damn! I wish we could get him, but I can't figure out how."

"Please allow me to do it, Hans."

"What?" Coldewe stared at Yoshida in surprise.

"It is not as if I had to lead a company, I would only be responsible for myself. I have one of the internal passports that Timo adjusted to fool the Ministry of Security's central data base. From Nagoya, I could take the train."

"How are we going to pick you up?"

Yoshida reached up and took Coldewe's hand in a very un-Japanese manner. "That is not a problem. After all, this is my homeland." He smiled, his face appearing surprisingly young. "I would like to take a recoilless gun. The security devices will not recognize it for what it is."

"All right," Coldewe said softly. "We've got an extra one somewhere. Mizo and I can handle the reporters. Get Thomas to fix you up. It's been a while since you've handled an eighty-eight, so ask Miinalainen to check you out."

When Yoshida left, Coldewe said conversationally to Platoon Sergeant Soe, who had overheard the exchange, "Mizo never liked Chiharu much. He's changed a lot since then. For the better. Some people do. Remind me to tell Mizo if he calls Chiharu 'Tingrin,' that blind or not, I'm going to pop him one. Oh, and get Thomas on the line—there's a change to the plan for the Ministry of Finance."

"Why?" Soe asked.

Coldewe grinned. "Aksa says the Minsistry isn't where it used to be."

While Coldewe and Aksu were busy with this, in a forested part of the Ise-Shima less than half a kilometer from a tourist trail, Danny Meagher's assault group set up a work area to modify the minivans. Rapidly and quietly, they equipped the two eight-passenger minis with a miscellany of curtains and opaque glass panels to conceal the fact that the rear seats would be full of armed soldiers. As an added touch, they made holographic images of the vans' interiors—empty—and used them to back the side and rear windows. It had taken them most of two weeks to refine the technique on Suid-Afrika, and it was with deep regret that Coldewe dumped the photographic equipment in the lake.

Meagher's group then attached sections of composite sheeting to the interior panels to make them bullet resistant, and fitted equipment brackets and mesh under the seats to hold weapons and bergens in place. Finally, they reinforced the noses of the two eight-passenger minis with lengths of molybdenum steel rod to withstand frontal impact.

After loading the third mini's utility trailer with water, cases of rations, communications equipment, and extra fuel bladders for the Sparrows, Coldewe transmitted a coded message to Vereshchagin to say that they were on schedule. Then he and Platoon Sergeant Soe, an Indonesian mortarman from No. 8, concealed their uniforms and weapons in the back and drove off to deliver drivers for the two panel delivery trucks that Mizoguchi and Aksu were renting. On the way, they stopped at a rest area to throw away the packaging from the box lunches. "Always leave a tidy battlefield," Coldewe explained.

Because Coldewe had deemed the delivery trucks to be too conspicuous to drive through the park, Snyman and Karaev and their thirteen-man assault groups bicycled through the forest to the outskirts of Uji to rendezvous with them. Well aware that a panel truck affords limited amenities, the last thing that Snyman and Karaev did before they left was to make sure their men used and then carefully concealed the tiny latrine they had dug.

Shortly before the park closed for the evening, Aksu and Mizoguchi returned the Toyota to Mizoguchi's cousin, and the five vehicles individually began the long drive to Tokyo-to along the Ise Expressway. Ten men and five Sparrow aircraft remained behind in the forest under Lieutenant Victor Thomas's command.

As Soe put Coldewe's vehicle into the computer-aided "speedo" lane and let the vehicle head itself north on the expressway, Coldewe asked Mizoguchi, "How long is it going to take us to get to Tokyo?"

"A few hours to Nagoya. From Nagoya to Tokyo on the express highway is five hours more."

"Good. That's about what I thought. Factor in a rest stop or two, and we'll have half the night left for mischief and sight-seeing before the fun starts.

"That sounds very ambitious to me."

"The alternative is to hole up for a day, which we really don't want to do."

"I would offer to drive, but I cannot," Mizoguchi said. His English was improving by the minute. He gestured to Aksu, who was already dozing off in the seat in front. "I feel as though I am useless."

"Useless? You're not. Aksu is good at looking and acting Japanese, but he's obviously not a local boy. If you hadn't come along, somebody might have blown his cover before we got started. Where did you get the notion you were useless?"

Mizoguchi inhaled deeply. "At times, some of my former

academy classmates would call to ask why I have not committed suicide to avoid being useless." He added bitterly, "Some of my neighbors have asked the same."

Coldewe sighed. "I'm sorry, Mizo. It's a nice bunch the Academy attracts. Although I was annoyed at the time, I'm glad that they were running separate classes for Japanese and *gaijin* officers when I went through. Otherwise, I might have gotten myself kicked out for breaking stuffy Japanese noses, and you wouldn't have enjoyed the pleasure of my company. As Schiller used to say, *'Mit der Dummheit kämpfen Götter selbst vergebens,'* which means, 'With stupidity the Gods themselves struggle in vain.' "

"You are reading Schiller now? I had thought that you mostly liked Westerns."

Coldewe gave Mizoguchi a very hurt look that Mizoguchi was in no position to appreciate. "I was filling in some of the holes in my education."

Mizoguchi sniffed. "I do not believe that our education system is very good. All the higher civil service positions and best jobs go to Todai graduates, but if you do not go to the best high schools and primary schools, they will not allow you to apply. We select our leaders based upon whether they pass examinations well as children."

"How did you ever end up as a soldier, Hiroshi?"

"I failed the examination to get into a certain high school," Mizoguchi said bleakly. "My father was very disappointed."

To change the subject, Coldewe said, "I've always thought that girls tend to be better students than boys."

"For women here, it is even harder. Virtually none of them are admitted into the higher civil service anymore. I think that we have fallen into bad practices." Mizoguchi stared sightlessly into the night. "My wife did not listen. She felt she should have been accepted to Todai. She was very outspoken about it. This caused problems when her parents tried to arrange marriages for her."

"Oh," Coldewe said lamely.

"She is still very unhappy, so I feel that she will understand what we are doing. I wish I could tell her what are our chances for success."

Coldewe coughed. "Let's see. If we hang around Tokyo long enough to do the reconnaissance we need, there's a high probability that we'll attract unwelcome attention, so basically we're trusting to luck and long experience at this sort of thing.

In sum, our operations plan is so truly hare-brained that I wish I owned stock in a carrot company."

He grinned. "We do have one thing in our favor. The Variag attended staff college here about twenty years ago, and one of his classmates offered to bet that Tokyo was impregnable to attack. Anton poked around most of the buildings we plan on visiting and cheerfully paid up—after filing away some ideas. So the Imperial Government truly 'nursed the pinion that impelled the steel.' "

Mizoguchi looked impressed. He leaned his head against the window frame. "I wondered why didn't you bring your own vehicles."

"The models and styles aren't the same, even apart from the fact that Suid-Afrikan models have the steering wheel on the wrong side. We would have stood out like Christmas trees. Also, we couldn't come up with a way to register them without attracting suspicion. It would have been embarrassing to have some policeman run our plates through his computer and haul us in for auto theft."

"There was also a slight problem with space in the shuttle," Soe added from the driver's seat.

Mizoguchi nodded and stretched. "So. Where are we staying tonight?"

"At the New Akasaki Prince Hotel."

Mizoguchi sat up. "What? That is a very expensive hotel."

"It's a nice place," Coldewe explained. "The Variag had dinner there about twenty years ago. It sits on a little hill right off of the Hanzoman subway line, and you get a beautiful view of the city from the upper floors."

Aksu stirred. "We are renting two rooms, and we have use of the roof-top 'Top of Akasaki' lounge after it closes for the night. I told them that we had a very new company and a very important business demonstration very early in the morning. They were very understanding—business is slow. They promised to have the lounge cleaned and the furniture moved out of the way by three o'clock."

He studied Mizoguchi's face. "Please trust me, sir. You do not wish to know what it will cost."

Coldewe grinned. "Don't worry. They'll earn every sen." He reflected, "I kind of liked alternate refueling plan five, which was the Aoyama Cemetery. A cemetery is such a peaceful, quiet place to spend the night."

Aksu answered Mizoguchi's question before he even asked it. "No, sir. He has not changed."

Back in the Ise-Shima, Timo Haerkoennen and Quartermaster Sergeant Vulko Redzup logged onto the evening paper and proceeded to read the closing stock prices into a data file. Shortly after dusk, the two of them flew north in a Sparrow. A few hours later, Thomas's other four Sparrows followed.

Central Tokyo, Earth

TOKYO-TO—THE GREATER TOKYO METROPOLITAN AREA—IS A HUGE area whose dense population spills over its boundaries into the neighboring prefectures. In the glare of the great city's lights, Vulko Redzup traced the mouth of the Sumidagawa River and began looking for the Imperial Palace's Outer Garden.

Spotting it, he quickly located the Babasaki Moat and used it to identify the wide sidewalks of the Marunouchi District, Japan's center of finance, and the uninspiring flat-roofed tower of steel and stone that was the Daikichi Sanwa Bank Building. Tilting his Sparrow's nose into the wind, Redzup gracefully landed on the roof, where he and Haerkoennen cautiously exited and covered their tiny plane with a lightweight gray tarpaulin.

Haerkoennen watched Redzup lay sensors to check for security systems. "You know, Vulko, I've always wanted to rob a bank."

"This is just the headquarters. They don't keep any money here. Maybe some securities."

Haerkoennen shook his head. "It's a lot easier to rob a bank with a briefcase than a gun. How does it look?"

Before switching to logistics years ago, Redzup had been, successively, a recon trooper and a combat engineer. He tapped the roof with his cutting bar. "There's a big air duct here. Once we get through the roof, we can crawl through the duct to get to one of the main corridors." He studied his readout. "The duct is clean, but it looks like they've got motion sensors in the corridors."

"Can you take them out?"

"Piece of cake," Redzup said as he pulled out a small battery-powered industrial saw to cut through the roof.

SHORTLY AFTER MIDNIGHT, AFTER POSTING LETTERS FOR Vereshchagin and stopping at the Sengakuji Temple to leave a "promissory note" at the museum dedicated to the forty-seven ronin, Soe parked Coldewe's van in the New Akasaki Prince Hotel garage, where they checked in.

Refusing assistance, the burly Soe carefully checked the communications equipment and fuel bladders packed in cardboard boxes and then manhandled the boxes upstairs himself. "Delicate equipment, highly sensitive," Aksu explained smoothly. Coldewe and Soe unpacked their uniforms and collapsed onto the futons. Aksu accepted the spare key to the open-air "Top of Akasaki" lounge from the hotel manager and went up to inspect it.

On his return, he pronounced himself well pleased. "The dance floor will make an excellent runway."

Coldewe lifted one eyelid. "Anything else worth knowing?"

"It is a karaoke bar." Observing the expression on Coldewe's face, he added, "Apparently it is popular again."

"Most people sing badly to begin with, and they sing worse when they get drunk, so it is compounding a felony," Coldewe observed. He told Mizoguchi, "We have about two hours yet, so we might as well sleep."

"I am too nervous," Mizoguchi protested.

Coldewe winked. "Mizo, I am shocked. An infantryman can sleep anytime, anywhere." A soft snore from Soe helped establish his point.

THE REMAINING SPARROWS REACHED TOKYO TWO HOURS LATER, dodging utility wires along the way.

"Is that the Imperial Palace?" Corporal Markus Alariesto asked from the rear seat of the lead aircraft. Alariesto had spent eight years in Thomas's reconnaissance platoon. Although his mind registered how impossible it was to see the tiny, partially translucent plane, he still felt naked under the glare of the city's lights as they passed the recently restored Tokyo Tower.

His pilot, Kokovtsov, nodded and continued to fly in the direction of the USS Building. The rumble of the traffic and the subway trains overwhelmed the quiet hum of his engine and its efficient scimitar-shaped prop.

Lieutenant Thomas was flying right behind Kokovtsov in a second Sparrow. The best shot in Vereshchagin's battalion, Thomas was also one of its best pilots. Orienting on the Imperial Palace complex and the tall, triangular National Police Headquarters with its queer little turret, Thomas found the broad Sakurada-dori crowded with pedestrians and flew parallel to it. Guiding on the green of Hibaya Park to his right and the Imperial Diet Building on his left, he found the cross-street that was the Kasumigaseki, the heart of official Tokyo, and drifted toward his target, with the third and fourth Sparrows following him.

The massive bulk of Tokyo's Central Station loomed to the northeast, only partly concealed by the tall buildings in between. As Thomas watched, a tilt-rotor took off from one of the heliports at the far end.

Slowing his craft and turning into the wind over the Ministry of International Trade and Industry building, Thomas angled the flaps and the blades of the propeller so that the little plane actually hovered a few centimeters above the roof of the thirty-story building. In the rear of the aircraft, Superior Private "Abdullah" Salchow carefully opened the panel between his legs and lowered his rucksack and the cylinder strapped to it onto the roof, then he gingerly lowered his body after it.

As Salchow shifted his weight from the plane to the building, Thomas skillfully adjusted to keep the aircraft almost completely motionless. When Salchow let go and crouched down, Thomas lifted up and away along the Kasumigaseki in the direction of the New Akasaki Prince.

Across the street, a similar operation was taking place on the saddle between the two built-up ends of the sleek new Finance Ministry. A few moments later, the fourth Sparrow deposited a recon team member on the roof of the Education Ministry a few blocks away.

On MITI's roof, Salchow laid down a sensor net and carefully studied his readings for alarms. Finding none, he identified the piping for the overpressure air system that protected the building against chemical and biological attack. Delicately, he carved himself an access hole with his diamond-tipped cutting bar and lowered himself into the building, pulling the bulky gas cylinder behind him.

Working in almost complete darkness with the aid of his night-vision glasses, Salchow patched the hole he had made in the roof. Then he cut open one of the ventilation pipes, inserted the cylinder, set the timer on it, and resealed the cut he had made.

Finding a small equipment closet, he pried it open and made himself comfortable for the night, jamming the lock shut so that no one could enter.

A kilometer and a half farther northeast, hard by Tokyo Station, Kokovtsov deposited Alariesto on the sloping granite top of the USS Building. There, Alariesto encountered difficulty. The roof itself was impenetrable to the tools he carried, and a door built into the side of the roof was securely locked and thoroughly wired to sound an alarm. The nearest windows were ten meters down. Alariesto let a coil of thin composite rope fixed to his belt trickle through his fingers and shuddered at the thought of trying to dangle himself off the roof and cut his way in.

He spoke into his wrist mount. "Recon point two. Break. Alariesto here. Coconut, I got problems. Get ready to pick me up if something goes wrong."

"Okay. Kokovtsov out."

Bending, Alariesto sent a short pulse of energy into the door frame to try to neutralize the alarm. Then he carefully began cutting around the frame. Suddenly, the sensors he had laid began lighting.

"Recon point two. Break. Coconut, I've got to abort. Pick me up."

"Okay. Kokovtsov out."

Alariesto carefully folded his sensors and stuffed them into his belt. While he had no doubt that he could kill every guard in the building, a few missing guards would arouse a certain amount of suspicion in the morning.

Getting off, however, was a problem in itself. Landing and taking off a small fixed-wing aircraft from a sloping roof of a building is normally not considered an insurable risk, and it wasn't something they had planned on trying.

"Hope the wind holds," Kokovtsov said to himself as he pointed his Sparrow's nose into the wind. He adjusted his flaps and altered the angle on his propeller, gently settling on to the roof a few meters away from Alariesto.

Adjusting the rucksack and gas cylinder on his back, Alariesto gripped the ridge of the roof with the climbing spikes on his hands and crawled to Kokovtsov. As he opened the entry panel to the rear seat from underneath, a sudden breeze stirred the plane, and Kokovtsov fought to keep it in place.

Alariesto cautiously climbed inside, telling Kokovtsov what he was doing so that Kokovtsov could adjust to the changing weight. The plane sank gradually until Kokovtsov's left wheel was touching. Then Alariesto shut the panel behind him, and

Kokovtsov changed the angle on his flaps and lifted, almost flying backward for a second before drifting off into the night.

Several moments later, the building's guards poked their heads out to check the roof. With his partner to hold his feet, the taller of the two cautiously crawled out to look. As he crawled back inside, his partner laughed and said, "Night birds."

Hovering a few blocks away, Alariesto called Coldewe. "Assault point one. Break. Alariesto here. Captain Hans, I aborted the USS Building. The place is wired and tough to break in. Request permission to refuel and try again. Over."

"Coldewe here. You trip the alarm, Marcus?"

"Yes, sir. But they checked it out, and even if I trip another alarm, the guards will think that it's a bad circuit."

"Kokovtsov, what do you say?"

Kokovtsov was listening in. "Wind's beginning to die down. If I have to pull him off again, it'll be a problem."

"We're also starting to run short on time before daylight. Request denied, Marcus. Come on in. We'll let Raul take it out in 'Speedy.' Coldewe out."

The last of the four Sparrows heading for New Akasaki Prince Hotel, Koskela touched down lightly on the dance floor and coasted to a stop near the bar where Coldewe had his communications equipment unobtrusively set up. Soe was already helping the other pilots to refuel their planes from the bladders and drape them in lightweight tarpaulins.

"We're rooming in 3440 and 3442 on the top floor," Coldewe told them. "So go inside and sack out. Marcus, you're going to help Soe out tomorrow, so I'll let him brief you."

Before going to sleep, Coldewe and Soe carefully hung out "Do Not Disturb" signs inscribed in seven languages.

Shoto Ward, Tokyo

DEKE DE KANTZOW'S TEAM, RIDING ONE OF THE TWO EIGHT-passenger minivans, had two night missions in Shoto, an ex-clusive section of Tokyo filled with old and very stately homes. At 3:30, he halted at 1-23-15 Shoto, and his engineer, Ketlinsky, slipped out the back.

Staring at the huge house for a moment, Ketlinsky rubbed his nose in silent reflection. Then he temporarily disabled the house's motion sensors and disappeared into the shrubbery near the front door. De Kantzow circled around to pick him up a few minutes later as he was stepping back to critically appraise his handiwork.

At 4:00, de Kantzow stopped his minivan in front of an even larger home at 1-16-32 Shoto where he and five men dressed as blacklegs slipped out and stealthily invaded the residence. Disabling four security systems and immobilizing two guards, they found their quarry asleep in bed with his mistress.

Private Dirkie Rousseaux shone a light in the man's face and poked the barrel of his submachine gun against his chest. Completely hidden by his face shield and uniform, Dirkie said in crisp and flawless Japanese, "I am Major Yosuhiro of the Imperial Security Police. Sato Shoji, you are under arrest for imperiling Imperial Security."

"What?" Shoji, the sole proprietor of Japan's largest venture-capital firm, attempted to crawl away from the barrel of the weapon that was imprinting a round circle in his skin. The girl beside him whimpered and buried herself under the bed linens.

As one might expect under the circumstances, Rousseaux had to repeat this comment twice before he was sure Shoji understood.

"Your company is intentionally lending millions to certain speculators with evil designs to manipulate the stock markets. Do you deny this?" Rousseaux hissed. "For the sake of enriching yourself and corrupt friends, you are destroying the Imperial way!"

"But, the prime minister himself—" Shoji tried to say.

"The prime minister is of no importance. This is an Imperial Security matter," Rousseaux said harshly, seconded by the uniformed men silently surrounding him. He gestured. "You must atone for your economic crimes. You must disappear."

De Kantzow, whose Japanese was minimal and overwhelmingly scatological, hesitated an instant before responding to his cue. He hauled up Shoji's mistress and roughly wrapped her in a blanket.

"Yoroshiku onegai itashimasu," Shoji gasped, an expression that defies precise translation, but that can be approximated as, "I ask you to look favorably upon me."

"Silence!" Rousseaux ranted.

Playing his part in the game, Section Sergeant Kaarlo Kivela, standing behind Rousseaux, said forcefully, "Wait. Let him speak."

"I am loyal. No one is more loyal than I," Shoji wheezed as Rousseaux's submachine gun poked him painfully in the belly.

"Maaa . . ." Kivela temporized, sucking in air.

"Honored sir, he must pay," Rousseaux said forcefully.

Kivela said, "I have made a decision. Sato Shoji, if you are indeed loyal, you will be given an opportunity to repair the damage you have caused. If you obey instructions, none of this will ever have happened."

"Honored sir, I protest," Rousseaux said, pantomiming outrage.

"My decision is made," Kivela said with finality.

"What must I do?" Shoji sobbed with relief.

"Call your office immediately," Kivela said, reaching for a telephone. "Leave instructions to call in loans you have made and to immediately sell off your stock holdings—all of them—as soon as the market opens. This will slow the manipulation of shares that you have helped initiate. If your employees obey, you will be released, and your arrest will never have occurred. You will even make a substantial profit. Make sure that you will not be disobeyed."

"Naruhodo, so desu ne?" Shoji said, meaning, "Naturally, why didn't I think of that?" He proceeded to do even better, leaving instructions with his answering service and calling his two principal subordinates to tell them to obey his instructions to the letter. As he was allowed to explain to them, it was an Imperial Security matter.

There were, of course, major holes in Rousseaux's story that Shoji would have noticed if he hadn't been sitting naked on the edge of his bed at four in the morning with several guns in his face. While the show was playing itself out, one by one, de Kantzow's soldiers stealthily made their way out to use the toilet.

As soon as Shoji was finished, he and his mistress were injected and left to sleep for the next twelve hours.

As the minivan pulled away, Filthy DeKe turned to Dirkie Rousseaux. "Frosting good, college boy. Frosting good. You too, Kivela."

Dirkie Rousseaux was another veteran of the *Boris Godunov* cast, chosen more for his acting ability than his singing. As a Boer militiaman during the Afrikaner rebellion, Rousseaux had been captured, and Raul Sanmartin had pulled much the same stunt on him.

Meanwhile, the governor of Tokyo, who lived six blocks away, blissfully slept through it all.

Ginza Ward, Tokyo

IN THE OTHER VAN, LIEUTENANT DANNY MEAGHER'S TEAM HAD A more prosaic task, which was to drive around the city dropping paper bags in trash cans and other likely spots. Each bag held a flash grenade and a smoke grenade attached to a timer, as well as a longish string of fireworks to simulate small-arms fire. Meagher's driver, Prigal, eventually found himself between the Ginza and the Port of Tokyo and stopped the van between two establishments whose massive neon signs read "Castle of Love" and "Romance Motel."

"Did you spot a dumpster?" Meagher asked him. "I'd really like to stuff one in a dumpster, for the reverberative effect you understand." The other five people in the back of the van were sleeping soundly.

"Ah, sir. Uh. Ah, I think we're lost."

Meagher pulled open the privacy screen. "I can't say this looks like the garment district."

Prigal began consulting the vehicle's computerized navigation system.

"Well, we need to kill some time, and no one would think twice about seeing a van here at this hour of the morning. Check the map, lock your doors, and get some sleep." Meagher tapped Yelenov awake. "Your watch, Mother Elena. Wake us up a few minutes before seven."

Yelenov stretched and rubbed his eyes. Then he looked out and saw the neon signs. "Prigal got us here?"

"He got lost."

"All of Tokyo to get lost in, and he ends up in the brothel district. It must be instinct."

"God's ways are mysterious," Meagher said, making himself comfortable. "It occurs to me that He has a rare sense of humor."

Central Tokyo

IN THE BOWELS OF THE DAIKICHI SANWA BANK BUILDING, TIMO Haerkoennen gave up at 4:40. "I can't get in without the access code," he said, disconnecting his laptop from the terminal on the bank's eleventh-floor stock-trading desk.

"Are you sure?" Redzup asked.

"I was sure fifteen minutes ago. Considering how many trillion yen this bank controls, I'm not particularly surprised that they want to keep people out of their data bases."

Redzup shrugged. "All right. Let's go back up and tell Coldewe it's time to go to plan B."

Coldewe wasn't surprised. At 5:00, after the other teams reported their progress, he pulsed another coded signal to Vereshchagin far out in space. He repeated the signal at irregular intervals until he got an acknowledgment around 5:13.

At 6:00, Aksu called room service and ordered four "Europe" breakfasts which everyone in the two rooms shared. "There is no need to advertise that we have more people here than that," he explained.

Alariesto studied a "Europe" bowl of oatmeal that had come up with a fried egg on top. He broke out a ration pack. "Europe has sure changed."

At 6:30, Aksu put on his impeccably tailored gray suit, stuck a briefcase under his arm, and prepared to catch the underground from the New Akasaki Prince to Tokyo Central Station.

"Look both ways when you cross the streets," Coldewe cautioned him. "The drivers here are crazy, which I can vouch for since some of them are ours."

Arriving at Central Station, Aksu presented his carefully forged internal passport and purchased a ticket at the heliport counter for the 9:16 flight to Narita International Airport. After buying his ticket, he spent a few minutes observing the heliport's boarding procedures and checking the inserts in his nostrils, then killed time eating noodles and looking through the shops.

At 6:47, Mizoguchi and Soe left to meet Mizoguchi's media acquaintances in the lobby. The first one arrived almost immediately, and he and Mizoguchi spent a few minutes chatting amiably. The second reporter appeared at two minutes after the hour with two other newsmen in tow, one of them from the prestigious *Asahi Shimbun*, Japan's leading newspaper.

After introductions and a brief conversation, the *Asahi* man said with charming candor, "Mizoguchi-san, you indicated that this was a very important story which would embarrass certain persons. I hope that you are correct."

Mizoguchi bowed low. "I think you will be agreeably surprised. Please come with me." They took the elevator up to room 3440, where Mizoguchi knocked twice and entered.

Armed and dressed in uniform, Coldewe and Alariesto were waiting to greet them. "Welcome. I am Captain Hans Coldewe, from Tübingen, commanding C Company, 1/35th Rifle Battalion, formerly the 1/35th Imperial Rifle Battalion. Do all of you speak English?"

"Yes," Mizoguchi said hastily, remembering Coldewe's command of Japanese.

The four of them looked at one another uncertainly. "English is fine," one of them said timidly at length. "Mizoguchi-san said that there was a newsworthy story here that we should cover. Are you his contact?"

"In a manner of speaking," Coldewe said ingratiatingly.

"What is this story?" the *Asahi* man asked.

"Japan was last invaded in A.D. 1274. Well, we're doing it again. It's not exactly third-page news, so we thought that people might want to know."

"Invading?" One reporter dropped his recorder.

"Yes. I am part of an expeditionary force—Mizo, you might want to translate this part to make sure they get it right—from the planet Suid-Afrika, which recently made itself independent of the Imperial Government. We are sincerely annoyed with a company called United Steel-Standard, and with its friends and associates."

Coldewe looked at his wrist mount. "In another two hours, we can let you begin broadcasting, so please allow me to fill you in on the background."

He added, misstating the truth only a little, "Our expeditionary force consists of forty-seven individuals, which is a fact your readers might find interesting."

Earth orbit

FAR OVERHEAD, THE FRIGATE *HENDRIK PIENAAR* BEGAN ITS APproach to Yamato Station broadcasting distress signals.

"Is this making history?" Henke said, staring into the viewscreen.

"Nudging it along," Vereshchagin said.

Detlef Jankowskie smiled as he maneuvered the ship. "Next stop, Yamato Station. Estimated time of launch is 8:50 Tokyo time." On the station, Jankowskie could already detect the thin tubes of lasers beginning to track them.

Shoto Ward, Tokyo

AT 7:50, SCHUNICHI GYOHTEN LEFT HIS HOME AT 1-23-15 SHOTO accompanied by two aides and a bodyguard. A corpulent, cheery, and ruthless politician, Gyohten was killed by his size.

Ketlinsky had set his sensor to react to two or more men moving, at least one of whom stood less than 1.8 meters tall and massed more than 110 kilograms. Gyohten and his party fit these parameters.

As they stepped toward the waiting limousine, two directional mines lodged in the bushes on either side of the door exploded and scythed them down. One aide, considerably in advance of the others, almost lived until the ambulance arrived.

The New Akasaki Prince Hotel, Tokyo

AFTER COLDEWE FINISHED EXPLAINING WHAT UNITED STEEL-Standard and the Imperial Government had done to Suid-Afrika, he opened the floor to questions.

One reporter timidly raised his hand. "But surely, if all of this is true, you will have accomplished your purposes merely by letting the Japanese people know that this has happened. What reason is there to conduct pointless attacks which will inevitably result in needless casualties?"

Coldewe wrinkled his nose. "If we wanted to send a message, we would have picked up the telephone. This sort of thing has been going on a lot, on colonial planets like Esdraelon and in places on Earth. There is an old, old saying in the military forces—we can't keep you from doing something, but we can make you wish you hadn't. We regret any *unintentional* casualties we cause."

Mizoguchi added politely. "If we Japanese continue to embark on an incorrect course, the generation of children growing up will be forced to experience sadness."

No one mistook his meaning.

When the questions ended, Mizoguchi bowed and put on his coat to leave. "Where are you going?" a reporter asked.

"Up until now, I have done very little to halt the drift in events. I have asked myself what is the responsibility of people who contribute to creating conditions in which nothing can be said."

"But you are blind!" the *Asahi* reporter protested.

"Captain Coldewe assures me that I am still a very good soldier, and other people seem to be more blind than I am," Mizoguchi said. "I hope that you will all take good care of your health."

"Please do the same," the *Asahi* man said in polite shock as Mizoguchi left.

"Where is he going?" the *Mainichi* man asked.

"There is a problem here in Japan that people who ask hard questions tend to get murdered. I told Hiroshi that killing one of your right-wing superpatriotic thugs was like killing one cockroach, but he told me it was a problem that the Japanese people had to resolve, and he wanted to make a start."

Central Tokyo

THE MISSION'S FIRST SERIOUS PROBLEM AROSE AT 8:20. ONLY A small percentage of people enter Tokyo each day by car, but that small percentage still represents an enormous number of vehicles. Native Edokkos zip through spaces with only a few centimeters' clearance, leaving visitors aghast. Shipboard computer simulations can only approximate reality.

As Prigal drove north on Sakura-dori, locked in a huge moving mass of cars, to link up with de Kantzow, a kamikaze driver whipped by him through a tiny opening. Prigal flinched—and nudged a *yatai* street cart selling snacks from the edge of the sidewalk. Prigal immediately stopped, halting traffic behind him.

"Lean out the window and apologize!" Meagher hissed from the other side of the privacy partition.

"*Shitsurei shimazi,*" Prigal stammered. "*Sumimasen. Sumimasen.*"

The *yatai* owner began murmuring polite responses as he inspected the dent in his cart.

"Give him money!" Meagher whispered, opening the privacy partition a hair and dropping bills on the seat.

Prigal lowered the window and thrust the money into the man's hands, repeating, "*Sumimasen.*"

The *yatai* owner murmured *dozo*s and protested that Prigal had given him too much.

Prigal pasted a fixed smile on his face and frantically waved him to take it.

The *yatai* owner smiled impishly in return and pushed a dozen skewers of *taroyaki* into the van.

"I see de Kantzow. Okay, get moving," Meagher whispered harshly.

Prigal pulled away, still waving at the *yatai* owner, and angled to avoid a small knot of schoolchildren in their blue uniforms. Before they'd traveled half a block, he sat bolt upright and whispered, "Oh, no," pointing into his rear view mirror.

A little policeman in white who had witnessed the accident was striding toward them, shouting, *"Orai, orai!"* and beckoning them to the side of the street. Traffic emptied out of the lane behind Prigal.

Meagher leaned across to whisper through the partition, "Ask him where you can get tickets to see the Takarazuka."

"Sir, he's going to want to see my license," Prigal whimpered.

"Tell him it's in your bag, and bring him on back," Meagher whispered, and motioned for Miinalainen and Kirponos to get ready.

As Prigal brought the white mouse around and slowly raised the back door, Meagher waited until the policeman's belt buckle came into view and shot him with a wave pistol on narrow beam at point-blank range. Almost before the man knew he was dead, Miinalainen gripped him by the front of his tunic and half lifted, half levered him into the vehicle, resting the body on the floor across everyone's feet.

Meagher hissed, "Prigal, shut the door and act normal! Get us out of here fast, but not too fast."

Prigal shut the rear door hastily and forced himself to walk around slowly and get back into the driver's seat. Meagher turned his head. "Mother Elena, get on the radio and tell DeKe and Captain Hans we've been blown but good. Tell them I'm going to advance our part of the schedule by ten minutes."

In the street outside, bystanders looked at one another uncertainly and wondered what they had seen.

As the vehicle squeezed back into the flow of traffic, Danny Meagher stared at the white-faced troopers sitting opposite him and pointed with his chin. "By the way, that's the National Police Headquarters up the street there. Well, with luck we can brazen it out for another twenty minutes or so."

Section Sergeant Yelenov nodded grimly.

"Do you know," Meagher the former mercenary said in a pleasant tone, "the last time I had a day this frosted, you lads were shooting at me. I hope this works out better." He turned and barked at Prigal, "Well, what are you waiting for? Pass some food back here!"

Guiding the mini with one hand, Prigal handed the *taroyaki* skewers back, saving one for himself. Numbly, he bit into it. "This is good."

"It's squid tentacles fried into batter balls," Meagher said, and watched Prigal almost swallow his skewer. Meagher added, "Try to remember you're not driving an armored car, and if you absolutely have to hit something else in the next ten minutes, try to hit a cart that sells something to go with squid."

Yelenov rolled his eyes. "I swear, if Prigal fell into a latrine headfirst—"

"Which he's done!" Miinalainen and Kirponos echoed in chorus.

Mother Elena concluded plaintively, "—he'd come up with a gold ring in his teeth. But why did he have to be in my van?"

Meagher stuffed money into the dead policeman's pocket and began writing a note of apology to the man's family on the back of his map. "Sorry, squirt," he said, absently patting the corpse. "You were in the wrong place. Of course, I've felt like doing that to officious traffic cops for twenty-five years."

Atsugi Air Defense Site, outside Tokyo

AT 8:35, INSIDE HIS PANEL TRUCK, PARKED JUST OUT OF SIGHT OF one of the six air-defense installations ringing Tokyo, Lieutenant Gennadi Karaev looked his men over and said stiffly, "Well, it is time. During the planning, I told Raul that this part of his plan was completely inane."

Section Sergeant Paavo Heiskanen gave him a quizzical look.

"Being the proud combat soldiers that you are, I told Raul that the lot of you were as innocent of parade ground routine as the birds of the air and the beasts of the fields, and the thought of finding a dozen of you who could actually march in step was preposterous."

Wolfish grins spread from face to face.

Karaev pointed his battered black umbrella from man to man. "Does each one of you understand what this mission means?"

"If we don't knock out the launchers and the lasers here, the Iceman can't land and nobody gets picked up," Tyulenov said.

"Close. Actually it means that after nine months, I don't

have to take any more acting or Japanese lessons, and I don't have to eat any more raw fish. But, as you say, if we don't succeed, no one gets picked up. So, please try not to embarrass me too much."

His men smiled, familiar with Karaev's eccentric brand of reverse psychology.

Tucking his umbrella—carefully patched to hide the more obvious bullet holes—under his arm, Karaev gestured munificently for Tyulenov to open the door.

Forming up, his three teams marched to the gate in the fence surrounding the air-defense center. Two men carried light machine guns and another held an s-mortar, which were the only heavy weapons that Karaev figured he could get inside the gate without attracting suspicion.

Spotting the rank insignia Karaev wore and the black stripes on his trousers, the two privates manning the gate hastily snapped to attention. "May we be of assistance, sir?" the senior of the two asked.

Karaev slowly removed his face shield. Karaev's grandmother had been a Khant, one of the native peoples submerged in a tide of Russian immigrants to Siberia, and Karaev resembled her in his straight black hair and epicanthic folds. Cosmetic surgery had done the rest.

"I am Lieutenant-Colonel Nakayama from Imperial Security." Karaev negligently held out a skillfully forged identity card in a leather case and snapped it shut. "*Stand at attention* when I address you! You will admit me to see your commanding officer immediately. We have reason to believe that your facility harbors politically unreliable individuals who are engaged in antigovernment activities."

"But, honored sir, my instructions do not—"

"You will be silent! My orders take precedence. I begin to believe that you are accomplices to treason! Sergeant, detain both these men until we can look into this matter."

Tyulenov reached through the window, plucked the rifle out of the unfortunate private's grasp, and snapped handcuffs on his wrists. His bewildered compatriot was treated with equal dispatch.

"Now, open this gate."

The two privates did so. Tyulenov took control of the guard box, and Karaev placed the two of them in the center of his little column. They marched in silence to the entrance of the command bunker where the corporal of the guard and the officer of the day rushed out to meet them. Recognizing the insignia Karaev was wearing, the officer stopped in his tracks and saluted. Karaev returned it with cold and studied contempt.

"Sir—" the officer began.

"Please be silent!" Karaev shouted. "I did not give you permission to speak. You will take me to your commanding officer immediately. This is a matter of extreme urgency, and I will not permit delays! Individuals may be destroying documents even as we speak."

Brushing by the young officer, Karaev entered the bunker. Pausing at the first armored blast door, he turned to two of his men. "You two! Stand guard here. Do not permit anyone to go by you."

Anonymous behind their masks, Thys Meiring and Toivo Virkki saluted crisply in unison and assumed menacing positions by the door.

Showing the young officer his phony identity badge, Karaev prodded him with his umbrella. "Lieutenant, you will accompany me. These two privates are under suspicion of complicity. You will take personal responsibility for them until we can ascertain whether or not they are implicated."

"Certainly, sir," the lieutenant said, absolutely convinced he was dealing with a madman.

As they stepped through the second blast door, Karaev observed the sergeant manning the security checkpoint frantically phoning downstairs. He took the phone out of the man's hand. "Lieutenant, arrange for your commander to be waiting for me. Inform him that this is a security matter of utmost urgency!"

The lieutenant did so, his eyes beginning to glaze over with fear, then he followed Karaev and his men into the elevator. As they descended four stories into the earth, Karaev ended the lieutenant's feeble effort at conversation with a harsh look.

When they reached bottom, the lieutenant-colonel commanding the site was waiting, absolutely livid with rage. Nevertheless, when Karaev emerged, he bowed slightly.

Ignoring him, Karaev walked past, motioning the officer to follow. As soon as they were past the last set of security doors, Heiskanen triggered the ambush. Within two minutes, Karaev's men had cleaned out the site's operations center with gas grenades and seized the arms room.

Taking advantage of the rumors that had undoubtedly preceded his arrival, Karaev went on the intercom to announce that the site's commanding officer had been arrested for conspiracy, and that Imperial Security had taken control. He ordered all personnel to assemble in the mess hall, where he locked them in as they arrived and tossed in a couple of incapacitation grenades while the team's engineer, Moushegian, cut power to the lasers and wired the operations center to detonate.

Returning to the surface where Meiring and Virkki had secured their retreat, they blew the elevator and left a note explaining that about 150 men needed rescuing. On their way out, they picked up Tyulenov, who was covering the puzzled perimeter guards.

Although every one of the site's lasers and missile launchers was physically intact, it would easily be a week before any of them could be made operable.

As Karaev's group climbed back into their panel truck, Heiskanen said, "Even money that the ones on the fence don't figure out what happened until their reliefs don't show."

"No," Karaev said. "In about ten or fifteen more minutes, every second officer in the Central Air Defense Force is going to want to know why this installation isn't taking calls, and eventually it will dawn on someone that they have a problem."

He looked around as the panel truck pulled away and said coldly, "This operation would not have worked if the soldiers here had not been conditioned to believe that blacklegs are not governed by normal laws and procedures. Nevertheless—" He banged the roof of the truck with his umbrella to emphasize his point. "Good job! Now, let's see if we can drive to Tachikawa before the traffic gets heavy."

Hachioji Air Defense Site, outside Tokyo

AT THE NEIGHBORING HACHIOJI AIR DEFENSE SITE, JAN SNYMAN'S assault group got as far the entrance to the command bunker before their imposture began to unravel. Playing the role of "Lieutenant-Colonel Nakayama," Platoon Sergeant Liu easily bluffed his way past the gate guards, but the duty officer was of a different caliber than the one Karaev had browbeaten. Although he came out to meet them, he left the armored door to the command bunker locked and steadfastly refused Liu entry until he could clear his presence with the Ministry of Security.

As the Ministry of Security had other things to attend to, minutes passed as the officer waited for a reply, politely ignoring Liu's increasingly pointed threats.

Abruptly, Snyman made up his mind and lightly slapped his hand against his side to signal Liu.

Responding to Snyman's cue, Liu turned, pointing to Pollezheyev and Swart. "You two! Return at once and report this. The rest of you may stand at ease."

Pollezheyev and Swart took off at a run. Snyman's other men began drifting out of formation to give themselves enough space to fight. Uborevich, carrying the s-mortar, calmly calculated the width of the firing slit in the pillbox covering the entrance to the command bunker; the machine gun inside could cut most of Snyman's assault group down in seconds. He nodded his head fractionally.

When Pollezheyev whispered over the radio that he was in position, Snyman wiped his nose with a white handkerchief. On a count of three, Uborevich pumped three s-mortar rounds through the vision slit of the pillbox. Isaac Wanjau shot the brave lieutenant who had thwarted them, while the rest of Snyman's men began picking off the perimeter guards in their assigned sections.

Venedikov had been left at the guard shack with a light machine gun. Shooting the two guards next to him, he opened fire on the main barracks. As Pollezheyev and Swart began firing an eighty-eight at the nearer of the two massive antiaircraft lasers, Wanjau led a four-man team around the side of the command bunker to eliminate the remaining guards on the far side. Hachioji's surprised defenders were in no position to reply effectively.

When Snyman took control of the site above ground at a cost of one man killed and one man wounded, the men inside the command bunker sensibly, if unheroically, left the armored door shut.

Taking advantage of the confusion, Snyman's engineer, Nikoskelainen, grabbed Liu and sprinted back to the truck for more explosives than Snyman's men were carrying. They came back dragging rucksacks stuffed with shaped charges.

"Police will be coming," Snyman told Nikoskelainen as Swart and Pollezheyev stalked the last laser. "Slap those things on the missile silos so we can get out of here." He keyed his wrist mount, "Assault three point Akita. Snyman here. Everybody, get ready to roll as soon as we blow the silos."

Nikoskelainen planted a twenty-kilogram shaped charge on the flat cover of a silo and ducked as he touched it off. Crawling over to inspect his work, he poked a penlight down the hole the charge had gouged out of the metal. Immediately, he began jumping up and down and swearing.

Snyman ran over at a crouch to avoid stray gunfire. "What's wrong?"

"Look at that! Barely a dent!" Nikoskelainen was exaggerating, but not much. "That charge should have knocked a hole in a battleship!"

"What if we used two charges for every silo?" Snyman asked.

"Then we'd have two dents, not one. Damn! Frosty damn!"

"Well, if they try to fire while we're here, we can just pitch in a charge when they open the covers." Snyman keyed his wrist mount. "Assault three point Akita. Break. Snyman here. Change in plan. It looks like we're staying."

Earth orbit

ABOARD THE *HENDRIK PIENAAR*, JANKOWSKIE WHISTLED. "I NEVER realized how big it was."

Floating in a stationary orbit 455 kilometers over central Honshu, the modules of huge Yamato Station were the dockyards for Earth's spaceborne traffic.

"What do they have berthed there?" Vereshchagin asked.

"Two corvettes, one frigate, and the battle cruiser *Mikasa*. Also a bunch of merchant ships that I don't think we need to worry about."

"Are there other warships that we need to take notice of?"

"There are two corvettes flying patterns down low over eastern Siberia. Everything else is at least three or four hours away."

From the seat next to him, Senior Communications Sergeant Poikolainnen looked up. "They're beginning to signal us, sir."

The men on the station obviously recognized the ship approaching them as *Maya*. Unfortunately, Jankowskie could not transmit the ship's identification code, which remained locked away in a part of the ship's data base that not even Timo Haerkoennen had been able to crack open.

Once they responded to sound and visual contact from the station, they would be hard-pressed to maintain their masquerade. There was, however, a gambit to try. "Flashing docking lights," Jankowskie said. Slowly, he began flashing in Morse code the message that the ship had suffered complete commu-

nications failure and was requesting permission to dock and
await repairs. As the seconds ticked by interminably, communications from the station increased.

"Continue to pretend that we cannot hear them," Vereshchagin
directed. "The next moment or two will be interesting."

The space station's duty officer only had a few minutes left
to come to a decision. The closer the ship came, the less time
the station had to react to an attack.

"Sir, they're flashing lights back at us. They are asking us
to hold position," Esko Poikolainnen reported.

"Keep coming at a steady speed. Tell them that we have injured men aboard," Vereshchagin directed.

Minutes passed.

"Sir, they are acknowledging," Poikolainnen said. "They are
telling us to dock in berth two."

Jankowskie exhaled a sigh of relief. "Fourteen minutes,
twenty-five seconds and counting."

Vereshchagin nodded, imperceptibly. "Begin speeding up
when we are twenty-eight thousand meters out. I believe that
the correct naval term is 'flank speed.' Fire at twenty-five
thousand meters. Advise Raul that that is when he should cut
free and engage ground targets. I believe that we can handle
the corvettes."

"The Japanese call unsettling events 'shocks.' What do you
think they will call this one?" Paul Henke asked.

"The Vereshchagin Shock," Jankowskie volunteered.

"They would never be able to pronounce it," Vereshchagin
said. "This will be the 'Suid-Afrika Shock.' "

At fifteen kilometers out, the *Hendrik Pienaar* simultaneously
sent a stream of charged particles to disrupt the station's laser
batteries and launched a cloud of missiles, including one with a
nuclear tip. Altering its vector, the ship began angling away
from the station at high speed as the corvette *Lightwell Gomani*
broke free and began descending into Earth's atmosphere.

Impelled by its rocket motor and the frigate's velocity, the nuclear missile struck Yamato Station squarely two minutes and
nineteen seconds later. A few fractions of a second later, the fusion bottle that powered the station lost its integrity and an explosion eddied through the space where the station had been.

"Inasmuch as we are still alive," Vereshchagin said a moment later, "we must compliment Lieutenant Reinikka's calcu-
lations."

"We have suffered severe damage, especially to our sensors," Jankowskie said, reading off his boards.

"Is this anything we can repair?"

Jankowskie shook his head. "Not really."

"Then we ought to see about those two corvettes without further delay."

As the *Hendrik Pienaar* moved out, Jankowskie paused to torch seven communications satellites along the way.

The New Akasaki Prince Hotel, Tokyo

AT 8:30, COLDEWE TOOK THE JOURNALISTS OUT ON THE ROOF OF the New Akasaki Prince Hotel and suggested that they look up at the sky.

"What are we looking for?" one of them asked, craning his neck.

"You'll know it when you see it."

Coldewe continued discussing the reasons impelling the expeditionary force's actions while the reporters taped him and improvised commentary. Between questions, he taught them verses to "The Whistling Pig." As Vereshchagin had recognized years ago, Coldewe made good copy.

Suddenly, one of the four exclaimed, "Look at that!" For a brief instant a bright light flared in the cloudless sky.

Monitoring the communications traffic with one ear, Coldewe said, "That used to be Yamato Station."

"There were hundreds of technicians there!" the *Asahi* man exclaimed.

"At the Academy, I was taught that lessons should be beaten into a pupil's head. Other operations are in progress. In fifteen minutes, you may begin transmitting if you wish to do so."

In the room below, Corporal Zerebtsov occupied himself by telephoning the banks and government offices on his list and making very realistic bomb threats in hoarse Japanese. He capped off his efforts with a call to the police to report that six armed terrorists were about to seize the Meiji Jingu Shrine. The shrine, built to honor the Emperor Meiji who ended the Tokugawa Shogunate and opened Japan to the world, was a national treasure packed with tourists. It was, of course, several kilometers away from where the real action was taking place.

While Zerebtsov was making calls, the bombs that Meagher and Prigal had set in various wards of the city began going off over a ten-minute span of time. In all, police officers manning neighborhood police boxes reported sixteen explosions followed by the ominous sounds of small-arms fire.

At the same time, Narita Airport, located about thirty kilometers east of Tokyo, was rocked by a series of explosive devices that Lebedyev had dropped from his Sparrow near the runways during the night. Even though the explosions didn't damage anything, noise and billowing clouds of smoke caused a modest panic. Like the other explosions and threats, this aspect of Vereshchagin's deception plan attracted its share of attention from the police, who already had their hands full with Gyohten's assassination.

The Daikichi Sanwa Bank, Tokyo

AT 8:40, TOXIC GAS BEGAN GUSHING INTO THE AIR-CIRCULATION system of the giant Daikichi Sanwa Bank. Crawling out from under a tarp on the roof, Haerkoennen and Redzup cautiously entered the building.

"Lock the doors. I'll meet you at the trading desk," Haerkoennen told Redzup.

Redzup rode the elevator to the ground level. Ignoring the limp bodies around him, including one unfortunate delivery boy, he grabbed the building keys from a guard who was slumped over and locked the front and back doors, pausing only to slap a sign across each door which read, "Temporarily closed by order of the Ministry of Health. Please excuse the inconvenience."

When he reached the stock-trading desk, Haerkoennen was already sitting in a dead man's chair furiously entering code. A window on the monitor in front of him was flashing the characters for "next transaction."

"Eureka," Haerkoennen said in a voice made tinny by the respirator he was wearing. "We're in. All right, financial wizard, give me a hand here."

Redzup smiled and pulled up a chair. "Well, the first thing we have to get around will be the safeguards they built in to keep employees from generating trillion-yen transactions."

"I'm working on that now," Haerkoennen said, executing keystrokes. He winked. "Piece of cake."

Central Tokyo

AT 8:49, THE GAS CYLINDERS HIDDEN IN THE MINISTRIES OF EDUCA-
tion, Finance, and International Trade and Industry hissed into
life. Within minutes, the air-circulation and overpressure systems carried the gas to every corner of the three buildings.

At 8:52, two blocks away, Meagher's and de Kantzow's
minivans circled the massive Ministry of Security Building for
the second time.

Prigal eyed the two armed guards lounging outside the entrance and muttered, "I hope this thing is built good." With his
free hand, he put his face shield on and pulled a section of
composite matting across his body.

Checking one last time to make sure that the equipment was
securely stowed and the body of the policeman was as tightly
wedged against the privacy partition as he could manage,
Meagher looked at the other five troopers in back and said,
"Tuck and brace, squirts! Let's go, Prigal, *ganbarimasho!*"
Then he leaned over and grabbed his knees to cushion himself.

As he brought his minivan abreast of the ministry, Prigal
whipped the steering wheel around, gunned the engine, and
drove at full speed straight for the doors. One of the guards
mistakenly stepped in front to try to wave him off and was carried like a broken rag doll into the interior of the building.

Prigal ran the van through a security checkpoint, killing two
more guards before he finally stopped in the center of the hall.
As he did so, DeKe de Kantzow's blue minivan came crashing
through the hole in the door and whipped around to face the
other way. The men inside the two minis came pouring out the
back and expertly shot up every blackleg in sight exactly as
they had done in rehearsals in the mock-up aboard ship.

Gamely, Prigal threw the composite matting aside, scattering
fragments of the windshield, and fired half a magazine from
his submachine gun at a startled security major who had just
raised a finger to admonish him. Within seconds, Meagher's
men had cleared the hall and secured the exits.

Pausing beside the buckled driver's door, Miinalainen
reached through the broken window. Grasping Prigal by the
collar, the big man pulled him free.

It was the sort of work that required iron nerve and left no
margin for thought, which was the reason that Vereshchagin
had selected Prigal.

While de Kantzow's team covered the main entrance and the

main stairwell, Kaarlo Toernvaenen's team tossed gas grenades and a scattering of antipersonnel devices into the fire escapes. Yelenov's team began clearing the rooms on the entry level. With little time for niceties, after Miinalainen put an 88mm round through the door, Kirponos tossed in a half-kilogram charge to make sure anyone inside stayed there. A blackleg who tried to short-circuit the process ended up with a bellyful from Yelenov's s-mortar.

An elevator grounded and a blackleg major emerged brandishing a pistol in either hand. Confronting Danny Meagher, he put one round through Meagher's arm and bounced another one off Meagher's body armor. Meagher calmly shot him four times in the body and twice in the face.

As Yelenov's people began work on the near side, one curious pedestrian stuck his head through the hole that Prigal's van had made. Although the trooper guarding the door refrained from shooting him, he was accidentally ignited by the backblast from Miinalainen's venturi.

Seconds later, the ready platoon of blacklegs came boiling up out of the first basement level. They ran into a hail of grenades and machine gun fire from de Kantzow, who began swearing in three languages. Meagher immediately diverted men to clean out that level.

After Miinalainen expertly ricochetted three 88mm antipersonnel rounds cut with a time delay around the corner of the staircase, DeKe de Kantzow stripped a twenty-kilogram satchel charge off little Ketlinsky's back and hurled it down the stairs. The resulting explosion caused the earthquake-proof building to quiver. Filthy DeKe's team descended to mop up and seal off the second and third basement levels.

As the gas in the stairwells began drifting into the building's upper levels, the riflemen covering the steps gunned down fugitives. Dirkie Rousseaux got three men with wet towels over their faces.

Meanwhile, Ketlinsky, momentarily distracted from his main mission, finally located the main power cables running underneath the floor. Hauling a rucksack with a thirty-kilogram shaped charge out of his van, he planted it and made the building rock again as the directed force of the explosion knifed through the armored floor and into the basement, cutting power. As the broken cables hissed and sparked, the windowless building's lights and power went down, and the alarms that had been going off since Prigal crashed the door finally stopped ringing.

Seconds later, the auxiliary generators began to hum. Automatic fuses reset, and the lights flickered back on. Ketlinsky pushed a dead guard away from the security switchboard. Exposing a length of cable, he attached an electronic device to it and touched it off. Seconds later, an enormous power surge ruptured the auxiliary system and plunged the building back into darkness.

As the lights went down for good, de Kantzow yelled, "There's a whole frosting company down here, and some of them made it into masks! Give me more frosting firepower!"

"Okay, DeKe." Meagher looked around. So far, Kirponos was the only casualty, and Miinalainen was using the brief respite to bandage his neck and arm.

"Kaarlo, I'm leaving you four men and the machine guns to hold this level. Keep an eye out for Kokovtsov and Thomas. The rest of you squirts come along." He shouldered a bergen full of demolition equipment and headed down the steps. "Remember, the biggest rats are in the deepest holes."

MEANWHILE, ON THE TOP FLOOR OF THE MITI BUILDING, ABDULLAH Salchow waited a minute or two for the gas to take effect and then hurried down to the tenth floor, shooting the two men he encountered who were capable of movement. With barely a glance at the corpses in the cubicles, Salchow pulled timed incendiary charges out of his rucksack and scattered them in corners. Running up the steps to the top floor on adrenaline, he hurriedly booby-trapped the four stairwells and slapped shaped charges on the wall above the elevator doors to cut through the cables.

As the elevator cars began dropping one by one into the basement and fire began to take hold on the tenth floor, Salchow took his flak launcher out of the closet and went out on the roof to provide Meagher with covering fire.

Spotting a traffic-control helicopter, he waited for his two compatriots on the Ministry of Education and Ministry of Finance buildings to announce that they were ready, then thumbed his wrist mount. "Recon point four-two and five-two. Break. Abdullah here. Ready. First copter's mine."

So saying, he shot the traffic helicopter out of the sky. Moments later, a second launcher on top of the Education Ministry took down a second police helicopter.

Salchow relaxed for the first time. With interlocking fields of fire and access to the tops of the ministries restricted, the three recon troopers were in a position to make life very miserable for the police for the next fifteen minutes or so.

"Recon point four-two and five-two. Abdullah here again. I hear sirens. Keep me covered. I'm going out to snipe at the cops in the street for a few minutes to let them know they're not wanted."

Tokyo Central Station, Tokyo

AT 9:01, RESIT AKSU PLACED HIMSELF FIRST IN LINE AT THE FOOT of the escalator leading to heliport 1. On the pad above, a tilt-rotor that differed only slightly from its military counterpart was disgorging the twenty passengers it had picked up at Narita Airport and preparing to take on twenty more for the return trip.

Aksu passed through the detector. The security guards and the clerk checking tickets waved him on with barely a glance at the wrist mount on his left wrist. As the escalator carried him to the top of the station, he punched a button on his wrist mount and stuck a hand into an interior pocket. When he passed the attendant who was greeting passengers as they boarded, Aksu pulled the pin on a plastic incapacitation grenade and flipped it on the ground behind him. The passengers behind him collapsed. As blue dust wafted in all directions, the horrified guard at the bottom shut off the escalator as the people on it began tilting over like a row of dominoes.

A second or two later, tiny explosions triggered by Aksu's wrist mount erupted on two concourses. Smoke and tear gas leaking from ruptured trash bins caused pandemonium.

Dropping to the floor of the aircraft to feign unconsciousness, Aksu tossed a second incapacitation grenade forward to make sure of the plane's crew. The pilot fell forward onto his instrument panel; the copilot, who was starting to come back to see what the problem was, reeled sideways and dropped into a row of seats.

Alerted by Aksu's signal, a Sparrow appeared a moment later and touched down lightly beside the tilt-rotor. Followed by Kokovtsov, Thomas sprang from the small plane and fired snap shots that dropped two security guards who were just coming over to take a look. While Aksu gently deposited the pilot and copilot on the pad, Kokovtsov prepared for takeoff and Thomas lit a smoke candle to cover their departure. Two minutes and eleven seconds after Aksu popped the first gas grenade, the tilt-rotor took off with Kokovtsov at the controls. Twenty minutes later, security personnel and medical crews were still sorting through the confusion inside Tokyo Station.

Subway police quickly interviewed seventeen eyewitnesses and obtained fourteen statements that bore a slight and largely accidental relationship to what had actually transpired. Before other events attracted attention, the police called the Ministry of Defense and the Ministry of Security to ask why uniformed military personnel had borrowed an airplane and left one of their own behind.

The response by officials at the MoD can best be described as incredulous. The phones at the Ministry of Security kept ringing.

Setagaya Ward, Tokyo

AT 9:03, A TAXI DROPPED HOROSHI MIZOGUCHI OFF AT AN ORNATE residence in Tokyo's Setagaya Ward, near the western edge of the city. With ill-concealed distaste, the driver escorted Mizoguchi to the door. Mizoguchi politely thanked him.

Knocking on the door, he was admitted by the maid, who led him into the house's study.

"Kozo-sama, your visitor is here to see you," the maid announced.

Mizoguchi smiled at her slip and bowed low. "I am greatly honored that a *nihonjinron* scholar of your stature would condescend to meet with me on such inadequate notice."

"I am honored," Kozo said, inclining his head slightly to acknowledge Mizoguchi's bow and puffing himself up a little. "Was your trip here pleasant?"

"When one is steadfast of purpose, inconveniences are of no great consequence," Mizoguchi said, listening carefully to ascertain where other persons were located in the professor's home.

"Yes, anything can be done if one sets one's mind to it. Life is merely a succession of moments, and what matters most is one's sense of purpose at any given moment," Kozo said inconsequentially, seating his visitor. He abruptly dispensed with pleasantries. "You said that you were interested in discussing the 'eight directions under one roof.' "

"Yes, it seems to me to be an important concept."

"Clarification of the fundamental principles of national policy leads inexorably to the concept that the eight directions must all come under a single roof through a process of spiritual mobilization."

"Naturally."

"While there are always unpredictable events, strength of purpose will carry one through."

"Of course, professor. I have become concerned, however, that there are certain dangers inherent in such a course, and that other peoples may not see benefits."

"The ways of heaven are not always apparent to lesser beings," Kozo said dogmatically. "As I have explained in my books, we must continue to strive to foster progress even though ignorant and ill-advised persons oppose us. How is it that you have become interested in this subject?"

"My experiences on colonial planets have convinced me that the situation on these worlds is becoming increasingly serious."

"I am pleased that you have become aware of the severity of the situation that faces us and of the need for complete firmness of purpose," the professor commented.

"Unfortunately, while I see the need for firmness of purpose, my experiences have convinced me that in striving to bring all peoples under the one roof of Imperial rule, some persons have caused great hardship and resentment. Although few books are printed with raised characters for a blind person to read, I recently read one book which had a profound effect on me. It had to do with the animals in the zoo at Ueno during the Great Pacific War."

"You should call it the Greater East Asia Co-Prosperity War," Kozo corrected impatiently. "What did the book say?"

"It mentioned that toward the end of the war, after the Americans had defeated our air and naval forces, the decision was made to destroy the animals which could become dangerous in the event that they escaped during an air raid. Among the animals which were to be destroyed were the elephants." Mizoguchi's voice softened.

"At first, the keepers decided to kill them by putting poison in their food, but elephants are very intelligent, and they refused to eat the poisoned food. The keepers loved them too much to shoot them, so it was decided reluctantly that they should be allowed to starve to death. Toward the end, it was very sad. Hidden behind curtains, the last two elephants would hobble to their feet with their remaining strength and perform tricks in the hope that any people watching them would take pity and feed them."

"Yes, it is indeed a very sad story." Kozo's eyes narrowed. "But what has this to do with anything? In comparison to the great task of bringing the eight directions under one roof that we are embarked upon, elephants are not of any importance."

"May I ask what time it is, honored professor?"

"It is a few moments after nine o'clock." Kozo's voice took on a strident edge. "You did say that you had to see me on a matter of great urgency, a matter of life and death, which is why I agreed to see you."

"I believe that people should be more sensitive about elephants. And also about people," Mizoguchi said, judging Kozo's exact position from the sound of his voice. He pulled the pin on a gas grenade and expertly tossed it in Kozo's lap before it burned his fingers as the chemicals inside reacted.

A few seconds later, Mizoguchi got up and left the room before the filters in his nostrils became impregnated. As he left, he calmly shut the door so that the professor's family would not become involved. Stopping at a pay phone, he used some of the money Coldewe had given him to call his wife.

The New Akasaki Prince Hotel, Tokyo

AT 9:11, ZEREBTSOV BROUGHT ALL OF THE ELEVATORS IN THE NEW Akasaki Prince Hotel to the top floor and locked them in place. Then he tossed a smoke candle down one of the stairwells and pulled the building's fire alarm.

Knocking on doors, Zerebtsov, Soe, and Alariesto preemptorially directed the people on the top floor to evacuate the area, patting their submachine guns for emphasis. As soon as they hustled them away, they booby-trapped the stairwells with hair-fine wire threaded to incapacitation grenades, pitched some more smoke candles down the stairwells, and used a bolt gun to secure alloy strips across the doors to hold them secure.

With the reporters broadcasting from the New Akasaki Prince, Zerebtsov expected the police to show, and as a good recon man, he had no intention of making their job easier.

Iruma Air Base, outside Tokyo

AT 9:09, THE *LIGHTWELL GOMANI* POWERED HER WAY INTO THE UP-per atmosphere over the headquarters of the Central Air Defense District at Iruma, northwest of Tokyo. The Central Air Defense District hadn't faced a serious foreign threat in a hundred years, and when Sanmartin and Malinov descended, it was at its fourth level of alert, which is to say it was completely unprepared.

Roused suddenly out of lethargy by the nuclear explosion in the vicinity of Yamato Station, Iruma lost precious minutes assuring itself that Yamato Station was indeed gone and more precious minutes recognizing that the explosion was not accidental. With no available officer senior enough to authorize a response, the command hastily dusted off its emergency procedures, with predictable results.

Ten kilometers above the base, Malinov let loose a hail of fusion-charged "chicken seed" that struck and released energy into buildings, parked aircraft, and radars.

Goaded into action, Central Air Defense District directed the Atsugi and Hachioji air defense sites and its own antiaircraft defenses to fire on the intruder. Atsugi failed to respond, since Karaev's men weren't answering phones. Before communications failed, Hachioji reported that it was under ground attack. The haphazard response by the base's own defenses was not enough to save it.

Taking minor damage from a laser battery, "Speedy" painted the base's operations center with a laser designator and released one of Reinikka's 210mm penetrators. Plunging, the missile struck one of the doors of the huge concrete structure at an oblique angle and drilled deep inside to explode twenty meters and three levels below the ground. A huge cloud of dust puffed out of the shattered armored door. Smaller missiles smashed hangars and mobile missile batteries.

Having neutralized Iruma, Sanmartin and Malinov leveled out the *Gomani* and headed south-southeast to bring themselves over Air Defense Command Headquarters at Fuchū. They gave key buildings on that installation a thorough seventy-second dusting with composite particles. Within minutes of the strike on Yamato Station, Tokyo's air-defense system was headless.

In a raspy voice, Malinov radioed, "Tora, tora, tora," to Vereshchagin and Coldewe, indicating surprise and success. As

Sanmartin aimed the corvette toward central Tokyo, Malinov asked, "You bring your handkerchief?"

Sanmartin had the handkerchief his wife had embroidered many years ago next to his skin and pulled it out for Malinov to see. "My little piece of Suid-Afrika."

Tachikawa Air Base, outside Tokyo

EVEN AS IRUMA WAS COMING UNDER FIRE, A SHUTTLE FLEW IN LOW over No. 3 runway at the interceptor base at Tachikawa, twenty-five kilometers west-northwest of Tokyo. Broadcasting clear-language distress signals, the shuttle touched down, ignoring communications from the tower, and the clamshell doors in back opened out.

A handful of security policemen emerged from the tower. After a short but animated discussion, they piled into a vehicle and drove toward the shuttle.

Within seconds, however, alerted by the Central Air Defense District, the control tower assumed the aspect of a disturbed beehive. Pilots and aircrew scrambled out to man the two ready fighter planes on runway No. 1, and a swarm of security policemen poured out of the building.

Suddenly, a bright bolt of lightning appeared from inside the shuttle and speared the security vehicle cruising down the runway. Two Cadillacs and two slicks under Daniel Savichev's command roared down the shuttle's ramp. One Cadillac had 1,200 rounds of 30mm ammunition on board, Savichev's had 150 rounds of 90mm, and Savichev didn't intend to take any of it home.

An infantry platoon and a mortar section followed to provide covering fire. Fanning out, Savichev's vehicles struck the air-defense lasers and then began systematically to take the airbase apart. One section of the Iceman's riflemen provided perimeter defense while the other two sections made certain of the buildings that the armored cars were ripping apart. The mortar set up in a small depression just off the runway and began laying smoke and white phosphorus.

A few more riflemen rolled a tilt-rotor out the back of the shuttle with its wings folded. Shielded by the smoke, they snapped its wings into place, and it lifted off to pick up Snyman's and Karaev's men.

From the base of the shuttle, Piotr Kolomeitsev watched the

action intently, occasionally relaying suggestions. The Iceman had sixty-seven men to hold his tiny airhead on Japanese soil and had no reason to believe he needed more. Although the base held several thousand men belonging to the Air Defense Forces, only a few were trained for ground combat, and less than half of these were armed.

It took the Iceman's men fourteen minutes to wreck every airplane on the base and reduce most of the buildings to burning ruins, including the ordnance sheds. Three Imperial maintenance men who had improvised a tank destroyer by mounting a launcher on a utility vehicle were dead, as was a brave pilot who attempted to use his aircraft as a stationary weapons platform. Altogether, nearly a third of the base's personnel were casualties, and the rest were leaderless and demoralized.

Daniel Savichev carefully backed his Cadillac up the ramp into the shuttle to top it off with more 90mm ammunition. Savichev's eyes glowed hotly. The intensity of the firing had partly deformed the barrel of his gun.

Interlude

AFTER A MOMENTARY BLIP CAUSED BY OVERSEAS TRANSACTIONS and by the sale of Shoji's stock, the Tokyo stock market settled down to an uneventful trading day.

At 9:10, the real excitement started shortly after the police evacuated the exchange in response to one of Zerebtsov's bomb threats. Because most institutional investors trade directly with each other electronically, evacuating the exchange did *not* halt stock trading. In fact, trading intensified six minutes later as Timo Haerkoennen began operating from the Daikichi terminal.

The first phase of the program Haerkoennen grafted onto the bank's electronic trading program was slightly mischievous. Following his preprogrammed instructions, the Daikichi Sanwa snapped up thousands of thirty-day put options on DKU group stocks. The options would allow Daikichi to sell DKU stocks at set prices for the next thirty days, leading anyone observing the market to conclude that the bank was betting heavily that the prices of these stocks would fall. Since the bank had been rigging DKU stock prices, to use Redzup's quaint phrase, "since Jesus was a lance-corporal," this sent a ripple through the financial world.

Despite sagging confidence in the market as a whole, most DKU investors expected that the Daikichi Sanwa would continue to intervene to keep DKU stock prices high. Few of them had hedged themselves against a drop in prices.

The market had recently been shaken by news that the directors of the Bank of Japan had failed to reach a consensus on raising the discount rate, and by an announcement that the government would recapitalize a public agency set up to purchase problem loans from banks, in effect providing banks with yet another subsidy. Although the move was intended to bolster confidence in the banking system, it had the unanticipated effect of convincing investors that banks would pursue even riskier ventures now that the government was prepared to protect them from the consequences of bad decisions.

In this context, Haerkoennen's opening gambit struck market observers as the initial salvo in some incredibly bold campaign to wring a quick profit out of the market: not only was the Daikichi prepared to let DKU prices fall, it was apparently going to push them down. Investors quickly began selling to protect themselves.

The second phrase of Haerkoennen's program capitalized on fears raised by the first phase. Quietly, at a speed that human operators could never hope to match, the Daikichi began liquidating its immense holdings of DKU group stocks and stock warrants.

Stock investors assume that a stock market is "efficient" in the sense that investors have equal information and price stocks such that the expected return on assets of similar risks will be equal. Japan's tax structure and the manipulative practices of the banks made the Japanese stock market inefficient, but even in an inefficient market, the price of a stock should not decline when a large seller gets rid of it, unless the fact that that particular seller wants to get rid of the stock constitutes new information for the market to react to. Unfortunately, the fact the parent bank of the DKU group was dumping DKU stocks in huge chunks was information for the market to react to.

Stock prices move quickly in response to new information, and investors who react first have decided advantages. Because market theory assumes that each player is attempting to make money, it didn't occur to anyone that Daikichi's trading was calculated to *lose* the maximum amount of money in the shortest possible time. Thus, when investors saw the Daikichi going berserk, they immediately assumed that the biggest gorilla in the game knew something very bad that they didn't—and tried to react first.

Despite this, for the first eleven minutes of the DKU fire sale that Haerkoennen initiated, as prices fell to lower than normal levels, big computerized trading programs executed automatic-buy orders, gobbling up huge blocks of shares. Unfortunately, no single entity had ever owned the quantity of stock that the Daikichi did, much less tried to unload it all at once. As the cost of the shares being liquidated exceeded the debt limits built into trading programs, the automatic-buy orders stopped—and prices plummeted.

Still, profit-seekers began rushing in to snap up bargains, and the market would likely have stabilized at much lower levels—particularly if the exchange directors had been present to halt trading—if more new information had not come in from the news media.

Stock prices reflect people's hopes and fears far more than they reflect the intrinsic cash value of a company's salable assets. The fact that warships in Tokyo's skies and hard-bitten infantrymen in Tokyo's streets were dedicated to ruining United Steel-Standard and other DKU companies explained to everyone's satisfaction why the Daikichi Sanwa was dumping stock. At computer terminals around Japan, investors took Daikichi's perceived assessment of the DKU group's future at face value. They panicked.

A panic is interesting to observe. Although intricate mathematical formulae generally describe the ways that markets and prices behave very accurately, a stock market in a panic takes on human characteristics. It becomes a game of musical chairs—no one wants to be the one holding the stock when the music stops, so everyone tries to sit at once. After decades of manipulation by the Daikichi Sanwa, the law of averages caught up with DKU group stock prices and mugged them.

The stocks that speculators had bought in hopes of quick killings fell the fastest. Within fifteen minutes, the shrewder investors were already unloading other stocks whose prices would fall in reaction to the collapse of the DKU group.

To heighten the effect, the third phase of Haerkoennen's program began liquidating the massive mutual funds that Daikichi managed, selling off corporate bonds and stock shares of unrelated companies.

"ALL RIGHT, MISTER FINANCIAL WIZARD," HAERKOENNEN TOLD Redzup, "the program is entered and running. Now, I think it's time for us to start thinking about getting out of here—what are you looking at?"

"This private phone directory we printed out has some very interesting numbers on it, you know." Redzup picked up the telephone and started dialing.

"Vulko, what are you doing?!"

"Is this the president of Dozan Chemical?" Redzup demanded in fluent Japanese. "Please never mind how I got your number. Are you aware of the uncertainty in today's stock market? . . . Please excuse, I have just purchased a majority of your company's shares. It would save considerable difficulty if you did not report for work tomorrow." Redzup slammed down the phone.

Haerkoennen crossed his arms. "Uh, Vulko, you realize that all of hell is breaking loose about twelve blocks away. Don't you think—"

"Just one more call," Redzup said, dialing another number.

AS FISCAL DISASTER LOOMED, INVESTORS FRANTICALLY LOOKED for Japan's banking system to pour in capital to cushion the radical adjustment in prices—as the banking system had done for two centuries. Unfortunately, the corpses in the Ministry of Finance were in no position to lead such an effort, and even as Japan's bankers began calling one another to discuss the crisis, Hans Coldewe came on the air to say that the corvette *Lightwell Gomani* was about to make a firing run on the Bank of Japan and the headquarters buildings of Japan's second, third, and fourth largest banks—and that the people inside had approximately ten minutes to get out. The moment for intervention passed. The market's safety net failed to operate.

For two centuries, stockbrokers in every department store and bank had been luring individual stockholders into the market in huge numbers. Periodically, stock prices were run up to staggering levels and a generation of stockholders who thought that the run would never end would be fleeced—in a crude sense, shorn of their wealth to fuel Japan's ever-increasing economic expansion—by insiders. The endless churning of portfolios made very few people wealthy and many poor, and the leveraged stockholders, who borrowed money to play the market and invariably bet on a sharp rise in prices, fell like moths in flames whenever prices dropped.

When the police allowed the traders back into the stock exchange, they found their terminals stuffed with unfulfilled sell orders at prices they couldn't believe. To save themselves, they called on investors who had bought on margin to put up more money and dumped onto a steadily eroding market the stock of the ones who could not meet margin calls. Within the hour, there was no market for USS stock and a few other issues at any price. The overheated stock market began to fall apart.

For decades, the only thing that had kept the irregular wheels of Japan's market turning was the expectation that the incestuous relationship between corporations, banks, and important politicians would never allow prices to drop too far. Beneath a massive wave of selling, that expectation died.

By 10:45, the market's last hope was for intervention by the large securities groups, which had cushioned crashes, often paying off the losses of favored customers. Unfortunately, the wall that had kept the banks from trading in securities had come down ten years previously, and without anyone's paying much attention, the banks had taken the lion's share of the securities market. The large securities groups were only a fraction of their former size. When the torrent hit, they blinked, consulted, and ultimately failed to act.

As Haerkoennen and Redzup had fervently hoped and prayed, the stocks on the Tokyo Exchange lost 19 percent of their value in fifty-nine minutes. By the end of the day, after two slight rallies, the market had lost 37 percent of its value, and most of the traders operating on margin found themselves wiped out.

The effects would continue to be felt far into the future. Many of Japan's smaller companies had gotten into the habit of issuing large quantities of short-term low-interest warrant bonds, which entitled the purchaser to convert the bond into shares of the company's stock at a fixed price when the bond came due—allowing the purchaser to realize untaxed capital-gains income instead of taxed dividends. Assuming that most of these bonds would be converted, the companies spent the cash received. As the market price of shares fell, these warrant bonds became ticking time bombs in the Japanese financial system.

As a final indignity, an ill-advised Ministry of Finance rul-

ing half a century old allowed banks to consider the full current market value of their stock holdings and real estate in de-
termining their loss reserves. Many of the smaller banks kept
no other assets to cushion themselves against bad loans. In a
matter of minutes, these banks found themselves undercapital-
ized, just as the dubious loans they had made began to surface.
The Japanese financial system, always viciously and inherently
unstable, began to boil.

In a word, a very small pin had burst a very large bubble.

By early afternoon, the decapitated Daikichi Sanwa was left
with a large, but finite, pile of cash and a legal mess that it
would likely take years to resolve. No one was very sure who
owned the companies it had once been associated with.

IT WAS A WHILE BEFORE ANYONE REMEMBERED TO TELL THE TWO
corvettes over Siberia that there was an invasion on. Additional
time passed before they were able to combine.

Niigata City, Niigata Prefecture

AT 9:35, FROM AN UPSTAIRS HOTEL WINDOW, CHIHARU YOSHIDA
put an 88mm antipersonnel round into a platform from which
Osachi Abe and five of his principal supporters were preparing
to dedicate a new municipal building. Leaving money with the
hotel's owner to pay for the damage to the walls from the
back-blast, Yoshida calmly walked outside, where he was arrested. The medical examiner eventually counted fifty-five
fléchettes that had passed into or through Abe's body.

Central Tokyo

TOKYO'S GUARDIANS REACTED. IN PARTS OF THE CITY, THE EARTH-
quake sirens sounded, and civil-emergency wardens evacuated
the population to surrounding prefectures along predetermined
routes.

Soldiers from the Military Academy deployed to protect the
Imperial Palace. The three Lifeguards battalions stationed at
Shibaura on land reclaimed from Tokyo Bay received ammunition and prepared to move to trouble spots as soon as the situation clarified.

The Tokyo police responded to the confused reports of

bombing and terrorist activity. Within minutes after the initial calls came in, seven companies and four independent platoons of armed and armored riot police moved out from compounds scattered around the city.

One riot company converged on the Kasumigaseki. As they arrived, they were greeted by the sight of two police helicopters crashing into the streets.

Unfortunately, their metal shields, helmets, and corselets were designed to protect them from staves and rocks, not assault rifles. Within minutes, Salchow and his compatriots on top of the ministries picked off five policemen and put an antitank rocket through the cab of an armored riot van. Screaming for reinforcements, the riot police backed away to regroup and bring in heavy weapons. A three-man reconnaissance team tried to enter the Security Ministry. None of them returned.

INSIDE THE SECURITY MINISTRY, AFTER CLEANING OUT THE BLACK-legs in the first and second basement levels, Meagher's men butted up against a final armored door.

"What do you think, Ketlinsky?" Meagher asked, shining an ultraviolet light.

The little engineer scratched his chin. "It must weigh a ton. With the power gone, we can't open it, and I doubt that they can either."

Meagher nodded. "All right. DeKe, you and Mother Elena leave me Miinalainen and Ketlinsky. Take everyone else—give Kaarlo a hand watching the door, and clear us a path up to the roof. I don't want to miss my flight."

De Kantzow and Yelenov took off with most of Meagher's men.

"Any ideas?" Meagher began rummaging through his bergen full of goodies.

"A thirty-kay shaped charge to blow a hole in the door, an eighty-eight–round through the hole to discourage anyone standing behind it, and then gas grenades," Ketlinsky said with authority, wanting to use the heavy charge strapped to his back in the worst way.

"Good, except they'll probably have masks, so the gas won't get to them," Meagher reflected.

"Smoke candles," Miinalainen volunteered unexpectedly. "Toss a bunch of them through the hole along with the gas grenades. There's no air circulating. They'll suck up the oxygen."

Meagher slapped him on the back. "You big squirt, you're a genius! We'll do it."

Five minutes later, they were headed toward the roof where Kokovtsov and Thomas were waiting in their stolen tilt-rotor. Miinalainen dropped his recoilless gun on the way to bring along Dirkie Rousseaux's body.

Hachioji Air Defense Site, outside Tokyo

CLUTCHING HIS SMASHED SHOULDER, JAN SNYMAN ASKED ISAAC Wanjau, "Any ideas?"

Snyman's men had penetrated the site's command bunker and blown the elevators to isolate the personnel below, and had beaten off a small detachment of riot police. Snyman's battle dress had largely absorbed a round from a policeman's submachine gun, but the impact had broken his collarbone.

The site's commander had made one attempt to fire off missiles, which had left two rather large holes in the ground.

"Major Kolomeitsev is sending a transport to pick us up, but if we leave, the police are going to move our charges and the moles in their holes get to shoot at us," Wanjau said happily. "It sounds like we got a problem."

"Liu is an armor puke and Nikoskelainen is an engineer, so we'll send them back along with the wounded. The rest of us ought to be able to hold this place for as long as it takes," Snyman thought aloud. "I guess we don't go back. God help Liu when he has to explain this to my wife."

A white grin split Wanjau's dark face. "Well, to tell you the truth, Jan, I'm not that fond of your planet. The natives aren't friendly. I still have family in Nigeria, cousins. Since we're here, I thought about taking some leave and going to see them."

"Your leave is approved, starting an hour from now." Snyman shook his head. "I wonder how Orlov is doing." Kirill Orlov had supervised Snyman's basic training.

Wanjau's eyes sparkled. "Kirill? He is at Tachikawa right now, happy as a bug moaning to everyone that he was an idiot to volunteer to come here."

"I bet you're right." Snyman tilted his head. "I never asked you why you volunteered, Isaac."

"You missed Ashcroft." For a moment, Wanjau's eyes burned. "The corporations made the planet what it was. We remember. Everyone the Variag recruited there came. What did you do to your mask?"

Snyman took off his face shield and examined it. "I don't see anything wrong."

Wanjau popped an incapacitation grenade under his nose. "I forgot to tell you, Jan. You're one of the wounded. Besides, I couldn't have let poor Liu face your wife."

Wanjau kept seven men and sent four men and one corpse back to Tachikawa on the tilt-rotor the Iceman had dispatched.

Shibuya Ward, Tokyo

"NOT MUCH PARKING HERE," MALINOV SAID AS THE CORVETTE *Lightwell Gomani* made its way toward the city's center. "We should help them build a few lots."

Sanmartin grinned. "When I make comments like that, Hans tells me I've been spending too much time with slugs and bugs."

"He's right."

Sanmartin had one ear monitoring Jankowskie. "We need to attract some attention."

"Targets coming up." In the Shibuya district, approaching the city center, Malinov planted a half-dozen five-hundred-kilogram projectiles on the Imperial Censorate Building and pushed a couple more through the windows of Dentsu-Hakuhado's offices.

Sanmartin shed some speed and jogged northeast. "O-Chan Pharmaceutical?" Malinov asked.

"They're on our list. The chairman of the board should have the biggest window."

Malinov ran a five-hundred-kilogram bomb through the chairman's window. As police milling around the Meiji Shrine Outer Garden ineffectually opened fire, Malinov hosed a few of the persistent ones with the laser.

"Imp aircraft are veering to intercept us. The corvettes still aren't taking the hint. Drop something on the offices of the patriotic organization up the street, and then get ready to let off some steam."

Malinov grinned and prepared to drop chicken seed into the moats around the Imperial Palace. With his hair gone and the skin stretched taut over his face, he looked hideous. The *Gomani*'s mission was to shoot up enough targets to create a diversion for the Iceman to get the assault teams off. Yuri Malinov intended to enjoy every minute of it.

Earth orbit

ABOARD THE *HENDRIK PIENAAR*, JANKOWSKIE SAID, "SIR, THE IMPE-rial corvettes are dropping low and veering south to get around us."

Oblivious to other threats, the corvettes from Siberia were converging on the city's center to intercept Sanmartin and Malinov.

"Ignore them," Vereshchagin ordered. "Position us so that we can cover Piotr's withdrawal."

The New Akasaki Prince Hotel, Tokyo

"KOKOVTSOV HAS GOTTEN MEAGHER'S PEOPLE AWAY," ZEREBTSOV reported to Coldewe, "and the cops are pounding on the door down there." Coldewe had already sent the rest of his people off.

"Parting is such sweet sorrow," he told the reporters. "None-theless, I bid you adieu. I suggest you stay here for about ten more minutes and keep watching in the direction of the USS Building. The corvette *Lightwell Gomani* should have one 210mm penetrator left, and you may find it interesting. You might want to lie down and pull some of those tarps over your heads."

"You are leaving?" The *Asahi* reporter was beginning to look frazzled.

"Yes, and with any luck, I won't be back. Remember, 'the Buddha forgives the wicked if they open their eyes to his wis-dom.' "

Zerebtsov already had the little Sparrow's engine running. Waving regally to the newsmen, Coldewe hopped in and told Zerebtsov, "Home, James."

Tachikawa Air Base, outside Tokyo

KOKOVTSOV GROUNDED HIS HIJACKED TILT-ROTOR NEXT TO THE one the Iceman had flown off, and Meagher's assault group climbed out to board the Iceman's shuttle. Zerebtsov landed the Sparrow with Coldewe a few moments later, and Kolomeitsev met them by the shuttle's crew door.

"I have begun pulling my men in," the Iceman said. "I sent one of your Sparrows to pick up one more of Wanjau's people, but the rest are staying to make sure that we get off. Who is still unaccounted for?"

"Mizo is staying, and Chiharu isn't going to make it back."

"I am not sure Chiharu wanted to," Kolomeitsev said. "We are still missing the intrepid duo of Haerkoennen and Redzup."

"Damn!" Coldewe swore. "They should be here by now." He tried calling them. "I'm not getting through."

A huge flash arc-lit the sky.

"That must be Raul. We have to get the shuttle turned around and out of here," the Iceman said inexorably. His two Cadillacs completed their final firing pass, and their crews were boarding and strapping in. The last of Kolomeitsev's riflemen followed them seconds later. Demolition charges in the armored cars and aircraft left behind began to explode.

As the shuttle's engines began turning over, Redzup's Sparrow appeared. Taking no chances, Redzup taxied it right up the shuttle's ramp. Willing hands strapped the tiny plane down as the clamshell closed and the shuttle began its takeoff.

Watching Earth's surface diminish, Kolomeitsev told Coldewe, "I am going to have to ask Timo why he keeps saying to Vulko, 'Just one more phone call, you said.' "

Central Tokyo

"I MAKE IT TWO MINUTES BEFORE THE INTERCEPTORS ARRIVE AND another nine before the corvettes join the party," Sanmartin told Malinov.

Malinov pointed to his instruments. "Tell them that. The interceptors are firing missiles at long range." He tossed a tiny squeeze bottle in Sanmartin's lap.

"What's this?"

"Imitation arak for the third toast. The real stuff would have eaten through the bottle."

Sanmartin laughed. "You realize that drinking on board is unmilitary as all hell, Battalion Sergeant. Give it to the ghosts we brought along."

"The Ministry of Security?"

"Go ahead."

Malinov fired the 210mm penetrator at the ruined Ministry of Security Building to make doubly sure of the people inside. Then Sanmartin pulled the corvette's nose straight into the sky over the Imperial Palace and engaged a preset navigation program. Missile batteries to the north and east that had been screened by the horizon locked on, and half a dozen missiles leaped into the air to follow the ship into space.

Twisting the *Gomani* around in the tightest arc its fabric would withstand, the automatic pilot whipped the ship around and aimed its nose at the ground below.

The missiles from the interceptors lost contact and passed by harmlessly. The pilots of the planes gaped, aghast at what they were seeing on their screen. Ships were not built to withstand the stresses involved, still less were the men inside.

At fifteen hundred meters over the ground, the corvette spewed its fusion bottle. Venting solar heat like an enormous laser, the ship continued to dive toward the ground. The flare lit the sky.

Plunging at a steep angle, the corvette struck the third floor of the United Steel-Standard Building. It buried itself in the subbasement. The building unfolded, scattering debris over a circle half a kilometer across. Two of the ship-killer missiles from the city's defense sites followed it down and hurled themselves into the growing hole where the building had stood. Every window in a ten-block area shivered itself apart.

Even as the force of the explosion buffeted the approaching aircraft, their pilots understood that if the *Gomani* had not vented its fusion bottle, their aircraft and a quarter of the city would have shared in the corvette's destruction. As it was, a crater graced the spot where the United Steel-Standard Building had stood.

Still looking for an opportunity to fire a shot, the two corvettes that had been picketing Siberia headed back out into space to try to engage the *Hendrik Pienaar*.

Earth orbit

ABOVE THE CITY, VERESHCHAGIN AND HENKE WATCHED IMPAS-sively. Vereshchagin said very quietly, "From dust we come. To dust we go." Esko Poikolainnen began broadcasting what the corvette had done, and why.

Obliterating USS corporate headquarters would deal the company a fatal blow, but Raul Sanmartin had argued long and hard that the expedition needed to tap into the thread of death and self-sacrifice that ran through Japanese culture in order to succeed.

Standing by the viewscreen, Vereshchagin recollected the points Sanmartin had made. To the Japanese, it mattered little whether the goal Malinov and Sanmartin had given themselves for was morally correct. What mattered was that by dying, they had proven their "sincerity." If self-sacrifice fascinated the Japanese, they had received a surfeit.

Vereshchagin came to understand that the Japanese people would not stand for the punishment his expedition had inflicted without this gesture. Still, it sickened him.

Coldewe had unwittingly mailed out information to every newspaper, and in the days to come, the Japanese would begin to understand what this war was about. It was Raul Sanmartin's goal to rub the noses of the Japanese people in it. After that, there was only hope.

One thought that particularly stuck in Vereshchagin's mind was Raul Sanmartin's comment that time dilation itself was a small death. They would leave Suid-Afrika for two years and return to find that seven had passed. Vereshchagin knew that Sanmartin had chosen a large death to escape a small one.

Jankowskie approached. "Sir, the shuttle's ready to dock."

"All right, Detlef."

"Sir," Jankowskie asked hesitantly, "we've done an awful lot of damage down there." Jankowskie could see where errant missiles from Tokyo's defenders had smashed into housing areas, and the area around the USS Building was a ruin. Like tiny ants in the ship's surveillance equipment, police and firemen were working to keep the fires in the ministry buildings from spreading.

"I think that there is one reason why they will not come after us, Detlef," Vereshchagin said carefully. "Given the history of military rule in Japan, the Japanese elite fear giving the military forces any role in governing the country. We have demonstrated that they cannot continue their current policies with military half measures. Given a choice between granting the military forces the power they would need to make Japan secure and letting the colonial planets and the nations on Earth travel their own road, I think that they will choose to let the colonies go."

"Do you think they might offer to let Suid-Afrika go in exchange for your hide?" Henke asked.

"I would go willingly," Vereshchagin said with a trace of humor. "But presumably they would have to try me, and I do not think that they would want that."

"Docking completed," Esko Poikolainnen reported.

"It is time to go home," Vereshchagin said.

When someone explained to Hans Coldewe what had happened with the *Lightwell Gomani*, he caught his breath and then buried himself in the frigate's library, to reread *Paradise Lost* and Milton's magnificent description of Lucifer's burning descent into hell.

Reprise

TAKEN INTO CUSTODY, CAPTAIN CHIHARU YOSHIDA WAS IMMEDIately tried in secret by a military court and executed. Several months later, Hiroshi Mizoguchi was brought before a civilian court and given seven years imprisonment. Leaving the courtroom, he was assassinated by a right-wing organization. His widow applied for permission to emigrate to a colonial world.

Several of Vereshchagin's staff college classmates received thoughtful letters from him that Coldewe had posted. At the height of the controversy, after the government resigned and clashes erupted between the violently patriotic societies and militantly antimilitaristic, anticorporate coalitions, the Keeper of the Privy Seal, another of Vereshchagin's staff college classmates, published a response to a letter he had received from Vereshchagin and passed on to His Imperial Majesty.

As one commentator explained, "A good war might unite the nation behind a single purpose. Unfortunately, Suid-Afrika is much too small and far away for this."

EPILOGUE _____

**In orbit, Suid-Afrika
Tuesday (789)**

MANNING THE INSTRUMENTS ON THE *HENDRIK PIENAAR*, NICOLAS Sery waved his hand excitedly. "Captain Jankowskie, there's a ship coming in!"

"All right. Everyone to action stations," Jankowskie ordered. As his crew took up their places with quiet efficiency, he asked Sery, "What kind is she?"

"It's a freighter."

Jankowskie whistled with relief. "All right. Get her in a parking orbit so we can make sure she's not a Q-ship, and let Matti and the Variag know."

"Sir, they're hailing us," Sery said. "They say that they have an envoy aboard."

ALBERT BEYERS ROSE TO GREET THE SLIM JAPANESE OFFICIAL WHO entered his office. "Heer Maeda. Welcome to Suid-Afrika."

"Thank you." Maeda offered his credentials.

"Please sit down," Beyers said, awkwardly playing the diplomatic game.

"Thank you." Maeda sat. "Please excuse me for asking, but was that a child that I saw working in your outer office?"

"Yes, that is my adopted daughter. She tells me that she will be the president of the republic someday. When she grows up."

"She seemed quite determined," Maeda said.

"Please excuse me for asking directly, Heer Maeda, but what is the position of the Imperial Government toward my people?"

"That is a difficult question," Maeda said, obviously amused. "There has been unpleasantness in the past and there are many issues which will need to be resolved."

"If the Imperial Government declines to recognize our right to self-government, I am afraid that there may be more unpleasantness," Beyers said with utter candor.

Noting his anxiety, Maeda unbent slightly. "Is that so? I assure you from my inmost feelings that the Imperial Government is committed to fostering cooperation and harmony."

"Hopefully, our people will be able to exchange the fusion

metals we have stockpiled on a more mutually advantageous basis than has existed in the past."

Maeda smiled. "You will have to discuss this directly with the company which succeeded to the interests of United Steel-Standard, but it is always better for different peoples to work things out on a mutually agreeable basis. Perhaps I can make inquiries."

"Perhaps. I will also see what can be arranged." Beyers hesitated. "I am reluctant to bring this matter up, but what is the attitude of the Imperial Government toward Lieutenant-Colonel Vereshchagin and the men who participated in the attack?"

Maeda's smile broadened. "Lieutenant-Colonel Vereshchagin? He and his soldiers died when they attacked the USS Building in Tokyo, neh? That is what the newspapers said. Such a tragic misunderstanding. Military operations of any kind are very costly. The clause in Japan's constitution which has always prohibited military forces other than self-defense forces is a very wise one. Still, one has to admire the sincerity of his purpose."

"Yes, of course," Beyers said, taken aback. "Of course."

Listening in on the conversation, Harjalo commented, "It's almost as if nothing happened."

Vereshchagin tapped his pipe against his thigh. Absently, he took out a small package of pipe tobacco, broke the seal on it, and began awkwardly stuffing it into the bowl of the pipe. "Sometimes, that is best."

As Vereshchagin patted his pockets for a source of flame, Harjalo grinned and handed him a lighter.

WHILE THE PEOPLE WERE STILL CELEBRATING IN THE STREETS, Albert Beyers made the Assembly swallow "The Whistling Pig" as Suid-Afrika's national anthem. After procrastinating for years on the issue to avoid irritating the cowboys and the sects, he told them it was that or bagpipes.

One of Hanna Bruwer's former pupils came up with a final verse for the song.

The pig came home from warring and began to sing a
*   song,*
*   "My planet isn't perfect but it's closer right than*
*   wrong."*
He wore a sprig of laurel, and he waved an olive twig,
*   And he whistled to the people so he'd be a whistling*
*   pig!*

Selected Verses from "The Whistling Pig," anonymous

"Oh, we're having a war, and we want you to come!"
  So the pig began to whistle and to pound on a drum.
"We'll give you a gun, and we'll give you a hat!"
  And the pig began to whistle when they told the piggies
    that.

The pig put on his webbing, and they marched him up and
    down,
  He did it with a whistle, so they gave him sand to pound.
He crossed the burning desert, and he trekked the arctic night
  And they made him do it over so he'd learn to do it right.

The pig cleaned up his webbing, and he shined his bayonet,
  Some people started shooting so he shot them with regret.
He couldn't work an office, and he couldn't be a clerk,
  For pigs who like to whistle like to whistle while they work.

The pig went on vacations, to planets near and far,
  For fighting wars on schedule, is very good PR.
The admirals love the piggies, and natives think them swell,
  At least they often say so after putting them through hell.

Wars are sometimes over and they debited his pay,
  They took away his hat and they took his gun away,
They told him they were thankful and they split him north to
    south
  And they fried him with a whistle and an apple in his
    mouth!